"SHALL I TELL YOU YOUR TRUE MOTIVES, CHANCE BALLINGER?"

Kathleen eyed him cynically, not waiting for a reply. "Your interest in me, in this ranch, lies only in whatever profit we can bring you." Her bright stare challenged him. "You're no different from those other backhanded suitors who came to my door looking for a profitable match, are you, Chance Ballinger?"

When he didn't respond, she braced herself against her unreasonable disappointment. "Even now, as you hold me in your arms, you're only waiting for me to make a mistake, to play the wrong card the way my brother did."

"No, Kathleen, *this* is what I'm waiting for. It's what I've been waiting for since the moment I set eyes on you."

As his mouth came down on hers, his teeth grazed her lower lip and excitement shook her. And the stunning knowledge that she had tried so hard to deny sprang to life. Her trembling body spoke the truth louder than a shouted confession. . . .

OUTSTANDING ACCLAIM FOR Laura DeVries
AND

GAMBLER'S DAUGHTER

"Gambler's Daughter is a western Americana romance with grit. Keep your eye on Laura DeVries."—Kathe Robin, editor of *Romantic Times*

"I loved *Gambler's Daughter!* It's a warm, wonderful book with honest, unforgettable characters. Kathleen and Chance are lovers to cheer for. They'll steal your heart as they stole mine."—Maggie Osborne, author of *The Seduction of Samantha Kincaid*

"Laura DeVries's historical debut is well written and the meticulous research brings the Montana Territory of 1875 to vivid life. Be sure to watch for more from this talented author."
—*I'll Take Romance!* magazine

"A delightful, sensual romp in the old west that lassos the reader from the first page and doesn't let go. Laura DeVries is a rising star . . . destined to become a satellite!"—Patricia Hagan, *New York Times* bestselling author

"Ms. DeVries's earthy characters and feisty dialogue add delightful spice to this Americana romance. A wonderful read!"—Sharon Ihle, award-winning author of *The Bride Wore Spurs*

GAMBLER'S DAUGHTER

LAURA DEVRIES

A Dell Book

Published by
Dell Publishing
a division of
Bantam Doubleday Dell Publishing Group, Inc.
1540 Broadway
New York, New York 10036

The trademark Dell® is registered in the U.S. Patent and
Trademark Office.

ISBN: 0-440-22136-6

Printed in the United States of America

Published simultaneously in Canada

March 1996

10 9 8 7 6 5 4 3 2 1

OPM

WITH LOVE,
TO MARY AND HERB DEVRIES,
WHOSE BIG-SKY ROMANCE LASTED
FOR OVER FIFTY YEARS

Chapter One

———◆———

YOUNG Danny McBride felt a cold chill climb his spine. Chance Ballinger's cool, blue-eyed gaze shifted from the small mountain of paper money and coins heaped in front of him to Danny's glistening face. "I didn't come here to watch you sweat, Junior. I came to play poker. If you're still in the game, show your money. If you're busted, give your chair to a man with a bigger bankroll and a drier shirt."

The drovers behind them at the bar broke into drunken laughter and Danny felt his face redden.

"Better listen to what the Texan sez, Danny Boy," the skinny bald-headed one they called Skeeter advised, "if'n you want to go home with that raggedy shirt still on yore scrawny back."

When their jeering laughter erupted again, Danny's nerves strained like a rubber band ready to snap. "I'm in, I'm in," he muttered grudgingly as he swabbed his sweat-streaked face with a grimy red bandanna and withdrew a small buckskin money bag from his shirt pocket. The satisfaction he saw flicker in Ballinger's eyes made his stomach roll.

"The man says he's in, Rubylee," Ballinger informed the voluptuous young woman at his elbow. The blond dealer smiled, batted her heavily kohled eyelids at the big Texan, and called out to the bartender for a fresh deck of cards and another bottle.

Danny focused on his opponent as Rubylee shuffled the new deck with practiced ease. Was Ballinger a professional? At first glance, he looked more like a common trail hand than the silk-suited, French-cuffed gamblers who usually held court at Bummer Dan's and the other saloons that lined the muddy streets of Alder Gulch, the gaming district of Virginia City.

But as the long night of poker and whiskey had worn on, Danny had begun to notice things that belied Chance Ballinger's ordinary appearance. Little things, mostly. Like the way he handled his cards and his money and the way he played—or, rather, the way he *outplayed* and outbluffed everyone all night.

Everyone but me. Danny clung to that distinction with fierce optimism. "Come on, Rubylee," he barked, buoyed by the sudden infusion of self-confidence. "Deal."

"Ante up, gentlemen," Rubylee crooned good-naturedly. The fitted bodice of her gold satin dress barely contained her ample bosom as she plied and worked the deck the way Danny had seen his sister knead bread. His teeth drew blood from his lower lip when he pushed his money to the center of the table. Still arcing the deck like a rainbow, Rubylee mixed, shuffled, and shifted the cards from one small pale hand to the other. When at last her hands and the cards were stilled, she set the deck down on the scarred tabletop in front of Danny. "Cut?" she asked him, her full, painted smile unoffending.

He divided the cards with reverence and Rubylee reclaimed the deck. As the cards flew from her fingertips, Danny's right eye began a betraying nervous twitch. He tried to will it still, but the harder he tried, the more the eye fluttered.

Snatching up each card as it was dealt to him, he drew a deep breath and studied his hand: two nines. *A damn good start!* A five. An eight. And another nine! *Good girl, Rubylee. These three nines should do just fine!* His eye still twitched, but inside Danny smiled and sat up straighter in his seat. He'd known if he just stayed with it, his luck was bound to turn. And now, it looked as though it had.

"Two hundred," he declared, and pushed his wager to the center of the table.

"I'll see that," Ballinger said, his words coming from between teeth clamped down on a thin, smoldering cigarillo. His stoic expression told Danny nothing. Whether the Texan held blank cards or a full house, Danny doubted his expression would have changed.

"Two cards," Danny said, discarding the eight and the five, swiping at his flinching eye with the back of his hand. He held his breath and snatched up the two new cards as fast as Rubylee dealt them to him. *The three of spades. And the fourth nine! The blessed nine of diamonds!* Danny wanted to shout, to jump up from the table and shove his winning hand under all their noses—the haughty Texas gambler, the big-mouth drovers at the bar.

Bide your time, Danny, an inner voice warned, reminding him that there'd be plenty of time for celebrating once he'd played his beautiful four-of-a-kind nines and won his money back. Trying desperately to remain stoic, Danny added the two new cards to the others in his trembling right hand and glanced across the table at his opponent.

"One card," Ballinger said evenly. Without emotion, he lifted the corner of the single card Rubylee dealt him before sliding it over to join the other four lying facedown in front of him. Each calm, deliberate movement proved torturous to his squirming opponent.

He's goin' for a straight, Danny's frantic mind concluded. Asking for one card was a dead giveaway. *Well sir, go ahead and play your straight. And just watch my four of a kind beat your blasted straight—it'll beat it all t'hell!*

Gulping the dregs of a warm beer, Danny cursed as a vision of Kathleen's face flashed before him for one terrible instant. And the heartrending disappointment lodged in her sad green eyes caused the bitter liquid to spew back up into his throat, choking him. The bitter mix of guilt and bile burned mightily, and he gasped and wiped his damp forehead and runny eyes with his bandanna again, and shivered despite the stifling heat of the crowded saloon.

"Are you still in this game, Junior?" the Texan asked, his silky drawl drifting lazily across the table.

"You're damn right I'm in!" Danny sputtered. "But it's gonna cost you another three hundred to see this hand." His chest swelled with his bravado.

"Well, well." Ballinger chuckled, and the harmless sound scraped across Danny's ragged nerves like a hacksaw across slate. "I guess you did come here to play poker after all. All right, then. Three hundred it is, 'cause I surely do want to see that hand of yours, Junior." He slid his money forward. "Yessir, I surely do. And just to keep it interesting, what say we add five hundred more?"

All pretense of good humor melted from the Texan's expression and the steely set of his jaw caused Danny's stomach to churn in earnest. The drops of sweat on his forehead turned to streams and his heart raced. *Five hundred?* Though he hadn't expected Ballinger to fold, he sure as hell hadn't expected him to raise the stakes!

Danny pulled the bandanna from his shirt pocket again, his frantic mind grappling for a way out.

"Have you got it, honey?" Rubylee asked in a nervous whisper.

"Aw, he ain't got it," someone murmured as the crowd gathered around the table moved in closer. "He's gonna fold."

"I ain't foldin'," Danny snarled over his shoulder. "Step back, fellas. Gimme some air. I *gotta* have air!"

No one moved until Ballinger gave a curt nod, and even then the expectant crowd edged back only a reluctant half-step. Danny felt all eyes on him, like vultures waiting for the kill.

"I'll see your five hundred," Danny said defiantly as he shoved his money to the center of the table. It was all he had, every last penny, but everyone could see it wasn't enough.

Rubylee picked up the bills and counted. "But there's barely . . . two . . . no, not even a hundred and fifty dollars here, Danny." Her eyes asked him if he knew he was treading on dangerous ground.

"Hold on, just hold on," Danny grumbled, and reaching into his shirt pocket, he pulled out the small stub of a pencil and a tattered piece of paper. He touched the tip of the pencil to his tongue and bent over the table and wrote. Fighting to steady his hand, he formed the letters carefully, just the way Kathleen had taught him.

It was the poker hand of a lifetime, he assured himself as he wrote. A man just couldn't walk away from a hand like that. It was fate, that's all. Pure, blessed four-of-a-kind fate! *Trust me, Kathleen. This time the McBrides win!*

He finished writing and confidently held the paper over the pile of money in the center of the table. But despite himself, he shuddered before he dropped it.

"What's this?" Ballinger reached for the note and with narrowed eyes read Danny's scribbling. "Twin Rivers? What the hell's a Twin Rivers?"

"It's my ranch," Danny sputtered indignantly.

"Your ranch?" Ballinger asked as he leaned back in his chair and stroked his thick dark mustache with his thumb. His eyes turned hard, the color of cold steel. He clenched the cigarillo between his teeth again and spoke around it. "And just what has your broken-down homestead got to do with me, Junior?" The smooth drawl had become an ominous growl.

Danny swallowed to find his voice. "I'm countering your bet with my half interest of a thousand acres of the richest grazing land in the whole Montana Territory. It's worth twice . . . maybe three times the bet." His voice rose with each word. "You could sell it off, if you had a mind, and come out real good." The betraying words tumbled from his mouth before he could stop them.

Lord knew the thought of selling out had occurred to him often enough. And he'd have done it, too, long ago, but for Kathleen's stubborn refusal. He was sure she'd die happy if she never set foot off Twin Rivers soil.

But as for Danny, well, he figured he'd die there, all right. Although anything but happy. Nothing but endless debts, bone-numbing blizzards, and dim-witted cows. No two ways about it, one or all of them would kill him in the end, of that Danny McBride was certain.

"Take it," Danny heard Rubylee whisper to the big man. "I heard the boys talkin' 'bout his spread. It sounded real nice—" When Ballinger shot her a menacing glare, she swallowed the rest of her advice with a gulp.

Ballinger threw the handwritten deed back into the pot. "Show us your hand, rancher" was all he said.

Danny held his breath as he fanned his cards out in front of him. Ballinger looked at Danny's cards and released a long, slow whistle of appreciation, leaned back in his chair, and stretched his long legs out in front of him. "Four of a kind. Well now, that's a damn good hand, Junior."

Danny finally allowed himself to breathe.

"Damn good," Ballinger repeated, shaking his head as he leaned forward slowly and flipped his own cards over one by one. "But not quite good enough."

The crowd drew a collective breath and Danny gasped. The air was being sucked out of his burning lungs faster than he could replace it. *It can't be!* Danny's startled mind screamed. It wasn't possible! And yet there it was. *A royal flush.* The Texan had himself a damn royal flush in diamonds!

Danny's staring eyes were at last shocked still. Numbed, he watched Ballinger collect his money and the handwritten deed. Waves of nausea broke over him in a suffocating tide. It'd been the hand of a lifetime. A sure thing!

"No!" The scream tore from Danny's throat, desperate and shrill. The reality of what had happened crashed down around him like a summer cloudburst.

Bolting out of his seat, he grabbed the edge of the table and heaved it with all his might, but in one fluid motion Ballinger was on his feet as well, avoiding the upended table as coins and paper rained down.

Danny reached for his gun, but Ballinger was faster. With hand frozen between hip and holster, Danny's heart sank as he stared without blinking into the black eye of Chance Ballinger's .45-caliber Colt. Danny felt the pulse at his throat throbbing. The ringing in his ears left him dizzy.

He squeezed his eyes closed and waited for the sound of the explosion, for the deadly blow that would shatter his chest and put an end to his nightmare. He waited. And the roaring silence that filled the astonished saloon threatened to split his reeling mind in two. And still he waited, on fire with the white-hot fear that engulfed his hammering heart. His short life was over, a bitter inner voice cried. Gunned down, dead broke and humiliated.

His arm ached. His fingers itched. If he went for his gun, he'd be dead before his fingers ever touched metal. If he didn't go for his gun, he'd die a coward. Danny screamed inside, knowing either way he was a dead man.

When he finally opened his eyes, the flinty gaze staring at him shifted an imperceptible inch. Danny flinched.

When Ballinger spoke, his words splintered the brittle silence like an ax. "You've lost your money and your ranch, Junior. Be a damn shame to lose your life as well."

The breath whooshed out of Danny in relief and his hand shot forward to catch the gold piece Ballinger flipped through the air to him.

"Now get the hell out of here before I change my mind. I don't care much for a man drawin' down on me and walkin' away to tell the tale." His teeth still clenched the smoldering tip of a cigarillo when he turned his back on Danny and eased his long frame up against the bar and accepted the drink Rubylee held out to him.

"Young fool," Ballinger mumbled before knocking back the amber liquid. He welcomed the pleasant stinging sensation when he swallowed.

Out of the corner of his eye, he watched Danny stumble toward the door, looking back over his shoulder, humiliation etched in his ashen stare. Pushing the hinged doors open with his shoulder, the young man shuffled out into the street like a sleepwalker.

Rubylee scrambled to gather up the money and the handwritten deed. Smiling triumphantly, she handed the jackpot to Chance. He nodded his thanks and held his empty glass out to her.

"Once more," he said.

Her powdered cheeks wrinkled into a wide grin as she bustled away for the bottle. He wasn't so much interested in a drink as he was in providing her with a reason to leave him alone to think.

Damn, but he was glad he hadn't had to kill Danny McBride. Likely the young whelp had a mama somewhere who would mourn his passing, or maybe even a young wife and some raggedy little mongrels depending on him.

Taking off his hat and raking his fingers through his thick black hair, Chance mulled over the question of how a man goes about telling his wife he's lost all their money and their land in a poker game.

On second thought, maybe he should have done McBride a favor and shot him after all, Chance told himself. A contrary woman could sure make a man's life miserable. He shook his head at that disagreeable thought and flipped his hat back onto his head. An adjustment with his thumb set it comfortably as he let his gaze wander absently down the row of grizzled miners and dust-choked drovers who lined the bar.

Virginia City. What a town. The back door to hell, someone had once said. But a lucky town for him, Chance figured. Three days in one place and no one had asked questions. But tonight he'd let his guard down and come close to killing a man. Another day and his luck might turn sour. He'd won some money and a ranch . . . half interest, McBride had said. Not a bad night's work.

Absorbed in thought, Chance hardly noticed when Rubylee moved up beside him and set the bottle down. He felt her brush her voluptuous body against his like a stray cat, and irritation pricked him.

He remembered she'd tried to tell him something when McBride had placed his last bet. "Rubylee, you know something about McBride's place?"

Her knowing smile made him wish he'd never asked. Rubylee didn't give anything without a price.

"Sure do," she said proudly. "Let's you and me go upstairs, and I'll tell you everything I know." Her invitation was a low murmur, nearly lost in the noisy din of whiskey-sated laughter and rowdy voices that saturated the smoky, blue air.

She leaned harder against him, letting her fingers play up and down the length of his shirtsleeve until he edged away from her. If she was offended, she didn't show it.

"Oh, now what's the matter, honey? Don't feel like playin'?"

"No more games tonight, Rubylee," he said without looking at her.

"The big rancher's all of a sudden too high and mighty for the likes of little ole Rubylee, is that it?" When he didn't respond, she relented. "Oh, all right. What do you want to know?"

"Forget it," he said, and lifted his glass again.

"Now don't go gettin' all riled." She smiled and looped her arm possessively through the crook of his elbow and leaned close. "Come on, honey," she coaxed. "Don't be that way. We've had us a good time these past few days, haven't we?" She pressed herself closer.

For some reason, tonight her attempts at seduction left him cold. It wasn't that Rubylee wasn't attractive, Chance told himself as he turned to look at her and she smiled. The body she displayed so brazenly was built to please a man, and her long, thick hair was the color of spun gold. He recognized that she'd been really pretty, once. But her natural attractiveness had been corrupted by the fetid air and the dark influences of places like Bummer Dan's. She couldn't be much over twenty, Chance figured, comparing her to the young women he knew back home. Although it was hard to tell; the kind of life women led working in saloons aged them unnaturally in body and spirit, as the lines already collecting around Rubylee's generous mouth and eyes attested.

With a resigned sigh, Chance reached into the

pocket of his split-leather vest and pulled out a small leather pouch. "All right, now tell me what you know about the McBride place," he said, pressing a gold piece into her cool palm.

She glanced down at the coin and her mouth puckered into a pout. "So you think that's all it takes, huh? Just this pitiful little piece of gold buys you everything I know?"

A wave of angry heat crept up his neck and spread across his scalp, but he added five more coins to the one already in her hand.

"It's only right," she insisted, her tone defensive. "I've been real good to you these last few days. I haven't been with any other man since you rode in." She batted her lashes and smiled innocently, but her attempt at portraying the coy maiden was hopelessly lost on Chance. "No one but you, honey."

"And now we're even."

Silently, Rubylee studied the coins, turning them over in her hand for a moment before suddenly shoving them back at him. "Take me with you, Chance," she blurted, clutching his forearm. "Please! Take me when you go." When he didn't respond, she added, "I'll pay my own way, Chance. You know firsthand the kind of money I can make in these mining camps and cow towns. I'll give you a share—"

"Stop it," he shouted, cutting her off in midsentence.

Her face fell. "B-but I dealt you that winning hand. I brought you good luck, didn't I?" Her voice dropped to a whisper. "I thought you were different. Not like the others. You were nice to me."

All contempt turned to pity as the hopelessness of her plight struck an all too familiar chord deep within

Chance. And although he could never allow her to go with him, the desperation he saw in her eyes touched him. That haunted look was the same one that stared back at him every time he looked in a mirror. A year of running took its toll on a man.

"Rubylee, I won that hand fair and square and you know it."

"Sure, I know you did. But lots of fellas think I really *do* bring them good luck. Now you take Cecil Moorehouse—that fella who wears the tall silk hat down at Sweeney's—he swears if I sit beside him during a game he'll win. You know Cecil?"

Chance could only shake his head.

"Well, anyway, if I was to go with you, maybe I could start bringing you luck like I bring Cecil." Her eyes were shining.

"I can't take you with me, Rubylee." Though his tone was soft, she winced as though he'd slapped her.

"Can't? Or won't?" she shot back.

"Both," he said quietly. If he owed her anything, it was the truth, but now it hung between them, ugly and black.

She glared at him, unblinking, as she raked the coins from his palm, her nails biting into his flesh. She shoved the money into the small, dingy satin bag that hung from a tattered black ribbon at her waist. "It's a big spread up in the high country," she said, her voice devoid of emotion. "Plenty of water and grass. But that boy—Danny, like he said, he didn't own all of it."

"Then who does?"

Her eyes shone with wicked pleasure as she dropped her voice conspiratorially. "Now, you understand it's only gossip, but they say some old maid relative runs roughshod over the place." She hesitated and made a ceremony of opening the small pouch again and peering disappointedly inside.

Chance ignored the greedy gesture. He'd already given her more than he'd intended. "Go on," he prompted her.

"Well, when Danny's pa got himself shot up in a poker game, the old man left the ranch split between 'em—the old gal and Danny. The way I hear it, she's the one who wears the britches now—if you get my meanin'." Rearing back, she placed a hand on each well-rounded hip and smiled. "Looks like you won yourself a ranch *and* a partner, Mr. Ballinger." One penciled eyebrow arched knowingly.

He finished his drink in one short swallow. Suddenly the cloying scent of rose water wafting around Rubylee's blond hair made him yearn for fresh air. Pushing past her, he stalked toward the door.

"Where you goin'?" she called, trotting after him. "Ballinger, you ain't leavin' already? Aw, come on back, honey. Don't be that way. I was only teasin'." She grabbed his arm. "Stay with me, Chance," she pleaded in a hoarse whisper. "Just one more night."

Her eyes, the pleading eyes of a stranger, begged him, and a foul-tasting mixture of disgust and pity roiled in his gut and soured in his mouth. "Good-bye, Rubylee," he said. "I hope your luck turns real soon." He shouldered his way through the crowd without looking back.

"My luck don't need turnin'," she sneered. "But I coulda brought you luck, Ballinger. I was born lucky!" she shouted at his back. "Everybody knows it. Damn you, Ballinger. You'll see!"

The bark of her shrill prophecy followed him into the street, its irritating echo still chafing his ears all the way down Alder Gulch as he walked quickly toward the livery.

He'd let her get too close, and he cursed himself now for his foolishness, for his lack of caution. Numbly indulging in the distractions she'd offered for the last three days had been too easy.

In the last year he'd spent too much time in Bummer Dan's and places like it. But at last he'd drunk his fill. He felt itchy, agitated, restless—more than ready to move on. Had fate and the deed to Danny McBride's ranch given him a somewhere to move on to?

But what about Canada? Chance asked himself. That hastily conceived plan, born on a dark, desperate night when he'd been running for his life, had been the thread he'd clung to for nearly a year.

Since the night of Jim's murder, he'd somehow managed to outrun and outwit his pursuers at every turn. But how much further would his luck stretch? Was tonight the beginning of another streak or the end?

Leaning against a tree outside the livery, he studied the glowing tip of his cigarillo and let himself indulge in the fantasy of what it would be like to ranch again. Oh, what he wouldn't give to feel the kind of satisfying tired that settled over a man at the end of a hard day's work, to lose himself in the blessed oblivion of one dreamless night, to take for granted again that easy peace of mind that only a pair of callused hands can bring.

When he tried to imagine that high-country ranch he could almost see its emerald meadows, taste the water dipped from its snow-fed streams, and smell its pine-scented air. Clean. Unspoiled. By God, a man could renew himself daily just by breathing that pure, sweet air!

Over his shoulder he could still see the flickering lights and hear the bawdy strains of the city's night music. The galloping melody of tinny pianos, drunken laughter, and shouted obscenities created the vulgar chorus of a song Chance had never grown used to singing, and had long grown tired of hearing.

Yet the memory of a time when he'd sought harmony in all that discord still haunted him. It had been another lifetime, he told himself. Or so it seemed to him now.

Dropping the glowing stub of his cigar, he ground it out with his heel, his boots throwing up dust as he strode into the darkened livery. He found his horse in the first stall. Saddling General quickly, he led him out into the night silently, his nerves humming, exhilarated by the possibility of a return to the life he'd once loved. After another tug of the cinch strap, Chance swung up into the saddle, kicked the powerful chestnut horse into an easy lope, and turned his back on Virginia City.

Ahead, by the light of a luminous moon, the rugged outline of the Rockies shrouded the horizon and showed him the way.

But even as he traveled toward that place just the other side of the sunset, a single thought nagged him, a grim companion, a constant reminder, and he knew that no matter how far or how fast he rode, the past that dogged his days and haunted his nights would always ride with him.

Chapter Two

———◆◆◆———

KATHLEEN could see her breath in short frosty bursts as she hurried across the yard between the barn and the cabin. Warm milk sloshed over the sides of the metal bucket she was carrying and sent a chill skittering through her when it splashed on her hand. Although the ground in the meadow was already spongy with the spring thaw, last night winter had snuck back in with a bone-numbing wind, and this morning's chill was a crisp reminder that spring came late to the Gallatin Valley.

Pushing open the wooden door, she stepped inside the pine cabin, and, as always, the cozy interior of her home reached out and cheered her like a hug from an old friend. The coals in the hearth had all but died, and Kathleen set the bucket down and stirred the smoldering embers with an iron poker until a small fire came to life. She'd need a steady fire, she told herself, to warm her hands before she began the lacework for Mrs. Settlemier's new gown.

A handful of kindling snapped and popped as it was devoured by the eager flames, and the cheery sound made Kathleen feel less alone. She knelt in front of the fire, rubbing her palms over the small flame.

How many times after Ma died had she knelt like this before the fire, drawing on its warmth to soothe her loneliness? Could she count the times she'd fallen asleep in front of the hearth, waiting for her father to come home? And when the fire died and the damp cold of early morning seeped through the plank floor and wakened her, how many times had she climbed the ladder to the loft only to lie awake in her bed until sunup, still wondering?

Finally she'd hear him come lumbering in, clumsily shuffling to his own bed at the back of the cabin to grieve alone. A familiar knot of regret twisted in her stomach. Perhaps she should have let him know she'd heard him crying. Maybe it could have made a difference.

Danny had been only an infant when Kathleen first began her fireside vigils. Only a child herself, she wondered what she would have done in those days if not for Uncle Jeb's constant comfort and support. She sighed, wishing Jeb were here now.

After a moment, Kathleen rose, leaving her fireside memories and a bit of her loneliness at the hearth. Two crockery jars sat on the wooden workbench in the kitchen, waiting to receive the milk she would strain into them. As she tied a clean square of flour sack over the mouth of each jar, she thought about Danny, wondered where he was, and whispered the prayer she prayed every day for his safe return.

Perhaps this would be the day, she told herself, that she'd look out the window and see his black gelding bringing him home. The thought cheered her and she hurried through her morning chores with a lighter heart.

When she poured the dregs of the sweet-smelling milk into a small saucer on the floor, a huge yellow cat crossed the room noiselessly and rubbed a thank-you against her skirt.

"Good morning, Gideon." She stooped to scratch the yellow cat's ears before going outside to the pump.

On the porch, she lifted her gaze to the mountains that ringed the long, lush river valley that was her home. The peaks wore a wispy crown of perfect white this morning, and Kathleen wondered if they'd seen the last snow of the season.

Pa could always predict the weather, using the mountains as his gauge. Towering clouds boiling up over rugged peaks in July meant a thunderstorm. A somber gray haze descending the rocky slopes in January would bring a silent snow in the night. Wispy feathers, like the ones today, brought the promise of a clear, cool afternoon and were his special favorite.

"How I miss you, Pa," she whispered. "You used to teach me so much." The pump handle's squeaky melody broke the silence of her reverie and her gaze wandered back to the mountains, then fell away and settled on the road snaking along the valley floor.

On this clear morning she could see more than a mile to where the ranch road forked. To the east it led to the Gallatin River and on to Bozeman City. To the west, the Madison River and bustling Virginia City, some thirty-five miles away.

She thought again about Danny in that wild mining town. In an attempt to beat the larger outfits to the hungry beef market, she and Danny had decided he should leave with the herd at the end of April. But now it was already mid-May, and she wondered if their decision had been a prudent one. By her calculations, Danny should have been home days ago.

Though Bozeman City would have been closer, tales of Indian attacks along the trail made heading west to Virginia City seem worth the extra miles. But in the end Kathleen couldn't help wondering if the white man's temptations in Virginia City hadn't proven to be a far greater risk for her brother.

After rinsing the milk bucket, she hung it upside down to dry and plopped down onto the wooden swing at the end of the porch. With one leg curled under her, she leaned back, tipping her face toward the sun and closing her eyes. The warmth caressed her cheeks, and bright sunlight illuminated a thousand unshed tears swirling behind closed lids.

With a shake of her head, she dispelled her gloom. Where was her faith? she scolded herself. This time things would work out. Danny understood the importance of his mission as much as she did. The very existence of their home, the survival of Twin Rivers itself, hinged on their ability to begin paying the mountain of debt Pa had left them.

She remembered how shocked she'd been to discover their father had left the ranch split between them. That Pa had decided she should inherit and hold property was a constant source of honor to her, though scalding to her brother's pride. He had to have known that to her, preserving Twin Rivers, the land and the family's legacy, represented no less than a sacred trust.

Gideon distracted her from her thoughts as he padded across the porch and leaped up onto her lap, landing heavily. She smiled down at her old companion and wiped dry the memories that clouded her vision, shaking off the sadness that inevitably descended with thoughts of her father's last, desperate gamble. The one that had cost him his life.

"Back to work," she declared, nudging the reluctant cat from her lap before rising to her feet. Gideon's tail swished his disdain as he followed her. Out of habit, Kathleen stopped in the doorway and scanned the horizon again. A movement on the road drew her attention.

Shading her eyes with the back of her hand, she squinted to see a solitary rider just a scant half mile away and moving steadily toward the cabin.

"Danny," she shouted, her voice full of joy. Gideon hissed at her outburst and skittered into the cabin.

Clutching her heavy muslin skirt with both hands, Kathleen bolted across the porch, skipped the bottom step and hit the ground running. Danny was home! Everything would turn out right. Why had she worried?

"Danny," she shouted as she ran, closing the gap between herself and the rider. Winded by exertion and excitement, Kathleen stopped a moment to catch her breath, staring harder at the man on horseback coming toward her.

"Danny," she called again, but his name died on her lips and her heart sank when she realized the rider moving steadily toward her was not her brother after all.

The faster the horseman bore down on her, the more clearly she could see the outline of the tall figure sitting comfortably erect and proud in the saddle could never be mistaken for her brother's slight form.

It had been only her own longing to see her brother's dear face that had made her lose her head, and now she rocked back on her heels, cursing the folly of the impetuousness that left her alone and vulnerable on the open road.

Her hands curled into fists at her side. Oh, why had she acted so impulsively?

Standing alone and unprotected, she felt an irresistible urge to run, but instinctively she fought against it. She had no place to hide; open meadow lined the sides of the road. Besides, revealing fear to a strange critter was the surest way to be bitten, Pa had always said. Best stand firm and face the beast head-on.

The horse, a powerful-looking chestnut with four white stockings, looked to be that rare combination of muscle and spirit that would leave a more timid rider wondering who was in charge. But watching this rider's effortless control over the magnificent animal left no question in Kathleen's mind who was the undisputed master.

Square-shouldered and broad-chested, the rider moved with the graceful rhythm of the horse's fluid gait. He was within ten feet of her now. She took a deep breath and told herself she must have been blind to have mistaken this big man for her brother!

As he moved closer still she could see that he wore gray britches fortified at the seams with buckskin, as was the style of most cattle drovers she'd seen wandering the streets of Bozeman. In a plain, collarless white shirt and a worn split-leather vest, the stranger looked, at first glance, much like any ranch hand in the valley.

Kathleen's mind leaped to that hope. Perhaps he was merely a drover, separated for some unforeseen reason from his companions, seeking assistance in finding his way back to his outfit. Perhaps he'd even passed Danny

on the road. With luck, he might even be bringing news
of her brother. But the smile that hopeful wondering
produced faded when the glint of cold steel from a
sidearm caught her eye.

A prickle of alarm needled across her scalp and her
heart picked up a beat. Clasping her hands in front,
she took another deep breath and braced herself for
the worst.

Paradise! By God, compared to the bone-dry desert
of West Texas, this Montana high country was sheer
paradise. Surveying the lush countryside that surrounded him, Chance decided the opportunity of a lifetime had fallen, quite literally, at his feet.

His heart pounding with boyish excitement, he'd
crossed the Madison River at daybreak to savor the
view of the Gallatin Valley at dawn. And even before
he'd topped the crest of the last foothill, he felt as if
he knew how the meadow on the other side would look:
a sea of brilliant green, shimmering beneath a translucent veil of silvery dew.

Without listening, he could already hear its gentle
sounds, those sparkling creeks and sudden springs mur-
muring their peaceful promises, with a scent so clean
and sweet, like white linen sun-dried on a clothesline.

A home place. That's what this place felt like to
Chance. A place to start over. A place to build a home.
A place for Jim Jr. and Callie. Reflecting a moment on
the mental picture of the children he carried close to
his heart, Chance could almost hear their excited
voices. How he longed to see them, to gaze again in
wonder at how closely they resembled their parents.

Callie May, delicate and fair, like the mother she'd
never known, who'd died giving her life. And Jim Jr.,

tall for his age and dark-haired, nearly a replica of the boy James had been.

And even as his hungry heart devoured the beauty and peace of this place, his soul grieved for the orphaned children, his niece and nephew left behind in Texas. Too young and innocent to realize why he'd had to leave them so suddenly or why their lives had been so brutally disrupted. They deserved better. Jim Jr. and Callie deserved a second chance, even if he didn't.

And one way or another, Chance vowed, he'd give them everything they deserved. "Well, children," he whispered to himself, "if there really is such a thing as a second chance, this looks like the place where we just might find it.'

Preoccupied by his thoughts, he didn't notice the slight figure up ahead until he was almost upon her. At first he thought he'd only imagined seeing someone or something in the road. He stared harder, squinting against the light.

She moved and he saw her again. Framed by the morning sun at her back, she seemed almost translucent, like the drawing of the saints in his grandmother's bible.

Fascinated by the sunlit illusion standing dead center in his path, Chance pressed General into a smart trot to close the distance between himself and his vision more quickly. He kept his gaze fastened on the motionless form, half afraid she'd vanish if he dared glance away, even for an instant.

An odd mixture of relief and disappointment settled around his heart when he finally drew within a few feet of her and realized his vision-lady was merely a woman. Wispy tendrils of auburn hair, freed by a gentle breeze from the braided coil she wore at her nape, played

across her freckle-dusted face. A pretty face, fitting
perfectly into its surroundings, he decided. Not the im-
passive face of a pious saint or an angel, but the lively,
fresh-scrubbed, healthy face of a woman, glowing with
life and as radiant as spring.

A wayward breeze pressed her blouse against her,
revealing the form of her very feminine, very human
figure beneath the soft white cloth. Chance felt his
senses quicken as his eyes drank in every delicate drop
of her.

"Stop! Stop right there," she demanded. Her voice
held less gentleness than he would have expected and
a great deal more volume than her angelic appearance
would warrant.

"Morning, miss." Chance touched his hat jauntily
with his fingertips. "It's a glorious spring morning,
wouldn't you agree?"

A scowl pursed her strawberry lips and a rush of
color stained her cheeks. "Don't move that animal another step."

The curious lilt in her voice had to be Irish, he decided. Or perhaps Welsh, like the miners he'd met at
the camps in Virginia City.

"You're trespassing, stranger," she said, her voice rising. "You're on private land. Twin Rivers land."

Chance smiled. "If that's the case, then I'm exactly
where I want to be," he drawled as his fastened his
gaze on her lovely mouth. "I've business with the mistress of Twin Rivers, a Miss McBride."

The young lady tipped her chin and almost smiled.
"Is that a fact?" she asked. Her narrowed green eyes
assessed him with open suspicion. "And you know Miss
McBride personally, I suppose?"

"No, I'm afraid I've yet to have the pleasure of making her acquaintance," he admitted. "But I've business with her all the same. So if you'd be an obliging girl and direct me to the lady, I'll be on my way."

Her expression grew hard. "Miss McBride doesn't do business with strangers," she informed him. "Now turn your animal around and ride out of here before the men in that cabin over there come out and help you on your way. And they won't be nearly as friendly as I've been, I promise you that."

Part Irish and part rattler, he decided, chuckling to himself. Now *that* was the more likely origin of her charming brogue. But Lord, what a terrible liar she was. Nonetheless her verbal curlicues fascinated him and snuffed out any spark of anger her impudence might have ignited.

General, frisky and impatient to be on his way, pawed at the ground and snorted. Chance checked his mount with a subtle touch of the reins, noticing with a measure of respect how the young woman stood her ground as the powerful animal pranced within inches of her. In fact, she gave General very little notice at all, save what Chance decided was a brief and admiring glance. Clearly the young woman was accustomed to good horseflesh.

"I appreciate your advice." Chance touched his hat again in a gesture of dismissal and moved past her. "And I'll keep an eye out for those fellas with the guns."

So, the old maid didn't live all alone, after all, Chance told himself as he rode past her. His interest piqued by the young beauty, he wondered if she might be related in some way to the McBrides. A niece or a cousin, perhaps.

"Hold up there, mister," she demanded, running to

catch up to him. The top of her head measured even with General's withers. The streaks of red in her hair shone like polished copper in the sunlight as she half walked, half ran to keep up with General's brisk pace.

"Haven't you heard one word I've said?" she demanded. "In Montana, we don't take kindly to trespassers." Her voice was angry and breathless, and her lips formed a stubborn pout that Chance found utterly and completely beguiling.

"Tell me one thing," he began, "do you treat all visitors to that same line of malarkey? Or am I the special exception?" He felt amusement tug at his lips.

"You sir," she declared, her tone haughty, her eyes shooting fire, "are not at all exceptional or special in any way, I assure you!"

The glint of satisfaction that sparkled in her spring-green eyes didn't escape him. Had she thought she'd bested him? Her fire appealed to Chance's affinity for a challenge.

Pulling up suddenly, he pivoted around in the saddle, obviously startling her. "My but I'd love to teach you some manners, missy." He watched the disdain spread across her face like the shadow of an angry storm cloud moving over the prairie. "And much as I'm sure I'd enjoy the teaching, that lesson will have to wait. My business with the mistress of Twin Rivers comes first." And with that he kicked General up into a lope and left her in the dust.

"Stop!" she yelled. "Blast you! Stop I say!"

Part rattlesnake, part *crow*, Chance amended his earlier conclusion with a hearty laugh as the sound of her screeching followed him down the road.

Entering the wide yard, Chance rode right up to the sturdy-looking little cabin and shouted, "Hello! Hello in there! Anybody home?" When there was no response, he dismounted and led General to a long watering trough filled with fresh, clear water. As his animal refreshed itself, Chance tipped his hat back and gazed in wonder at the massive gray peaks that surrounded the valley. "We're a long way from home, boy," he murmured, patting the horse's neck affectionately. "A long way." And with any luck, maybe just far enough.

From the porch he noticed white ruffled curtains at the windows, through which he caught a glimpse of shining pots and pans hanging on the walls. A cheerful picture of loving care and feminine attention. A picture that, for the next few seconds, lulled Chance into bittersweet reverie.

The door stood slightly ajar and he called out again. "Hello inside. Is anyone home?" Silence greeted him, the place was obviously deserted, but all the same he rested his fingers on the butt of his .45 as he nudged the door open with the toe of his boot.

He peered in and saw no one. It seemed that army of menfolk his little road angel had spoken of had better things to do than await her order to murder trespassers.

The smell of coffee drew him inside to an iron stove set to one side of the room. While hunting a cup, he saw a plate of biscuits sitting on the warmer and his stomach lurched. For a moment, he contemplated helping himself, but on second thought he resisted. His welcome at Twin Rivers so far had been a frosty one, and after he broke the news of his part ownership to Miss McBride it was likely get a whole lot colder.

The room was neat and cozy. Four ladder-back chairs were arranged around a rough-hewn pine table.

A jar brimming with a riotous bouquet of wild flowers graced the center of the table and added a delicate scent to the air. Here and there pieces of white lace decorated the sparse pine furnishings and made him keenly aware of the road dust that covered him.

Opposite the wooden work space that designated the kitchen hung a quilt that partitioned the otherwise open room. Colorful rings formed an intricate and graceful pattern across the coverlet. There was little room for doubt that he had entered a woman's domain.

Beyond the half-drawn quilt curtain he could see a four-poster bed. A one-eyed yellow cat raised its head and watched him with mild disinterest.

When Chance lifted his gaze to a loft encircled by a pine railing, his mouth gaped open in surprise. Dragging his hat from his head, he ran his fingers through his hair. "What the . . . hell . . . ?" he breathed.

Draped all along the length of railing hung every manner and form of lady's undergarment. He whistled low, shook his head, and stared.

Pantalets, petticoats, and nightgowns. More lacy white things than he had names for, each more frilly and fragile than the last. Good Lord, endless bleached yards of the stuff! White lace and white cotton, white ribbons and white bows, a veritable army of white!

"What the hell kind of place is this?" he asked the big cat who'd moved up noiselessly beside him. But except for a friendly rub and a hoarse mew, the feline offered no explanation.

Chance turned back to the coffeepot at the same moment the young woman from the road burst through the door, her cheeks bright from exertion and her long, thick hair a wild wreath around her shoulders. The ribbon that had held the braided coil now dangled down her back, tangled in a long mane of cinnamon-colored curls.

The woman glared at him, sailing past him without a word, leaving a gentle trail of lilac in her wake as she disappeared behind the quilt partition. The unmistakable sound of shells being shoved into a shotgun chamber rang through the cabin. Alerted, Chance slid his .45 from its holster.

"Now get out!" she ordered, stepping back into the room toting a gun big enough to stop a charging buffalo at twenty paces. Unbelievably, she seemed oblivious to his drawn six-shooter.

"I swear, little gal, you really *do* lack manners," he drawled patiently.

"Get out of my house and off my land or I'll blow a hole in you big enough to herd cattle through," she threatened.

" 'Fraid I can't do that, missy." He pulled a prerolled cigarillo from his breast pocket and bit off the tip. "Who are you anyway, miss, and what's your connection to Twin Rivers? Are all those petticoats yours?" he asked, fighting a smile.

As he eased down onto a pine chair near the stone fireplace that dominated the north wall, Chance kept his gaze and his Colt trained on the little lady with the big gun.

"Who am *I*?" she sputtered, her indignation causing her voice to skip a notch higher. "And by what right, I'd like to know, do you invade my land, break into my house, and start asking all manner of personal questions?" She waved the shotgun around the room wildly, indicating the extent of his intrusion. "Just *who* the devil are *you*?" she demanded.

There it was again, that delightful brogue. The faster

she talked, the thicker the accent and the more she charmed him. Chance was certain now that the lace that trimmed her petticoats and the brogue that decorated her speech were both unmistakably Irish.

"Stop waving that gun around, gal, before you hurt yourself."

"It's not me who'll be hurting, mister," she spat out. "Now be on your way. You've pushed your advantage and tried my patience long enough. I'll not be responsible for the harm that will come to you if you do not leave at once." She tightened her grip on the shotgun and tilted her chin stubbornly.

The defiant determination with which she confronted him was not without its effect. It made her seem older than he'd first thought. Twenty, he guessed now, or maybe twenty-one. More fully grown than at first glance, too. He watched the rise and fall of high, firm breasts beneath the blouse she wore knotted at her slim waist.

"Well, I guess you've got me," he relented.

Distrust colored her eyes a darker shade of green when he lowered his gun and stood up.

"I know when I'm outgunned."

She took a wary step forward and lowered the barrel of the shotgun as he made a move toward the door. Suddenly she gasped as he reached out with blazing speed and snatched the shotgun, ripping it from her grasp. Stunned, she could only stand blinking in empty-handed silence.

"Have a seat, miss," he ordered politely, easing his own frame back into the chair, the shotgun in one hand and his Colt in the other.

Stubbornly, she stood her ground, arms folded tightly across her middle.

"Sit." He raised his voice and felt it fill the small room to bursting.

She didn't budge, but continued to defy him, standing at indignant attention, stiffening her already rigid spine. "Well, what are you waiting for?" she demanded. "Kill me, then! Go ahead. Kill me. I'll gladly die before I'll cower to your brute force."

Oh, but she was the stubborn one, Chance told himself, straining to keep a straight face. Such a prideful little package was in dire need of a lesson. "Well, suit yourself," he said, and sighed as he raised his Colt and took careful aim. "Though death seems a pretty harsh penalty for bad manners. But then again, I *am* a stranger to the Montana Territory and unaccustomed to its ways." He choked back the chuckle that rose in his throat.

He had to give her credit for nerve. Even with his Colt trained squarely at her heart, she never flinched but merely continued to glare down her pretty nose at him, her eyes blazing a haughty challenge. The color, however, *had* drained from her face and her pulse fluttered wildly at the hollow of her graceful throat.

Chance became momentarily fixed on that silky spot, wondering for a moment what it would feel like to kiss it. His eyes roved back to her face and saw that his brazen appraisal hadn't gone unnoticed. She blushed, but jutted her chin higher and pursed her lips disapprovingly until they were only a thin pink slit in her heart-shaped face.

"Well, get on with it," she ordered, her eyes filled with contempt.

What a crazy woman she was! All haughty and full of herself, not at all like one about to be murdered. Well, she didn't bluff easy, he'd have to give her that.

"Look here," he said finally. "Let's start all over, shall we? I've come a long way, and I have business with the mistress of this place. I'd be happy to let you live, and I'll even try to forgive your ill-mannered welcome, if you'll just tell me where I might find Miss McBride."

She hesitated only a moment, glaring at him before she blurted out, "I *am* Miss McBride, you silly fool!"

He felt the surprise register on his face. "Well, I'll be damned." He pushed his hat back farther on his head with the tip of his six-shooter before shoving the weapon back into its holster.

So this fiery little thing was the old maid of Twin Rivers ranch—now there was an interesting piece of news.

"Which Miss McBride?"

"Kathleen McBride."

"But you're no old—" He checked his choice of words. "Kathleen McBride, you say?" He'd given some thought to the old maid Rubylee had told him about and decided buying her out would be his best bet. If she wished to stay on, he'd figured on hiring her as a cook, a housekeeper, and if she proved an amiable old gal, maybe even a nanny to the children. But this young woman . . . well, he just hadn't figured on someone like her. He hadn't figured on her at all.

"So, you're Danny's sister?" he asked stupidly, still not quite believing.

His question went unanswered as she deluged him with a flood of her own questions. "You know my brother? How is he? Where is he? When will he be home?" The emotion that had seeped into her cool reserve softened her voice and her pretty face pleasantly. "Oh, please tell me, when did you see him? Is he well?" Looking past him toward the window, she asked again, "When will he be home?"

"Whoa, whoa, hold up there, young lady. One thing at a time," he admonished her. "The only thing I know about your brother is that he's a pitiful, poor card player."

She appeared stricken by his words, a grave shadow doused the spirited light flickering in her eyes, and though she tried to hide it, she even wavered a bit.

"I think you'd better sit down, miss," he suggested. "You don't look well, all of the sudden. And I've got some news that might come as a . . . well, as a bit of a shock. Here . . ." He motioned to the chair by the hearth. "Sit down."

For the first time, she abandoned her proud stance. All the blood drained from her cheeks, leaving her face and lips ashen. Her shoulders slumped and she brought her hands up to cover her mouth.

"Dear God," she whispered, and covered her eyes with her hands for a moment before taking a deep breath, straightening again, and clasping her trembling hands in front of her. "Go ahead," she said quietly. "Tell me, how did it happen? Where's the body?"

"What?" Chance rested the shotgun against the fireplace and moved over to her as the full impact of her misunderstanding hit him. "No, no, Miss McBride. You don't understand. Your brother isn't dead!"

He watched the relief wash over her, and the look of cool detachment returned with lightning speed to her face when she became fully aware of how close he was standing beside her.

"He's broke, that's all," Chance explained, gently. "Dead broke, I reckon."

She swallowed hard and when she spoke, her voice

shook. "Sir, kindly tell me whatever it is you know about my brother." Despite her obviously reeling emotions, she instructed him in the same condescending manner a schoolmarm might use to address a dull-witted child.

"As far as I know, he's still in Virginia City," he began. She still didn't look all that steady. "Miss, you really should sit down," he suggested again, motioning to the rocking chair.

She dismissed his concern with a quick, impatient wave of her small hand. "Please . . . just tell me what you know."

He hesitated only a moment, still worried about the extreme lack of color in her cheeks. "Your brother played poker in Virginia City and he lost. As near as I could tell, he lost everything." He watched his words scorch a trail of pain across her face.

"The money from the herd?" she whispered.

"Gone."

"The cattle?"

He nodded. "The money he was betting came from the sale of your cattle, I'm sure. And that money is long gone. The ranch, or at least, his half of it, he lost when his cash ran out. He lost it all, Miss McBride. Everything." He watched her proud expression wilt into one of abject humiliation and pain. Looking at her, he felt as though he'd crushed a vibrant rose beneath his heel. *Damn you, Danny McBride,* he cursed to himself. *This is your story to tell, not mine!* If only there had been some way he could have pulled the punch, protected her a little from the blow.

She stood stock-still, though her hands shook, and he knew that inside she was reeling. But she wasn't the fainting type, he told himself, wagering it would take a whole lot more than a sudden shock to make this little spitfire keel over.

"Thank you," she whispered when he pulled the rocking chair forward and eased it under her. She folded into the chair numbly. As he studied her face, he felt an unexpected lurch in his gut at the tears shimmering in her eyes.

"Water," she whispered, and pointed.

Looking around, he saw a bucket sitting on the wooden drainboard in the kitchen. Quickly, he crossed over to it, ladled a cupful and brought it back to her. With both hands, she guided the cup unsteadily to her lips and drank.

For a long moment after she swallowed, she stared into the cup and then suddenly rose and walked stiffly toward the window, as if she were made of glass and the slightest jar might shatter every bone in her body.

Without turning around she spoke, her voice a whispered version of the lilting soprano he'd already grown accustomed to hearing. "I wish to apologize for my behavior, Mr. . . . ?"

"Ballinger," he supplied. "Chance Ballinger."

"Mr. Ballinger. It's just that I was *so* depending on . . . That is, we needed those funds so badly and . . ." The words died on her lips. She stood without speaking, seemingly unaware of his presence for a long moment, and when at last she turned to face him, her expression was soft and kind.

A weak smile was all she could manage, but she gave it to him graciously. "May I offer you a warm meal before you leave, Mr. Ballinger? I know it seems little by way of repayment, but under the circumstances . . . well, I hope you understand. It was good of Danny to send you, and so good of you to come. I hope he paid you your wages before he . . . well, I hope you got your pay."

He watched her with growing admiration. She'd recovered from the stunning news with all the pride of a seasoned field general, and he found himself wishing he could think of a way to soften the next blow. But nothing came to mind.

Straight out was the best way, he assured himself. Besides, he reckoned that was how she liked to handle things: Direct. Head-on.

"Miss McBride," he began. "Kathleen." He savored the first taste as her given name rolled off his tongue like the title of a cherished song.

"Yes," she murmured, her emerald eyes shimmering with the threat of sudden tears.

"I think you'd better sit back down, Miss McBride," he said softly. "I've more to tell you. Much more."

And this time she did not ignore his suggestion.

Chapter Three

———❖———

"AND that's the long and the short of it, Miss McBride," he said quietly. "Your brother lost and I won. Fair and square. Simple as that."

Kathleen felt him searching her face, and she forced an expressionless stare that belied the utter turmoil that raged inside her. Hearing the grim details of Danny's disastrous gamble brought back every bitter memory of her father's death, but she'd be damned if she'd let this stranger see her pain. The McBrides had lost enough at the gaming tables; her pride, at least, could be salvaged.

Ballinger's eyes never left her face as he leaned back in the chair, stretched his long legs out in front of him, and folded his arms across his chest. His presence filled the room, his very male presence that produced a distracting self-consciousness in Kathleen and blessedly numbed the effect of his unbelievable story.

"So you see," he went on, "Twin Rivers isn't lost, it's just changed hands, that's all."

Was she supposed to take some kind of comfort in the fact that this gambler held all the money she had in the world and half of her birthright? Her outrage choked her, making speech a momentary impossibility.

"Now, I know for a fact that a man can make good money in cattle," he went on, "and that's exactly what I intend to do here at Twin Rivers."

Kathleen cringed. Despite his melodic drawl and his calm, southern manner, something warned her that once Chance Ballinger made an oath, he wouldn't back down without a fight. The proud set of his solid jaw, the intensity of his blue-eyed stare, were the characteristics of keen intelligence and dogged determination.

"Wouldn't you agree?" he asked, his sudden question jarring her from her open study of his face.

"I—I . . ." she stammered. Oh Lord, what had he said?

"Maybe you don't see it that way, but I for one can't see any reason why this place shouldn't pay its own way and turn a pretty profit, as well. Good grass, plenty of water . . . and the army always needs beef. Driving cattle to Fort Benton two, maybe three times a year makes more sense than a long drive through hostile territory to the railhead. And after I've secured the army's contract, I plan to begin—" He stopped suddenly. "Excuse me, Miss McBride, but you look confused. Am I going too fast? Do you have any questions?"

She shook her head numbly, trying to clear the jumble of thoughts that fought for her attention. *Fort Benton? The army? Did she have any questions?* Oh, she had questions, all right! Plenty of them! But none she'd give this stranger the satisfaction of asking.

Now as for Danny, that was another matter. She'd

have plenty of questions for her brother when he finally came home with his sorry tail tucked between his legs.

She felt his eyes on her as he waited for her response. In an effort to buy time, she rose and walked across the room, her hands clasped and her mind scrambling for the right words. This man, this gun-toting stranger believed he had some claim on Twin Rivers. Incredible, but true. She must set him straight, here and now, but she'd need to speak cautiously, measuring her words and his responses carefully.

So far he seemed cordial, but the gleaming sidearm slung low on his narrow hip was a constant reminder of his dangerous lifestyle.

Her mind grasped at a thread of hope. His demeanor *did* suggest an exposure to manners, perhaps an upbringing in the South. With luck, the remnants of a gentlemen might lie somewhere beneath his toughened exterior. Perhaps she could appeal to his sense of chivalry.

"Mr. Ballinger," she began, granting him a tenuous smile. "Surely you see the terrible mistake that's been made here. You seem to be a reasonable man, a man of basic intelligence. . . ."

He nodded, acknowledging her compliment, and an amused smile bloomed beneath his thick dark mustache.

What on earth did he find so amusing, Kathleen wondered, averting her gaze from him to gather the thoughts his maddening grin had so thoroughly scattered. Once composed, she met his eyes again. "You wouldn't really expect me to hand over fifty percent of my ranch based on some . . . card game played between you and my brother, now, would you, Mr. Ballinger?"

"Poker," he said.

"Pardon me?"

"It was poker, ma'am," he said, smiling obligingly.

"Be that as it may . . ." She bit the inside of her lip, struggling to maintain her poise. "As I was saying, as a *gentleman* I know you will be sensitive to my position," she said. "Just as I am trying to understand yours—and I *am* trying to understand," she added quickly.

"And I *do* appreciate that, Miss McBride." His tone was distinctly mocking.

She set her jaw and clasped her hands tighter, trying to somehow bind the frayed edge of her nerves for a few moments longer. "I realize you've come a great distance," she began again, "and Lord only knows what you expected to find. But Twin Rivers is owned and operated solely by the McBride family." She took a deep breath and tried to read a reaction in the intense stare beneath the thick, dark slashes of his brows. Failing at that, she went on.

"We already have one hired man and Jeb is really more a member of the family than an employee." She glanced out the window at the small two-room bunkhouse south of the cabin, wishing her old friend and adopted uncle were there now instead of a half day's ride away in Bozeman City. "We haven't much money—as you are no doubt aware from your dealings with my brother."

"I am aware of that," he said, nodding. "And I quite agree with most everything you've said so far. There is no need to hire another hand at this time."

Undaunted by what she decided was his intentional lack of understanding, she charged forward again. "However, I am not an unreasonable person and I am prepared to offer you food and lodging in exchange for labor until my brother returns from Virginia City. Perhaps longer, if need be, at least until this misunderstanding can be straightened out." She paused, hoping her meaning had at last sunk in. But instead of agreeing, he only watched her, intently staring with a look of complete concentration on his face.

"I think my offer is more than generous, under the circumstances," she prodded him. "And if you are sincerely interested in ranching, the lessons you learn here will serve you well on your own place someday." Hardly daring to believe the air had been so easily cleared, she offered him a polite smile and braced for his reply.

But for the moment he only sat, silently contemplating. When finally he rose, he moved toward her in the kitchen. Like a big cat he moved noiselessly, covering the space between them with unexpected fluidity for a man his size.

Kathleen drew a quiet breath, but instead of its having a steadying effect, she experienced quite the opposite. The mingled aromas of tobacco, leather, and musky male caused her nerves to hum, and she realized with a shock that his rugged scent seemed to have oddly stimulated her quickened senses.

Without warning, he reached for her. Startled, she stepped aside. He reacted instantly to her movement. She moved again. He moved back, and for an uneasy moment she felt as though they were engaged in some peculiar dance.

Uncertain and disoriented, she jumped when he moved toward her again. When they almost collided, a startled cry escaped her lips.

"Water," he explained, indicating the bucket behind her on the drainboard. "Just a drink of water, if you please."

"Certainly," she said, awkwardly backing away.

She watched as he filled a cup and brought it to his lips. When he drank, the cords in his muscular neck constricted and expanded. Studying his face, Kathleen found his features irregular and jagged when taken one by one, yet startlingly handsome in total.

Shrouded with blue-black beard stubble, the proud set of a square chin and the rise of sharp cheekbones lay in stark contrast to the penetrating clear blue of his eyes. Like her beloved Rockies, the angular length of his face was a study in light and shadow. A powerful visage; once seen, not easily forgotten.

The collarless shirt he wore open at the throat revealed the beginnings of a coarse dark thatch of black that she could envision spreading down and across his broad chest. When her gaze traveled back to his face, she found him smiling at her over the rim of the cup.

Realizing he'd been fully aware of her study, she lowered her lashes and cursed her curiosity as well as the rush of heat she felt flooding her face.

"Delicious." He swallowed again. "Spring water or well?"

"Well," she answered flatly, ignoring her racing pulse. If he was stalling to unnerve her, it was working.

"Delicious," he proclaimed again.

"It's only water." She glared at him, unblinking. The man was truly maddening. Her proposal of room and board had been a generous one—in these times, more than generous! "Mr. Ballinger, I don't wish to seem impatient, but did you quite fully understand my proposal of room and board in exchange for labor?" She knew her tone sounded shrill, but her irritation was mounting and at this point she didn't much care how she sounded.

"Fully," he said with a satisfied smile. His eyes

moved over her freely, making her feel uncomfortable, yet oddly excited in a strange and thoroughly confusing way. A trickle of chilling perspiration slid down her spine, and a tiny shiver rippled beneath her skin from her scalp to her toes.

At the same time a wariness crept over her as the vulnerability of her immediate position dawned. She was completely alone with a darkly handsome, ominous stranger. The frightening fact that he was bigger, stronger, and faster than she was seeped into her consciousness.

Danny was obviously still miles away. Jeb wasn't expected to return until week's end. And although Ballinger's manner until now had been perfectly harmless, albeit teasing and mocking, the physical aura he radiated was commanding, almost frightening in its quiet strength.

She squared her shoulders and cleared her throat before speaking again, lest something in her demeanor betray her growing apprehension. "If you truly understood my good-faith proposal, Mr. Ballinger, then why haven't you given me the courtesy of a reply?" she demanded. She knew pushing him could be dangerous, but she couldn't seem to stop herself.

"Ah, but I'm afraid it is you who do not fully understand our situation, Miss McBride." Leaning one hip against the drainboard, he crossed his arms over his ample chest. "Please allow me to simplify the matter for you. First, the McBride family no longer has sole ownership of Twin Rivers. Second, I'm willing to give you a fair price for your share."

"Fair price! Mr. Ballinger—"

He went on as if she hadn't objected, his tone firm

and uncompromising, yet oddly gentle. "Third. If you agree to sell your share, but feel inclined to stay on, I'm sure we can come to some mutual agreement that would make that possible. I've seen what you can do with a needle and thread, and I'll be needing a cook and a housekeeper, as well."

His cook! His housekeeper! Stunned by the absurdity of such a notion, Kathleen could only stare at him in shocked disbelief.

"But if you refuse to sell out, or to hire on as my housekeeper . . ." he hesitated only an instant before he added, "Well then, I guess that would make us partners, wouldn't it?" He smiled. "I'm here to stay, Miss McBride," he said with finality. "I aim to turn this place into a money-making operation as quickly as I can." His gaze shifted past her and a spark of some dark emotion she couldn't read flared in his eyes. "God willing, I aim to make this place my home," he said quietly, almost to himself.

And then, in a gesture of complete dismissal, he drained the last of the water and set the cup down behind him.

"Now, I'll gladly accept that offer of a hot meal you mentioned," he informed her, all smiles again. "Been three days since I had decent grub. Where do I wash up?"

She watched the deep creases that had moments ago made his expression seem cold and ominous melt away. The now-familiar grin was firmly in place; his light, easy manner completely restored.

Kathleen felt numbed, stunned, unsure of where to go from here. Unbelievably he thought the matter was resolved. *Dear God*, her mind shrieked, what nightmare had sprung to life before her very eyes? Why, the man was nothing more than a saloon gambler! A gun-slinger as well, judging by the way he handled his gun.

His own, he'd said. *Twin Rivers, he aimed to make it his own!* Half owner and full partner!

The thought jarred her out of her voiceless stupor, prodding her into action. Drawing up to her full height, which still left her a good six inches shorter than the dark-haired stranger, she struggled for whatever measure of control would allow her to speak coherently.

"Stay on?" she said, her voice jerky. "Why, thank you *ever* so much for allowing me to stay on in my own home." She answered his patronizing smile with a haughty scowl. "And what do you know about ranching?" she demanded without giving him time to answer. "What do you know about cattle? Or a home, for that matter?" Control be dashed, the man's gall would provoke a saint! "*A home,* you say! Well, Mr. Ballinger, this is *my* home and I'll not sit idly by and watch it be stolen by the likes of you."

His eyes narrowed and his jaw tightened. "Careful, gal." His voice had grown ominously low again. But rather than intimidating, his warning only incensed her further, her anger rendering her fearless.

"Only the lowest scoundrel would take advantage of a boy, a young man barely eighteen. A low scoundrel, I say!" She was shouting as she paced, her fists clenched at her sides. The pulse in her throat throbbed harder as her estimation of his character spilled with brutal eloquence from her mouth, the words and the courage to say them fueled by an inner rage that burned ever hotter each time she looked at him.

"I detest your kind!" she spat finally. "With no future and a dark sinful past, no doubt. Men like you who prey on the weaknesses of good, honest men. You steal their very hopes, their dreams—" *Their lives,* an inner voice whispered as the memory of her father's sudden and cruel death sprung stingingly to her mind's eye. Her voice cracked. "Well, you'll not waltz in here and steal *my* dreams," she informed him, her voice ragged with emotion, "not while there's breath left in my body!"

Drawing boldly within an arm's length of him, she stood with her hands planted on her hips and stared at the pulse that pounded at his temples. The rage registered in his face hardened his features into chiseled granite. Had she been less livid his dangerous expression might have caused her to fear for her very life, but as long as her anger filled her it gave her the raw courage of a wounded lioness defending her young.

"You say you'll buy me out," she went on. "And with what money, might I ask, do you intend to purchase my ranch?" Her voice broke again and she swallowed hard.

He didn't answer but only glared at her, his eyes icy and searing at the same time.

"No, Mr. Ballinger," she spat out. "No, I'll not be bought out, not with my own money or with anyone else's. Twin Rivers is not for sale. Not now! Not ever!" And with that she spun on her heels, turning her back to him to swipe at the sudden tears that scalded her eyes. "Now I suggest you move on, gambler, before I fetch the law," she finished with breathless outrage.

For a long moment neither of them moved nor spoke. Her outburst left her feeling drained, depleted. When at last she found the courage to turn around and face him, she found him stroking his mustache thoughtfully with his thumb.

"Good Lord," he muttered, shaking his head. "Do you always go on like that?" Clearly he was more exasperated than angry. "Someone really ought to teach you some manners, gal."

"No one has to teach me anything," she snapped. "And certainly not you!"

Taking his hat off with one hand, he raked his long fingers through his thick inky hair with the other. After replacing the hat firmly on his head, he stared at her for a moment longer and then started slowly toward her again.

With each step he moved forward, she stepped back one. Just as in the kitchen around the water bucket, Kathleen felt their wary dance begin again. Not until he was so close that she could see tiny sunbursts of silver-blue in his eyes did her common sense beg her to bolt and run. But she would not listen; her pride and an uneasy yet compelling fascination held her in lockstep with the dark-haired stranger.

"You're wrong, Miss McBride," he said as he continued to move steadily toward her. "There are a great many things I could teach you."

She tipped her chin and folded her arms across her middle to still her quivering senses as the sound of his butter-soft voice slipped down her spine.

"I can assure you there's nothing I care to learn from the likes of you," she declared, sounding not half as repelled as she would have liked.

He moved closer and she saw his jaw clench as they continued to move as one across the room. Without warning she backed into something solid, the rocking chair by the hearth.

Her knees folded and she tried to duck past him, but

before she could slip away, his hands came down on her shoulders and he pressed her gently but firmly into the rocker.

Inexplicably, his touch triggered a shock wave of heat that zipped through her body like a miniature bolt of lightning. Her mouth went dry. Her lower lip trembled. She wanted to cry out, but she knew it would be useless, that her voice would fail her. Bracing against myriad dizzying sensations, she made her body rigid beneath his touch.

When she was finally sitting, he lifted his hands from her shoulders. And though untouched, now, she still felt oddly bound where she sat. The stunning realization that he held her by the sheer power of his presence shook Kathleen's confidence to the core.

She grappled with this bewildering realization. Never had another human being held such control over Kathleen McBride.

Her eyes followed his hand as he slowly reached into his vest pocket and pulled out a piece of tattered paper. Tossing it onto her lap, he commanded, "Read it."

Her hands shook as she lifted the document and read. By Danny's own hand, it was all there, and duly signed. *Dear Lord, Danny,* she cried inwardly, *what have you done?* The bitter truth burned her eyes as she reread her brother's mutinous contract.

"It's legal," Ballinger said, in the tone of voice one might use to comfort a frightened child. When he reached for the handwritten deed, his fingers lingered on hers for an instant. His eyes softened and he seemed almost ready to console her.

A burning lump rose in her throat and she averted her eyes quickly. Bitter disappointment and frustration engulfed her, but she fought the defeat that despair would bring. Shedding her tears now would be the same as surrendering, she told herself.

She flinched when he touched her chin, despising his touch and yet strangely drawn to his warmth. With his thumb and forefinger, he tipped her face, forcing her to look up at him. She watched his languid gaze rove over her features, one at a time, stopping for a long, breathless moment on her mouth.

Instinctively she moistened her parched lips with a quick flick of her tongue. His own lips parted slightly and his eyes blazed.

"Lesson number one," he whispered gruffly. "Listen when I tell you something."

She held her breath, imagining that if she dared breathe or make the slightest movement, the air between them, already crackling with tension, might explode.

"Lesson two. I take orders from no one. I'll come and go and conduct the business of Twin Rivers ranch, our ranch, the way I see fit."

She felt the power of each word reverberate against her senses like rumbling thunder. When he dropped his hand away from her face, his heat remained. And although he no longer touched her, she found herself transfixed by his gaze.

How long she was held there, she couldn't say, but finally, mercifully, he looked away, shattering the spell she knew in some primitive way had held them both, one to the other, binding them together as surely as if they'd been tied with the strongest ropes.

She inhaled sharply, trying to refill her burning lungs, to steady her racing heart and still her reeling senses.

"I've cash for the mortgage note," he said evenly.

"Now that I've got it, I will not lose this ranch to debt, that much I promise you." He reached into his pocket again and laid two twenty-dollar gold pieces down onto the table. "Household money. Use it as you see fit . . . partner." His eyes flicked over her face again and his slow, intimate smile pulled a knot in the pit of her stomach.

Not trusting her legs, Kathleen remained seated. The reality of the situation stung like a cold-water dunk in the Gallatin River. Everything she'd worked for, all her dreams, were disappearing like frost on the pump handle beneath the spring sun.

Clinging to her pride, she gripped the wooden arms of the rocker for strength. "You may stay . . ." she began, but upon hearing the humiliating catch in her voice, she cleared her throat before continuing. "You may stay in the bunkhouse until such time as I can raise the necessary funds to buy out your . . . your . . ."

"My half?"

"Your half"—she swallowed—"of Twin Rivers." She swallowed again and stared at him, praying her expression reflected more strength than she felt.

When he reared back and laughed, she jumped. And he laughed again. And the harder he laughed, the longer he laughed and the air rang and shook and shuddered with the sound until Kathleen thought the very walls might burst.

Utterly confused, she could only sit and stare and listen as his laughter pelted her like rain from a cloudburst on a summer afternoon.

At last he inhaled a ragged breath, and wiping his glistening eyes with the back of his hand, he said, "Oh, yes . . . yes, ma'am," he said with feigned reverence. "I *do* think I'd prefer the quiet comfort of the bunkhouse, thank you, over a house infested with a screeching female. And now if you'll excuse me, I'll go wash up."

He headed for the door. "I take my eggs over easy, my biscuits light and my steaks rare," he informed her over his shoulder. "Oh, and one more thing, partner." He paused with his hand on the doorknob and turned and lifted his eyes dramatically to the loft. "Your petticoat's showing." And with that he left her, his laughter echoing behind him as he went.

The door had hardly closed when the cup that had so recently touched his taunting lips flew across the room. But the crashing sound it made when it shattered against the door gave precious little release to the anger that choked Kathleen.

From the window she saw him at the pump. When he looked up, she ducked behind the curtain and watched him drink his fill and then dunk his bare head under the gushing stream of clear water.

"Drown, damn you!" she cried, closing her eyes as the tears fell. *He's won*, she told herself miserably. The insufferable, strutting, stretching rooster had called her bluff and won as surely as he'd beaten poor Danny out of half of everything she held dear. Dear Lord, had a more detestable, galling man than Chance Ballinger ever been created?

She swiped savagely at the tears cascading down her burning cheeks, even as she peeked again between the curtains. He was still chuckling when he shrugged out of his vest and in one graceful motion peeled off his shirt and stood shamelessly bare-chested in the sunlight.

And just as shamelessly, she watched as sparkling rivulets of water trickled through the dark coils of hair on his chest and streaked his firm belly, making his sun-burnished skin glisten.

Suddenly, viciously, Kathleen jerked the curtains closed, disgust filling her—disgust toward him, the gambler and gunslinger, and toward herself, as well, for the undeniable control his physical presence held over her.

Oh, she should have blasted him when she'd had the chance, she told herself. An acquittal would have been assured! He was so smug, so sure. But worst of all, he held all the cards. Her money. Her ranch. Hadn't she seen Danny's handwritten betrayal with her own eyes?

But I'll not be defeated so easily, Mr. Ballinger, she vowed as she slammed her hand down on the wooden drainboard and cursed the day he was born. She refused to be defeated by him, she told herself. And certainly not by her own emotions. Deadly blizzards, flash floods, destitution, even the death of her dearest loved ones, hadn't defeated her yet.

And one way or another, if it was the last thing she ever did, Kathleen McBride vowed to rid Twin Rivers of this latest plague now visited upon her in the person of one Chance Ballinger.

Chapter Four

———————◆———————

A dozen small wooden bobbins wound with white thread dangled from the cylindrical pillow Kathleen settled onto her lap. When she finished, the lace she was weaving tonight would trim the collar on Ida Settlemier's gown. Passing the bobbins over and around the intricate pattern pinned to the pillow, Kathleen's fingers moved quickly. Her mother had taught her to weave lace before she'd taught her to read, and the young Kathleen had learned quickly, duplicating the traditional rose-and-shamrock patterns easily. Soon even the most complicated designs came second nature.

But tonight her fingers felt unusually clumsy and she tended to bobble a stitch here and there as she sneaked a look to see if a light still flickered from the bunkhouse window.

What was he doing over there? Why didn't he go to bed? How could she possibly rest easy with a gunslinger, a gambler, prowling only a few hundred feet away?

This had been one long torturous night so far, one Kathleen wouldn't soon forget. Nervous, edgy, and tired, she longed for sleep. But like the shadows cast from the oil lamp dancing across the cabin wall, the unbelievable events of the day flickered and flared through Kathleen's mind, making any hope of rest impossible.

Her mind labored late into the night as steadily as her fingers worked the bobbins, searching for that thread of hope to soothe and calm her agitated spirit, searching for a way out of the despicable tangle into which she'd been unwittingly trapped. Her spirits rose and fell as each new plan took form, only to be quickly discarded as unfavorable or impossible.

Finally, as certain reality dawned, Kathleen's hands fell idle and she sighed wearily. There really was only one way out: Somehow she had to obtain enough money to buy back Danny's share of Twin Rivers. But how?

With quick mental tallying, Kathleen reviewed the sewing projects she still had outstanding. First, there was Ida Settlemier's new gown and three lace altar cloths for the church, and Mrs. Newcomb had delivered material for two more lace-trimmed petticoats just last week. Then there were the pantalets and Sunday dresses for the Jensen twins—the sisters always paid promptly, Kathleen tried to cheer herself by remembering. And perhaps she could convince Ben Allerby to carry sunbonnets like the ones she'd fashioned for his mercantile store last summer.

But even as she hoped Ben might agree to sell her bonnets, Kathleen wondered where she'd find the time to make them. She'd already taken on more projects now than she had time for, and even if she could somehow find the time, where would she find the money she'd need to buy the extra supplies?

Her defeating thoughts caused her lips to draw together in a tight frown. Hopelessness settled over her like a sodden blanket. The money brought in from her sewing, though a blessed supplement, would never be enough to buy the gambler out.

Besides, how could she even think about taking on more sewing projects, Kathleen chided herself, when she hadn't even started setting the sleeves on the dress Daphne Brewer planned on wearing to the Spring Social, and she'd promised Ida Settlemier a fitting day after tomorrow.

At the thought of seeing Ida, Kathleen's mind leaped to Ida's husband, Charles, the banker. Three years ago Pa had strained his friendship with Charles to the breaking point by mortgaging Twin Rivers past its value. Only with Kathleen's solemn assurance that a substantial payment would be made when Danny returned from Virginia City, had Charles agreed to stall foreclosure procedures this long.

Kathleen shuddered to think about what could happen when Charles learned that Danny had lost his share of Twin Rivers in a poker game.

She would have to plead with him for more time and more money. If only the bank would give her another chance, she'd buy out the gambler, find Danny, bring him home, and life on Twin Rivers could get back to normal, the way it used to be.

Well, maybe not *exactly* the way it used to be. Many things would need to change, Kathleen knew. And the first change would have to come from Danny. Though her deep love for him made her loath to admit it, no one was more aware of her brother's shortcomings than Kathleen.

Sometimes she wondered if he would ever grow up, if he would ever take hold and start acting like a man. Was she partly to blame? she wondered. Perhaps she'd made it too easy for him by continually forgiving him, by always helping him out of whatever scrape he found himself facing.

The last time his shenanigans had come close to landing him in jail, and Kathleen had thought he'd learned an important lesson. She could still remember his promise to change after the fiasco last fall cost the family precious funds—funds they could ill afford to lose.

It all started when Danny and his friend Billy Franks were target practicing with their rifles too near Hiram Bonner's barn and a stray bullet wound up killing Bonner's bull. As if killing the animal hadn't been bad enough, Danny and Billy had run away without telling Bonner what they'd done.

When the truth finally came out, old man Bonner understandably screamed for Danny's hide. In the end, Kathleen had been the one who'd placated their neighbor, agreeing to pay five hundred dollars—more than twice what the old bull had been worth—to keep Bonner from going to the sheriff and swearing out a complaint against her brother.

Even after a heated discussion on the grave consequences of his actions, Danny hadn't really seemed to understand the seriousness of what he'd done, dismissing it as a freak accident that could have happened to anyone.

Well, now he'd gone too far, Kathleen told herself.

This time it wouldn't be so easy to undo his mistake. And despite her deep love for her brother, what he'd done wouldn't be simple or easy to forgive.

Kathleen glanced down at the lace in her lap and realized she hadn't the heart to continue her work. Setting aside the half-finished collar, she doused the light and crawled into bed, her heart heavy and her mind burdened. Bitter thoughts swirled as one inescapable thought tormented her: The arrival of the gambler at Twin Rivers meant that nothing would ever be simple or easy again.

Hours later the smell of coffee tugged Kathleen from sleep. She groaned and rolled over, her body sore and stiff from too little sleep and too much worry. But her mind had already begun to stir, and when her thoughts finally cleared enough to equate the smell of coffee with the presence of someone else in the cabin, she bolted upright in bed. "Danny!" she cried.

Danny's come home! her mind insisted as she threw back the covers and swung her feet over the side of the bed. The morning chill nipped at her feet as she ran across the wooden floor, eager to see her brother sitting at the kitchen table sipping from a steaming mug. Tears of joy sprang to her eyes and made her vision shimmer.

But almost immediately, keen disappointment replaced her excitement as one glance at the cabin's small interior told her she was alone. A fire snapped in the hearth and a load of wood stood in a neat stack beside the door. A single cup and saucer sat on the table and the coffeepot gurgled merrily on the warmer above the cookstove, but Kathleen's spirits sagged.

Someone had brought in the wood, built the fire, and

made the coffee, but it hadn't been Danny, she realized sadly. If her brother had come home, he would have awakened her.

Mingled with the coffee, another scent, oddly pleasing and yet strangely disconcerting, teased at her nose. Tobacco! Her anger flared. The gambler! The arrogant, trespassing, heathen gambler had walked right in and made himself a pot of coffee as she'd slept in the next room completely unaware.

Kathleen glanced at the unbolted door and cursed under her breath. She should have known better than to leave herself so vulnerable. Despite Uncle Jeb's harping over the years, Kathleen had never acquired the habit of routinely locking doors and latching windows. Like the reassuring ring of peaks that surrounded the valley, feeling safe and secure had been a constant in her life at Twin Rivers. Until now.

Now things were different. Everything had changed, she told herself bleakly. And that grim realization twisted a knot of fresh resentment deep inside her. She poured herself a cup of coffee, cursing the hands that had prepared it.

But slowly, into her dark thoughts a distant and steady pounding sound gradually intruded. Its persistence drew her to the window. When she pushed the crisp white curtains aside her eyes landed on something that hadn't been there the night before. And her jaw dropped in astonishment.

Fence posts! Eight . . . ten, no, eleven posts stood like silent sentinels in a line across the meadow. And even as she watched, the gambler tamped the twelfth one in place.

Seething anger clouded her judgment and banished caution as she jerked open the cabin door and ran barefoot out of the cabin. The gauzy skirt of her white gown billowed out behind her like a sail as she breached the yard and entered the meadow. Her wrath made her oblivious to the small stones and weeds that pricked the bottom and sides of her feet.

A fence! The gambler was building a fence across her meadow. Indignation bubbled inside her, a roiling, churning cauldron of anger. Who did he think he was? What gave him the right?

Squinting against the brightness of the morning light, she stopped short, drawing within a few dangerous feet of him. Stripped to the waist, his muscled frame wore the glistening sheen of perspiration from his labor, making him appear golden in the sunlight. His waist tapered down from his firm flat stomach, and the sharp definition of muscles sculpted his broad tanned back.

When he saw her he stopped working and greeted her with a curt nod. For a moment, she stood transfixed, staring at his shimmering sun-kissed body in utter fascination—aside from her brother and her father, she'd never seen a man bare-chested before yesterday. And now, for the second time in twenty-four hours, she gazed upon his seminakedness in wonder.

He'd shaved his mustache, making the chiseled angles of his rugged features appear even more dramatic and his full mouth more compelling. A wry grin touched the corners of his lips. Was he laughing at her?

Kathleen's hands curled into fists at her side. "And just what do you think you're doing?" she demanded, glaring at him, trying to ignore the delight with which he openly took in her fresh-from-the-bedroom appearance.

"And a bright good morning to you, too, partner," he said cheerfully.

She ignored his mocking salutation, focusing instead on the fence posts. She stared at the first tangible proof of how much her life on Twin Rivers had changed and sputtered, "What the devil is all this?"

His expression was all innocence. "Why, it's the meadow," he proclaimed, smiling. "Wild flowers, grass, morning dew, and God's own blessed sunshine." He closed his eyes and inhaled deeply.

But when he opened his eyes again, Kathleen met his devilish smile with a blistering glare. "And just what do you think you're doing to my meadow, gambler?"

"Fencing it," he said simply, and turning his back to her, proceeded to resume his work.

"Fencing it, you say? Well, I'm afraid you've wasted your time with your fencing. Now, I demand you take those wretched posts down. Dig them up. Get them out of my meadow. Right now! Every post!"

He kept working as though he hadn't heard her.

"Every one, you hear?" she said louder, her hands planted firmly on the curve of each hip. An enemy of the rancher as surely as any blizzard or mountain lion, her father had always said about the twisted wire that kept a man's cattle from fresh water and open grazing land. The fences Kevin McBride had cursed were the illegal fences land-grabbers used to stake claim to public grazing lands. And although the land that Chance Ballinger fenced this morning was private land, to Kathleen any fence was an illegal fence and the idea of stretched wire on Twin Rivers's soil seemed obscene.

But even as she simmered, the gambler kept working, tamping each post deeper into the rich, black earth, his every movement incensing her further.

Yet, somewhere at the edge of her anger, she couldn't help noticing the way he wielded the shovel and the hammer effortlessly in his powerful grip, the way the muscles in his arms bunched beneath his golden skin.

Perhaps she should have felt afraid of all that blatant strength, but instead of frightening her, his arrogant actions served only to inflame her senses and jostle her pride further.

"Listen to me," she demanded, her voice rising as she edged around in front of him. "Twin Rivers cattle have always roamed freely, grazing side by side with our neighbors' stock until fall roundup." The well-known battles for land and water that had raged across the vast prairies of Texas and Colorado, Nebraska and Kansas, had served as lessons to the inhabitants of the Gallatin Valley. For a generation peace had reigned in the valley and Kathleen had no intention of letting her new "partner" start a local range war.

"Do you wish to see my cattle mangled on those wretched barbs, to see my neighbors turn against me?"

"I'm not fencing off the entire ranch," he explained patiently as he continued to work. "I'm merely closing off this section of the lower meadow to make a number of chores easier. Branding, for one. Doctoring and de-horning, for another."

Despite her desire to defy him, she felt relieved until he added, "And as for my neighbors, why I doubt they'll even take notice of this little bit of wire."

"*Your* neighbors!" she gasped. Dear Lord, they *were* his neighbors now. "I'll thank you to remember that I still own one half of Twin Rivers," she informed him hotly. "And I don't recall giving you permission to build a fence, even a small one, on any portion of this land!"

His eyes narrowed dangerously as he let the handle

of the shovel slide through his big hand, the head coming to rest on the ground beside his feet. "And I don't recall asking," he said simply.

His direct challenge shook her, but she held her ground, resisting the urge to shrink back and run. Damn him and his blue-eyed gaze that scorched her from head to toe. "Very well," she said, jutting her chin. "You leave me no choice but to dig them up myself."

He didn't make a move to stop her when she gathered up the skirt of her nightgown, snatched up the shovel, and stalked past him to the first pine post. Thrusting the shovel's nose snug up against the base of the post, she stomped down on the shovel's ragged metal rim with all her might.

A cry of startled pain tore from her throat as the edge of the spade dug deep into her tender instep. Dropping the shovel as though it had seared her hands, she might have fallen had not his two strong arms caught her from behind.

"Little fool," she heard him mutter under his breath, and before she could protest, he swept her up into his arms and started purposefully toward the cabin.

Tears of pain and anger stung her eyes. She felt blood trickling from her foot and cursed her impetuous actions. His arms felt like solid bands of steel around her body. She squirmed, fighting against his hold, but her efforts proved futile. He seemed to hardly notice her wiggling as he stalked across the meadow.

The pain from her injury forced her to give in to his rescue, but prudence demanded that she at least try to adjust herself away from his sun-warmed chest. But soon she realized the hopelessness of that effort as well. No matter which way she shifted, the steady rhythm of his stride forced her helplessly against his nakedness.

"Keep still," he ordered without looking down at her.

Where her cheek met his moist brown skin, she felt his strong, steady heartbeat and her own pulse quickened. Gritting her teeth seemed to dull the edge of pain in her foot, but nothing stopped the deluge of uncertain feelings that assaulted her from within.

As he walked, her awareness of his raw power grew. He held her with supple strength, one arm securely under her bottom, the other wrapped firmly across her back. She'd never been this close to a man before and an odd mixture of vulnerability and excitement fought for possession of her emotions.

The smell of moist earth and pine mixed with his own distinctive scent, and she inhaled the provocative scent of him despite herself. Suddenly she felt uncomfortably warm, warmer than she ever remembered feeling, yet some inner struggle made her shiver. The gambler responded by tightening his hold, and she shivered again.

"These days a fence is a necessity on a ranch," he explained in a low, even voice that she felt and heard at the same time, its resonance coming from deep within his ample chest. "It might take some getting used to, but in time I know you'll come to see the practicality of that enclosure as clearly as I see it now."

Her argument clogged in her throat when he adjusted her in his arms and she felt through the thin material of her gown a pleasant prickling from the springy black mat of hair on his chest.

Through the fringe of her lashes, she peeked at his rigid features. *Ah, but he is handsome, Kathleen,* she admitted to herself. By far the most handsome man she'd ever seen. What would he do, she wondered, if he knew what she was thinking, if he knew that in his arms she had all but forgotten that miserable fence?

No doubt he'd find it amusing, her common sense shot back. And there was less doubt that he'd use her private thoughts against her if he could indeed manage somehow to read them.

Kathleen, what's gotten into you? she asked herself. Perhaps the strain of the past twenty-four hours had affected her mind. For the man who held her in his arms wasn't just another harmless suitor. He wasn't a neighbor or a friend—no, not even a friendly acquaintance. What he was, despite his practiced southern charm and his easy drawl, was a ruthless and dangerous man, a threat to all she held dear. A gunslinger and a gambler. A common thief. A thief of the worst sort, a thief of hopes and dreams.

"You're going to be all right," he said when he felt her stiffen in his arms.

Kathleen's good sense screamed at her to raise her guard against his soothing assurances, but the sound of his silky drawl warmed her like golden sunshine after a spring flurry, numbing her judgment and disarming her defenses.

"It's a bad cut," he went on, "and I know it hurts like hell, but I've seen worse. You'll be all right," he promised, not bothering to apologize for his profanity.

She nodded but said nothing, biting the inside of her cheek to keep from crying out against the pain in her foot and the confusion playing havoc with her emotions.

And somewhere in an obscure corner of her brain a crazy notion was beginning to form: Maybe they could strike some sort of compromise.

Despite her brother's name on the title at the bank, the responsibility of Twin Rivers had been hers alone for some time. And although she loved her home, cherished her way of life, sometimes the responsibility *did* feel unbearably heavy for one set of shoulders.

The gambler seemed genuinely interested in the welfare of the ranch—which was more than could be said for her own brother. But what could a gambler, a gunslinger, possibly know about ranching? she asked bitterly, shaking herself back to reality.

He'd called Twin Rivers his home. But what did he know of the hard work, devotion, the sacrifices that had been made to build this home? And what in the name of God was she thinking? A compromise with this man? Never!

He had stolen her brother's birthright. To even consider a legitimate partnership with such a man was sheer lunacy. Surely it would take more than a pair of sky-blue eyes and a satiny southern drawl to obliterate her sense of family loyalty and her own good common sense, wouldn't it?

In the next moment, an unsettling answer came to her when a breeze ruffled through her hair and for a brief moment she imagined it had been the gambler's lips and not the morning air that had kissed the top of her head.

The fantasy forced her to face reality. Somehow, some way, somewhere in the last twenty-four hours, she had, indeed, lost her mind! And, unbelievably, a little piece of her heart as well.

* * *

Chance inhaled deeply, filling his lungs with the clean lilac scent of her. Combined with the warmth of her body against his as he carried her, her delicate scent caused subtle desire to ripple through him in disconcerting waves.

By God, Kathleen McBride was a beautiful woman. The loveliness of the vision he'd seen on the road yesterday paled by comparison with the flesh-and-blood woman he held in his arms. Her face, a delicate heart shape, intrigued him. Her cheeks wore a perpetual rosy blush, the exact color of a Texas sunset. And though her eyes had done little more than shoot fire at him from the moment they'd met, he found their emerald beauty arrestingly alluring.

The comb that contained her thick auburn mane had fallen away when he'd scooped her up into his arms, and now a shimmering cascade of autumn-colored curls fell across her shoulders and danced teasingly across his bare skin.

On impulse, he'd brushed his lips across the top of her head a moment ago and felt his heart hammer in response. It was only the pain of her injured foot, he reminded himself, that caused her to cling to him so tightly. Nothing more. She loathed and despised the very sight of him. If she knew he'd stolen a kiss, she'd reach for her father's shotgun again. And this time she'd probably use it.

At the cabin, Chance kicked the door open and stepped inside. Shouldering past the quilt partition, he lowered her onto the unmade bed. The big yellow cat, interrupted from his morning nap, dropped off the bed and sashayed indignantly out of the room.

And when Chance set Kathleen down on the bed, his heart felt as empty as his arms.

She couldn't explain the vague sense of loss she felt when the gambler set her down on the bed and turned and walked out of the cabin. Was he just going to leave her here? An odd feeling of relief and disappointment played tug-of-war with her emotions.

But before a winner could be declared, he came back, striding into the bedroom, carrying a small brown bottle. "Drink this," he ordered. The unmistakable smell of liquor emanated from the bottle he uncorked and held under her nose.

"I most certainly will not," Kathleen huffed, shoving the hand that held the pungent-smelling liquor aside.

He shrugged and set the bottle down beside the bed. "Have it your way. But it'll be here when you change your mind."

He left again, returning this time with a pail of water, a cake of soap, and a towel. Kathleen recognized the clean white strips he'd torn into bandages as the scraps she'd hoped to use to line the cuffs on Ida Settlemier's gown.

The mattress sagged with his weight as he sat down facing her. Unceremoniously, he pushed her nightgown up to expose her bare calf. Embarrassment in heated waves traveled from her toes to the top of her head.

"Steady, partner," he cautioned as he gently examined the wound.

"Must you keep calling me that?" she asked through clenched teeth.

"What? Partner?"

She glared at him.

"But that's what we are." He placed a folded towel carefully under her foot.

"I do have a name, you know," she informed him, her teeth still gritted against the pain.

He smiled. "I know . . . Kathleen."

She meant to glare at him again, but something about the way he said her name, the way he seemed to savor each syllable, doused her anger and she shivered.

"Seems running around in your nightclothes has given you a chill."

When he reached for the quilt to cover her, she shoved his hand away. "I'm fine, thank you." How had she managed to wind up dependent on the one person in all the world whom she longed to owe nothing? And all before breakfast! It served her right, she supposed grudgingly, for running across the meadow half naked. Would the good Lord never see fit to bestow upon her the gift of patience?

The gambler walked out of the room again and the bedroom felt strangely empty and cold. Perhaps he was right. Perhaps she had caught a chill.

"A cup of coffee will warm you," he said when he came back and noticed that she'd wrapped the quilt around her shoulders.

"That really won't be necessary."

"Oh, no bother." He turned and headed back toward the kitchen.

"You needn't continue your charade of good manners," she called after him. "My constant prayer is to find a way to remove you from my property and reclaim what rightfully belongs to this family. It will do you no good to feign friendship, either. You'll find I'm not as easily duped as my poor brother."

Her words stopped him halfway across the room. He turned and strode back to her bedside. Standing over her, she thought she saw an expression something akin to regret flickering for an instant before he fastened a steely, unreadable gaze on her face. It was the same expression she'd seen yesterday when he'd backed her down and laid out his rules for this unholy alliance he persisted in calling a partnership.

She swallowed hard. "If you think I don't see through you, through your pretense of . . . of concern, then you're sadly mistaken," she sputtered. "I know that your sole purpose in playing the gentleman lies in your desire to wrest the remainder of Twin Rivers ranch away from me." She finished her accusation in a breathless rush, feeling her courage flagging as his midnight gaze scorched her.

Swallowing her fear, she figured since she'd come this far, she might as well go all the way toward antagonizing him. "I shall find some way to endure our situation," she said firmly. "But I assure you, I will never, never accept it." She hugged her arms across her chest in a futile effort to still her shaking.

"You wouldn't care to place a small wager on that, now would you, partner?" he said, jolting her with his words.

Oh, the man was impossible, mocking and impudent!

"Not interested?" he goaded, a crooked smile tugging at the corner of his mouth. "Well, I shouldn't wonder. You're a bright woman, Kathleen. I think you know as well as I do that in the end you will accept our situation, a situation that could prove beneficial to both of us."

"Never," she spat out.

He smiled and sat back down on the bed, facing her. Edging closer, he reached out and smoothed an errant auburn curl from her cheek. At his touch, her mutinous heart fluttered uncertainly against her chest. "You will accept our situation," he assured her. "And someday, Kathleen," he murmured, "you might even come to enjoy our . . . partnership."

"Never," she gasped again, shoving his hand away from her cheek, desperate to extinguish the burning his touch had ignited inside her.

"By the way," he drawled easily, "I have a name too. I think Mr. Ballinger is a bit formal and 'gambler' a bit cold, don't you?"

She answered him with a silent scowl, too taken aback by his lack of rancor to respond.

"The name's Chance," he said before returning his attention to her wound. "Now, we'd better see to that foot. I wouldn't want my new partner to bleed to death before we'd even struck a proper working agreement."

Instantly he abandoned his teasing and focused his attention on her wound. Kathleen was surprised by his gentleness, but when he pressed a wet rag to the cut, she cried out. He reached for her hand. Oddly his touch calmed her, and in that moment Kathleen somehow knew that the gambler would never hurt her—not physically anyway.

He wouldn't shoot her with his Colt revolver, he wouldn't wring her neck with his huge, callused hands—even though she suspected that a few moments ago, when his eyes had blazed in anger, the thought might have crossed his mind.

Fresh waves of pain washed over her, distracting her from her thoughts as he flushed her wound with warm water. She grabbed the quilt and brought it to her mouth. Hearing her muffled cries, he reached for the whiskey bottle.

"Drink," he commanded.

The throbbing pain forced her to do his bidding without argument.

Wrapping trembling fingers around the bottle, she closed her eyes, intending to take only a sip to placate him. But at the very moment she touched the glass rim to her lips, the gambler tipped the bottle suddenly and in one breathless gulp, Kathleen downed a long, fiery swallow.

"D-damn you," she sputtered. Her mouth and lips felt seared. Her chest and throat burned. A violent shudder shook her whole body. Through watery eyes she saw him grinning and she cursed him again.

"You'll thank me in a minute," he promised.

A rolling wave of nausea hit her. She closed her eyes and felt light-headed. When she opened her eyes again, it seemed strangely difficult to steady herself and she decided to focus her attention on the gambler's head as he worked over her foot. Unexpectedly, she found herself oddly intrigued by the inky waves that swirled down his nape.

But when he swabbed the deepest part of the wound, the pain shot through her again, and Kathleen clutched the mattress until her knuckles ached. She bit her cheek, stubborn pride keeping her from crying out again, and common sense preventing her from fighting him. Merely knowing that a cut not properly cleaned could result in a dangerous infection or even deadly gangrene did little to ease her agony.

"Again," he said, handing her the bottle.

This time she accepted the whiskey without protest, knowing it would do her no good to refuse and praying for whatever numbing powers the liquid possessed to take effect quickly. Strange how this second swallow didn't burn as much, she mused.

Though she couldn't be certain, for she had never consumed liquor before, she sensed the subtle change it was making inside her. So this was a sample of how her father had sought to dull the pain that had raged inside him, Kathleen thought sadly.

And in a moment her own pain did begin to subside. Her arms felt leaden, her tongue thick and lazy. She felt wonderfully sleepy, the muscles in her neck and shoulders liquid and warm. As she watched the gambler wrap the wound, she found she felt strangely distanced and detached from the scene. When he tied the final dressing securely around her ankle, she felt hardly more than a light pressure.

Through her sleepy gaze, she saw his eyes rove over her face. She became vaguely aware of his hand resting lightly on her calf. "Feeling better?" he asked, his voice low and gentle.

"Hmm." This tender, compassionate side of the gambler confused her. She could fight him head to head, but how could she deal with this? A distant warning sounded through the fog in her mind as she studied the delicious curve of his full mouth. He could easily disarm her with his southern charms.

"Don't you worry, partner," he assured her, "you'll be up and around, giving orders and riding roughshod in no time." A teasing grin split his mouth as his thumb and forefinger grazed her cheek.

She wanted to jerk away, to scald him with a quick retort, but a lazy "Uh-huh" was all she seemed able to manage.

"For now, let's declare a truce, shall we?"

Kathleen nodded. Her mind felt pleasantly clouded, her body relaxed, and her spirit calm. She felt him gather her hands between both of his.

"Good enough," he whispered. "Now, let's shake on it to seal our bargain."

She *had* tried to resist when he'd kissed the palms of her hands, hadn't she? She must have tried, she told herself, for a lady would never have allowed such familiar behavior without loud protest.

"You can trust me," he murmured, adding a whispered "partner" as an easy smile spread across his handsome face.

Kathleen's hands felt lost in his much larger ones, cradled in the unexpected tenderness and warmth of his touch for a long dreamy moment. The next thing she knew, she felt herself being eased down into the bed.

"I'm here," he murmured. "You're not alone anymore, Kathleen. We're in this together now." Had the gambler really uttered those promises, she wondered through the gauzy curtain of half-sleep, or had she only been dreaming?

As she felt the covers being drawn gently over her languid body, her eyelids drooped and finally closed, shutting out the cool blue light of midmorning. Somewhere in the distance she heard someone humming a low, sweet tune. The melody was unfamiliar but pleasant, and soon the easy sound and the gentle tug of sleep pulled her into blessed oblivion.

But just before she feel asleep the gambler must have opened the window. How else could that spring breeze have crept into her room to feather a soft caress against her cheek?

Chapter Five

———◆◆———

THE sun felt good on his bare back. The smell of wild flowers and the soft murmurings of the small spring nearby brought a peace to his turbulent soul. For the first time in months, the weight that had pushed Chance farther and farther from Texas seemed a bit lighter. Gone was the feeling of eyes boring into his back and the suspicious mutterings he'd imagined hearing for the last thousand miles.

He straightened and stretched, surveying the expanse of the mountain-ringed valley that surrounded him. The new cattle he planned to purchase would thrive in these lush pastures, he assured himself again. He hadn't felt this hopeful in a long time, not since the early days with James in Texas.

He and James had taken care to choose the finest stock, building the herd slowly and carefully, paying special attention to proper breeding and crossbreeding. And Chance would do the same here at Twin Rivers, with one important exception: He would never again take his life for granted.

He wouldn't be lured by the glitter and excitement he'd imagined a different life might bring. If Twin Rivers proved to be the second chance he longed for, he'd give it all he had. And with luck, his efforts would be rewarded, as James's and his efforts had been rewarded in Texas.

Within five years of staking their claim, the Ballinger brothers' spread had come to be known as one of the best-run cattle operations in West Texas, though by no means the largest—that unique distinction belonged to the J. D. Holcomb ranch and had for the last twenty years.

Along with his two bear-sized sons, Will and Seth, J. D. ran roughshod over the territory, grabbing grazing rights and water from the smaller spreads.

Thoughts of his deadly dealings with the Holcomb clan drove a hard line across Chance's forehead and he gripped the shovel tighter in his fist. As it always did whenever he thought back to that last terrible night in Texas, his past threatened to overwhelm his sense of the present. Rage went slicing through him at the thought of his brother's cold-blooded murder at the hands of J. D. Holcomb.

When it had happened, Chance had been away in the Panhandle, searching for the excitement he'd thought he'd find in the city. Upon his return, he'd learned of James's murder and something akin to insanity seized him. When he confronted the sheriff and discovered that the local lawman was willingly looking the other way, Chance's wrath had known no bounds.

"You better think twice, Ballinger," the sheriff had

warned him, "before you go and do something you'll be sorry for."

"No one will be sorrier than J. D. Holcomb," Chance had promised as he stormed out of the sheriff's office that evening almost a year ago.

He'd left town in a grief- and guilt-induced rage, and by the time he rode onto the Holcomb ranch, night had fallen thick and black around him.

From horseback, Chance had called J. D. out of the house. When he closed his eyes, he could still see J. D.'s sneering smile. "So the prodigal Ballinger has come home." He'd laughed, and the next thing Chance knew he was on the ground and his hands were at J. D.'s throat.

The nightmare that followed was one of shouts and fists and gunfire. And when it was over, J. D. lay bleeding. Like the foreboding rattle of a sidewinder poised to strike, the rattling sound from deep within Holcomb's chest had proved a grim prophecy of more trouble to come for Chance.

That night when he rode back home and told Grandma Logan, James's mother-in-law, what had happened she'd begged him to run for his life.

"They'll never believe it was self-defense, Chance," the old woman had said, her face a mask of grief. "Not so long as there's a Holcomb left to testify against you."

Hearing the commotion, the children, Callie May and Jim Jr., sat up in their beds, their eyes wide and uncomprehending.

But despite Grandma Logan's urging, Chance made the decision to stay and try to clear his name. Running from a fight was something he'd never done before, and now, with his brother's orphaned children depending on him, he wasn't about to start.

But in the dusky hours of late the next evening a trusted friend rode into the yard of the Ballinger homestead and Chance had been forced to change his mind.

"They're coming, Chance!" his friend had warned breathlessly. "J. D.'s boys and a posse! They aren't planning on taking you in. And they're bringing a rope!"

"You've got to go, Chance!" Grandma Logan cried, her face pale and her wrinkled hands shaking. "You're a good man and God willing you'll have your day in court. But for now, for the children's sake, you've got to run! You're all they have, Chance," she added when he hesitated. "They can't lose you too."

Chance looked into the frightened faces of his brother's children and knew Grandma Logan was right.

"Get out of Texas, Chance," she made him promise as she rushed with him to the back door. "Find these children a home. I'm an old woman and this is where I'll die, but I'll send the children whenever you call for them."

Chance kissed the children at the door. "I'll send for you," he promised. "I'll find us a new home."

"But Uncle Chance—" When Jim Jr.'s frightened voice broke, Chance's heart broke with it.

"It's all right, son," he promised, drawing the trembling boy and the confused little girl into his arms and hugging them to his chest. "You two take good care of Grandma and I'll send for you just as soon as I get settled."

"Good-bye, Uncle Chance," Callie May whispered. "Don't you cry now and I won't either." But her lip had trembled and so had Chance's heart.

"God bless you, son," Grandma Logan said as she tucked the egg money and a small black Bible into his hand. "Soon you and these children will be together again. I'm sure of it."

With a final glance at the faces of all those he held closest to his heart, Chance rode north into the darkness. That night Chance knew there would be no going back, that there would be no trial, no jury, and no justice for him in Holcomb, Texas.

His plans were formed over the next few days somewhere along the trail. Remembering what he'd heard and read about the lush, uninhabited plains of Canada, Chance figured those northern prairies offered the best choices for a new start.

He had no doubt that he could begin again; he and James had had plenty of experience in starting over. After the war had devastated the Ballinger family home in Natchez, Chance and James had ridden west to stake their claim. The only difference now was that Chance was alone.

He trusted Grandma Logan to take good care of six-year-old Callie and eight-year-old Jim Jr. until he could send for them. But the old woman's health was failing, and Chance knew he couldn't afford to wait too long.

And so, with firm resolve never to abandon the responsibilities left him by his older brother, Chance had pressed on.

He'd been on the trail for more than three months when he'd met up with a cattle drive outside of Santa Fe headed for Virginia City. They were moving north. Chance figured hiring on with a drive would give him the anonymity he needed to continue traveling through the vast Wyoming and Montana territories.

But everything had changed when he'd met up with Danny McBride in Virginia City. Fate had dealt him an unbeatable hand.

Why hadn't he just thrown it in, he asked himself now. He could have walked away. He wondered now if he should have. What made him think he had a future in Montana? Was he a fool to believe that at Twin Rivers he could forget his past and build a future?

And even as he tamped the next post into place, he asked himself the questions that had been nagging him from the moment he'd tucked Danny's handwritten deed into his pocket: Was there truly a new life for him anywhere, a new life for Jim Jr. and young Callie May?

If he stayed hidden in this vast valley long enough, would the world forget he ever existed?

And more importantly, in these gentle high-country pastures, could Chance Ballinger forgive himself his own mistakes, the mistakes he believed with all his heart had cost his brother his life?

Though kneading the clump of cream-colored dough mounded on the drainboard helped to vent some of her anger, it did little to relieve the dull headache that had awakened Kathleen an hour ago. As she worked, the thudding in her head continued, and she felt like someone had embedded grains of sand in her eyelids.

The events of the morning played over again in her mind and she jammed both fists back into the sourdough, folding and kneading and pummeling even harder. She'd always looked forward to bread-making day, taking pride in adding just the right amounts of flour and sugar and eggs to carefully measured cups of sourdough starter that she kept in a jar in the pantry. Before today, working the dough, kneading it to just the right consistency, being careful not to overwork and toughen the dough in the process, had given her great satisfaction.

Until today, the distinctive scent of sourdough filling the cabin's interior had always stimulated her appetite and boosted her spirits.

But today something different happened when she smelled the savory aroma of the starter sitting in an open jar at her elbow and it made her stomach roll.

Covering the jar quickly, she hurried out onto the porch for the third time in the last ten minutes, for another gulp of cleansing air. As she watched the sun make its gradual descent, her stomach calmed and she felt relieved that this day was almost over—this day which had been a horror from the moment she'd opened her eyes, she reminded herself. And the sight of a dozen more fence posts dotting the meadow told her it wasn't going to get any better tomorrow.

As her eyes followed the line of posts, she saw the gambler still working. Despite herself, she couldn't help remembering how he'd looked this morning—his muscled and bronzed body glistening in the sun. The memory set her senses thrumming.

Defiantly, a picture of Chance Ballinger's knowing smile appeared before her mind's eye, and despite herself she stared a moment at that compelling apparition. A churning began again in her stomach that had nothing to do with the lingering effects of the whiskey or the scent of sourdough and everything to do with a half-remembered dream, spun sometime during her uneasy afternoon sleep. As the dream stirred to life at the corners of her mind, she strained to remember the details that had left her tangled in her bedding, her gown coiled around her legs, her skin and hair damp with restless excitement.

Disconnected and hazy pieces drifted back to her. The flickering images finally provoked a memory, soft and smooth, like fine satin. And as the memory began to insinuate itself more clearly into her mind it seized her imagination, and she felt her heart flutter.

And suddenly there he was. The tall, dark-haired stranger who had been the center of her dream. At first he was nothing more than a shadow figure, this man who'd held her in his arms, who'd danced with her in her dream. But then she remembered more, remembering how they'd moved together gracefully, effortlessly to the sound of some distant melody—a strange, unfamiliar tune whose distant strain echoed hauntingly through her mind even now.

She recalled with startling clarity the feeling of liquid pleasure that had flowed through her as he'd held her in his arms. The memory of his slow, rhythmic movements, frighteningly intimate, blatantly seductive, and shamefully irresistible, caused a disturbing tightness in the pit of her stomach.

Involuntarily she smiled as her memories drew her back into his arms. Her breath caught when she remembered how, without a word, he'd spoken to her with his eyes, how easily she'd become a willing captive to his charms.

Captured by her memories, Kathleen gave herself up again to the heady sensations. She strained to remember every movement shared, every sigh that had passed between them. She could almost feel his breath on her cheek.

She closed her eyes and suddenly she saw his face. "No!" she cried.

The figure from her dreams was no stranger, and the spell he'd cast upon her while she slept was the same spell he'd used to mesmerize her yesterday! His quiet authority and masculine presence produced the same hypnotic effect under which she'd fallen today as he'd carried her to the cabin and tended to her wounds.

"Dear God," she whispered, clutching the railing for balance in a world suddenly and wildly spinning out of control. The man in her dreams and the gambler were one and the same! It wasn't enough that he'd invaded her home; now he'd invaded her dreams.

The tumultuous emotions that shook her caused her body to tremble and her thoughts to whirl. She couldn't ever remember feeling more uncertain. And as she stumbled back into the cabin, she cursed both the feeling and the man who'd caused it.

On the drainboard, the unwieldy concoction of sourdough, overworked by her preoccupation and left sitting too long in the cool evening air, had taken on the same dull, grayish color as the ash-and-mud mixture Uncle Jeb used to rechink the cabin in the spring. Kathleen shook her head miserably, realizing the bread from this batch would be anything but the light, crusty delight her starter usually yielded.

By giving into her shameful daydreams of Chance Ballinger, she'd wasted not only precious ingredients and time but had succeeded in making the whole batch of sourdough fit only for the hogs to fight over.

With a heavy and guilty heart, she scooped the dough into a large bowl and covered it with a flour sack. She would take it to the animals when she went out to do her evening chores. Maybe tomorrow, she told herself wearily, she'd have the heart—and the stomach— to attempt another batch.

Just then the cabin door flew open with a startling bang. The swirling draft caused a great cloud of smoke to belch from the cookstove.

"Close it quick," Kathleen shouted. "Close it!"

Coughing, she fought the smoke that rasped against her throat and burned her eyes. "D-didn't anyone ever t-teach you to knock?" she sputtered angrily without turning around.

"Now what kind of greetin' is that for an old friend?"

Kathleen could hardly believe her delighted ears. "Jeb!" she cried, whirling around to face him.

"Howdy, missy."

The welcome sound of that gravelly old voice warmed Kathleen's heart and caused tears of joy to spring to her eyes. "Oh, Jeb!" she cried, and rushed across the room to hug him, the rough nap of his woolen mackinaw scraping pleasantly against her cheek as she did. "It's only that old stove . . . and the smoke," she explained. "I couldn't even see your dear face. Oh, but I see it now! And you'll never know how glad I am it's you."

A raspy chuckle wheezed its way past Jeb's lips. "Well now, who else would you be expectin' this evenin', missy?"

Kathleen took a step back and shook her head. "I haven't the heart to tell you on an empty stomach. Sit down. I'll get you something to eat, then we need to have a long talk." Taking his callused hand in hers, she pulled him to the table.

Jeb dragged his battered leather hat off his head and Kathleen hung it on a peg near the door. As he shrugged out of his coat, she poured a cup of coffee and set it down in front of him on the table. After filling his plate with cold biscuits, sliced beef, and canned peaches, she brought her own cup to the table and sat down across from him.

"Our little talk wouldn't have anything to do with that young man out there in the bunkhouse, now would it?" He cast a sidelong glance at her as he folded his bulky form down into a straight-backed chair. "Or maybe we'll be talking about that bandage wrapped round your foot?" Worry creased a series of leathery folds in his weathered and wizened face.

"Both, I'm afraid," Kathleen admitted.

"Thought so," Jeb said simply, and wrapped his hands around the coffee cup, warming his crooked fingers, bent and gnarled by time and hard work.

"So you've met him?" she asked without looking up.

"When I rode in he was working on the new fence. We had us a chat while you were sleeping."

She looked up to see him studying her over the rim of his cup as he took a long, noisy sip of coffee. Color swept her cheeks. "And did he tell you what brought him to Twin Rivers?" she asked, knowing full well Jeb would have demanded that Chance explain his presence.

"He did." He lowered his gaze and seemed to concentrate unduly on buttering his biscuits.

The weight of her brother's betrayal pressed down heavier than ever on Kathleen's heart. "Jeb, why didn't Danny come home and tell me himself?"

"Too ashamed, I guess," Jeb muttered.

"Yes," she said softly, imagining the hangdog expression in her brother's round eyes. "But where is he now, Jeb? And what do you think he's doing?"

The old man didn't answer.

"We've got to find him. We've got to go after him. Bring him back. This is his home," Kathleen said quietly, blinking back tears dangerously close to spilling.

Jeb reached across the table and covered her hand with his. "First light I'll ride out after him."

She sensed his reluctance. "But you don't want to go after Danny, do you, Jeb?"

He dragged his hand through his thinning hair and pushed back in his chair, focusing his wise gray eyes on hers. "No, I don't, missy," he admitted. "Danny's done a terrible thing and he ought to be man enough to come home and face up to what he's done." He shook his head wearily and sighed. "But I reckon it's a lot to ask of a young man." He studied his coffee a moment longer before he said, "I'll go get him. I'll haul him back home by the scruff of his scrawny neck, if that's what you want. But dag gummit, he ain't a kid anymore."

Kathleen heard the anger in Jeb's voice and understood his frustration. Without their mother's steadying hand, Danny had grown up wild and irresponsible. After Mama's death, Pa, immersed in his own grief, had neither the time nor the patience for his high-spirited son. Even now it was difficult for Kathleen to think of Danny as anything but an unruly boy, even though she knew many men Danny's age, some even younger, who had assumed much greater responsibilities than her brother had ever willingly accepted.

In her heart she knew Jeb was right. Though sometimes Danny still acted like one, he was no longer a child.

"We'll wait a while longer," she said softly. "Danny should come home on his own, when he's ready . . ." Her voice trailed off as she refilled Jeb's cup.

"I think it's best," Jeb said, his own voice low.

"He'll be back." She tried to reassure them both even as another disturbing thought struck her. "Surely he knows he's welcome to come back home . . ."

The old man nodded. "'Course he does."

Kathleen sipped her coffee as Jeb finished his meal.

"Jeb," she said finally, "what are we going to do? About Ballinger, I mean."

"What do you mean?"

"Well, we certainly can't let him get away with this. Cheating Danny, stealing half of everything I own."

"Cheatin', stealin' . . . those are some mighty powerful accusations, missy." Jeb's eyes narrowed. "How do you know he cheated Danny?"

"Why, of course he did," she insisted. "Ballinger must have seen Danny bringing the herd into Virginia City and coaxed him into a crooked game, knowing his pockets were full and ripe for the picking." She bowed to Jeb's dubious expression. "Well, if he didn't cheat Danny outright, he definitely took advantage of his inexperience and innocence."

Jeb shook his head again. "I'll wager it took darned little arm-twistin' to get Danny into that game." His conviction gave his voice a harsh quality Kathleen had never heard before. "Danny took his chances and he lost."

Kathleen winced. Hadn't the gambler said essentially the same thing, even used those exact words? "But why, Jeb?" she asked. "Why would he do something like that to us? He must have thought he had a good chance. An even chance, anyway," she added. "Why else would Danny have taken that kind of crazy risk?"

"Maybe he didn't see it as that big a risk."

"What do you mean?"

His expression softened. "Missy, you know as well as I do that that boy has never cared two hoots about Twin Rivers."

She folded her hands in front of her and lowered her eyes, feeling her brother's shame twisting another pain-

ful knot in her stomach. The truth, even coming from
a dear old friend, was difficult to accept.

"If you ask me, it's a blessing," Jeb declared before
bringing his cup to his lips and draining it again.

Kathleen couldn't believe what she was hearing. "A
blessing!" From the beginning she'd planned to enlist
Jeb's help in devising some way to get out of the dreadful partnership into which Danny's actions had forced
her, but now everything seemed turned all around,
confused and distorted.

"This Ballinger fella seems to know what he's doin',"
Jeb said. "He's got big plans for this place, missy."

"Oh, he does, does he?"

Jeb nodded. "Yep, he's bent on improvin' the herd.
Tomorrow or the next day he's ridin' over to Richardson's place to look at the new breeder stock they got
over there. First part of his plan." Jeb smiled.

"His plan!" she gasped, disbelieving. How, she wondered frantically, had Ballinger managed to win Jeb
over so quickly, so completely? Evidently while she'd
slept, the two men had done a lot more talking than
she'd first suspected.

"And what is this *plan*?" she demanded, fighting to
keep the anger boiling inside her from spewing out at
Jeb. But it wasn't easy. The thought of Ballinger pro-
ceeding as if he had full run of the place caused a blaze
of fresh resentment that wasn't easily contained.

"Didn't he tell you?"

She shook her head. "We . . . haven't talked much
since he arrived." She couldn't very well tell Jeb she'd
spent most of the day sleeping off the effects of her
first disastrous encounter with liquor.

"Well, he's chock-full of moneymaking plans and
schemes," Jeb went on, his expression bright. "Says

folks are real pleased with this new stock—Herefords, he called 'em. Says they're a whole lot beefier breed than their scrawny Longhorn cousins. Hale and hardy, better suited to winter in the mountain valleys. Ballinger says these critters come down out of the high country in the spring fat and sassy. Hold their weight through the long drives, too."

Kathleen found her voice as she jumped to her feet. "Jeb, stop! Just listen to yourself! 'Ballinger says this. Ballinger says that.' Why, you've hardly met the man and it sounds like you're ready to turn Twin Rivers over like an orphaned calf to a new mama. Maybe you've forgotten who owns this ranch?" she added pointedly.

The wounded look in his eyes caused a stab of instant regret to pierce her heart. Unable to face the hurt she'd inflicted on her oldest friend, Kathleen turned away to stare out the window into the Montana dusk. Her throat burned and her eyes stung. The silence between them was brittle.

At last Jeb rose and pushed into his jacket. "No, Miss Kathleen," he said, his voice solemn, "I haven't forgotten whose ranch this is. First, it was Kevin McBride's ranch," he began. "He staked his claim in 1856 when he rode into the territory with Nelson Story and the first bunch of Texas Longhorns to see Montana soil." His voice dropped another notch. "And next to his dear Emma and you children, this land was the one thing he cared for most in this world. He worked dawn to dusk, winters and summers, trying to keep this place alive."

Kathleen swiped away the tears gathering at the corners of her eyes before turning around slowly to face her old friend.

Jeb went on, "And in all that time, he never stopped

trying to make things better, improving things where he could, learning what he could from the new ranchers that settled in. He always talked to folks, worked with his neighbors. But when he lost his Emma, he lost his partner and his best friend. And along with her . . . well, it seemed like he kinda lost his will to go on."

He cleared his throat before continuing. "Your pa always knew . . . he knew even after his heart had gone out of this place that if he left Twin Rivers to Danny it would've been lost the first day. That's why he left the place split between the two of you. He knew you loved Twin Rivers, had dreams for it the way he used to."

Jeb's words packed the force of a physical blow. Kathleen moved over to the table and dropped down into her chair. For the first time since his death, she wondered if her father had placed in her a trust she might not be capable of fulfilling.

Blinking back the tears that swam in her eyes, she watched as Jeb sat back down in his chair. He was her family's oldest and dearest friend; she couldn't allow a rift to come between them now.

"Jeb, can you forgive me?" she asked, reaching across the table to touch his arm. "I'm sorry for what I said. I know you care every bit as much about this ranch as I do. I don't know what's gotten into me. I— I just haven't been myself all day."

He nodded and smiled a sad, understanding smile. "It's all right, missy. I know you've had a shock."

"But you do understand, don't you? I can't just let some stranger ride in here and snatch away my dreams. Somehow I've got to get Twin Rivers back. For all of us."

He patted her hand still resting on his sleeve. "But

missy, don't you see? You ain't lost nothing, yet. Nothing at all."

Kathleen stared at him a moment longer before she reached for the coffeepot and filled their cups again.

"Go on, Jeb. Tell me what else Ballinger told you."

"Well, like I said, he's got big plans." The flame of open enthusiasm burned in Jeb's eyes. "Improving the herd is just the beginning. He's plannin' to talk to the army about becoming the sole supplier of beef for the troops at Fort Benton. Now, don't that beat all? The army'll pay a damn sight better than the auction in Virginia City, I'd wager, and we won't run the risk of a long trail drive." Jeb rubbed his hands together and smiled. "I swear, just talking about this place makin' some money for a change makes it feels like the old days, don't it?"

"But Jeb—"

He held up a hand, interrupting her protest. "Now missy, you know how I got a feel for people. Always have." Jeb's eyes twinkled with a sudden merriment that both perplexed and annoyed her.

"Yep," he declared, rising. "If you ask me, any rancher in this valley would be mighty lucky to fall into a partnership with the likes of this young Ballinger."

Jeb's words stunned her. "Lucky?" The word burst from her lips at the same moment the cabin door swung open and the woodstove belched another gust of acrid black smoke.

Chance Ballinger's long frame filled the doorway. "Evening, partner." She acknowledged his presence with an indifferent nod. Partner, indeed, she grumbled to herself as she rose and went into the kitchen. If he really considered her his partner, why hadn't he told her about his grand plans to improve the herd?

"How's the foot?"

"Much better, thank you," she answered tersely.

"Good, good," he said, nodding.

She watched him inhale deeply, his broad chest expanding as he shrugged out of his split-leather vest. "Hmm. Sourdough," he exclaimed. As a smile of hungry anticipation played across his rugged features an irresistible idea seized Kathleen.

"Yes," she replied vaguely. "Sourdough." Perhaps her bread-making efforts hadn't been a total waste after all. *His eggs over easy. His biscuits light.* And how did her partner like his sourdough biscuits? she wondered wickedly as she busied herself at the drainboard.

Surely the man who held an opinion on every other subject on God's green earth held one on the proper preparation of biscuits as well. But alas, it seemed he'd forgotten to voice his preference. Ah, such a pity. Well, this was one batch he'd find unforgettable, Kathleen promised herself, coughing to suppress a throaty chuckle.

With a new sense of purpose, she worked quickly, dividing the weighty mass into small round sections. Her heart felt lighter as each biscuit landed with a hearty thud onto a pan smeared with fat. With any luck at all, her new partner would carry the memory of this sourdough like an anvil wedged in the pit of his stomach for at least a few hours—a subtle reminder that it'd be a hot and sultry Montana winter before Kathleen McBride would be the last to know her *partner's* plans for *her* ranch.

"Jeb, pour Mr. Ballinger some coffee, will you?" she sang out cheerily. She slid the pan of biscuits into the oven, before setting a place for the gambler at the table. As she worked she hummed a lively Irish tune her mother had taught her.

"Sit down, sit down," she implored him. "Help yourself to beef and potatoes. The biscuits will be out soon."

"Kathleen makes the best sourdough biscuits this side of Kansas City," Jeb declared.

At his praise, she managed a modest smile. "Too bad you've already had your supper, Uncle Jeb. But I promise I'll bake something special for you tomorrow."

"I guess it's lucky I came in late," the gambler remarked. "If those biscuits taste half as good as they smell, I'm sure they'll be worth the wait." He offered her an easy smile.

Kathleen bit her lip to suppress an evil grin. *Good* just wasn't the word to describe the biscuits she'd made especially for Twin Rivers's newest resident.

"Eat hardy, Mr. Ballinger," Kathleen encouraged, moving over to the table and setting the platter of beef and potatoes at his elbow, before offering him peach preserves. "I'll be offended if you don't."

Sudden suspicion sparked in his eyes. "Why, thank you, ma'am. And to what do I owe this sudden display of hospitality? Aren't you the same gal who welcomed me just yesterday with the business end of a shotgun?"

Jeb's laugh was only a snort and when Kathleen wheeled on him, he coughed to cover it. "Coffee must have gone down the wrong pipe," he explained hoarsely.

Kathleen merely nodded before turning her attention back to Ballinger. "As I recall, I wasn't the only one whose weapon was drawn."

"A man has the right to defend himself, Miss McBride."

"And a lady has the right to defend her home," she countered.

The gambler's eyes sparkled with devilish delight; he was clearly enjoying their verbal duel. "That she has," Ballinger agreed. "And I for one have always admired courage in either sex." His drawl had never been smoother. "And as for the potatoes and the meat . . . thank you, ma'am, I believe I will have a large helping of each."

"Wonderful." She smiled, watching him begin to eat. "And I was afraid I had prepared too much food, that it might go to waste."

"Oh, I wouldn't worry about waste, missy," Jeb put in as he watched the Texan devour his food. "By the looks of that meadow, your partner put in a good day's work. And by the looks of his appetite, I think he can handle whatever you dish up."

This time it was Chance who coughed.

As for herself, Kathleen found she had to fight to hide a smile of satisfaction. Quite innocently, Jeb had taken the conversation in a most fortuitous direction. "Is that true, Mr. Ballinger? Whatever I dish up?"

One dark eyebrow arched wickedly. "Absolutely." His gaze was steady and unyielding.

"You seem quite sure of yourself," she taunted.

"That I am," he said, folding his arms over his chest in a gesture of supreme confidence.

"Then how about a friendly wager?"

Jeb was at the door, preparing to go out onto the porch to enjoy an after-dinner smoke, but Kathleen watched the turn of events pull him back inside, and when he sat back down, his old eyes twinkled and the corners of his mouth twitched with amusement.

"A wager, Miss McBride?" the gambler asked, for

the first time appearing slightly disarmed. "And just what kind of wager did you have in mind?"

Being careful not to appear overeager, Kathleen moved into the kitchen and pulled the pan of biscuits out of the oven. "Oh, just a bit of fun, Mr. Ballinger. A wager all in good fun," she said lightly. "Let's see, what could it be?" She didn't give him time to respond. "I know, I'll bet one of those gold pieces you left on the table yesterday against another one just like it, that you can't finish your supper."

The gambler's eyes narrowed and darkened to a velvety blue that caused a strange and disturbing stirring of Kathleen's senses. His expression told her he'd play along, but it also said he mistrusted the very air she breathed.

"But how, in good faith, could I allow you to make such a foolish wager, Miss McBride? The food you prepared was quite delicious, and as you can see, I've nearly cleaned my plate already."

"As I said, it's all in fun, Mr. Ballinger," she responded. "The biscuits are ready," she announced gaily.

"Well then, bring them on," he said good-naturedly. "The smell has tempted me all through supper and I've saved room for at least three."

"Then you accept my wager?"

"I will and I do," he said congenially, and as if to show his good faith, he scooped up the last bite of potato and ate it with a smile. "Although I must admit," he said between swallows, "I feel a little guilty winning so easily."

"Ah, but you haven't won yet," Kathleen reminded him as she slid a plate bearing three biscuits in front of him and gave him her most innocent smile.

"Three?" he said, almost laughing. "Just three?"

"Just three." *Three will be enough,* she told herself triumphantly. The gambler had more to lose than just a gold piece; he had his teeth to consider, she told herself with an inner smile.

"Here," Jeb said, sliding the bowl of blackberry jam across the table. "Missy's biscuits are so light, they darn near float away if you don't weight 'em down with some of her homemade jam."

Kathleen beamed innocently under Jeb's compliment and watched with barely contained delight as Ballinger slathered all three biscuits with jam. The hangover she'd suffered was almost worth the revenge, she told herself as she watched him lift the first biscuit to his mouth.

The realization that he'd been duped flashed like fireworks in his eyes from the moment he tried to take his first bite. And in his eyes, she saw something else as well. A message that Kathleen heard as clearly as if he'd shouted it, the message that although she'd won this round, he intended to win their wager.

Even if it cost him every tooth in his head.

Chapter Six

—◆—

THE sun was up when the clattering sound of the team pulling the wagon out of the yard woke her. Shrugging off the covers, Kathleen padded to the window and peered out, her eyes still fuzzy with sleep. She sighed with relief when she saw that it was Chance who was leaving. Her gaze lingered on him for a moment as she took in how easily he controlled the powerful team.

Hadn't Jeb said something about Chance picking up cattle at the Richardson ranch? More than likely that was where he was headed now. If that was the case, Chance would be gone for at least a day, perhaps longer.

And this morning of all mornings, Kathleen was thankful that he wouldn't be about. Ida Settlemier was coming for her fitting this morning, and although Kathleen hated to admit it, trying to explain the presence of Chance Ballinger to the town busybody had been a chore she'd been dreading all night.

There was enough gossip circulating along the wide Bozeman City streets about Kevin McBride's snooty, property-holding daughter. Kathleen could well imagine the rumors that circulated about her treatment of the various suitors the town's do-gooders had seen fit to send to her doorstep since her father's death.

Over the past year they'd come one after another in a steady stream, like ants at a Sunday school picnic. And one by one they'd hightailed it back down the road after having been put off by Kathleen's frank questions concerning their motives and intentions.

Looking back, she had to admit that one or two of these eager young men might actually have held some measure of true affection for her. Men like John Miles and Ray Chandler, whom she'd grown up with, were both of them good, decent young men in their own way, she supposed. But despite their best intentions, the result was always the same. When the subject of property arose and Kathleen stated, without hesitation, her uncompromising opinion that a woman held the same rights as a man to keep and hold property, they turned cold and ran.

Unlike John and Ray, some of her more recent would-be suitors hadn't even pretended a romantic interest, but simply stated what they deemed the obvious: A woman alone couldn't handle a ranch the size of Twin Rivers. It wasn't possible. It wasn't even right, for Lord's sakes. She need a husband, and by all that was right and holy, they told her that she ought to know it.

But those who'd come and those who'd sent them hadn't counted on Kathleen's pride, a pride instilled deeply by the confidence her father and mother had placed in her at an early age. Yes, she'd learned to garden, to cook, and to make the delicate lace that was a family tradition dating back to her mother's Irish heritage, but she'd also learned a great deal from her father.

From him, Kathleen had learned to ride like an Indian scout, to throw a rope and shoot a rifle as well as any boy her age. She'd learned the value of work, sharing chores and working from dawn to dusk with the rest of the family at roundup. She could fish and track wild game, and doctor sick animals and people as well. And she was proud of her accomplishments.

Whether dealing with a flighty colt, a stubborn steer, or an intricate design for a lace tablecloth, Kathleen had learned to trust the instincts experience had given her.

But it was more than her innate pride and confidence that her suitors had to face in their efforts to win her hand; an even greater obstacle was Kathleen's own ideal of what a marriage should be.

It was a picture clearly drawn and locked tightly away in the most private place in her heart. Kathleen knew what she wanted in a husband. Her mother and father had shown her how it could be between a man and woman. She'd grown up watching them work side by side, hand in hand, true partners, neither subservient or inferior to the other, each respected for their individual abilities and strengths.

She took for granted that her parents had always loved each other. If there had been one backward glance or a single secret regret for either of them, their daughter had never seen or sensed it.

Just knowing that kind of love could exist between a husband and wife, Kathleen had never for one moment considered settling for anything less.

And so, one by one, the suitors had quit coming, those eager young men, those proponents of a marriage of convenience. As for the others, when words didn't penetrate their thick, greedy, land-grabbing skulls, Kathleen didn't mind letting the sight of her father's shotgun do her talking for her.

She sighed, remembering their confrontations as she sat down on the edge of the bed and stared at the dresses hanging in her small closet. If "old maid" was the name given to a woman who refused to compromise her pride, her principles, and her property, then she guessed she'd fully earned the title.

She was worlds apart from the fawning females she'd seen in Bozeman City, those young women who had come to the male-dominated territory for the express purpose of finding a husband. Their flirting games struck Kathleen as dishonest and demeaning. Why on earth would any decent woman feel she needed to go to such lengths to trap a man?

How an intelligent man could fall so easily under the paint-and-powder spells conjured by these crafty females escaped her. And why any woman would want a man she could outsmart was beyond Kathleen's reasoning. But then, to her the whole courting game, at least the way she'd seen and heard it played, seemed like nothing more than a tawdry game of lies and deceit. And Kathleen McBride wanted none of it.

She glanced idly out the window again. The wagon was crossing the meadow. Yes, she told herself again, a morning without bracing her emotions against the inevitable encounter with Chance Ballinger would be a relief. Much as she hated to admit it, the gambler, with his wavy black hair and sky-blue eyes, had the handsomest face she'd ever seen on a man.

And for the last few days that face had been the first one she'd seen every morning and the last one she looked upon every night. Was that what it would be like to be married? Kathleen wondered.

The thought made her gasp. Dear God, how had marriage, that blessed union that bound two decent individuals who'd willingly pledged their eternal love and respect, become jumbled with thoughts of Chance Ballinger?

The answer came back to her in a flash of dangerous insight, in another question that brought a rush of heat to her cheeks: Why, of all the men in the territory, was it Ballinger who stirred her senses, captured her imagination, and disturbed her dreams like no other ever had?

Skittering like a spring colt from that dreadful question, Kathleen dressed quickly, choosing a long-sleeved green muslin dress and a white gingham apron with two deep pockets on either side. She'd need the pockets today during Ida's fitting to hold her pins and thimble, scissors and thread.

Remembering that Ida had promised to arrive early, Kathleen hurriedly unbraided her hair, swept it over one shoulder and ran a brush quickly through her long, shimmering mane. In less than a minute she'd re-braided it, securing the thick plait that hung past the middle of her back with a white ribbon.

She scolded herself guiltily for oversleeping again, as she hurried to finish dressing, pulled on her shoes, and thought about the milk cow in the barn waiting to be relieved of her burden. Though she'd worked late into the night getting Ida's gown ready for the fitting today, it was an excuse she wouldn't allow herself to accept. There were chores to be done. And a milk cow couldn't wait.

Draping a gray woolen shawl around her shoulders,

Kathleen hurried through the empty cabin, grabbing the pail from its peg as she stepped out onto the porch. As always the crisp morning air of the high country invigorated and enlivened her, and the heaviness in her limbs melted away.

At least *some* good was coming from the odd restlessness that had plagued her of late, Kathleen told herself as she opened the barn door and stepped inside its musty interior. Last night, before she'd finally surrendered to sleep, she'd nearly finished Ida's gown and the night before that she'd completed the altar cloths for Henry Draper's Community Church. The delicately embroidered and lace-trimmed stack now lay in the corner, starched and pressed and waiting for Henry to fetch them.

Thoughts of Henry's reaction to Chance Ballinger's presence at Twin Rivers stopped Kathleen cold. Mercy, how would she handle that one? Long after all the others had given up, Henry, a friend since childhood, still kept calling. And as a result of his persistence, Bozeman City's lay minister was the closest thing Kathleen had to a beau.

Before her father's death, Henry had proven himself a good friend to the family as well, visiting Ma regularly during her illness and comforting the rest of them after her passing.

And then in that awful time after Pa's murder, Henry had become a confidant and special friend to Kathleen, one who seemed unusually blessed with the gift of understanding.

In the last six months Henry's visits to the ranch had become more regular and his escorts to and from Sunday services more frequent. Kathleen enjoyed their friendship. Henry Draper was an interesting man, well read and well traveled. Often on their rides to and from town, they'd engage in long conversations on a variety of subjects—the same kind of pleasant, rambling talks that Kathleen missed having with her father. But lately, she'd sensed Henry wishing that their friendship would bloom into something more.

And why shouldn't it? she asked herself honestly. Henry Draper was a good man, an interesting, dependable, God-fearing man. He was nice-looking, polite—*Stop it, Kathleen!* she checked herself, suddenly ashamed at how unemotionally she'd been summing up Henry's attributes like a prospective bidder sizing up a prize bull in a sale ring.

Henry deserved better. He deserved a woman whose heart turned over at the sight of him, whose senses hummed at his touch, whose dreams were spun around his kisses. And although Kathleen longed to experience all those delicious emotions, she'd begun to wonder if she would ever feel them for him.

And if not for Henry, then for whom? Did the man exist who could fulfill her expectations? Or were her romantic notions nothing more than foolish dreams?

When she entered the stall where the family milk cow was waiting, the long, plaintive moo that greeted her reflected Kathleen's mood exactly.

"What do *you* think, Gracie," she asked as she took the three-legged stool from its peg, swept it under her and sat down and began milking. "Is there such a man anywhere?"

"Are you looking for me, partner?" His voice came out of nowhere, startling her. Reflexively, Gracie reacted to Kathleen's rude yank, pawing at the bucket with one hind foot and emitting an indignant bellow.

"Gently, gently," Chance chided, giving the old cow an affectionate pat on the rump..

"I know how to milk a cow, thank you," Kathleen shot back, her cheeks burning again.

"You may know how," he drawled, "but by the looks of that swollen udder, I'd say you forgot when."

Kathleen almost tipped the stool over wrenching around to glare at him. "I thought you'd gone to Richardson's."

"Now, would I up and leave my partner without so much as a fare-thee-well? Did you really think I'd left you, Kathleen? Did you miss me already?" he taunted, smiling wickedly as he moved around beside her and leaned one hip against the railing that separated Gracie's stall from the next.

Kathleen fumed. How was it that he always managed to find a double meaning in everything she said?

She felt his amused stare still resting on her face, but she refused to look at him. "I happened to see you driving the wagon down the road, that's all. And since most people only harness a team and hitch a wagon if they plan on going somewhere, I merely assumed you were leaving. But I assure you that whether you come or go is of no interest to me at all." It was a lie and they both knew it. Kathleen's nerves had been taut as piano wires since the first moment Chance Ballinger set foot on Twin Rivers soil. His every movement was of great interest to her, because she never knew what he'd do next to keep her off-balance, uncertain and edgy.

"I used the wagon to haul the last rolls of wire out to the fence line," he explained. "I expect to finish building it today."

"And I suppose you expect me to rejoice at this bit of news?"

She heard a soft chuckle bubble out from deep within his chest, and despite herself, she found the sound pleasing.

"No ma'am," he said, shaking his head. "I don't suppose I expect you to do anything of the kind." His easy drawl had a hypnotic effect on her senses she realized with the next jerk that made Gracie cry out again.

"Sorry, girl," she muttered.

"I know you'll change your mind come branding time," he said brightly. "That fence'll prove to be a godsend. You'll see."

Trying to ignore his unsettling presence and unswerving self-confidence, Kathleen finished milking, pulled the bucket from beneath the cow, and gave Gracie an extra bucket of grain to make amends for the discomfort she'd inflicted. "My father never needed a fence to get the job done," she declared, heading for the door without looking back.

When he came up beside her and his fingers slid around the handle, the weight of the bucket shifted from her hand to his. She tightened her grip on the handle and the pail jerked, causing some of the frothy liquid to slop over the side of the pail and spill onto the ground. Realizing how foolish a battle for control of the milk pail was, Kathleen relinquished her hold and walked stiffly beside him out of the barn and toward the house.

A sideways glance at the comfortable smile set in his handsome face caused her to walk faster. "Thank you," she said curtly over her shoulder at the cabin door. "Just set the pail down on the drainboard before you go."

"My pleasure, ma'am," he drawled. "Always glad to help my partner."

The frayed ends of her patience finally snapped. "Mr. Ballinger," she said, whirling around to face him. "Why *do* you persist in calling me that? Isn't our situation difficult enough without you goading me at every turn?"

"Chance," he interrupted. "Just plain—"

"Fine. Fine," she said with an impatient wave of her hand. "Just plain Chance, then."

"Well, partner—that is, Kathleen," he drawled, his eyes roving lazily over her face. "It just seems kind of natural, I guess. A term of endearment, you could call it."

She drew a quick sharp breath. "An endearment?" His choice of words stunned her. Surely he was only mocking her, common sense shouted. Why then did the mere suggestion that he might find her endearing cause her heart to break into wild hammering?

"I think you'd better leave, now." She turned away, flustered. His steady scrutiny made it impossible for her to recapture the poise his careless words had scattered. "I have a lot of work to do this morning." She grabbed two empty milk jars and covered the mouth of each with a flour sack filter. "And I'm sure you must have plenty of chores to attend to as well."

She felt him move up behind her, and out of the corner of her eye she watched him lift the milk pail. As he poured the liquid into first one jar and then the other, she inched away from him, trying to ignore the feeling of being trapped in the small kitchen where, suddenly, there didn't seem to be enough air for both of them.

The distinctive scent if him—that strangely pleasant tobacco and leather smell—filled the air again, permeating her senses, leaving her feeling anxious and agitated.

When he finished pouring, he set the bucket down and edged closer to her. "Would you really find it so hard to believe, Kathleen?" he asked.

She stared at him, helpless to avoid his knowing eyes and the clear blue light coming from them. Somehow it felt as if he were staring straight through to her heart, and she found herself suddenly unable to look away. "Why, I'm sure I don't know wh-what you're talking about," she stammered.

"Oh, but I think you do, partner. And I wonder why it's so difficult for you to imagine that a man like me might find a woman like you endearing." His eyes held her motionless.

Her breath caught when without warning he reached for a curl that had escaped its pins and fallen onto her cheek. With a gentleness that belied his size and strength, he tucked it behind her ear, letting his fingers rest a moment on her face.

The color rose to her cheeks as time hung suspended, as in that breathless moment waiting for the thunder after lightning slashes a midnight sky.

She backed up against the drainboard when he moved closer, but she didn't flinch when his fingers began gently to caress her cheek. And still his eyes held hers.

"Did you know that I thought you were an apparition that first day we met out on the road?" His eyes were a cloudless summer sky, his breath the sweet summer breeze on her cheek, his voice pure velvet. "Kathleen," he sighed. "An angel in gingham," he whispered, his eyes caressing her face, resting for only a heartbeat on her lips before locking again on her eyes.

A sudden light-headedness seized her, a disturbing and delicious disorientation.

"Kathleen," he murmured again as he took both her hands and, with his eyes never leaving hers, his lips grazed her skin. "An angel's name. An angel's face."

A shiver slid down her spine and she swallowed hard. Mesmerized by his voice and his lips, by his overwhelming presence and his slow deliberate movements, she felt the warmth beginning to spread inside her, increasing to a flame, a fire she'd never experienced before leaping to life somewhere deep within her heart.

In his eyes she saw that he meant to kiss her. And suddenly, she wanted nothing more. For one crazy moment she longed for him to press his mouth against hers, to hold her, to crush her against him again, the way she'd been pressed against him when he'd carried her across the meadow.

And just when she thought this strange longing might overwhelm her, might steal the very breath from her lungs, he spoke again, his voice a low, velvety drawl. "So tell me, partner mine," he implored her, his eyes turning a dark and dangerous blue, "would an angel of God really try to kill a man with sourdough biscuits?"

The breath came back to her lungs with a gasp and she blinked in shock and outraged disbelief. In an instant her passion changed to white-hot anger. She jerked her hands from his. Sudden, bright embarrassment flooded her, bathing her neck and face in simmering scarlet.

She raised her hand to slap him, but found her wrist instantly captured in his iron grip.

"Why you! You bastard . . ." she gasped.

A sound behind them jolted her back from the edge of her rage, back to sanity with dizzying speed as she whirled around to face the door. In her haste, she would have fallen against the cookstove had Chance not grabbed her and hauled her into his arms as she stumbled.

A voice called out from the porch. "Kathleen? Are you in there, dear?"

Instantly, Kathleen recognized the high-pitched female voice and desperation squeezed her heart. But before she could form another thought, Ida Settlemier's pinched face appeared in the doorway, wearing an expression of complete shock as her quick brown eyes interpreted the scene being played out in the kitchen.

"Ida!" Kathleen gasped as she wrenched out of Chance's arms. "You're . . . you're early," she stammered.

"Indeed," the older woman sniffed, "it would appear that I am!" Ida looked down the length of her nose, her eyes narrowed in unconcealed disdain.

"Miss McBride, you really should take more care the next time you strain the milk," Chance chided, his voice fairly oozing with concern as he grabbed a flour sack, dropped to the floor and swiped at an imaginary spill. "Lord only *knows* what might have happened had I not walked in when I did. Why, you might have fallen against this hot stove and received grievous burns." As he tossed the rag onto the drainboard, he gave her a satisfied smile.

Kathleen felt Ida's eyes on her, waiting to measure her response. "Why, thank you, Mr. Ballinger," she replied, cursing the tremor in her voice as she smoothed her skirts and willed the color from her cheeks. "I assure you I'll remember every single word you've said. Every word," she added pointedly.

He smiled again. "I'm only too glad to be of service, part—"

"Thank you again, Mr. Ballinger," Kathleen interrupted curtly, grabbing his elbow and escorting him quickly past the curious Ida Settlemier, who was still standing in the doorway.

"Then I'll say good-day, ladies," Chance drawled at the door, gallantly tipping his hat to Ida, though how he was able to perform this simple physical feat Kathleen would never know, since the sheer power of the glare she locked on his heathen face should have rendered him forever paralyzed where he stood.

"Such a nice young man," Ida noted as Kathleen closed the door in his face.

"Hmm. I'll go get your gown, Ida," Kathleen managed through clenched teeth. "Let's get to your fitting, shall we?"

And as she hurried to the loft to fetch Ida's gown, Kathleen told herself that if God really did give second chances, Ida Settlemier would never notice that the cookstove was stone-cold.

Chapter Seven

———◆———

OVER the course of the next few days, Kathleen came to realize that she and Chance seemed to be operating under some sort of unspoken truce. She'd given up the idea of trying to chase him away with her cooking, and he seemed content to ready the ranch for the new cattle he was still intent on buying.

In their day-to-day contact, they treated each other with wary respect. And although she still viewed him suspiciously, Kathleen couldn't help but appreciate his hard work and his seemingly genuine interest in the ranch. And because of this growing, albeit grudging, respect for him, she treated Chance with the same courtesy she would have extended to any hired hand doing an able job.

Though her pride still stung, Kathleen conducted herself like a lady, outwardly giving the appearance of cool control.

Unfortunately, her inner turmoil wasn't so easily managed. At night, in her most quiet moments, she worried about the strange and growing attraction she felt toward the tall, attractive gambler. In those dusky moments, when she had too much time to think of him, an aching longing plagued her. She remembered how his lips had felt against her skin. She heard his voice again, low and sensual against her ear.

And so by night Kathleen battled her mutinous desires, and by day she acted as though nothing more had passed between them than the mundane and impersonal business of the ranch. In a way she was two women, battling for control of her emotions and her heart.

To her amazement, Jeb and Chance worked together as though they'd known each other all their lives. Kathleen cooked their meals, washed their clothes, worked in the garden, and tended to her barnyard chores as she always had. With the extra pair of hands Chance lent, she'd even been able to catch up on her sewing. And for that she was most grateful, for her sewing money was the only money she could truly call her own, the only money to which her *partner* held no legal claim.

The Jensen twins had paid her just this morning for the gowns she'd made them for the Spring Social. The money was still up in the loft where they'd had their fitting and Kathleen, remembering it now, went to fetch it. She counted it, smiling as she climbed down the ladder and hurried into the kitchen and stuffed the cash into the sugar bowl she kept in the corner of the cupboard.

Her spirits were high when she sat down at the kitchen table to record her latest earnings in her father's Bible-sized leather-bound ledger. Her hands even trembled slightly as she recorded the sum: four dollars, more money than she'd ever earned at one time for sewing. It was an incredible amount!

But even as she scanned the previous rows of her carefully penned entries, she wondered how much larger the balance would have been had Danny come home with the money from the herd. She felt her optimism wilt like roses in the snow.

With a defeated sigh, her eyes came to rest on the debit side of the ledger. The note payment at the Cattlemen's Bank in Bozeman stared back at her. A measly four dollars wouldn't go very far toward reducing that sum.

How much money had Chance brought with him to Twin Rivers? she wondered. Had Danny been his only victim that night in Virginia City, or had Chance Ballinger bilked other men out of their earnings as well?

She wished she knew the answer to those questions. And as his *partner,* didn't she have the right to know? she asked herself. Just how much had the herd brought at auction? She had a right to that information too.

But more important were the questions for which she had no answers: How much was needed to buy back Twin Rivers? How many satin gowns and lace collars would she need to make? How many table runners and petticoats would be enough? There was only one way to find out.

Kathleen slapped the ledger closed and took a deep breath. This evening she'd ask him, she resolved. After supper, with Jeb present to act as her witness, she'd confront Ballinger and demand answers. If she had any hope of buying him out, she had to know just how much money it would take.

She rose, invigorated by her resolve, and moved over to the fireplace. Grabbing a long-handled spoon hanging by a leather strap over the hearth, she lifted the lid on the cast-iron pot and savored the beef-and-onion smell of the stew she'd been simmering over a low fire since morning.

Next she wrapped cold biscuits in a flour sack towel, placed them in a metal pan, and shoved them into the corner of the hearth to warm. As she lit the oil lamps on the mantel and set the table, her gaze moved sadly to her brother's empty place.

Where was Danny? Had someone taken him in? Was he getting enough to eat? Did he have a warm bed on these cold spring nights? If he'd lost all his money in Virginia City, how was he managing to survive? Had he found work in exchange for room and board?

Kathleen pulled the coffeepot from the stove and a frown set her mouth in a firm line when she remembered her offer to let Chance stay on in exchange for his keep. Uh! she snorted, remembering *his* offer to let her stay on at Twin Rivers as cook and housekeeper. His cook! His housekeeper! The thought of it scalded her pride again.

But wasn't that exactly what she'd become? she asked herself abruptly. Sinking down into a chair, lost in thoughts of her awful predicament, she glanced idly at the ledger again.

Her mind swirled as she stared down at the book for another long, hard minute before opening it again. The handwritten deed Danny had lost that fateful night at Bummer Dan's was folded and placed in the back, but she refused to read it again. The grim fact that Chance Ballinger owned half of Twin Rivers was a reality. It was his money—money he'd won from Danny—that would pay the bank note and buy the supplies needed to maintain the ranch.

The awful truth was that she would remain in his debt so long as he worked the ranch and held the hand-written deed over her head. But what of his debt to her? she wondered as an idea suddenly presented itself to her troubled mind.

Didn't Chance take all of his meals at her table, filling himself with food prepared by her hand? Didn't he expect his clothes to be laundered and mended? And what about the feed his horse consumed while it grazed alongside Twin Rivers stock? Did that make his horse the property of the ranch? Of course not, she told herself logically; Ballinger had brought the horse with him and would take the animal when he left. She had no quarrel with that and sought to place no claim on the big chestnut stallion.

But since General wasn't part of their shared livestock, wouldn't it follow that Chance owed for the animal's keep?

Kathleen felt a triumphant smile growing inside her as the extent of Chance Ballinger's indebtedness began to take shape in the form of real money. She picked up the pencil and started to write with an excited hand.

Oh, she'd gladly launder and mend his clothes, she told herself, and prepare his meals. She'd perform each chore happily now, with a glad heart and great satisfaction, knowing that as she worked his indebtedness steadily increased and her own decreased.

With every day that passed, the scales would be further balanced. She'd own a larger share of Twin Rivers and Chance Ballinger less. Just thinking of the day when she could present him with his bill and order him off her property made her feel giddy.

For nearly an hour Kathleen bent over the ledger, intent on figuring. Based on the prices for the butter and eggs she took to town and sold once a week at Allerby's general store, she estimated the cost of each meal Chance consumed. Coming up with a fair figure for boarding his horse was a bit more difficult.

A twinge of guilt nipped her when she came to the final grazing figure. It was high—maybe too high, she worried. After all, she'd always prided herself in fairness. But then again, General *was* a big horse, she consoled herself. And it figured that he would consume more grass and oats than her own petite mare, wouldn't he?

A dollar a week for laundry, a dime for each piece she mended. That seemed reasonable. Each sock darned cost an additional nickel. Potatoes and biscuits. Eggs and gravy. Nothing came without a price.

And on and on it went. And as the list of Chance Ballinger's debts grew, so did Kathleen's hopes of someday soon being able to recover her brother's birthright.

When she heard the cabin door open, she slammed the ledger closed and with her heart pounding as if she were a youngster caught behind the barn smoking corn husks, she jumped to her feet, hoping her guilt didn't show on her face.

As he closed the door and shrugged out of his vest, Kathleen hugged the ledger to her chest, protectively wrapping her arms over it.

"Evening, Kathleen," he drawled as he hung his vest on the peg beside the door.

As always when she was unprepared for the sudden sight of him, she felt her senses quicken. "Good evening," she said, trying with mild success to make her voice sound as steady as possible. "Your supper's nearly ready."

"Smells good," he said, moving to the fire and rubbing his hands over the flame.

"Sit down. You must be famished." *And I intend to see that you eat hearty, Mr. Ballinger. After all, you can afford it!*

"Where's Jeb?" she asked over her shoulder.

"He rode into Bozeman this afternoon. Said he'd be back by supper, but I haven't seen him yet."

Her eyes posed the question.

"You were busy with the Jensen twins when he left. He said to tell you he had some business to tend to."

Kathleen nodded, but a nameless anxiety gnawed at her. She'd planned on Jeb being there when she confronted Chance about the money from the herd.

"I guess that leaves just you and me for supper," Chance said, smiling.

Kathleen swallowed as she walked past him and reached for the coffeepot sitting on a warmer over the hearth. The thought of a supper alone with Chance Ballinger set her nerves on edge.

"In a way it's good that Jeb is away," he said, startling her by contradicting her very thoughts. "It'll give us a chance to talk."

Kathleen nodded stiffly.

"Partners need to talk," he declared as he sat down at the table and she filled their cups with coffee. "Keeping things out in the open, aboveboard, is the only way to avoid misunderstandings. It's the best way for business partners to get along, don't you think so, Kathleen?" he asked pleasantly.

"Hmm, yes," she managed, panic seizing her when she realized the ledger was still on the table, mere inches from his elbow. She swallowed hard, willing her eyes not to look at it, to resist in any way calling his attention to the incriminating book.

He brought his cup to his lips and smiled at her over the rim as she brought the kettle to the table and filled his bowl with stew.

"I'm thoroughly pleased with the way things are going so far. I know it was a bitter pill for you to swallow at first," he allowed. "But didn't I tell you things would work out? This partnership isn't so bad, now is it, Kathleen? Twin Rivers has another able-bodied hand, one who cares about the long-range outcome of our decisions."

She stared at him, unblinking.

"And as for me, well . . . life here has exceeded all my expectations," he said jauntily. "You provide me with room and board. And good food"—his eyes twinkled—"for the most part. Jeb offers me friendship and the wisdom of his experience."

She lowered herself stiffly into her chair.

"How about it, Kathleen? Haven't things worked out better than you'd first thought?"

She'd barely heard a word he'd said; all her thoughts were focused firmly on how to get the ledger off the table without drawing his attention or arousing his suspicions.

"It isn't all that bad having me around, is it? Well, is it?" he prodded.

She shook her head absently.

"There. See? It didn't hurt you to admit it. I told you we'd both benefit from this arrangement. And if my plans for the herd work out, we'll reap even greater rewards . . . partner," he added with a playful smile. Just then he reached for his fork, and as he did he

umped the ledger with his elbow and it fell to the
oor with a thud.

Kathleen's heart stopped.

"What's this?" he asked, reaching for the leather-
ound book at his feet.

She swallowed a gasp when he picked it up and
urned to the first page. "Nothing," she replied tersely,
eaching over his plate to snatch the record book out
f his hands.

She saw in his intelligent eyes that he wondered at
er undue concern, and instead of relinquishing the
ook, he tightened his grip.

"Is this some sort of ledger? Is that what it is, Kath-
een? A record book of figures for the ranch?"

She knew he was trying to gauge her response, but
he merely nodded.

Averting her eyes from his, she pretended to con-
entrate on her food as she forced herself to take a
mall bite of stew. Perhaps after he scanned a few
ages, he'd lose interest and turn his attention back to
is supper.

"Your food's getting cold," she warned. "I'm sure
here's nothing in that old ledger that you'd find very
nteresting." She struggled to make her remarks sound
s offhand and innocent as possible, even as she silently
emoaned the fact that she'd never learned to tell a
elievable lie.

"Give it to me and I'll just put it away . . ." she said,
eaching for it again.

He turned in his seat, just enough to put the book out
f her reach. "Hold on, hold on," he murmured as he
egan to turn each page more slowly, studying closely
he figures and notations that filled each column.

Although she chewed her stew to dust, she still
couldn't swallow it.

"I see you keep a detailed record of expenses and
income in this book."

She nodded, feeling more desperate by the moment.
"My father taught me."

He offered her a wry smile. "Quite a partner I have.
She cooks and sews, rides and ropes, tends the garden
and the livestock, and keep the books as well."

She accepted his praise with a nervous smile and
reached for the book, but once again he pulled it away
before she could take it.

"Maybe I ought to take a closer look." He rose from
the table and moved over to the rocking chair by the
hearth with Kathleen hot on his heels.

"I assure you my records really won't mean a thing
to you, Mr. Ballinger . . ." She changed it to a friendly
"Chance" when he started to interrupt. "It's just a lot
of chicken scratching you wouldn't understand. I'll be
happy to tell you anything you'd like to know about the
business," she offered, trying to hide the desperation
in her voice.

"But it all looks quite legible, very understandable to
me," he said. "Every entry neat and well organized."
He nodded appreciatively as he flipped through the
pages. "Yes, all very clear."

And as he skimmed page after page, row after row
of the figures that reflected the past year's earnings and
losses, Kathleen's dread grew. When he reached the
final page of entries, her heart sank.

The further he read, the more his eyes narrowed.
Finally, still reading, he rose slowly, one eyebrow lifted
accusingly, his eyes still locked on the page. "What the

. . . ?" he muttered, moving toward her. Instinctively, Kathleen braced herself.

"What is this? Laundry? Mending? Coffee and jam?" His eyes seared the page with such intensity, she imagined that if he didn't look up soon the ledger might burst into flames in his hands.

"Flour, bacon, beans? Sourdough!" he yelled, his gaze finally lifting from the book in fiery accusation. "You'd have the nerve to charge me for those lead weights you call biscuits?"

She swallowed her retort, but tipped her chin with a defiance she felt wavering as his anger grew.

"General's grazing fee!" he roared, slapping the ledger closed and wrapping a clenched fist around it. "Is this your idea of how it goes? Of how a partnership is supposed to work?"

"L-let me explain," she stammered.

"There's nothing to explain, partner," he boomed. "We're keeping score, keeping a strict tally, is that it?" He ran his large fingers through his hair and shook his head, muttering to himself angrily. "Well, I reckon two can play at that game." As he shoved the ledger at her, he commanded, "Sit!"

His barked order stunned her into speechless obedience, and Kathleen felt her knees go weak as she dropped into one of the straight-backed chairs at the table.

"Put this in your ledger, partner," he ordered, shoving toward her the pencil that still lay beside his plate. "Fifty-two fence posts at . . . ten cents a post."

When she started to protest, he pointed at the ledger and glared at her dangerously. "I'm not finished. Ten dollars for the wire. Write it down."

"Ten dollars?" she gasped.

"Ten dollars," he repeated firmly. "And then there's the matter of my labor . . . but I'll figure that up later. And the doctoring. And the whiskey! Hmm. I don't remember exactly what I paid for that . . . oh well, hell, for now just put down fifteen dollars, total."

She jerked her head up to glare at him.

"Put it down," he said, and sat down in the chair beside her. "Put it *all* down. Every penny! If we're keeping a tally, we want to be accurate, don't we?"

She could feel the flood of crimson wash over her face.

Chance riveted his gaze on her lovely mouth, saw her lower lip tremble, and reminded himself of what he'd always known: A contrary woman could make a man's life a living hell. Damn, had he *ever* encountered a more irritating, vexing female than Kathleen McBride? And damn it all, had he ever seen a more beautiful face? An angel's face, he told himself, fighting to maintain the anger he felt slipping.

"The trimming of horses' feet," he continued, reminding himself of his indignation. "Ten head at a dollar apiece."

"Ten dollars!" she cried. "Why, that's robbery!"

"Ten dollars," he repeated loudly. "Now, as for the daily wood chopping . . ."

She slapped the ledger closed, flung it at him and jumped to her feet, tipping the chair over backward as she did. "Enough!" she shouted. "And I'll thank you to stay away from the woodpile in the future. I'll chop it myself, from now on. At your prices, I could never afford to fire up the stove again."

Chance shoved his own chair back and rose slowly, finding his patience stretched to the breaking point.

"Now that," he roared, the deep timbre of his voice filling the room and reverberating off the rafters, "would be a blessing indeed, if that damned sourdough is the best that blasted oven can produce!"

For a breathless moment they stood eye to eye, glowering at each other, sparks flying between them. And then without warning, he saw her lovely lips begin to twitch and curl into a smile.

"Was it really so awful?" she asked, fighting for a straight face as her voice cracked and she giggled.

He shook his head and made a terrible face. "Awful doesn't even come close."

She clapped her hand over her mouth as if to recapture the burst of laughter that had escaped. The musical sound tripped delightfully over his senses and melted Chance's anger like fresh butter on steaming hotcakes.

He tried to frown as he rubbed his jaw comically. "With the first bite, I thought I'd broken a tooth," he informed her, feeling the contagion of her laughter curling inside him. "Just getting it down was one thing, but keeping it down, well, that was another matter!"

"Oh . . . oh, no!" she howled, wrapping her arms around herself as her shoulders shook. "I-I just couldn't help myself," she admitted, fighting to catch her breath. "I just couldn't." A fresh wave of convulsive laughter seized her.

"I know . . . ," he assured her, his own voice cracking as he laughed. "I know what you mean. And I'd planned to even the score until that nosey old biddy from Bozeman came calling and ruined my plan. . . . I'll never forget the look on her face!" He finally let his laughter flow.

Kathleen could only nod, the memory of Ida's startled expression sending her into a fresh fit of convulsive laughter. Chance was as helpless as she was to control his howling. His sides ached, his head hurt, and he couldn't remember the last time he'd had so much fun.

Though they tried to regain control, every time they looked at each other their shared laughter exploded anew, rising to a new crescendo and crashing around them in waves.

"P-please," she begged, reaching for his arm. "Stop. Oh, stop . . . I can't . . . breathe." She swiped at the tears as she staggered to the drainboard and leaned over it, gasping for breath.

He gulped for air as he moved up behind her, watching her fall apart all over again. She looked so pretty when she smiled, and downright irresistible when she laughed.

Suddenly he realized he should never let anger come between them again. Her laughter was pure gold, a healing balm for his troubled soul. Looking at her now, he couldn't bear the thought of watching her smile disappear, to see this easy time together end.

And he knew he couldn't go another day without kissing her.

When he touched her shoulders and she whirled around to face him, he decided the smile that graced her lovely mouth was the sweetest, dearest sight he'd ever seen. His breath burned in his lungs, but the laughter froze in his throat when he touched her cheek and let his eyes devour her face.

"Chance?" she whispered, her lips parted seductively as she gazed up at him. Her eyes, glistening emeralds, smoldering with distant desire, seemed almost child-like, so endearing with bright innocence.

He felt control of his emotions strain against the

flood of his desire. "Kathleen," he groaned as he reached for her.

She sucked in a sharp breath, but didn't pull away when he slid his arm around her small waist and pulled her against him. His heart raced and his senses burned with the nearness of her, with her scent all lilacs and sunshine.

Her gaze locked on his rugged features. His eyes sparked a deep sapphire blue. Instinctively she recognized the hunger she saw simmering there, and she knew that he meant to kiss her. And in an instant of naked self-awareness, she knew full well she meant to kiss him back.

In that secret place in her heart hadn't she longed for this to happen? she asked herself. Hadn't she dreamed of his touch in the aching darkness of her restless nights?

An inner voice urged her to protest when she felt his fingers tangle in the hair at the nape of her neck, when she felt herself grow light-headed as his muscular length pressed against her. That inner voice grew louder, urging her to run for her life from the swelling tide of her own emotions that threatened to pull her down into the dark waters of her longing, into the depths of that swirling pool from which, if she survived at all, she knew she'd emerge forever changed.

But the wondrous and mysterious melody that had begun playing in her heart with his first touch, deafened her to all warnings. The fire in his eyes mesmerized her and drew her toward an irresistible flame she longed to touch.

Her throat constricted and her heart pounded painfully in her breast as he lowered his face to hers with agonizing slowness. His breath felt warm against her mouth as his lips hovered over hers for the space of a heartbeat.

Involuntarily her eyelids fluttered closed and a shiver of anticipation sent a shuddery sigh quivering through her.

"Kathleen." He whispered her name like a prayer seconds before his lips claimed hers.

His kiss was a gentle caress, a feathered promise, a reverent vow that made her breath catch in her throat. In the next moment his kiss grew hotter, more demanding.

She melted against him, reveling in the delight that filled her heart. She laced her arms around his neck and drew him even closer. How could she have known it would be like this? How could she have known she was capable of feeling such desire?

And just when she thought the emotions coursing wildly between them might engulf her, his kiss ended.

"Listen," he murmured against that sensitive spot just below her ear. "I think we've got company."

With an inner agony she'd never known, she pulled away from him and, peering out the window, saw Jeb and their neighbor Sam Coulter crossing the porch headed for the cabin door.

Kathleen ran a hand quickly over her hair, hoping the masculine fingers that had so recently been buried there had left no trace. Touching a trembling hand to her cheeks, she felt the heat and could only hope Jeb and Sam wouldn't notice.

Reluctantly, Chance moved away from her and back to the table before the door opened.

"Evenin', Chance," Jeb said as he clambered in. "This here's our neighbor and good friend Sam Coulter. Sam," he said, "this here's the fella I been tellin' you about."

Chance nodded. Kathleen marveled at how completely composed he appeared.

"If anyone can tell you what's ailin' that horse of yours, Chance can," Jeb declared.

Sam nodded hopefully. "Kathleen," he greeted her with his familiar smile. "Etta sends her best."

"Hello, Sam. How's she doing?" Kathleen said, forcing a steadiness into her voice that belied the tremors still tingling through her body.

"Well as can be expected, I suppose, with the baby so close to comin'," Sam said, his brown eyes sober. "She's awful tired these days." Etta Coulter was within a few short weeks of delivering the couple's first child, and seeing Sam tonight reminded Kathleen that she'd need to hurry to finish the quilt she'd started for the new arrival.

"Won't you stay for supper, Sam?" Kathleen asked.

The tall, sandy-haired young man nodded appreciatively. "Thanks, something smells mighty good."

"I'll get a chair," Chance offered, and followed Kathleen into the kitchen while Sam and Jeb moved to the fire to warm themselves.

She was reaching for two more plates when Chance came up behind her. Her senses quivered with an overwhelming awareness of him.

"One kiss," he uttered in a low voice that only the two of them could hear, "no charge." His mouth tilted in a wry grin, but his eyes still smoldered with desire. Before she could respond, he grabbed the chair from the corner and was gone.

And as the three men seated themselves at the table

and became immediately immersed in conversation concerning Sam Coulter's ailing stallion, Kathleen served their supper and wondered how in the name of heaven she'd survive a partnership with the blue-eyed gambler who'd laid claim to half of everything she owned, including her heart.

For the women who plied their trade in the rooms above the bar at Bummer Dan's, morning always came too early. But for Rubylee Tyler, this morning couldn't have come soon enough. Last night she'd packed most of her belongings, and later today when the stage pulled out of Virginia City headed for Bozeman, she meant to be on it.

That bunch of godforsaken drovers who'd stumbled into Bummer Dan's last night had made her decision final—trail-filthy, half starved, and pauper-poor, the lot of them. Their scraggly herd, or what was left of it, wouldn't have been enough to meet their payroll had all the drovers who'd signed on survived the drive.

Rubylee had heard the trail boss tell the bartender about the renegade band of Indians they'd run into some twenty miles south of town. It was a gruesome story, one the people of Virginia City thought they'd heard the last of when the army had moved into Fort Benton a few years back.

In the past, Indian raids on a trail drive often consisted of nothing more than a few braves creeping up into the herd during the night, then jumping up and shouting and waving buffalo blankets to start a stampede. In the confusion that would ultimately follow, the Indians usually made off with only a few head of steers and a couple of horses.

Most outfits had come to expect a more open confrontation and had learned to dicker with the ragtag bands of three or four braves when they saw them along the trail. Safe passage could usually be bought with no more than a steer or two. Though some renegades might come back in the night to steal and loot the supply wagons, most were hungry beggars, eager to take what they were peaceably given.

Sure, a man could get himself killed during an Indian raid by stampeding cattle or spooked and frightened horses running wild. Despite the bragging done around the campfires, however, open hostilities between cowhand and Indian had been rare.

But lately things had been changing. As more settlers moved into the territory and the Indians were pushed farther north, they'd become more hostile, more desperate and savage. A band of Sioux from the Dakotas had moved into Wyoming. The army had resumed regular patrols near the old trail that back in the fifties had come to be known as the Bloody Bozeman. The Indian bands that confronted the drovers now were becoming more vicious. Their attacks more brutal. Their raids more deadly.

Rubylee had heard that this last outfit had been hit the hardest, losing more than half the herd and all but a handful of resourceful drovers. The worst attack had come two nights ago.

When the raid began, panic spread like cholera through the herd. Half a dozen drovers deserted the fight. The trail boss figured his fleeing comrades were riding hell-bent to Fort Benton to summon the army.

But whatever their intended destination, the trail hands never made it. Their mutilated bodies, relieved of their scalps and other vital parts, were found three days later, grisly markers beside the trail.

Men who'd survived what this bunch had survived, seen what they'd seen, and lived to tell about it needed a lot of whiskey to ward off the inevitable night terrors that would visit them. Once they reached the safety of civilization, they drank and bragged and gambled away their pitiful bankrolls, feeling damn lucky just to be alive.

At the gaming tables up and down Alder Gulch there were always the dandies whose luck was calculated to relieve the trail hand of his meager earnings. Virginia City was a mining town. A gambling town. A town built on luck. But the unsuspecting trail hand learned too late that the luck that had brought him safely to Virginia City soon deserted him in Alder Gulch.

And Rubylee had seen enough bum luck and busted cowhands to last her a lifetime. Why, the pittance she'd made last night would barely last a week paying room and board in Bozeman City.

As she jammed the last of her belongings into the overstuffed carpetbag, she glanced scornfully around the dingy room and decided whatever awaited her in Bozeman had to be better than what she was leaving behind.

The faded paper was peeling and cracking off the walls. The curtains, once lacy and white, had turned to yellow tatters from the heat and dust of too many summers.

This morning Rubylee felt as old and faded as the ragged spread hanging unevenly off the thin mattress. At twenty-two, but feeling more like forty, she knew she wasn't leaving Virginia City a moment too soon.

As she secured the drooping feathered hat to the mass of blond curls pinned on top of her head, her gaze slid to the letter lying beside her bag on the bed.

If she played her cards right, the letter she'd intercepted a week ago would mean her passage out of
places like Bummer Dan's and into a legitimate world
she'd never known—the world of starched linens, fancy
wallpaper, and clean-smelling air.

That letter was her last ace, and she fully intended
to play it wisely.

She hoped delivering the letter to the man to whom
it was addressed, to Chance Ballinger, would bring her
his gratitude. Perhaps he'd reward her handsomely
enough to wipe the smell of trail dust, rotgut whiskey,
and cow manure from her senses forever. If she were
really lucky, he might even begin to see her in a new
light. Rubylee closed her eyes and let herself imagine
what it might be like to walk down a proper city street
on the arm of the handsome Texan.

She sighed when she thought about the possibilities
and smiled as she picked up the envelope with his
name scrawled across the front. A knot of anticipation
tightened in her stomach as she shoved the letter into
her well-worn reticule and drew the strings closed.

Ballinger had won big the night he'd left Virginia
City. He was one of the last big winners she was likely
to see for some time, with the Indian situation the way
it was.

He was a man of property now as well. A big man
in the Gallatin Valley. A man with a future. But as it
turned out, according to the letter, he was a man with
a past, too. Well, that past only mattered to her in the
way she could use it to help herself. She had a past,
but that didn't mean she couldn't do better. And with
Ballinger's help—the help that letter would prompt
him to give—perhaps she could start over.

If he could forget his past, so could she. In her mind,

it wasn't blackmail, it was merely playing the lucky hand she'd been dealt. It was surviving the only way she knew how.

Right now Rubylee was as anxious to ride out and grab that future as Ballinger had been the night he'd turned his back on her and ridden out to his high-country ranch.

But nothing came easily or without a price. Five years of working a dozen bars and whorehouses in Virginia City had taught Rubylee that much. And while she meant the big man no harm, she knew that the letter from Texas and her silence about what she'd read had to be worth something.

It was her chance. A chance to start over, she reminded herself as she descended the backstairs of Bummer Dan's for the last time. A smart girl didn't ignore opportunity when it knocked.

And Rubylee Tyler had heard it knocking and was more than ready to open the door.

Chapter Eight

———◆———

DANNY fanned the mound of smoking pine needles vigorously, trying to coax a blaze to warm his trembling body and dry his soggy clothes. His hands shook as he scooped more needles and dried grass onto the sputtering blue flame. Good Lord, had he ever been this cold? If he didn't get warm and dry soon, he'd be doomed.

He was doomed anyway, he thought miserably, if he crossed paths with that gang of men he'd seen on the trail this morning.

When Danny had crawled out of the beaver pond where he'd hidden until he thought it was safe to come out, he'd decided to keep going as fast and as straight as he could for Bozeman, even if it meant traveling through the night. After what he'd witnessed, the bone-numbing cold of a night out on the mountain seemed like a pleasant alternative.

The men he'd seen—six or seven of them—must have been vigilantes. He'd heard about them, a local

bunch who operated in the name of justice, leaving a
trail of corpses hanging from the cottonwoods from Virginia City to Bannack. It would do a man no good to
plead his case once this group drew a bead on him.

The way Danny had heard it, many of the victims
were small cattlemen or homesteaders whose only
crime lay in the threat they posed to those whose intent
it was to gather all the prime acreage in the valley for
themselves.

Whether the hanging he'd witnessed this morning
had been at the hands of vigilantes or not, Danny didn't
know. As far as he was concerned, it didn't make much
difference. Either way, if that bunch knew what he'd
seen, he'd be a marked man.

Danny shuddered, trying to dispel the terrible images that haunted him. He'd never forget the wild terror blazing in the eyes of that poor devil perched
astride the big gray. He couldn't imagine what any man
might have done to warrant the kind of brutal punishment that poor bastard had suffered.

The gruesome scene lingered in fresh detail in Danny's memory. The man's face, beaten to a bloody pulp.
His arms hung limp in their sockets—broken, Danny
figured, when the wretched soul had tried to put up a
fight.

"Poor SOB never had a chance," Danny muttered to
himself, shaking his head. When the horse had been
slapped into motion and the rope had snapped tight
around the man's neck, Danny had stumbled backward
into the brush—half running, half crawling—terrified
for his own life.

He had no idea if the vigilantes had seen or heard
him. And he sure as hell hadn't waited around to find
out. When a beaver pond blocked his trail of retreat,

he'd jumped in headfirst without hesitation and stayed there for what seemed like hours. Only when he'd felt certain the mob had moved on had Danny forsaken his soggy hideaway.

He clamped his chattering teeth together now as a series of convulsive shivers shook him back to his present predicament. He couldn't let that bunch catch him out here alone on the trail. After tugging on his still-damp clothes, Danny stamped out the small fire. He needed to get moving again.

"Damn horse," he swore under his breath. His gelding had come untied in the night and he'd been tracking the animal when he'd come upon the hanging party. But maybe it would work out better this way after all. A man on foot made a hell of a lot less noise than a horse crashing through the timber.

He pulled a piece of wet jerky from his pocket, yanked off a mouthful, and started walking east cursing his rotten luck, which had been bad enough in Virginia City but seemed to be turning worse by the hour.

It was just after daylight when Chance rode out the next morning. After a stop in Bozeman City to post a letter to Callie and Jim Jr., look around for Danny McBride, and visit the banker, he planned to head straight for the Richardson ranch.

As he rode across the meadow, Chance urged General to quicken his pace. Thoughts of riding out to buy cattle, of building a herd, made him feel revitalized, invigorated with a renewed sense of purpose.

But implementing his plans for Twin Rivers wouldn't be easy, he reminded himself. The ranch was heavily indebted. The first step in putting his plans to work involved convincing the banker to carry them another season, to make Charles Settlemier see that what little capital had come from the sale of the cattle in Virginia City would be better spent strengthening the herd than applied to the promissory note.

Chance smiled to himself, convincing the banker to give him more time couldn't be any harder than convincing Kathleen to give him her trust.

Last night after Sam had left, Chance, Jeb, and Kathleen had discussed the Herefords. At first Kathleen had been openly skeptical, even angry. She wasn't a lady who accepted change easily, and she wasn't accustomed to taking risks. But as he'd told her more about other ranchers' successes with the hardy breed, Chance had seen the excitement sparking in her eyes. His own hopes had soared when she'd finally come round to his way of thinking. And in the end, the decision to buy the Herefords had been made with the consent of both partners.

Now he was excited to finally be getting down to business. But first there were some personal matters that needed attending to, and the matter of reuniting the McBride family was at the top of his list.

If he ever hoped to win Kathleen's confidence, Chance knew that finding Danny McBride and bringing him home was something he couldn't afford to put off any longer. Though Kathleen hadn't yet met him dead center, he could feel her beginning to edge his way. She'd shown good faith in trusting him with the decision concerning the new stock, and she'd even given her grudging acceptance of the fenced meadow. Sometimes it almost seemed like a real partnership might actually be taking shape—after all, Chance reminded himself, Kathleen McBride was a practical woman. She appreciated good, sound horse sense, even when it came from him.

But she was also fiercely loyal, and as long as she held him responsible for tearing her family apart, for chasing her brother from his rightful home, she'd never find it in her heart to truly trust him, or accept him as a full partner.

Looking back, Chance guessed he'd known all along that he'd eventually have to go after the boy, from that very first day when he'd witnessed the depth of Kathleen's devotion to her brother, and felt the first tug of guilt.

His decision to combine his cattle-buying trip with finding Danny had been cemented last night after Kathleen had gone to bed, when Sam and Jeb said they both thought Danny would likely be found hanging around Bozeman in one of the local saloons.

"The way I figure it, the boy's too ashamed to come home," Sam had stated regretfully. "Poor Kathleen," he said, shaking his head.

"Sometimes I wonder if Danny will ever turn himself around," Jeb had said angrily. "I care about the boy, I really do. But what he's doing to his sister—well, it just rips my hide to see him grieve her so. What with her Pa dyin' the way he did, and now Danny goin' off half-cocked—well, it just don't seem right. She deserves better."

Chance couldn't have agreed more. But finding Danny and bringing him home and purchasing a few head of stock was just the beginning, Chance warned himself as he topped a hill and caught sight of the first buildings at the edge of town. In ranching the risks were always high. Drought, disease, predators, or a killing winter, all could strike without warning and destroy his dreams—not to mention a murder charge that haunted his every move.

But Jim Jr. and Callie were depending on him to succeed, to fulfill his promise of finding them a home. And now Kathleen and Jeb were depending on him too. When he thought about all that he had riding on his shoulders and all that was pushing at his back, he realized the odds against him had never been higher.

But then again, Chance reminded himself with a wry smile, he'd always played best when the stakes were high. This time fate had dealt the hand and he was playing to win. And with the memory of Kathleen's honeyed lips still lingering on his tongue, how could he play for less?

An hour later, Chance's eyes fought to readjust to the semidarkness of the cavelike interior of the Bozeman establishment simply called Hoffman's. The stale air hung in a gauzy curtain of smoke-sated gray and carried the sounds of rattling poker chips and boozy voices.

Shouldering his way past a knot of swaggering trail hands, Chance scanned the dingy room for a moment. He'd chosen Hoffman's as the first place to look for Kathleen's wayward brother after thinking back to the times when he'd been seeking a place to lick his *own* wounds and deciding this dark, anonymous hole seemed the perfect choice. When his gaze came to rest on the slumped figure at a table in the corner, he knew his instincts had been right.

As he moved closer to Danny, Chance frowned, remembering how Jeb had declared Kathleen's younger brother an undependable cur, whose boozing and gambling had cost his sister more than her share of sleep-less nights.

Standing over the dozing boy, Chance reminded himself once more of just why he was here. Kathleen worried and grieved every day over the loss of her brother. Jeb had said she wouldn't rest until she knew for sure that her brother was safe. All right, then. He'd do what had to be done. He'd drag Danny McBride back home. He'd do it for Kathleen, he told himself.

But deep down inside, Chance knew he'd be bring-ing Danny back to Twin Rivers for an even more per-sonal reason.

By offering Danny McBride a fresh start, Chance figured he'd be paying back at least a portion of the debt he owed his own brother. Like Kathleen, James had spent one too many sleepless nights and given more than one second chance to his wild younger brother.

Now that Chance had learned what a home and a family could mean to a man, he was determined to try to show Danny before it was too late. Who knew? Per-haps all the young man needed was the chance to prove his lessons had already been learned.

The subject of these speculations snorted loudly in his sleep, bringing Chance back to his present di-lemma. Now that he'd found the boy, how the hell was he going to convince Danny to trust him?

Chance took a deep breath and almost gagged; he'd walked past stock pens that smelled a whole lot better than Danny McBride did this afternoon. "Wake up, Junior," Chance ordered gruffly as he clamped one hand onto the young man's narrow shoulder.

"Wh-what? What the . . . ? What's goin' on?" Danny sputtered toward consciousness.

"Get up, Junior." Chance grabbed a handful of dirty coat and hauled Danny up out of his seat.

The half-dazed young man didn't put up much of a fight as Chance dragged him through the darkened barroom and out onto the wooden sidewalk. Once outside, Danny rubbed his face with both hands, mumbling a curse at the brightness of the sunshine that stung his red-rimmed and bloodshot eyes.

"Why, you're—you're him . . . !" Danny exclaimed when full consciousness finally returned. Eyes blazing, he struggled against the steely grip that held him upright.

"That's right. It's me," Chance growled.

"Lemme go. I don't owe you nothin'." Danny's bravado was as transparent as his bluffing in Virginia City had been. He was clearly on the losing side of a long bout with bad whiskey. One look told Chance the young man was not only dead broke, but half sick and wholly scared as well.

Chance released him and Danny staggered and nearly fell until Chance grabbed him again and ushered him across the street to a long, low watering trough in front of the general mercantile store. Against Danny's weak protests, Chance dunked the young man's head under the dark water.

He came up sputtering and choking and grabbing for his wide-brimmed hat. "You son of a bitch! You're tryin' to kill me!

"Hold your tongue, boy," Chance ordered as a wagon carrying a man, a woman, and three small children pulled up beside them. "No one's trying to kill you." Chance retrieved Danny's sodden hat and jammed it onto the young man's head, sending streams of water streaking down his unshaven face. "Though you look and smell as though you'd given it one whale of a try yourself."

Danny staggered and shook his head. "Wake a feller up. Haul him out and try to drown him," he muttered sullenly. "Wh-what do you want with me, anyway?"

"Hell if I know," Chance drawled as he grabbed Danny's arm and shoved him back onto the sidewalk. "But I'll think of something once you're cleaned up and had a decent meal."

At the mention of food something sparked in Danny's green eyes. For the first time Chance saw a glimmer of familial resemblance and felt something soften inside him. "Hungry?" he asked.

Danny nodded, his expression grim. "But I don't have any money. You took it all, remember?"

Chance stopped in his tracks, whirled around and grabbed Danny by the shirtfront. "I didn't *take* anything from you, Junior."

"Well, what do you call it, then?" Danny demanded, shrugging away from Chance's grip.

"Luck."

"Bad luck," the young man grumbled.

"Maybe," Chance growled. "And maybe not. But you played the game and you lost. I won that money from you fair and square. No one forced you to sit in on that game, Junior."

Danny stared at him, confusion clouding his eyes. "What do you want with me, anyway? You took—"

Chance cut off his accusation with a murderous glare.

"All right, all right," Danny relented, "you *won* everything I had. What more do you want from me?"

It took almost more patience than Chance possessed to keep from turning and walking away from Kathleen's belligerent young brother. "I want you to do what's right," he said angrily. "I want you to go home and set things straight with your family, with your sister."

"But why?" Danny asked.

"Because you can, Junior," Chance said quietly.

Chance watched Danny deciding whether or not to trust the man who'd cleaned his pockets the last time they'd met. In the end it seemed his basic needs made the decision for him. "You asked if I was hungry. Well, I am," Danny declared, his eyes still narrowed with suspicion.

Chance acknowledged his admission with a curt nod. "Then let's get you some dinner."

"B-but I haven't any way to pay you back," Danny said uncertainly.

Chance clapped the young man on the back and smiled as they started down the street together. "Don't worry, Danny. I'll work it out of you, if you're willing. You feel like herding some cattle?"

"Well, I don't know," Danny said uneasily. "Well, yeah, I guess I could use the work. But—but what cattle? Most of the herd was auctioned off in Virginia City. There won't be any Twin Rivers steers ready for market till fall."

"Not the old herd," Chance explained. "New cattle. Hereford cattle. Every heard of them?"

Danny shook his head.

"Well, you will," Chance assured him.

"Then she hasn't done it yet." Danny shook his head and smiled a grim smile.

"Who hasn't done what?" Chance asked as they stepped inside the lobby of a two-story hotel at the end of the street.

"My sister. Kathleen," Danny explained. "I figured she'd have run you off by now."

Chance laughed. "Not yet, Junior."

Danny stared at him with a look of open admiration. "Well, I'll be damned."

Behind the gleaming counter, a middle-aged woman in a long calico dress covered with a starched white apron shot them a disapproving look. Chance could hardly blame the woman. Danny looked and smelled like he'd been plucked from the dung heap.

"Good afternoon, ma'am," Chance drawled easily as he doffed his hat and leaned one arm on the counter. "I think you'll agree that my friend here could use a bath and a fresh set of clothes."

The woman nodded her agreement, pointedly ignoring Danny while offering Chance her warmest smile. Chance had grown accustomed long ago to the admiring glances he garnered from members of the opposite sex, and he returned the clerk's smile and decided that the woman behind the counter had a prettier than average face.

But as he studied her more closely he noticed that she wore too much powder and rouge for his taste, and she'd smeared too much red tint on her lips. It surprised him when he caught himself comparing the woman to the mental picture he now carried of Kathleen.

He couldn't resist smiling at the image that formed so easily in his mind. With her fresh-scrubbed loveliness and shining auburn hair, his partner could certainly teach the ladies he'd encountered along the trail between Texas and the Montana Territory a thing or two about beauty.

"And what can we do for you?" the woman behind the counter asked seductively, batting her lashes.

Chance shook his head as he plunked two gold pieces down onto the counter. "Nothing for me, ma'am. But if you could take good care of my young friend, here, I'd be much obliged. See to it he gets whatever he needs, and keep whatever's left for your trouble."

Slender fingers reached out, slid the gold pieces across the counter, and dropped them into the cash drawer. "This should more than cover everything," she assured him. "And thank you, Mr. . . . ?"

"Ballinger."

"Ballinger. I'll remember that," she assured him, flashing a sweet smile.

Ah, now there was something this city gal could teach Kathleen. He'd give three times the amount of gold he'd just spent on her brother to see Kathleen smile that way at him more often.

Good Lord, Ballinger, an inner voice chided, *one would think you loved the woman!* The thought shocked him. Was he in love with Kathleen? he asked himself. In love with the lady who haunted his dreams as he lay in her blasted bunkhouse torturing himself with thoughts of her next door in that big four-poster? In love with the same stubborn Irish lady who wished to heaven she'd never laid eyes on him? The lady who if she ever learned about the past he was trying to outrun, would gladly turn him over to the nearest lynch mob to regain control of her family's ranch?

Fascinated, yes. Intrigued, definitely. Desirous, more often than he cared to ponder. But in love?

Yes, he *could* love her, he heard his heart whisper.

It would be so easy to fall for that very same lady, the lady that any man would be proud to call his partner.

Danny tugged Chance out of his startling reveries when he dragged his hat off his head and muttered, "Afternoon, ma'am," parroting Chance's display of manners. The clerk glared at the dirty water still dripping from Danny's clothes and pooling on the floor at his feet.

"I guess his hat could use a little cleaning too," Chance explained apologetically. "Can you see to it?"

"Why, yes. Yes, sir, Mr. Ballinger," the woman replied pleasantly. "I'll see to it myself."

"I'd appreciate that, ma'am, I truly would," Chance drawled in his best southern style, and enjoyed watching the color rise to the woman's pleasant face. "And after he's cleaned up, get him a steak—a big one—and plenty of potatoes, biscuits, and coffee. Lots of coffee," Chance added as he headed for the door. "I'll be back in an hour, Junior. You get yourself ready to go to work, and then we'll see about getting you home."

Danny stood speechless for a moment, blinking in numbed disbelief. "Yes, sir," he said slowly, his voice cracking a little when he added, "I—I surely am ready to go home."

The next morning dawned unusually hot for spring. Chance and Danny had been on the trail since before sunup and both men could feel the heat building. So far it had been an easy drive, Chance told himself. Then he chuckled, remembering the vast herds he'd pushed across the wide Texas plains. Forty head of domestic Hereford cattle hardly qualified as a trail drive.

What Chance had heard and read about Herefords

was already proving true. The reddish-brown animals with the distinctive white faces were a docile breed, a quality Chance was quick to appreciate as they trailed the cattle over the rough terrain outside Bozeman City. At this rate they'd be home in less than four hours, Chance estimated.

If the cattle remained cooperative, he warned himself, and *if* the Indian scout he'd seen watching them from a butte on the horizon an hour ago decided to let them pass unmolested.

There was a wide spot in the creek up ahead. Chance had made a mental note of its location on the ride out to Richardson's. He saw now that the young heifers in the lead had already discovered the water and were bunching around the shallow banks.

As he eased his horse closer to a clearing by the stream, Danny rode up beside him, his face flushed and his breath coming in short gasps.

"Did you see them?" Danny asked, his voice tight with apprehension. "The Indians?"

"I did," Chance said without turning around.

"What should we do?"

"Nothing to do, yet," Chance drawled as he dismounted and dipped his hat into the cold, clear water. Danny was at his side in an instant.

"But we can't just pretend they ain't out there."

"Be patient, Junior," Chance said, before tipping his hat and taking a long, slow swallow of the icy creek water. "I figure they'll make their move soon enough."

"Make their move?" Danny blurted out. "Attack us, don't you mean?"

Chance shook his head. "If that was their plan, they've had the advantage all morning. No," he said easily, running a wet hand through his hair before settling his hat back onto his head, "I reckon when they finally come out into the open they'll be more interested in trading than fighting."

"Are you betting my scalp on that, Ballinger?" Danny grumbled.

Chance gave him a wry smile and slapped him heartily on the back. "Mine and yours, Junior."

As Chance shoved his foot back into the stirrup and prepared to mount up, he heard a soft crying sound coming from within a stand of trees on the other side of the stream.

Danny heard it, too, and his eyes bulged. "Did you hear that? It's them, isn't it? It's some kind of signal. They're going to ambush us right here at this water hole and murder us where we stand."

"Calm down," Chance ordered in a low voice, "and stay here with the cattle while I go take a look."

Danny's brows shot up in panic.

"I'll be right back, Junior. Keep your eyes open and stay calm." But as he rode across the creek, Chance heard Danny grumbling something about scalps and savages and cattle being the death of him.

The whimpering grew more desperate the closer Chance rode, and in a moment he spotted the source of the mournful sound. An Indian child, curled up with her arms wrapped pitifully around herself was lying in the tall grass, crying.

Chance dismounted without a sound and eased over to the crying child. When he laid a gentle hand on her back, she jumped up, fear etched on her small golden face.

"Easy, easy, little one," Chance murmured gently.

Her glistening black eyes viewed him with hostile suspicion. The child, clothed in a soft deerskin dress and tattered moccasins, couldn't have been more than five or six. Around her neck she wore a braided chain of colorful wild flowers that hung down past her swollen belly.

Anger and pity choked Chance as he noted the all too familiar sight of an Indian child in the throes of slow starvation. Why was it when men went to war it was the innocents who always seemed to suffer the most?

"I won't hurt you," he assured her as he moved over to his horse and took a handful of jerky and a biscuit out of his saddlebag.

The little girl took the food from him cautiously, but soon hunger overpowered her fear and she began to devour the jerky with ripping, tearing animal bites.

"Are you lost, little one?" Chance asked.

"Washita," she said, between mouthfuls.

Chance shook his head. He had not yet learned the language of the Montana tribes: the Crow, Flatheads, Kootenais, and others.

"Washita?" he repeated clumsily. "I'm afraid I don't know what that means, little one."

"My name Washita, not Little One," she shot back, her chin tipped proudly and her dark eyes snapping.

The feisty comeback, spoken in near-perfect English, startled Chance and caused him to rear back and laugh. His outburst startled her, and she edged back into the trees, but a moment later a slow smile began to blossom at the corners of her pink mouth.

"Well, Miss Washita," he said, "where did you learn to speak the white man's language so well?"

"Reservation," she said flatly. "They teach us."

Chance nodded. If Washita came from the reservation, it was unlikely that she'd wandered all this way on her own. Somehow she must have become separated from her family, from a band of Indians who were in all probability on the run.

"Are you lost?" he asked.

She stared up at him, her great round eyes filling with tears. "Washita right here," she said. "Father and brother, they are lost!" she declared with bright emotion. "Washita search all night but cannot find them."

The tears slipping down her cheek tugged at Chance's heart. The child was so much like Callie May. And like his pint-sized niece, this spirited little maiden had more pride than size.

"I think I saw your father this morning," he said as he took her hand, and she let him lead her to his horse. "And I bet he was looking for you."

She stared at him, confused.

"Would you like me to help you find your father and brother?"

Her pretty face broke into a relieved smile and she nodded vigorously.

"Well, then, climb aboard," he said as he lifted her up onto General's back. Reaching into his saddlebag, he handed her another biscuit before he took up the reins and led the horse and passenger back toward the stream.

Washita patted General's neck and talked to him in low, soothing murmurs.

"You like this big old horse?" Chance asked.

Washita nodded and smiled.

"His name is General. I named him after a great general I once knew and admired very much. General Lee. Have you ever heard of him?"

Washita scowled and shook her head. "Is your horse a great general too?" she asked.

"Well, he's smart and strong. And his heart's about as big as he is. Now that you mention it, yes, I guess that makes him a great general too."

Washita nodded her agreement. "I like General," she declared. "I think he is a fine brave soldier."

Before they could cross the creek, the sound of water churning and splashing drew Chance's attention to the other side. The sight that met his eyes made him curse quietly under his breath.

Danny, his hands bound behind him, was being forced across the water by six Indian braves.

Chance brought General to a halt, assessing the situation as he waited for the men to approach him. Two of the braves carried rifles. The other four carried bows.

Danny's eyes were wide with fright. "We're done for," he cried. "Didn't I tell you? They're gonna scalp us and leave us for dead!"

"Shut up, Danny," Chance ordered harshly.

When the Indians were within a few feet of Chance and the child, they trained their weapons on him.

The tallest brave flicked a dangerous gaze between Chance and the child seated on General's back.

"Is that your father, Washita?" Chance asked quietly.

The child nodded.

Chance turned to lift Washita down, but froze when he heard the rifles being cocked.

"Father, no!" Washita cried. "White man help Washita find you. He give Washita good food," she said, holding out the half-eaten biscuit and the remaining jerky as evidence. "White man and General are Washita's friends," she declared, ducking her head to remove her flower necklace and drape it gently across the horse's neck.

Chance felt the Indian's eye rake over him with open hostility. For a moment no one made a move. Finally Washita's father barked an order to his men and the rifles were lowered. Danny's sigh of relief was audible as another brave moved around behind him and untied his hands.

"Washita run away," her father explained in a voice brittle with exhaustion. "Silver Elk has searched all night for his daughter."

The other braves stood in stoic silence as Silver Elk walked past Chance and lifted Washita down off General's back. "Silver Elk owe white man for the safety of his daughter."

"Silver Elk owes nothing," Chance said evenly, lift- the flower necklace from General's neck and hold- it gently between his hands. "Washita has already id."

The girl's father stared at Chance; his dark, intelli- gent eyes seemed capable of boring through a man's soul and finding the truth in a man's heart. With a curt nod that barely disturbed a strand of the blue-black hair that fell past his shoulders, Silver Elk gave his sol- emn acceptance of the situation.

"White man has many beef cattle," he said as the entire group moved together across the creek.

Chance studied the man's proud visage for a moment before he spoke. A glance at the braves who rode with Silver Elk was deceptive. Their lean, muscled bodies gave the illusion of health and strength, but their young faces were unduly haggard and gaunt. Chance figured the women and children in Silver Elk's band were probably in similar stages of starvation.

"Yes." He nodded. "I have many cattle," Chance said as he tipped his hat back and stared at the Herefords milling around the stream bank. "Too many, perhaps. Just take a look at those scraggly heifers," he said, shaking his head. "A couple of those cows probably won't survive the trip over that next bunch of hills. Probably have to shoot 'em halfway home just to keep the rest of the herd moving."

Danny started to speak, but was instantly silenced by Chance's pointed glance. "Seems a pity to waste the meat, though . . ." Chance murmured, almost to himself but just loud enough for Silver Elk to hear. "You wouldn't be interested in helping me out, would you?" he asked, keeping his eyes trained on the herd.

He could feel Silver Elk studying him, weighing his next move. "I will trade for your cows," the Indian said finally with an expressionless stare.

Chance feigned surprise. "Well, now, it just doesn't seem right to push those scrawny beeves off on you, but if you'd be willing to take them off my hands . . ."

Washita's father motioned for one of the braves to hand over his rifle. "It is a good rifle," Silver Elk said simply as he placed the gun in Chance's hand.

As Washita, her father, and the Indian braves rode away, herding the two heifers with them, Danny took off his hat and scratched his head. "If those heifers were on their last legs, I'm Abe Lincoln," he grumbled.

Chance gave him a dry grin as he swung up into his saddle. "Well, then, mount up, Mr. President," he drawled, "if we push these critters a bit, we might just make it home in time for supper."

Chapter Nine

———◆———

KATHLEEN was in the chicken coop gathering eggs when Henry Draper pulled his fancy cloth-topped buggy into the yard. As she hurried toward the house, she noticed that Henry, dressed in his customary black woolen suit and starched collar, looked strangely smaller, more narrow in the shoulders and chest than she remembered.

He heard her coming up behind him and before she could say hello, he blurted out, "Well, there you are! Thank goodness." His expression was one of open relief.

"Hello, Henry," she said, relinquishing the basket of eggs when he offered to carry them for her.

"I was beginning to worry," he said, following her into the house. The grim line of his mouth alarmed her. Perhaps he'd brought bad news. Immediately her thoughts flew to her brother and she laid her hand on his arm.

"What's the matter, Henry? What's happened?"

"Happened?" His face went blank. "Nothing's happened. It's just that when I found your door unlocked, and no one around, I began to worry that something might have happened to you."

"I'm sorry you were worried, Henry." Why did his undue concern irritate her? she wondered, and dropped her hand from his sleeve, took the egg basket, and walked past him into the kitchen. "We hardly ever lock our doors at Twin Rivers, you know that," she reminded him in a friendlier tone. "Now sit down, Henry. I'll put the eggs up and warm some coffee for us. And for heaven's sakes, smile," she said over her shoulder, at the same time obeying her own order. "By the look on your face, you'd think someone had died."

Henry's mouth softened into a smile and he pulled his black narrow-brimmed hat from his head and sat down. "I'm sorry if I've irritated you, Kathleen," he apologized. "But I missed you last Sunday and the two Sabbaths before . . . and . . . when I asked members of the congregation about you, and no one had seen either you . . . or Jeb or Danny lately . . ."

Three weeks? Is that all the time that had passed since Chance Ballinger had ridden onto Twin Rivers and turned her life upside down? Kathleen could hardly believe it.

"We've been . . . busy," she explained. "There have been some . . . changes at Twin Rivers that have required a great deal of my attention," she added uneasily as she set the coffeepot on the stove and stoked a flame to life beneath it.

"I understand how hectic early spring can be for ranchers in the valley," Henry put in.

She stared at him, wondering how she could begin

to explain to her old friend that *hectic* didn't begin to describe her situation.

"Is there something more, some other problem that kept you from services, Kathleen?" Henry's face tightened with concern again.

For no good reason she could name, she felt alternately flustered and defensive. "There's no *other* reason, Henry," she lied. "We're busy, that's all. Running a ranch this size takes a great deal of time and work."

"Oh, I know. I know," he conceded quickly and rose and walked around the cookstove to stand beside her as she worked. "And I wasn't scolding, really I wasn't. I was only concerned."

She felt his eyes searching her face and felt guilty for the peevish attitude she'd taken. "Everything's fine. I'm fine," she assured him again.

His relief was nearly palpable when he smiled. "It really *is* so good to see you again, Kathleen. I've missed talking to you, being with you."

She took two cups out of the cupboard above the drainboard and poured the coffee. As she poured she didn't look at him; for some reason she couldn't seem to meet his eyes, or face the expectant look she knew she'd see in his expression. *I've missed you, too,* he was waiting to hear her say, but for some strange reason that innocent reply caught in her throat and a feeble "It's always nice to see you, too, Henry" emerged in its place.

He smiled again and took the cup she handed him, hiding his disappointment well.

But she *had* missed him, Kathleen's conscience insisted. And most days she really did welcome Henry's company. What was so different about today? And why had Henry's concern on her behalf irritated her so unreasonably?

The answer came back to her in the image of the tall, dark-haired gambler who had taken up residence in the bunkhouse. Lately, thoughts of Chance Ballinger had changed how she reacted to everything, it seemed. The realization disturbed her, and she gave herself a mental shake and turned to Henry with a too-bright smile. "Come. Let's sit down. Catch me up on all the news, Henry," she urged him, determined to restore that easy, comfortable feeling that normally passed between them.

As soon as Henry sat down he began talking. "I received a note from Mother last week."

Gerta Draper had been one of Ma's close friends. "I hope she's well."

Henry nodded. "Very well, thanks. And she sends her best to you. She's planning a visit soon. The groundbreaking for the new church has her very excited. Mother's a generous contributor, you know. She has very definite ideas about how the building should be arranged."

As Henry rattled on, Kathleen studied him. Except for the blond mustache, and the hint of creases in the fair skin at the corners of his soft brown eyes, Henry didn't look that much different than he had as a boy. She knew his face by heart, she realized. Almost as well as she knew her own brother's.

Was it that familiarity, she wondered, that smothered any spark of romance she might be otherwise feeling?

Like Kathleen, Henry had lived in the Gallatin Valley nearly all his life. They'd attended the same one-room territorial school when the winter snows hadn't kept Kathleen stranded on the ranch. Henry had always

been at the head of their class. As the only child of a
mother widowed at a young age, he was raised differently from the other boys growing up on farms and
ranches in the territory.

Gerta Draper, a tall, rawboned, no-nonsense woman,
had been one of the territorys' first schoolmarms. In an
area starving for eligible females, Gerta's inborn work
ethic and strict German background made her a prime
candidate for remarriage. But she chose to remain single, devoting the sum of her energy to her son, doting
on him, tutoring him—which accounted for his extended education, as well as his tendency to expect to
have things his own way.

Then, quite unexpectedly a few years ago, Gerta met
and married a widower whose vast cattle ranch lay west
of the Yellowstone River. Though Henry was a young
man by that time, he accompanied his mother to her
new home. Within a year he came back to Bozeman
and started building his congregation.

Self-appointed and self-anointed, Jeb had cynically
said of the young, fair-haired Community Church minister, but Kathleen had thought Jeb's assessment too
harsh. Although Henry had been no saint growing up
and still sometimes exhibited a single-minded determination to have his way, he seemed genuine in his
devotion to the church and quite sincere in his calling.

To the settlers still moving into Bozeman City, Henry's church offered an oasis of comfort and civilization
in the primitive and harsh existence many of them
found in their new frontier homes. As a result, the congregation had grown steadily over the past few years as
the influx of homesteaders had increased.

To the trail-weary cowhand, Bozeman City was a
place to indulge in all the worldly pleasures he'd only

been able to dream of along the trail. But to the settlers, and the stream of merchants, lawyers, teachers, and doctors who settled in behind them, Bozeman was home. For the last three years, Henry's ministry had been embraced enthusiastically by the residents of the Gallatin Valley, and Henry had become an admired and respected community leader.

As much an expression of confidence in their young pastor as a symptom of growth, the plans for a new church building had become the pride of the community. The new structure would replace the weatherbeaten clapboard structure that held fewer than fifty people comfortably.

"Oh, it will be just *perfect* for weddings," Astrid Olsen had confided to Kathleen one Sunday after services. "My Sven is heading up the building committee, you know," she'd added, referring to her husband with pride. "And Pastor is all in favor of my idea for a padded kneeler at the altar to accommodate young couples when they take their wedding vows."

Kathleen had forced a polite smile and tried to slip away gracefully, but Astrid wouldn't be put off, and she followed Kathleen to the wagon where Jeb and Danny were waiting. "He won't wait forever, you know," Astrid had warned, her voice low and conspiratorial. "Henry Draper is a fine man, Kathleen. Your ma and pa always thought so much of him."

The new church. The successful young preacher. The eligible spinster from Twin Rivers. Kathleen was all too aware that folks were expecting a wedding.

"Now, about these changes at Twin Rivers," Henry said, jarring her back to their conversation. "Do they have anything to do with the man Ida Settlemier said she met in your kitchen? Ida said he was a stranger," he added before Kathleen had a chance to reply. "Was he just passing through, or have you hired another hand?"

With his eyes trained on hers, Kathleen silently willed her quivering nerves steady. "It's rather difficult to explain," she began. "What did Ida tell you, exactly?"

"Not much, really. Only that she met him briefly when she came for her fitting. But frankly, I have to tell you that I was quite disturbed. And your visitor seems to have caused a bit of a stir with others, as well. Several concerned ladies of our congregation have questioned me about this . . . Mr. Ballinger, I believe Ida said his name was? Rumor has it he's actually living here now."

Kathleen nodded. A strange heat crept up the back of her neck, her pride scalded at the thought of her personal life becoming the source of Sunday gossip. "Chance Ballinger," she said evenly. "And he's not a stranger. And he wasn't just passing through."

"A distant relative, then?"

"No," she said quietly, holding her temper. "No, he's not a relative, either."

Henry stared at her, waiting. The ticking from the clock on the mantel seemed unduly loud in the silence.

Finally Kathleen rose and walked a few feet across the room before she turned and said, "You might as well know, Henry. Word will get around soon enough. He's my partner. And he's the reason I haven't been to Sunday services. Danny lost his share of the ranch in a poker game. Mr. Ballinger held the winning hand," she said, remembering as if it had been yesterday the exact words Chance had used when he'd told her. *It's as simple as that.*

She could almost hear Henry's jaw drop. He sat in stunned silence, his eyes wide and unblinking.

"And as a matter of record," she continued hotly, "I believe Mr. Ballinger was trying to kiss me the day Ida Settlemier walked into the cabin." She couldn't quite believe she'd said it, and Henry's gasp told her he couldn't believe it either.

"Now you have the facts, Henry." She fought to suppress a perverse smile. "You may go back to Bozeman and report to any curious parishioners exactly what Ida Settlemier witnessed that morning in my kitchen." She folded her hands in front of her. "Are there any more questions?"

She continued to stare at Henry defiantly and watched the blood drain from his face and disappear beneath the rim of his starched white collar. A tug of satisfaction at having shocked him into an uncustomary silence made Kathleen want to giggle like a schoolgirl. After all, she wasn't yet promised to him, she told herself, regardless of what the town busybodies would like to believe.

"Would you care for a slice of pie, Henry?" she asked brightly as she turned on her heel and walked into the kitchen, sensing she should give him a bit of breathing room in which to recover from the shock she'd just delivered.

Henry only stared after her and shook his head, his expression glazed and disbelieving as he ran a hand absently over his wavy blond hair. "B-but this is unbelievable!" he sputtered, finally finding his voice. "He kissed you?"

Kathleen drew in a deep breath, knowing full well she was about to skirt the edge of truth. "I said, I think he *wanted* to kiss me." What was the eternal penalty, she wondered, for lying to a man of the cloth? In fact, there was no guessing about it, she knew darned well Chance Ballinger had wanted to kiss her—almost as much as she'd wanted to kiss him.

And technically she hadn't lied at all, she consoled herself. For it had been several days *after* the incident in the kitchen when Chance had finally fulfilled his desire to kiss her.

"I—I just don't know what to say—" Henry sputtered.

"Why not?" she pressed him. "Do you find it so unbelievable, so shocking that a man other than yourself might want to kiss me?" Suddenly she didn't care that she was taunting him, making him squirm in his seat. He deserved it, didn't he, for assuming a claim without consent?

Henry rose from his seat woodenly. "What I find difficult to believe, Kathleen, is your casual and accepting reaction to such an indecent gesture. A gentleman—a God-fearing gentleman would have awaited your invitation before assuming such liberties," he declared, his voice shaking. "I assume he received no such invitation?" he added, one blond brow arched suspiciously.

She met his inquisition with an icy glare and stood toe to toe with him. "A gentleman," Kathleen informed him, "a *real* gentleman would never ask a lady such a question!"

At least he had the good grace to lower his eyes. "I'm sorry, Kathleen," he muttered.

Immediately Kathleen felt sorry too, sorry for the tension she felt stretching uncomfortably between them. After all, she and Henry were friends. But weren't friends supposed to turn a deaf ear to gossip?

Didn't true friends resist passing judgment? As hard as it was to see the pain she'd inflicted, Kathleen decided Henry had needed this lesson in friendship. If he felt sheepish now, or even ashamed, it wasn't any of her doing, she assured herself.

"I'd better be going," he said softly, his face unusually pale. "I planned to drop in on the Coulters this afternoon on my way back to town. Etta is very near her time, you know."

Kathleen reached for his sleeve. "Wait. Henry— don't go just yet. I don't want to quarrel with you—"

He turned to her, his face eager, his expression hopeful.

"And I'm sorry I snapped at you, but you know how I detest the way they gossip about me." She pulled her hand away. "I guess I'd hoped you were different. I thought we were friends . . ."

"Friends," he said gravely.

"Yes. Good friends."

He swallowed hard and Kathleen felt her own throat tighten, but she stood her ground. "Kathleen, I only want what's best for you."

"I understand," she said, resisting the urge to ask him who would know better than she what was best for her.

"The Spring Social is next Sunday evening," he said, reaching for his hat. He didn't look at her but fidgeted with the buttons on his coat as though they were suddenly an incomprehensible puzzle.

"I remember."

"I don't suppose you'll still allow me to escort you . . ."

"Well of course you'll still be escorting me," she said graciously. "I'd be pleased to be your part—" She al-

most choked on the word. "That is, I'd be pleased . . .
to accompany you, just as we'd planned."

He nodded, his expression brightening considerably.
"Fine. Then I'll be round shortly after noon to collect
you."

"I look forward to it." She hoped by Sunday she
would feel more enthusiastic.

Henry touched her arm as she moved past him toward the door. "I care a great deal for you, Kathleen,"
he declared intently, his gaze resting a disturbing moment too long on her mouth.

She opened the door. "I know, Henry. We've been
friends a long time."

For the first time she detected a spark of resentment
in his eyes. "I'd always hoped we could someday
be more," he confessed. "If you'd only give me a
chance—" Without warning, he captured both her
hands, startling her.

But why? she asked herself. Hadn't she allowed him
to hold her hand after Sunday services? Didn't she respect and admire him for the good and decent man he
was? And although he'd never said it in so many words,
hadn't she come to expect that he'd someday propose
marriage? The answer to each question was an undeniable yes.

Then why all of a sudden did her hands feel uncomfortable in his? And why did the thought of Henry Draper kissing her make her feel slightly afraid?

"What's the matter, Kathleen?"

She shook her head and pulled her hands gently, but
firmly, from his grasp and backed away from him.

What is the matter? she asked herself. Why did her
old friend seem like a stranger? She turned to avoid
his eyes and when she did, she saw Chance's beaded

tobacco pouch where he'd left it on the mantel. And the answer to her question blazed forth in a startling realization that shocked her: She felt bound to Chance Ballinger, and for some inexplicable reason she'd felt disloyal when Henry touched her.

Somehow she knew now that from the moment the gambler's lips had touched hers, she'd been possessed by him, branded in some irrevocable way. Without a word, that kiss had sealed her fate. The realization startled, excited, and terrified her all at once.

Chance Ballinger. The gambler. The gunslinger. The drifter. A man with a shadowy past and an uncertain future. A man who'd stolen her brother's birthright—for her familial pride *still* insisted Danny must have been cheated.

Her partner. Chance Ballinger. The name echoed tauntingly through her mind. A man who mocked convention and propriety, who didn't wait for a lady's invitation to kiss, but instead took what he wanted without apology. A man to whom marriage, commitment, and trust—those values Kathleen held most dear—obviously held little or no meaning.

Why then, in the name of heaven, was Chance Ballinger the man to whom Kathleen felt strangely and hopelessly honorbound, possessed by and promised to? And all by just a single kiss.

"Kathleen?" Henry had moved up behind her and he spoke her name tentatively, as though he were waking a sleeping child. "What is it, my dear? What's the matter?"

She shook her head, unable to answer.

"I think I can guess what you're thinking," he said, causing her to jerk her head up to look at him, stunned by the possibility that what he'd said might be true, that he really had guessed what she'd been thinking and who she'd been thinking about.

"You can?" Her voice was trembling.

He nodded and frowned. "Don't you think I know what they say, that I've heard what they call you? The old maid," he said in a low, angry voice. "I'm sorry, Kathleen. It's so unfair. And we both know it isn't true. That you're only waiting for that special love to come along and claim you, waiting for the one man who can give you the love, respect, and honor for which you long, and so richly deserve."

Kathleen's mouth was suddenly as dry as parchment.

"I know you," he said gently, his eyes beseeching. "And I know that someday you'll give your heart and your hand to that man." He paused and took a deep breath before continuing his prophecy. "And when that day comes, there'll be no more talk of business arrangements. For it will be you and"—he smiled—"and your husband who'll be the master and mistress of Twin Rivers ranch, and there'll be no room for anyone or anything else."

Despite the warmth of the fire, Kathleen felt his declaration drive a chill straight through to the center of her being.

He took her hand again and kissed it. But Kathleen was too numbed even to feel the pressure of his lips against her skin. "And I'll wait, my dear," he promised. "I'll wait for as long as it takes." He smiled, a smile that Kathleen used to think was endearing but that now seemed irritating. "Isn't that what you want? For me to prove myself, to show you just how much I care, how much I'm willing to bear to get what I want, what we *both* want," he amended quickly.

The sound of horses pulled Henry's attention to the

yard and granted Kathleen a blessed reprieve not only from answering his questions but, more important, from facing the disturbing questions about her future and Chance Ballinger that burned in her mind.

When Kathleen spotted Danny stepping up onto the porch, she rushed past Henry and out the door.

"Danny!" she cried. "Oh, Danny, you're home! You're safe! Oh, thank God!" She threw her arms around her brother's neck and buried her face in his coat. The tears that sprang to her eyes came from a heart brimming with relief and joy.

Danny returned her hug and gave his sister a sheepish smile. "I wasn't sure you'd be so glad to see me, Kathleen."

She studied her brother for a moment. He looked tired, and road weary, but happier than she remembered seeing him in a long time. "Of course I'm happy to see you, Danny," she said, letting her gaze drift past him to see Chance leading their horses to the watering trough. He smiled when he saw her watching him.

"You must be hungry," she said, taking her brother's hand and leading him toward the door.

"Aren't I always?" he asked, casting a glance backward at Chance, who had crossed the yard and was moving up onto the porch. "But I can wait. We had us a big meal on the trail at noon, didn't we, Chance?"

The big man nodded as he moved up beside them. Understanding finally broke through and Kathleen now realized that Chance and her brother had ridden in together. But how? And why?

"Ain't they beauties?" Danny said, swaggering proudly as he turned and pointed to the cattle in the meadow.

Following his gaze, Kathleen saw about thirty brown-and-white animals grazing in the near pasture. Enclosed in the circle of fence Chance and Jeb had so recently completed, the animals were grazing contentedly.

"We figure they'll bring nearly twice the amount at auction as the Longhorns," Danny declared proudly, glancing over at Chance for confirmation.

Chance nodded and a lazy smile played at the corners of his mouth. Kathleen had grown used to the tugging feeling in her heart at the mere sight of him, but at the moment, seeing Chance standing there beside her brother and knowing that somehow he was responsible for finding and bringing Danny back to her, caused her heart to reach out to him as never before.

Danny pulled the cabin door open. "Do I smell coffee?"

"It seems I owe you a debt of gratitude for my brother's return," Kathleen said as she and Chance followed Danny inside.

"No thanks needed," Chance assured her. "I figured we could use another hand this summer, and this young man was able-bodied and willing."

"Good to see you back in the bosom of your family, Daniel," Henry said, pulling back the door wide to allow them all inside. Taking up a position at Kathleen's side, Henry extended a hand to Danny, but Kathleen sensed that his sole interest was fastened on the tall, dark-haired cowboy who had moved over to the hearth in search of the tobacco he'd left there.

As she made the introduction, Kathleen watched each man size up the other warily. The smile vanished from Chance's face as he met Henry's stare with a stony gaze.

Kathleen set about pouring cups of coffee for her brother and Chance and refilling her own and Henry's cups still sitting on the table.

"I see that you carry a Colt, Mr. Ballinger," Henry said, casting a glance at the gleaming sidearm slung low in its leather holster on Chance's lean hip.

"Never travel without it."

Henry nodded approvingly. "In these uncertain times many believe it is a prudent practice to bear arms whenever traveling. I regret that the criminal element seems to have spread from the mining camps of Virginia City into our own peaceful valley. Innocent folks have been forced to arm themselves and take on the task that, under more civilized circumstances, would fall to a duly elected peace officer."

Henry paused to accept the cup Kathleen held out to him. "Thank you, my dear," he said, smiling.

As she filled Chance's cup, Kathleen felt him searching her face, pausing on her mouth, and holding her gaze for an instant before she remembered there were others in the room.

If Henry had seen or sensed the intense unspoken communication that had passed between them, he did not show it, but rather went on with his diatribe. "It is a perilous time we live in," he said, his expression grave as he shook his head to emphasize the importance of his declaration. "The innocent-looking stranger one meets on the trail today could easily turn out to be a notorious cattle rustler or robber. Cutthroats, con men, all manner of criminals have gravitated to our fair territory."

Chance did not respond to Henry's comments, but kept the preacher under steady scrutiny as he pulled a match from his vest pocket, struck it to life with his thumbnail, and held the flame to the tip of a slim cigarillo.

Kathleen saw something dark and chillingly unsettling glinting in Chance's eyes as he stared back at the white-collared preacher.

"It might interest you to know," Henry continued, "that many of our neighbors have organized. Their numbers increase every day. Once you've settled in, you might want to consider joining their group."

"Vigilantes," Danny muttered. All eyes shifted to him, and Kathleen saw her brother's face suddenly grow pale as he dropped into a chair at the long plank table and studied the dark liquid swirling in his cup.

Henry nodded. "That's what some folks call them, Daniel. But really they're nothing more than your neighbors and friends, brave men who've decided to take a firm stand against the forces of evil that threaten to corrupt their communities. Have you heard of these citizens' groups as well, Ballinger?"

"I've heard," Chance said quietly.

"Then you've no doubt heard of the law and order they've restored to places like Virginia City, Bannack, and other areas once besieged by ruffians and outlaws. They act with the Lord on their side, in the name of justice."

"Some might call it justice," Chance drawled, but he scoffed to himself. He'd seen this same style of vigilante justice firsthand in Texas the day J. D. Holcomb and his boys had ridden onto James's place and killed him in cold blood for violating the so-called water rights—the water rights that favored the Holcombs and left Ballinger cattle, as well as the other smaller ranchers' cattle, dying of thirst.

"And what is your opinion of this citizens' movement, Mr. Ballinger?" Henry queried, dragging Chance's grim introspection back to the present.

Chance considered the question a moment before answering. Then, with an innocent smile, he folded his long frame into the rocking chair and took a slow sip of coffee. "Well, to tell the truth, I don't believe I have an opinion worth sharing on the subject. Haven't given the matter a whole lot of thought lately. Been too busy trying to make a living."

Henry nodded, obviously placated by Chance's simple reply. "Admirable," he said. "Admirable, indeed. But there comes a time when a man's got to decide on which side of the fence he walks. Someday you may have to give this matter some consideration, Mr. Ballinger."

Henry may have been satisfied with Chance's evasive reply, but Kathleen's curiosity was piqued by her partner's uncharacteristic disinterest. Though she had to admit that there were still a good many things she did not know about Chance Ballinger, she knew all too well that he held a firm opinion on every subject from cattle to sourdough—the thought of sourdough and Chance's "no charge" kiss caused a secret smile to bloom inside her.

But as she studied Chance's pensive expression the smile faded, and she wondered about his true feelings on the subject of vigilantes. At the moment, however, there were no clues. In fact he seemed to be avoiding her gaze, his intelligent eyes hooded by the dark slashes of his brows, making his thoughts maddeningly unreadable.

"If ever you find yourself interested in learning more about the cause, just let me know. I'm sure you would be a welcome addition," Henry said. "You too, Daniel."

Chance shook his head. "I've never been much of a joiner."

"Me neither," Danny chimed in quickly.

"Well, perhaps you'll change your mind," Henry said, still directing his remarks to Chance. "After you've lived in the Valley for a while, witnessed firsthand the criminal activities that threaten our homes and families, you'll decide the cause is indeed a good one." Henry inhaled, drawing himself up to his full height. But even with his spine ramrod-straight, Kathleen observed, he was still a good two inches shorter than Chance.

Rolling the thin cigarillo between his thumb and forefinger, Chance sat studying it as though its glowing tip held all the secrets of the universe.

"So the prodigal returns," Henry said, turning his attention to Danny.

Kathleen felt herself bristling as she sat down in the chair across from her brother and tried to capture his eyes. Henry took the chair next to Danny and leaned close.

She could see Chance past Henry's shoulder, watching from the hearth with what she decided was a distant, almost amused expression.

"And where were you holed up this time, Daniel? In the back room of the local saloon?" Henry prodded. "Or was it in some more despicable house of sin and degradation?"

Kathleen's anger flared, but before she could speak, Chance's voice shattered the tense silence. "Danny was on his way home when I met up with him in Bozeman." He stood slowly and walked toward the stove to refill his cup.

Danny exhaled the breath he'd been holding and nodded eagerly. "That's right."

"So you were on your way home." Kathleen sighed, giving her brother a gentle smile.

"Y-yeah, I was headed this way, but I kind of—well, I kind of fell on hard times," Danny said without looking up.

"All that matters is that you're home now," she said softly, touching his hand.

"You do him no favor by coddling him, Kathleen," Henry muttered. "I know it is only out of the goodness of your own heart that you make excuses for him, but he's none the better for it."

"I make no excuses for my brother," Kathleen shot back, her anger rekindled. Why was Henry acting so terrible? Was it for her benefit that he thought he needed to scold Danny, Kathleen wondered, or was his pride still stinging over the stolen kiss between her and Chance Ballinger?

"You put your sister through untold worry, young man," Henry informed Danny. "In my opinion, you owe her not only a full explanation of your whereabouts and activities, but an apology as well."

Danny's gaze slid between Kathleen and the preacher.

"What Danny does and does not owe is between the two of us," Kathleen told Henry, speaking carefully, trying her best to contain her temper.

The slow smile she glimpsed tugging at Chance's lips made her doubly determined to hold her tongue in check. "I appreciate your concern on my behalf, Henry," she said, forcing a tight smile. "But this is a family matter, something my brother and I will discuss after he's settled in and rested."

Kathleen watched Henry's face turn a deep shade of crimson. Looking past him, she saw Chance cross his arms over his chest and lean one hip against the drain-board, watching the drama being played out at the table as if he were an amused front-row spectator at a sideshow.

"Do I smell biscuits?" Danny asked meekly, but no one, least of all Kathleen, seemed to hear his question or respond to his attempt to steer the conversation to a less volatile subject.

"Kathleen," Henry implored her, "if you'll just consider the matter for a moment, I know you'll see that I'm right. Your love for your brother has blinded you to what's best for him."

Kathleen leaped up out of her chair, her cheeks burning. "This is none of your business, Henry!"

Her verbal punch was received with an audible gasp from the red-faced preacher. Danny coughed nervously and Chance stood listening impassively as Kathleen shot them each a searing glance.

"But *someone* has to take charge of the moral conduct of the men who reside on this ranch," Henry declared desperately. "Lord knows, if anyone had been on guard against these kinds of corrupting influences, your own dear father might still be with us today."

His words left her breathless. Inside she felt herself reeling. Henry knew how much she'd loved her father, how she cherished his memory, and how deeply she grieved his passing. That Henry would hurt her now, in such a manner was nearly incomprehensible.

She was momentarily stunned speechless, her glance ricocheting between her brother and Henry. Danny kept his eyes downcast, unable to meet his sister's gaze. He shifted in his chair uneasily, looking like a nervous colt ready to bolt and run. Henry continued to stare at her, his face etched with his own pain.

And when her gaze finally traveled to Chance, she shuddered at the dark, murderous glint in his eyes.

"I think you'd better leave now, Henry," she said in a low, tight voice. She walked quickly around the table to the door.

Henry didn't move, but stared at her a long moment before he shifted his gaze to Chance and then back to Kathleen. "I'm sorry," he muttered. "Please—please forgive me. I seem to have overstepped my bounds."

"Henry," Kathleen said, fighting for control, "I'd like some time alone with my brother." She opened the door and he hurried toward it, stopping to plead in a low voice.

"Please, Kathleen, walk with me to my buggy." When she hesitated, he asked again more urgently, "Please, I can't leave with these angry words still between us."

Kathleen gave him a curt nod and walked woodenly out the door in front of him, across the porch, and down the steps.

Acutely aware of Henry's hand at her elbow and Chance Ballinger's midnight eyes on her back, she held her head high and looked straight ahead.

At his carriage, when he believed they were out of earshot of Danny and Chance, who had moved out onto the porch, Henry touched Kathleen's arm. "Kathleen, I'm truly sorry I've upset you. Forgive me. Please. I don't know what got into me. I only want—"

"What's best for me?" she cut in bitterly.

He nodded, his expression miserable. "I'm afraid I didn't handle myself at all well in there. But sometimes it just makes me so angry what that boy puts you through, how he's deserted you and this ranch since you lost your father."

She held up her hand. "Please, Henry—"

"And I know how difficult it's been. Remember? I'm the one you've turned to, the one you've confided in. I've seen the unfairness of it all, the burden you've had to bear all alone. Kathleen, I beg you. Please don't blame me for caring. And please, think about what I've said. This place needs a firm hand, the hand of a decent God-fearing man." He eyes begged her to listen. "What I witnessed in there between you . . . and that . . . drifter, well . . . I am not a blind man, Kathleen—" His voice cracked and she found she had to look away. "Nor am I a man without feelings."

Before she could reply, or try once more to put an end to an awful situation that was becoming worse by the moment, the lurid words of a raucous Irish melody drifted out of the bunkhouse, riding high on the thin mountain air. Kathleen watched each spicy syllable land like a physical blow on Henry's ears.

His eyes narrowed. Behind them Danny fell into a sudden fit of coughing, and Chance flipped his cigarillo into the mud.

When Jeb emerged from the bunkhouse the saucy serenade grew louder and louder, only to end in a strangled gasp when he stumbled into the yard and finally noticed Kathleen and the preacher standing beside the buggy.

"Evening, missy," he sang out gaily to the tune of his Irish serenade. "Chance, I see you made it back," he said as he headed for the cabin. "And Danny, my boy! Now there's a sight for these weak old eyes! Good to see you found your way home, son. By God, it's good to have you back!"

Danny smiled with his whole face as he jogged down the porch steps to greet his old friend with a hearty embrace. But Jeb's smile faded when his eyes met Henry's. "Evenin', Reverend."

Henry frowned. "Jebediah." He regarded the older man with disdain before turning to face Kathleen again and saying in a low voice, "Need I say more? Jeb is so drunk he can hardly walk! What in heaven's name are you going to do about all of this, Kathleen?" His expression was one of complete exasperation. "Kathleen?" he prodded.

"Oh, Henry!" she snapped. "Please, please just say good-day and don't press me further, or I fear I shall say something for which we'll both be very sorry."

When she turned to walk away he reached for her hand, but quickly released it when she whirled around and stabbed him with a scorching glare.

"Kathleen . . ." He took a deep breath. "If there is something you wish to say to me, say it now. For I cannot possibly ride out knowing this terrible chasm of misunderstanding has opened between us."

"Don't push me, Henry," she warned. "I'm so angry—I swear if I hear one more word out of your mouth, I think I shall scream!"

Henry recoiled as though she'd slapped him. "Do you know who you are talking to?" he gasped.

"Yes," she shot back. "Yes, I do! I am speaking to *you,* Henry Draper, to the man who at this moment is the most self-righteous, sanctimonious, pious . . ." She inhaled sharply. "How dare you berate my family, my friends, my own good name—"

"Kathleen!" He cut her off in a loud voice that seemed to shock even him. Two bright spots pulsed at his temples; his hands shook. "I'm leaving now. . . . Perhaps you're right," he said, his voice tight as he strained for control. "Perhaps we've both said enough for now.

And when you've—that is, when we've both calmed down, we'll discuss this further."

"Why, thank you ever so kindly, Henry," she said, her voice dripping with biting sarcasm. "How very Christian of you to concede that I *might* be right!" She turned on her heels and marched away from his carriage, the anger pounding behind her eyes.

"Oh, and another thing," she shouted, spinning around to face him for the last time. "You can forget about taking me to the Social. I'm quite sure I shall not have sufficiently *calmed down* enough by then!"

The sound of Henry's whip being laid to his gray gelding's backside made Kathleen's anger sizzle hotter. Blinded by her scalded pride and her raging anger, she brushed past the three men on the porch with their curious stares and sheepish smiles.

It was bad enough that Henry had acted the role of the jealous fool, but to have lost control in front of the smirking Chance Ballinger—well, that was enough to try the patience of a saint!

Stomping into the cabin, she slammed the door in the faces of the men staring at her on the porch.

But in the next instant she stormed out of the cabin again, milk pail in hand. She called over her shoulder to the startled threesome, "There are chores to be done before supper. None of us has time to stand around gawking."

But by the time she reached the barn door and closed it behind her, she'd forgotten all about her own chores. For the next minute she stood and fumed and released a string of words that should have, as her father had always said, "turned the blessed air blue."

Chapter Ten

WHEN Chance opened the barn door it took a moment for his eyes to adjust to the darkness. Then he spotted her, slumped on a pile of fresh straw, her head in her hands and her shoulders shaking.

"Lovers' quarrel?" he asked when he was beside her.

Her head jerked up and she swiped quickly at her eyes, but traces of her tears still lingered. At the sight of them, Chance had a strong urge to ride out after the high-handed preacher and batter some sense into his thick, self-righteous skull. But in the end, his common sense prevailed.

Chance couldn't afford to let his temper rule his head—not this time, not when his new life seemed so ripe with promise.

"Go away," she sniffed. "Leave me alone. I'm in no mood for your teasing." She didn't look at him when she stood and straightened her skirts. But as she walked away, she stumbled over a clump of hay. Chance caught her from behind and dragged her up against him and held her.

"Steady, partner," he murmured. The huge grain door above them in the loft was propped open and the yellow-gold of sunset filtered in. Her eyes still glistened and her hair shone a deep burgundy in the light. Chance felt his senses stirred again by her natural beauty and by the sweet floral scent of her, mingled with the heady smell of fresh hay and molasses-rolled oats coming from the open grain bins.

"You can let me go now," she said curtly. "I'm just fine."

"But if I let you go, you'll bolt out of here without hearing what I came to say."

"Oh? And what did you come in here to say?" she demanded, twisting around in his arms and staring defiantly into his eyes. "Did you come in here to tease me, to mock me some more?"

"You're a harsh woman, Kathleen. You wound me with your unkind accusations. I only came in here to thank you."

"You can save that smooth southern drawl for someone who finds it charming, Mr. Ballinger. Besides, what could you possibly have to thank me for?"

Chance focused his attention on her delicate mouth as the memory of its honeyed taste sent desire sweeping through him in long tantalizing waves. "I could thank you for a good many things," he said softly, brushing an errant curl away from her forehead. "But especially for coming to my defense today, for standing up to your suitor—"

"He is not my suitor!" Kathleen snapped. "After today, he's not my anything," she murmured miserably, almost to herself.

"Then I apologize for the faulty assumption. But when Danny and I rode in, and I saw you and the preacher alone together I just assumed . . ."

"Oh, you are maddening!" she sputtered as she twisted away from him and plopped back down on the mound of hay. "Haven't you and I been alone together many times over the past few weeks?"

He sat down beside her, remembering the taste of her lips the last time that happy circumstance had occurred. He smiled. "Why, yes, now that you mention it, I suppose we have."

"And would anyone in their right mind call you my suitor?"

He found himself unreasonably disappointed that she found the possibility so absurd. "I guess I see what you mean," he said, picking up a piece of hay and twisting it around his finger.

"I'm sure you *do not*," she said, sighing wearily.

For a long moment they sat side by side, she studying her hands and he absorbed in the straw he continued to weave around his fingertips, neither intruding on the other's private silence.

It was she who finally spoke, and when she did her voice was soft. "When my father died, he left the ranch split up between the two of us, Danny and me. I know it hurt Danny's pride." There was a note of uncharacteristic weariness and defeat in her voice that worried him.

"In Bozeman, tongues are probably still wagging over the way my father died. Did you know that his murderer was never apprehended?"

He shook his head and studied her face as she continued, wishing he could somehow erase the hurt he saw inscribed too deeply in her sad emerald eyes.

"Some folks don't even deem it a crime to shoot a man over a hand of cards. Did you know that, Mr. Ballinger?"

Chance acknowledged this dubious fact with an uncertain nod.

"Yet those same decent folks think it highly improper, immoral, even illegal for a woman to hold and manage property the way I do."

"Damn fools," he muttered.

She stared at him a moment, as though she was trying to decide whether or not to trust him.

"Go on," he prodded gently.

"After my father died, Danny took no interest in the ranch. I had no choice but to carry the responsibilities of managing Twin Rivers, keeping it afloat and one step ahead of the banker. I'm not complaining," she was quick to add. "Twin Rivers means more to me than just about anything in this world. Anyway, I went to some of the businessmen of Bozeman for help, but those good folks had already passed judgment on my situation and were prepared to sit back and await my downfall."

"But what about Ida Settlemier and the Jensen twins?"

"Ida and the other ladies only come to see me for their sewing and lacework. The men stopped calling on me when they discovered I wasn't about to turn my property over to the first one of them who chose to make me an honest woman." She laughed, but the sound was dry as dust and completely without humor.

Chance noticed that in her reverie, her eyes had turned a fascinating shade of blue-green.

"Aside from Sam, Etta, and Jeb, of course, there are few in this valley I'd call true friends."

Chance wondered if the day would come when she'd consider him her friend. "What about the Reverend Draper?" he asked. "Isn't *he* your friend?"

She nodded and lowered her eyes. "I was coming to him," she said. "Henry Draper *has* been my good friend. For the last two years, I've counted him as one of my closest."

Why her admission had the effect it did, Chance didn't begin to understand, but something in his gut started churning, sending a burning sensation all the way up to his throat. "I see" was all he said, but his mind raced.

Why had he come out here after her in the first place? he asked himself now as he rose to his feet. Had he hoped in some way to console her? Or was it his own selfish fascination with the feisty Irish beauty that had driven him to her again? He'd been a fool to toy with the emotions of this decent young woman, he scolded himself.

What she needed was a friend. A real partner. And what did he have to offer her? For the first time, she'd shown him a glimpse of the burdens she carried, burdens she shouldered with quiet pride and dignity: the weight of her father's mistakes, her brother's weaknesses, and the censure of the community.

And now, although she had no way of knowing it, she'd taken on the added burden of a business partner with a price on his head. If he had a spark of decency, he told himself, he'd mount up and ride out of the territory tonight and never look back.

"Wait." Her softly spoken request startled him out of his thoughts and seemed to speak to his troubled heart. Her eyes and her voice drew him to her with an invisible force he felt nearly powerless to resist.

She stood up to face him, her eyes bright with curiosity. "I owe you a deep debt of gratitude for bringing my brother home. I was afraid I might never see him again," she confided. "I don't know if he would have had the courage to come home if you hadn't somehow persuaded him. It was kind of you to offer him a job, a way to save face. Thank you, Chance."

She looked him squarely in the eye and added, "It seems despite my efforts to get even, I am once again in your debt." She laughed and shook her head. "So now go ahead and tell me whatever it was you came out here to say. Lord knows if you do owe me something, I'd be pleased to hear what it is."

For a moment Chance felt he'd lost his sense of place and time. She was standing so close, smelling so fresh, looking so beautiful, he found himself desperately distracted by her disturbing presence.

"Chance?" His name had never sounded so good as it did when it came from her lips. "Are you going to tell me what you came to say, or must I start guessing?"

He studied her another long moment before taking her hands in his. "I wanted to thank you for defending me to the preacher," he said finally.

"Defending you? I didn't defend anyone."

"Oh, yes, you did. You defended me," he insisted. "You defended us all. I heard you give that pompous— I mean, that friend of yours a hearty piece of your mind. I assumed you were defending all who reside on Twin Rivers soil, all those you hold near and dear to your heart." His gaze moved to her lower lip when it started to tremble. "Kathleen," he murmured in a gruff whisper as he drew her slowly to him, barely able to contain the desire welling inside him, "will you accept my thanks?"

She stared at him, unblinking, and in that taut silence she hardly dared to breathe; his touch had stolen the air from her lungs. Her heart hammered against her chest and her mind raced. Was he teasing her again the way he'd teased her that day in the kitchen? Was this another trap into which she might unwittingly step and find herself caught once more in his wily game, a game where he made all the rules and in which she had no hope of competing?

"And why do you pretend to care who I defend?" she asked, aware of the slight tremor in her voice.

He smiled at her and pulled her tighter into the circle of his embrace. "I do care," he said, his voice low and tender. "I care about everything you care about, Kathleen."

She drew away from him a scant few inches, eyeing him suspiciously.

"Shall I tell you your true motives, Chance Ballinger?" She continued to eye him cynically, not waiting for a reply. "Your interest in me, in this ranch, lies only in whatever profit it can bring you." Her bright stare challenged him. "You're no different from those other backhanded suitors who came to my door looking for a profitable match, now are you, Chance Ballinger?"

Convince me, a small voice cried inside her. *Convince me I'm wrong about you, Chance. Convince me you really do care for me, for my dreams.*

When he didn't respond, she braced herself against her unreasonable disappointment and prepared her next words carefully, despising the truth she knew they held. "Even now, as you hold me in your arms, you're only waiting for me to make a mistake, to play the wrong card the way my brother did that night in Virginia City."

She watched a tiny pulse working in his clenched jaw as he matched her steady stare. Did she only imagine it, or was that spark in his steady blue gaze one of regret?

"You accuse me unjustly, partner," he said quietly

"Do I?" she asked, hoping, praying for him to do or say something, anything, to prove he cared. But instead of convincing her with words, his intelligent eyes continued to move languidly over her face, gleaming with anything but innocence.

"Leave me alone, Chance," she blurted out, pushing away from him.

"I will do that, Kathleen, if that's what you want," he said, his tone surprisingly conciliatory.

"It is," she insisted, adjusting her skirts again and arranging her hair, busying herself with anything to keep her eyes from meeting his. In some strange way she feared that if she dared look again into those blue depths, he'd be able to view the deepest recesses of her heart and know that she was lying.

"Then I'll go."

Her heart felt crushed by the disappointment that settled there.

"I'll go," he repeated in a velvet drawl, "but not before you let me express my thanks." And without another word, he kissed her.

As his mouth moved over hers, irresistibly caressing, Kathleen felt a subtle change. This kiss, this slow, careful kiss, was very different from that first hungry, almost desperate one that still sizzled like a fresh brand in her memory. It was as though he'd been aware of all the tenderness she'd felt for him less than an hour ago when she realized he'd brought her brother home,

for his kisses caused that tenderness to well inside her
again.

And her deep feelings for him washed over her now,
like a warm summer rain. As his lips covered hers more
completely and his kiss grew deeper, her thoughts
clouded. His passion became hers, her body seemingly
taking on a life and a mind of its own as she thrilled
to the sensations his mouth and hands and tongue sent
darting through her.

Her resistance dissolved, all pretense of struggle
ceased as her arms slid up around his neck and she
pressed her body against his, her fingertips tangling in
the thick, dark curls at his nape.

He kissed her again and again, all the while mur-
muring softly, seductively, hypnotically. His hand slid
up from her waist and moved across her breasts, igniting an explosion of desire inside her.

Spinning deeper and deeper under the spell from
which she no longer cared if she ever emerged, all
sense of time and place was lost. Startling physical sensations blurred reality as she felt herself being lowered
slowly into the soft hay as his hands continued their
gentle probing.

As his tongue tantalized her quivering lips, she felt
as though she would burst with the emotions filling her.
He kissed her again, deeply, thoroughly, leaving them
both breathless.

When he finally lifted his lips and opened his eyes,
the naked desire she saw burning in them sent a new
blaze of heat scorching through her. She nearly
shrieked with joy when he pulled her to him again.
Clinging to him, she urged him with her body to go on
kissing her, touching her, forever.

His hungry mouth obliged, claiming hers again as he

pressed her down, covering her body with his own. The
evidence of his desire pressed against her through her
gown, and a low moan of animal pleasure escaped her
parted lips.

And when the primitive sound registered in her startled mind, it turned into a deafening alarm, clamoring
like a thousand shrieking bells inside her head, a startling call to her dazed senses that brought reality crashing back like a sudden clap of thunder.

"No!" she gasped, rolling away from him. "No.
Please, let me go."

He released her immediately and fell back into the
hay, where he lay on his back, his chest rising and falling with each ragged breath. She sat up, trembling,
fussing with her skirts, desperately trying to ignore the
physical sensations that left her quivering and the extraordinary heat that emanated from the length of the
muscular body lying beside her.

He rolled over on his side, propping himself up on
one arm, his gaze smoldering. "You are so beautiful,"
he whispered. "I've never wanted a woman more than
I want you, Kathleen."

His words washed over her, nearly drowning her in
a heady flood of feminine power. A surge of her own
desire begged her to fall back into his arms, to forget
who and what he was. And what of her? Who was she?
Was she the wanton woman willing to risk all for an
afternoon in his arms?

The irony struck her with bitter clarity. Chance Ballinger had ridden onto Twin Rivers ranch looking for
an old maid, a spinster. And when the day came when
he left—and one way or another, he *would* leave, either when she finally bought back her brother's birthright or Chance gambled away his share in some dark

barroom—he'd be leaving that old maid, that spinster, for Kathleen knew her heart had been given. And she knew she would give it only once.

The stunning knowledge that she had tried so hard to deny sprang to life inside her: She'd fallen in love with Chance Ballinger. A gambler, a gunslinger, a man who'd stolen her brother's birthright, a man probably cut from the same cloth as the man who'd murdered her own father. That horrible possibility made her shudder.

She closed her eyes to steady her reeling emotions, and when she opened them again, she found him still staring at her. His eyes had turned a softer shade of blue that made her heart turn over.

Oh, how she longed to ignore her head and follow her heart, to give herself up to the electric longing one look from those eyes set pulsing inside her.

But he'd said nothing about love, marriage, devotion—those romantic notions were scorned by his type, no doubt. He'd merely said he wanted her. And she wanted him. The shameless admission caused a surge of bright heat to course through her, singeing and chilling her at the same time.

Without thinking, she reached out and touched the stray lock of shining blue-black hair that had fallen across his forehead. Without a word, she studied him, committing his rugged features to memory. Perhaps the memories would be enough, she told herself, feeling the sting of sudden loss.

For if she gave in to her passions, gave herself to this man who could never care or love her in the way she'd always dreamed a man should love a woman, memories would be all she'd have left.

His eyes held her for another long moment, and then

suddenly she rose, gathered her skirts in her hands, and ran out of the barn like the devil himself was chasing her.

Chance could only stand and watch her go. Every instinct cried out for him to follow her, to pull her into the heart of his embrace and kiss her until her resistance melted in his arms and she succumbed to their mutual passions.

But instead he merely watched her leave him, reminding himself he had no right to follow.

He saw Jeb and Danny coming in from the meadow, where the younger man had no doubt taken Jeb to view the new cattle. Chance decided he'd been right not to follow Kathleen into the cabin. She needed a few moments to collect herself before she was forced to face her brother and Jeb.

The old man was no fool. His devotion to Kathleen was complete, like that of a father's. If the man she lovingly referred to as her uncle had seen her running out of the barn with her hair and clothes disheveled, Chance knew he might well be facing the business end of Jeb's buffalo rifle.

Regret welled inside him and he vowed to conduct himself with more control in the future. If by some quirky twist of fate he ever found himself standing at the altar beside a woman like Kathleen McBride, it would be because he loved her and not because he'd been forced.

Staring a moment longer at the cabin door, Chance asked himself the question that had been burning a hole through his mind for days: What was it about Kathleen that drew him to her, rendering him nearly helpless to control his passion whenever she was near?

Was it the tantalizing scent of her—that lilac scent that seemed to follow her like a gentle shadow? Was it her enchanting brogue, which delighted his senses whenever she spoke and grew especially thick and charming when she was angry? Was it her rich red hair or her fascinating green eyes? Her indomitable spirit? Her fierce loyalty and stubborn pride, the pride she'd displayed so valiantly today when she'd shown the pious preacher the gate?

Chance drew a deep, stinging breath, the reality of his situation hitting him full force. It was all of that, he told himself and much, much more. The sum of all the intricate parts that made up his beautiful and bewitching partner intrigued and captivated his imagination and spoke to his soul. A subtle mix of all those things that made her different from any other woman he'd ever known.

The inner woman, whose deep and abiding passion for all she held dear, ignited in Chance a desire he never knew he possessed, the desire he'd felt growing inside since the first day he'd laid eyes on the "old maid" of Twin Rivers ranch.

He smiled to himself when he saw her feminine silhouette move across the window. His heart lurched at the possibility that she might be looking for him.

"Now look what you've done, you damn fool!" he swore to himself as he stalked out of the barn and headed for the bunkhouse. "You've gone and fallen in love!"

Chapter Eleven

———◆———

THE sound of a shrill whinny jolted Chance back to the moment, reminding him that he'd left General tied to the trough outside the yard. In a few moments he'd unsaddled his horse, led him to the fenced meadow, and carried his own gear into the bunkhouse.

He noticed a bedroll and a bundle of what he guessed were Danny's clothes on the cot at the far side of the narrow room. Chance wondered briefly why Danny had chosen to take up quarters in the bunkhouse. Perhaps he'd decided a hired hand didn't have the right to sleep in the cabin.

Chance shook his head, smiling, knowing that he wouldn't be getting much sleep tonight if this afternoon had been a glimpse of things to come. As they'd ridden home, Danny had hardly taken a breath between words. For twenty miles Chance had listened patiently as the young man had related one long-winded tale after another of his exploits and close shaves with disaster at the gaming tables.

Chance figured Danny had stretched the truth at times in an effort to spice up his stories, trying to impress his older, more experienced companion. But despite Danny's exaggerations, by the time they'd herded the white-faced cattle onto Twin Rivers, Chance had come to the conclusion that if ever there were two more different people than reckless Danny McBride and his dependable sister, he'd never met them.

He smiled at the thought of the way Kathleen had looked as he held her, her green eyes sparkling with desire, her hair and clothes seductively disheveled from their embrace. He felt gratified, knowing instinctively that he was the first man ever to glimpse the passionate side of the always responsible and dependable Kathleen McBride.

Was he a fool to think he could build a life with her? The question surprised him. Had he not said himself on many occasions that a contrary woman was a curse? And had she not told him herself, time and again, that he represented all she despised in a man?

Ah, but her actions spoke so much louder than her words, he reminded himself as he sank down onto his cot, remembering the way she'd clung to him, kissed him, and, with the language of her supple body, urged him to go further.

Besides, contrary was not the right word to describe Kathleen McBride, anyway. Independent, strong-willed, proud—those words provided a far more apt description. And it was those very qualities that he admired in a partner, in a lover, in a wife. . . .

"Damn it all," he muttered to himself. He was nine kinds of a fool to ignore the circumstances that had brought him to Twin Rivers in the first place. It was those circumstances that made all his wild imaginings about a life together with Kathleen McBride the dreams of a fool. Perhaps he just should have kept running, or stayed at Twin Rivers only long enough to sell his share.

That money could have seen him to Canada. Was he crazy to believe he could hide in the Gallatin Valley forever?

He was a hunted man, a criminal on the run who by now probably had a sizable reward on his head. When he'd struck out that night at his brother's murderer, he'd dealt a death blow to his future. A future that had held no meaning for him then, but taunted him now with thoughts of what might have been.

Chance picked up a long thin strip of leather and a bridle that Jeb had told him needed mending. His hands worked steadily, but his thoughts shifted to the chain of dark events of almost a year ago in Texas.

His hatred was still bright for the man who'd orphaned Jim Jr. and Callie. Sometimes that hate was all he had. It gave him a reason to go on.

But hadn't there been enough hating? he asked himself bitterly. Enough loss? The loss of his father in the war, the loss of the children's mother who'd died giving birth to Callie while the ranch had been under siege by a band of renegades. The loss of James. Hate and loss, sometimes it felt as though his life had been filled with little else.

James was dead. By Chance's own hand J. D. Holcomb was dead as well. Too many deaths, too many losses, Chance repeated to himself. Too much hatred. When did it end?

Was there a way to finally bury his dead, cover his losses, and start living again? Didn't he owe that much to those left behind? If not for himself, for James's children?

Jim and Callie would love Montana, he told himself.
On a ranch this size, with acres of lush meadows to
roam and explore, animals to tend and daily chores to
be done, their young minds and bodies would flourish.
He closed his eyes for a moment, bringing his memories of them into focus.

Little Callie, soft yellow hair glistening in the West
Texas sunlight. Thoughts of the high-spirited child
made him chuckle despite his inner agony. She'd get
along well with Kathleen, he'd wager. Even at her
tender age, his niece possessed that same brand of feminine fire.

And then there was Jim, reed-thin and wiry like his
father had been. Serious and intense—a gentleman already.

It wasn't hard for Chance to picture their life now
and what it must be like for them in a town where
their uncle was wanted for murder. His hurt went all
the way to the bone, filling him with deep guilt that
wasn't easy to swallow.

But picturing the children at Twin Rivers brought a
very different response. Callie would mother every
newborn orphan calf with that innate tenderness she'd
inherited from her father. Perhaps Kathleen could
teach Callie to make those fancy lace patterns, the ones
he'd seen her making the last three nights as she'd sat
quietly by the fire.

He could teach Jim Jr. to use a rope. In the fall,
during roundup, he'd have plenty of chance to practice.
Or perhaps they could spend a day on the river together, where Jim would feel the thrill of hooking his
first glistening rainbow trout.

A familiar ache settled in Chance's heart as he tried
to focus on his work. But the pain persisted; he missed

his brother's children and he wondered when he dared take the chance of sending for them. When the time came to tell them, would they understand why their uncle, their guardian, had abandoned them, run out on them in the middle of the night? It was a lot to expect. They were only children, after all, and thanks to J. D. Holcomb, orphans.

Looping the last strand of leather around the head-piece, Chance tied it off and hung the bridle on a peg beside the door before he stepped out into the cool evening air. The Hereford cattle cast long, bulky shadows where they grazed in the near pasture. The hush of evening fell over the valley like a veil. The peaceful scene presented a stark contrast to his inner turmoil.

Maybe his charade as a respected landowner and cattleman could succeed. Maybe he could somehow manage to win Kathleen's love and someday send for Callie and Jim Jr. and make this beautiful Montana land their home.

And maybe he could learn to shrug off the hate, maybe she could heal him. But could any light, even one as strong as the light of her love, banish the memories of his dark past?

Slamming his fist against the door frame, he watched a plume of dust motes fill the dusky light.

Henry Draper certainly had more right to her heart. Danny had told him as much when they'd ridden into the yard. Henry had stood by her through the tough times. He'd been her friend when she needed him most. Today the preacher had gotten his hackles raised, but it wasn't too difficult to imagine why. Had it been Chance in his place, watching the kind of looks exchanged between another man and Kathleen, he'd have owned a piece of the interloper's hide.

And more important, Henry Draper had never killed a man. He was a man respected in his community. A man with a future. Unlike himself, a man whose past shrouded his days and haunted his nights, a man whose past would always mock his dreams for the future.

A man who had no right to love a woman like her.

An unexpected commotion at the front of the cabin tore Chance away from his inner tauntings. With his senses tuned, he moved quickly toward the yard.

He saw someone cross the porch and pound on the cabin door. When Chance saw Kathleen open it, real alarm rose inside him until he recognized the lathered stallion tied outside the yard as Sam Coulter's mount.

"It's Etta," Chance heard Sam say as he walked up behind him.

Kathleen's face lost its color. "Go home, Sam," she ordered. "I'll be right over."

"Please, hurry!" Sam pleaded as he turned and raced past Chance to his horse. "She's in terrible pain."

"Gather whatever you need," Chance said. "I'll hitch the wagon."

Kathleen flew into action.

Three hours later, Chance stood beside the fire in the Coulters' small, cramped cabin, watching Sam pace the floor. For the last ten minutes there had been an increase in the whimpers and groans coming from behind the door of the small bedroom.

"What's going on in there?" Sam asked impatiently, turning accusing eyes on Chance when the sounds abruptly stopped.

"Maybe it means it'll be over soon," Chance tried to assure Sam, though something inside Chance told him the night had just begun. "Smoke?" Chance offered, and Sam gratefully accepted a thin cigar.

"I think I'll go out to the barn and check on the animals," Sam said.

"Good idea. Need any help?"

Sam shook his head and privately Chance was relieved. He needed a break from Sam's incessant pacing and impossible questions as much as Sam needed a breath of fresh air to clear his frantic mind.

The cabin door had no sooner closed than the bedroom door opened and an exhausted Kathleen stepped into the cabin's main room.

Chance met her halfway across the room. Dark smudges of violet rimmed her eyes, damp tendrils of hair clung to the sides of her pale face. The blue cotton gown she wore clung to her body, damp with perspiration.

"Where's Sam?" she asked, her eyes searching the small room.

"Outside. He needed to move around a little. Should I go get him?"

Kathleen shook her head. "No, let him be."

"What is it, Kathleen?"

"Etta will be fine," she said softly. "But the baby . . ."

If it were possible, Chance would have gladly taken upon himself all the anguish he saw in her eyes. He took her hand and squeezed it gently. His heart lurched when her fingertips tightened for an almost imperceptible moment around his.

"Oh, Chance," she whispered, "they wanted that baby so badly." Her hands flew up to her mouth to stifle a sob.

He pulled her into his arms, and felt her shuddery

sigh. Her pain sliced through him and he searched his heart for a way to comfort her. But as he rested his head against the top of hers, he could think of nothing better to do than hold her.

In a moment, she pulled reluctantly out of his embrace. "I've got to get back to Etta," she said, swiping at the moisture collected at the corners of her eyes.

"I'll tell Sam," he said solemnly.

She nodded, and somehow he knew, without words, the depth of her gratitude.

Two days later, under a cloudless sky and to the sounds of nest-building birds chattering overhead in the pines, Henry Draper conducted the funeral services for the tiny stillborn Rachael Marie Coulter.

Etta Coulter stood numbly between her husband and Kathleen, her face ashen. Her eyes were glassy and vacant and mirrored her boundless grief.

After the miniature wooden coffin was lowered into the damp spring soil, a small knot of neighbors gathered around Etta and Sam to express their condolences before returning to their homes and their own lives. Some dabbed at tears as they walked away, tears for Etta and Sam, for the tiny life that would never be, or perhaps for their own distant losses that this morning's grim ceremony had brought back achingly to them.

They would hug their rosy-cheeked children a little tighter as they lifted them up onto the wagon seat, and hold the hands of their loved ones a little longer on the silent ride home.

Unexpected death was a grim reality the settlers of the lush and untamed Gallatin Valley had come to expect with grudging acceptance. But like the early frost that swooped from the north and destroyed their gardens before harvest, that threatened their very existence through the harsh Montana winter, the death of their young laid waste to hope and devastated their dreams.

Danny, Jeb, Chance, and Kathleen bore that hopelessness as they walked together across the meadow to the Coulter cabin. Kathleen helped Sam support Etta on what seemed to Kathleen to be the longest walk of her life. Her own arms and legs felt leaden, her heart laden with grief. She was only vaguely aware of Henry at her side.

When they reached the cabin's front door, Kathleen turned to Sam. "I'll see to Etta and then set out some dinner." The neighbors had been generous with their gifts of pies and cakes and covered dishes.

Sam seemed not to have heard. "Thank you, Kathleen," Henry offered in his stead. Their eyes met and she gave him a weary smile.

It had been a long day, and Henry's somber face attested to the toll this afternoon had taken on him, as well. Though hell's fire and brimstone and ridding the territory of criminals was more his style of shepherding, Henry had shown deep compassion from the moment he'd arrived at the Coulters' door.

And at a time when there really was no consolation, he'd done his best to assure and minister to the devastated couple. During the funeral service Kathleen had even heard his voice crack and hadn't dared let herself look at him for fear they might both break down.

Yes, it had been a long day for everyone, too long and too grueling to carry a grudge any further, Kathleen decided. Henry returned her kindness with a weak smile of his own, before his attention was pulled away by a group of neighbors paying their respects.

Before she closed the cabin door, Kathleen's eyes searched the yard and found Chance standing in quiet conversation with Danny and Jeb. The sight of him, his very presence, made her feel immeasurably better.

Through it all, Chance had been a rock of strength for Sam and Etta, and for her too. Lending his quiet sympathy throughout the difficult and agonizing hours of Etta's ill-fated labor, he'd torn rags, carried hot water, and in the end, helped her through the agony of preparing the infant for burial.

Kathleen had expected Chance to leave the Coulters' ranch the morning after. She'd been tending to Etta, trying to get the weakened and heartbroken woman to down a cup of sugary tea, when she heard Sam ride out before dawn toward Bozeman to fetch Henry.

When she'd heard Chance ride out an hour later, she hadn't really been surprised. But when he didn't return at lunchtime or for supper, she'd secretly mourned his absence.

Of course he had gone home, Kathleen had told herself, trying to be practical and ignore her welling disappointment. He didn't have the deep emotional attachment to Sam and Etta that she did. They were her friends, she reminded herself, not his.

Chance Ballinger had his own interests, interests that lay solidly in his share of Twin Rivers ranch and the profits he planned to derive from it. He had every right to attend to those interests, she had reminded herself sternly. Just because he'd helped her through a crisis, there was no reason for her to believe he'd stay longer.

After Etta had fallen asleep, Kathleen had heard a noise outside the cabin. Her brain told her that it had to be Sam riding in from Bozeman, but her heart hoped it would be Chance she'd find when she slipped out to the barn in the moonlight.

A light flickered at the back of the barn. As soon as she'd walked in, and seen General unsaddled and standing quietly in a stall, a surge of pure joy bolted through her. Her eager eyes had scanned the shadowy interior of the barn for a long moment before she saw him.

His back was to her as he crouched next to the small pine box she realized he'd spent the day building and sanding to a smooth finish. A white satin sheet lined the interior.

But where had he come by the satin? she'd asked herself. Etta and Sam would never have had such a lovely piece of fabric on hand.

An understanding of the events of the day gelled in her mind all at once when she recognized the satin as the swatch of fabric she'd saved from a wedding dress she'd made for Caroline Simmons's wedding last spring.

Immediately Kathleen knew where he'd been all day, why he hadn't come into the house for meals. At first light he'd started building the small coffin. And sometime during the day, he'd ridden back to Twin Rivers for the satin lining. He'd done what had to be done to prepare for the funeral the next day.

And as she'd watched, by the lantern's flickering light, he worked to finish his labor of love for Etta and Sam. His actions touched her deeply as she'd watched him dip a brush into the jar of white paint sitting on the ground beside him and make long, careful swipes across the small wooden cross he held reverently in one hand.

As he'd worked and she'd secretly watched from the shadows, the love she felt growing inside her for the tall, dark-haired cowboy with the midnight blue eyes doubled. She'd had to fight the impulse to go to him and proclaim her love, there and then.

But what if he'd laughed at her silly notions of love and lifelong partnerships? Or worse, what if finding her confession embarrassing or pathetic, he remained silent? After all, he knew they called her an old maid, didn't he? What if he deemed her profession of love the rantings of a desperate spinster?

And so with those agonizing thoughts blazing a trail of pain through her mind and heart, Kathleen had slipped quietly out of the barn, her silent tears gone by the time she returned to Etta's bedside.

This morning she'd said nothing about what she'd witnessed last night. When Chance brought the coffin into the house, together they'd washed and dressed the tiny corpse and laid the still, small figure onto the satin lining.

The memory of Chance's quiet kindness, of his unselfish gesture, made Kathleen's heart race again as she saw him now, standing beside her brother across the yard, tall and strong, his hair a glossy blue-black beneath the midmorning sun.

A few minutes later, after Kathleen had helped Etta back into bed, she stepped out into the sunshine and crossed the yard to her family.

"I'll be staying on with Etta for a couple of days," she explained to the men. "She's still very weak."

Jeb rested a hand on her shoulder. "Don't you worry

'bout a thing back home, missy. We'll take care of everything."

Danny nodded solemnly as he and Jeb walked over to the porch, where they mumbled a final few words of consolation to Sam. Kathleen went back to the house to lay out dinner for Sam and Henry and to make another cup of sugar tea for Etta.

"I'll be home, later," Chance told Jeb and Danny as he walked with them to their horses hitched outside the barn. "I reckon Sam could use a hand with his chores."

Jeb studied Chance's face for a moment. True, Ballinger was the kind of man to offer a helping hand to his neighbor, Jeb had seen enough of him to know that. But there was something more, Jeb knew, that kept Chance from riding back to Twin Rivers with them.

Though Ballinger's face was a rigid mask, unreadable and stoic, Jeb found it easy enough to guess why Chance was staying on at the Coulters'. He'd seen it coming from the beginning: The man was plum taken with Kathleen and he wasn't about to leave her alone with Henry Draper, and that was the long and the short of it.

Jeb had noticed Chance Ballinger watching Henry Draper hovering around Kathleen and seen the dark jealousy that flared in his eyes. Frankly, Jeb couldn't be more pleased.

As far as he'd been able to tell, Chance Ballinger was the one man strong enough, virile enough, to take Miss Kathleen and her ranch in hand—a hell of a lot more man than any Jeb had seen come calling on her in the past, that was for damn certain, especially when one compared him to that mama-coddled young preacher.

Jeb wasn't blind. He knew that Ballinger had probably stolen more than one kiss from Kathleen. But Jeb didn't disapprove. If ever a gal needed kissing . . . Lord knew she'd waited long enough. Why, if Ballinger hadn't come along when he had, Jeb figured Kathleen just might have become that old maid folks accused her of being already.

There was no doubt in Jeb's mind that Chance wanted Kathleen. And though she'd probably deny it with all the fury of hell, Kathleen wanted him just as badly.

"You keep daydreamin', old man, and that horse of yours is goin' to walk right into that river and drown you both," Danny chided him, jolting Jeb out of his reverie.

"Well, maybe you just best keep an eye on your own nag, youngster," Jeb drawled as he eased up beside Danny's long-backed bay gelding and gave the animal a sound smack on the rear.

When the horse bolted, Danny laughed and grabbed at the reins to keep the animal from running out from under him. "You reckon he'll be home tonight?" he asked, looking back over his shoulder at the Coulter homestead.

Jeb studied the younger man with narrowed eyes. "I reckon he'll be home when he's damn good and ready."

Danny's smile was knowing. "My money says he won't be leaving before the preacher does."

Jeb bit off a piece of plug tobacco and settled it firmly in his cheek before he said, "Now there's one bet you just might win, Danny boy."

It was a long time after sundown before Etta fell into an exhausted sleep. Kathleen waited an hour longer before she tiptoed out of the room to see Sam's lanky frame wrapped in a blanket on the floor in front of the fire. She moved over to him without making a sound.

"Sam?" she whispered as she bent and touched his shoulder.

He awoke with a start, his red-rimmed eyes bright with alarm. Kathleen instantly regretted waking him.

"Wh-what is it? Is she all right? What's wrong?" he demanded in a voice still thick with sleep.

"Nothing's wrong," Kathleen soothed, taking his arm and helping him to his feet. "Etta's sleeping. Why don't you go in?"

Sam shook his head. "Best I stay out here and let her be," he said, the sharp edge of his pain slicing through every word.

Kathleen knew that Sam had been shocked and deeply disturbed when Etta, realizing her infant had died, threw herself wildly into her grief. Her wailing and moaning had been the pathetic sounds of a wounded animal as she cried out against the anguish that threatened to consume her. Etta's grief had terrified her husband, making the normally soft-spoken, genteel woman seem a virtual stranger to her stunned spouse.

Kathleen had stayed beside Etta through it all. Not really knowing if what she said was getting through to her grief-stricken friend, Kathleen had just kept talking, soothing, comforting, even when it seemed there were no more words of comfort or consolation left to say.

She had hardly seen Sam in the first hours after the baby's death. Silently, stoically, he'd carried his grief alone, inside. If he'd confided in Chance, Kathleen had not seen it. Sam had seemed to avoid Etta, seeming not to want to be alone with her, even for a few moments. It was as though he was afraid that if he ever let go of the pain and the rage burning inside him, their combined grief would be too great for either of them to survive.

And then suddenly, late last night after he'd come back from Bozeman, something seemed to snap inside him. He rose up like a wounded bear and grabbed the cradle he'd built for the baby. With hands trembling with his rage, he'd snapped the wooden slats like kindling into a thousand splintered pieces and thrown them into the fire.

Hearing the commotion, Etta had staggered out of the bedroom, hysterical. One look at his terrified wife and Sam had stormed out of the house for the night.

No one saw him again until a few moments before Henry began the funeral service. Then Sam had strode silently across the meadow, moving up beside his wife and standing wooden and unblinking throughout the ceremony.

"Go to her, Sam," Kathleen urged him now. "She needs you."

Sam lifted his eyes and stared at her uncertainly as he slowly shook his head. "She said she didn't want to live anymore," he murmured, anger, confusion, and grief choking his voice. "She hates me. I did this to her, didn't I? And now she doesn't want to live. She doesn't want me," he added in a ragged whisper.

"No, no, that isn't true, Sam," Kathleen insisted, touching his big arm. "She was out of her head with grief. You both were. You did nothing to hurt Etta. You love her and she loves you. She needs you, Sam."

His eyes told her he longed to believe what she said was true.

"She needs you," Kathleen insisted again. "And you need her," she added softly. "That's what a husband and wife do for each other, Sam. They're lifetime partners who give each other a reason to go on."

She saw his tears glistening and felt her insides knot. A searing lump lodged in her own throat. Little Rachael Marie would have had her father's mournful, doe-eyed expression, Kathleen thought sadly.

"Etta's your partner, Sam. She needs you now to help her get through this terrible time. You can help her. You're the one she wants. The one she needs." She took his big callused hands in hers and squeezed them. "Both of you will survive this, I promise. Etta is young. She's strong. You'll have other children."

Unchecked, his tears streamed down his ruddy cheeks and dripped onto his shirt collar as Kathleen continued to speak to him in soft, reassuring tones as she led him toward the bedroom.

"Sam Coulter, you and Etta are going to have fine healthy babies," Kathleen declared, feeling her own strength somehow renewed. "Round-faced, brown-eyed babies," she said with a faint smile as she blinked back the tears nipping at her own eyes. "Though you'll never forget that little angel who visited us for a brief moment in the night, you'll smile and laugh with those other babies, Sam. You'll hold them and rock them and teach them how to be good, fine people, just like their mother and father."

Sam nodded and wiped his eyes as he turned to go into the bedroom. "Thank you," he whispered before he opened the door and walked through, closing it behind him without a sound.

Kathleen sagged against the door and released a long shuddery sigh. Her arms and legs felt heavy, as though the last ounce of energy had finally been drained from her body.

Out of the corner of her eye, she saw a sudden movement at the other end of the room. It startled her and she gasped.

"Who's there?" she asked, her voice shaky. When she'd come out of the bedroom, she'd just assumed everyone had left and that she and Sam were alone.

"Kathleen." The sound of his voice wrapped itself around her like a hug.

"Chance," she whispered.

He was by her side, his hand sliding over hers and pulling her to him as together they stepped outside. She fought the tears that burned her eyes and swelled in her throat until she heard the door close behind them.

But with the sound of the door came a signal of a release, and in the next moment she was in his arms, sobbing against his chest. Once again his steady presence was a reassuring beacon of light through the darkness of death and black desolation. But would he always be there for her?

Kathleen didn't know the answer as she leaned into his embrace and let his soothing words ease her sorrow.

But standing here in the moonlight with his arms around her, somehow tomorrow didn't seem to matter. He was here, now. And for the moment, that was enough.

Chapter Twelve

———⟡———

FOR Kathleen full spring could never come quickly enough to the Gallatin Valley. When it finally arrived, it was a time of rejoicing, of marveling at the wonders of nature. To her and to her neighbors, spring was traditionally a time to celebrate the long-awaited awakening of the firmament.

By June the meadows and woodlands were finally in full bloom, decorated in a profusion of delicate color as if they'd been placed there by the careful strokes of an artist's hand. Each sunlit day lasted a bit longer, and echoed more loudly the promise of the long, languid summer just around the bend for a winter-weary population.

For the McBrides, as well as many other ranchers of the Gallatin, this spring was the best yet. Their herds' latest arrivals, all bug-eyed, gangly, and bawling out for their mamas, had been counted and branded. Since last winter had been relatively mild, most the neighbors hadn't found too many unpleasant surprises, and were pleased to find a large number of surviving young.

By now, most of the calves in the valley were thriving and the more mature beef had been gathered for sale to passing drovers heading east. Plans for the second busiest time of the year, the fall roundup, were already being made.

It was late spring and that rare time in the cycle of seemingly endless ranch work when the cattleman paused to take stock of himself, to measure his worth and to assess his chances of succeeding at his chosen vocation for another year.

In the final assessment the future looked bright, and it was a time to celebrate. And, as had become a tradition in the valley, it was time to socialize. The McBrides and their neighbors looked forward with eager anticipation to coming together after the long winter months of isolation. Next to Christmas, the annual Spring Social was the biggest event in the valley.

The female population spent all their time baking the week before the event. The cookies and candies, cakes and pies, brought to the event usually filled two or more long tables. After the baking was finished, they pressed their best Sunday dresses, added a bit of new trim to an old bonnet, gave their husbands a much-needed haircut, and forced an unlucky few into starched collars. In the evenings before the Social young men were taught the proper dance steps and practiced for hours on their long-suffering mothers and sisters.

Kathleen could remember being allowed to attend Spring Socials when she was too small to climb up onto the wagon seat without her father's help. She especially remembered the Socials her family had hosted, so many years ago when her mother had still been alive. Long before dawn her mother would be absorbed in the preparations. When the guests began to arrive a special electricity always seemed to charge the air.

Tonight Kathleen tried to draw on those golden memories to brighten her mood, but to no avail. Even the lilting sounds of fiddle music coming from the group of musicians positioned at one end of Jacob and Daphne Brewer's barn did little to lift her spirits. It just didn't seem right, all the laughter and the celebrating, while only a few miles down the road from the Brewer homestead the shadow of Sam and Etta's personal loss still hung over the valley like a funeral shroud.

As Kathleen watched, smiling couples moved onto the makeshift dance floor, where a thin layer of straw had been strewn to keep the dust down. The Brewers' barn had been cleared of its animal inhabitants earlier in the day and then decorated gaily with paper streamers and bouquets of wild flowers.

The musicians broke into a rollicking song that pulled more dancers onto the floor. Men and women lined up facing each other for a feisty reel, and Kathleen moved behind the long pine-plank table that Henry had helped Jacob set up for refreshments. As more couples joined the growing lines that divided the middle of the floor, she saw Henry striding purposefully toward her. She glanced away, immediately busying herself by filling cups with punch and arranging the plates and silverware that would be used to serve the generous variety of cakes, pies, and sweet rolls.

"Oh, thank you, Kathleen," Daphne Brewer said, breathlessly rushing up to stand beside her behind the table. "I was just about to start serving. Jacob tells me they'll be a hungry and a thirsty bunch once they really start dancing."

Tall, blond Jacob Brewer ought to know, Kathleen thought, and smiled. He'd attended as many Spring Socials as she had. His German immigrant family had arrived in the valley just after the McBrides, their homestead butting up against Twin Rivers on the south.

The Brewers understood very little English and spoke less, but as a twelve-year-old Jacob was eager and ambitious and he'd learned quickly. As the eldest son, he soon became the spokesman for the clan.

For years the Brewers had been good neighbors and good friends. Kathleen and Jacob had gone to the territorial school together and shared more than one waltz at past Socials.

Last July when Kathleen declined Jacob's offer to buy Twin Rivers, she knew their long-standing friendship had been strained. A month later, Jacob had proposed to her. "A practical solution," he'd called it, benefiting them both. He would hold title to the largest, richest share of the valley, he'd explained with chest swelled, and she would have a handsome and prosperous young husband.

How could she have refused such a *romantic* offer, Kathleen asked herself now, with a silent chuckle she felt obliged to hide from Jacob's wife.

"It *is* exciting, isn't it?" Daphne's exclamation pulled Kathleen out of her thoughts. "This is all so new to me," Daphne said, rolling her big brown eyes dramatically. "But Jacob insisted we take our turn as hosts, and now I'm so glad we did!"

Daphne was a newcomer to the valley. After a whirlwind courtship, she and Jacob were married just after the new year. Daphne had grown up in Philadelphia, the daughter of a prosperous banker and financier. She was well traveled and educated.

When her father died last fall, and her older brother and his wife moved to Bozeman City to open a restaurant and bakery, Daphne had come with them. Rumor had it that Daphne's share of her father's inheritance was substantial.

Kathleen and Daphne had met in church, and later in Ben Allerby's mercantile store. The two women struck up an immediate friendship, and if Daphne Brewer knew about Jacob's previous proposal to Kathleen, she'd never mentioned it.

Although Daphne was several years older than Kathleen, she had a delightful, almost childlike enthusiasm that Kathleen found charming. And so when Daphne had approached her with several sewing projects, Kathleen had been eager. She enjoyed the challenge of trying to copy for Daphne the new look of gowns featured on the pages of the newspapers Daphne had brought with her from the East, or lifted from plates found in *Godey's Lady's Book*—Daphne's favorite reference for the latest in fashion.

The green dress Kathleen wore tonight was one of their joint creations, one of which she was especially proud. The scalloped collar and dainty cap sleeves were trimmed in delicate white lace, through which Kathleen had threaded a pale green satin ribbon. Layers of matching lace adorned the petticoat that showed discreetly at regular intervals where the skirt was caught up at the hem in gentle gathers by small bows of matching ribbon.

Though Kathleen had done all of the sewing and the

lacework, Daphne had inspired the design. It was during their sewing sessions that Kathleen and Daphne's friendship had really blossomed. And tonight, with Etta and Sam's absence an acute reminder of the sadness that still hung over her heart, Kathleen was especially glad for Daphne's friendship.

In fact, Daphne was the main reason Kathleen had agreed to attend this year's Social at all. Her involvement with the tragedy at the Coulters' would have given her the perfect excuse to beg off, but Kathleen had promised to help Daphne through her first duties as hostess.

"Everything looks wonderful," Kathleen remarked sincerely. "Yours is one Spring Social that won't soon be forgotten, Daphne."

"Thanks in large part to you," she reminded Kathleen. "I don't know what I would have done if you hadn't come over this morning and helped get things set up." But even though they'd swept and cleaned all morning and opened the doors at both ends to air the place out, the barnyard aroma was hardly obliterated. Daphne made a comment about the lingering smell and made a face, pursing her small mouth disapprovingly.

Kathleen's smile was sly and she put her arm around her friend's shoulder. "Jeb says the smell of cattle is the smell of money."

Daphne stared at her a moment, then laughed. "Speaking of Jeb, I was surprised when you came back with him this evening. I thought Henry was to be your escort tonight."

Kathleen set to filling a plate with pralines and peanut brittle. "We had a—a slight change of plans. . . ."

"An argument?"

"Hmm."

"I remember Jacob and I couldn't seem to agree on anything in the weeks just before our wedding." There was a wistful look in her eyes when she patted Kathleen's hand. "Don't worry. I'm sure you two will work everything out—"

Breathless and laughing, Selma Nygood and Buddy Wilhelm rushed off the dance floor and hurried up to the table for punch, distracting Daphne from completing the assurances Kathleen didn't really want to hear anyway.

As the young couple engaged their hostess in conversation, Kathleen scanned the crowd, searching the spot where only moments ago she'd seen Henry. But now he was nowhere to be seen.

Perhaps he'd decided to leave, she thought with guilty relief. She'd seen him arrive, and watched him making his way through the crowd. From where she'd stood watching, he certainly hadn't appeared to be enjoying himself. And when their eyes had finally met, she'd received the distinct impression that he'd purposely headed the other direction to avoid her.

Of course Henry would still be smarting from their recent encounter. And although Kathleen still felt justified in everything she'd said to him, she was sorry to think that their friendship might have been damaged beyond repair.

Henry's kindness to the Coulters had softened her feelings toward him to the point that she was ready to speak to him again. Although she realized fully that things could never be the same between them, she hoped at least to come to civil terms with the man—

after all, they had been good friends, once. Now all she wanted was to clear the air between them as quickly and painlessly as possible.

But mending their rift tonight seemed unlikely. She'd happened to catch the look on Henry's face when Chance Ballinger had arrived. If possible, the preacher's mood had seemed to grow even darker than it had been before—not that Chance's presence was doing much to improve Kathleen's mood either, she admitted to herself.

But to say it was his presence that upset her wasn't exactly the whole truth. What irritated her most was the constant flock of young women who'd gathered around him from the moment the music had started. Though she hadn't yet seen him ask any of them to dance, she knew they'd keep trying.

She could hardly blame them. All evening she'd found it difficult to stop watching him, finding herself struck anew by his startling good looks.

Her eyes traveled to him now, and she realized she'd never seen him looking more handsome than he did tonight. Dressed in a snowy white shirt beneath a black topcoat and black britches that hugged his lean hips and emphasized the long muscular lengths of his legs, Chance Ballinger was, without argument, the best-looking man at the Social. She could not read the expression in those sparkling azure eyes from this distance, but even across the room, she felt the effects of his wry smile when his eyes met hers, and she knew he'd seen her studying him.

She returned his smile before forcing herself to look away, pretending interest in Selma and Buddy's happy chatter. But when her gaze was inevitably drawn back to him, her smile faded.

A woman she didn't recognize had emerged from the crowd and sidled up to Chance. She offered him her hand and he took it. The look that passed between them was unmistakable and caused Kathleen's heart to sink.

The woman, a curvaceous blonde, dressed in a bright blue satin dress cut low to expose the creamy white mounds of her full breasts, had a pretty face. Her hair, arranged in soft ringlets, was the color of honey. When she smiled at Chance with open familiarity, Kathleen felt as though all the air had been sucked out of her lungs.

". . . it's such a *large* barrel," Daphne was saying. "I don't think we could manage it. I'll ask Henry or Jacob—if I can find them—to bring it in after the next reel. Buddy, be a dear and see if you can locate either of them, will you? Where could they have gotten off to?"

The realization that Daphne had been talking to her startled and embarrassed Kathleen. Had she been talking the entire time Kathleen's wayward gaze and distracted mind had been otherwise occupied on Chance Ballinger and his mysterious lady?

"Kathleen? Are you all right?" Daphne's voice sounded impossibly far away. "You don't look well at all. You're very pale all of the sudden. Maybe you should sit down or go into the house and lie down for a while."

"Uh, n-no. No. I'm fine." Kathleen's own voice sounded hollow and she wouldn't meet Daphne's eyes. Somehow she couldn't seem to tear her eyes away from the dance floor, where the woman in blue satin and Chance were moving together to the strains of a lilting waltz.

The blonde's expression was one of obvious delight, but Chance's expression was torturously unreadable.

Before she could look away, the blonde turned her stare directly at Kathleen and smiled. Their gazes held for a moment before the woman lowered her face and whispered something to Chance and they both laughed. Kathleen felt a stab of searing jealousy knife through her.

When Daphne touched her arm, she jumped. "Kathleen? What's wrong? I'm worried about you. You face is as bright as a beet!"

Kathleen hands flew to her cheeks. The fire under her skin singed her fingertips. "I'm fine," she insisted breathlessly. "It's so . . . warm in here, don't you think? I could use a glass of cider. What was it you were saying . . . about the cider . . . ?"

Daphne studied her skeptically. "Well, if you're sure you're all right . . . I was just saying that if I could find Henry or Jacob, I would have them fetch the keg of cider up from where it's been chilling in the creek— oh, here they come now!"

Jacob Brewer talked to his neighbors as he moved through the crowd, but it was easy to see that he only had eyes for his wife as he swept around the table and slipped his arm around her small waist and drew her from behind the table. "Did you miss me, honey?" Daphne giggled as her husband hugged her to him.

"Ladies." Henry greeted them with a curt nod. "The Social seems to be a resounding success, Daphne."

"Why, thank you, Reverend." Daphne beamed under Henry's compliment.

His eyes shifted to Kathleen and then down. "Is that your apple pie, Kathleen?"

"Why, yes, yes it is, Henry. Would you care for a

slice?" She was relieved to have the ice between them so easily broken. Perhaps Henry wanted to make amends as badly as she did.

"Maybe later."

"We'll put a slice back for you, Henry," Daphne offered.

"Now, Kathleen, will you just look at these two!" Daphne demanded gaily. "Are we or are we not in the company of the two most handsome gentlemen at this year's Social?"

"*This* or *any* year!" Jacob corrected playfully before planting a kiss on her cheek and whirling her out onto the dance floor. "Come on, you two!" he urged them. "They're playing one of my favorite songs."

Left abruptly alone with Henry, Kathleen felt strangely trapped and uneasy. She could feel his eyes move over her in a way they'd never done before; from the gathering of lace at her throat to the glimpse of lace petticoat skimming the tops of her cloth slippers, he took in every detail. Something uncharacteristic about his demeanor set off a vague warning in Kathleen's brain, and if she hadn't known better, she would have sworn she detected a hint of whiskey on his breath.

He offered her his hand. "Kathleen?"

"Come on!" Daphne shouted over the rollicking music. "It's a Virginia reel!"

Henry offered her his hand again.

Oh, why not, she asked herself, and smiled. And in the next moment she and Henry were gliding around the floor with the other dancers. The gaiety of the music and the crowd was infectious and in a moment they were both laughing and dancing and moving among their mutual friends with familiar ease. Henry's mood seemed immeasurably improved and he smiled and quipped good-naturedly in a merry voice to those who called out to him.

When the reel ended, the band settled down to a waltz and Kathleen slid her hand from Henry's and started off the floor. He reached for her and caught her hand and turned her gently back to him.

"Once more?" he asked.

"I really should get back to the refreshment table . . . I promised Daphne—"

"You're still angry with me," he said quietly, his expression dejected.

"No. Not anymore," she said simply, meeting his eyes directly for the first time.

"Then dance with me, Kathleen."

Still she hesitated, and his expression was a mix of hurt and disappointment as he followed her to the edge of the floor. "If you're not still angry," he challenged, "then why are you running away from me?"

She stood her ground, facing him. "I'm not running, Henry."

"You must know how badly I feel. How this awful silence between us has tortured me. I miss you. I—I—" He swallowed the catch in his voice before continuing in a rush of words. "You must forgive me, Kathleen. I know I overstepped my bounds that day. I . . . said . . . some things, things I . . . shouldn't have said . . . not then, anyway. And certainly not in the way that I said them." He took her hand again and squeezed it ardently. "You know how I feel about you—how I've *always* felt about you—"

"Please," she cut in, edging a step back from him and pulling her hand from his again. "Please, Henry. Don't say any more."

"But I must. Don't you see? I may not have another chance. I can't let you just walk away from me. Say you forgive me," he pleaded. "Say we're still friends."

"Well, of course we're friends . . ."

He took a deep breath. "Then show me. Dance with me again, Kathleen. Just once more."

"But I promised Daphne I'd serve punch and—" When she glanced over her shoulder at the refreshment table, all she saw was a blur of blue satin as her eyes clouded with mind-numbing jealousy. She blinked and her vision cleared enough to see the blond woman still nestled against Chance's arm accept the punch he handed her. When she thanked him by planting an ardent kiss on his cheek, Kathleen could stand no more. She whirled around to face Henry so fast, she nearly stumbled.

"All right, Henry. Let's dance," she declared, promising herself that the moment this waltz was over, she'd find Uncle Jeb and leave.

As Chance watched Henry move with Kathleen across the dance floor, his grip on his partner's hand tightened unconsciously. Rubylee, taking his gesture to mean something else, giggled and pressed herself closer to him.

At that precise moment his eyes met Kathleen's and the spark of anger he saw there was unmistakable before she shifted her gaze past him and smiled vacantly, as if he'd become invisible. It galled him to have her dismiss him so easily and to see her in the arms of the young preacher. But then again, what was more fitting? Would it have been better if she were in the arms of a wanted man?

"A girl could get downright lonely dancing with you,

Ballinger," Rubylee informed him with an exaggerated pout on her pretty lips.

"Sorry, Rubylee," Chance muttered. "Now, tell me. What brings you to Bozeman?"

"That's better," she cooed. "For a minute there I was beginning to think you'd never ask. You remember that night you won so big in Virginia City?"

"Sure I remember."

"Well, it was that night that I realized you were the best friend little ole Rubylee ever had."

"The way I remember it, you were mad as a wet hen and when I left you were calling me names that would have made a mule skinner blush."

"Oh, well," she said, dismissing the memory with a quick wave of her hand. "My mama always said I had a hair trigger. But you know I didn't mean it. Why, how could I stay mad at the man who turned my luck around the way you did, who changed my whole life the way you did?" She smiled up at him innocently and batted her lashes.

Chance couldn't help laughing at her theatrics. "And just how did I manage to do all that, Rubylee?" he asked good-naturedly.

"Why, with those lucky gold pieces, that's how. I sat in on a game a week later with that money you gave me, and I won! A week later, I took them gold pieces and sat in on another game, and the week after that another one. And I won, Chance! Every time I opened with them lucky little gold pieces, I won. By last week, I'd won enough to get the hell—" Her voice rose and a couple next to them stared. She lowered her lashes and muttered, "Sorry," and dropped her voice a notch and went on excitedly, "I won enough to buy myself a couple of dresses and a ticket to Bozeman and still have enough left to tide me over until I get my new business started."

Chance stopped dancing and held her at arm's length. "New business?" he asked, one dark brow arched suspiciously.

"A *legitimate* business," she informed him hotly, before smiling and sliding back into his arms. "I grabbed that second chance, same as you did, Mr. Rancher," she declared with a proud smile.

"Oh? And just what kind of business did you have in mind, Rubylee? If you don't mind me asking."

"Why, not at all," she said graciously. "Although my new endeavor will be something nice and respectable it won't be anything quite so grand as ranching," she teased. "But something nice, all the same. With the last of them gold pieces, I bargained for half a dozen bolts of ladies' dress material from a peddler heading west. I'm gonna open me a dress shop, Chance! Say, you wouldn't know a good seamstress, would you?" Before he could reply, she asked, "How 'bout that old maid you're hooked up with? From what I hear she's a whiz with a needle and thread—"

Chance pushed her away from him. "Don't ever call her that," he said, the level of threat in his voice surprising even him.

Rubylee winced. "Sorry!" she said, her eyes wide. "I didn't mean nothing by what I called her, Chance. It's just what I heard them sayin' in town, what the boys called her in Virginia City, that's all. I didn't mean no harm."

He took her hand again and they moved with the other couples across the floor, but his heart wasn't in the music and it certainly wasn't with his dancing partner.

"Kathleen. That's her name, isn't it?" Rubylee asked

after a moment's silence. "She's pretty. I saw her. Strange how she never found herself a man . . ."

"I'd rather not talk about Miss McBride, Rubylee."

"Well sure, honey." She stared up at him, her eyes narrowed. "Anything you say."

The music stopped and he dropped her hand. "Good luck, Rubylee. I wish you well in your business endeavor." She followed him when he walked off the dance floor. "Your dress shop should do well. Bozeman is growing by leaps and bounds."

"Hey, you ain't leavin', are you, Chance honey?"

"Morning comes early when there's cattle to feed."

Rubylee's face mirrored her disappointment. As he stepped out into the black night, heading for the corral where General was tethered along with the other guests' horses, he heard her still behind him.

"That's no way to treat a lady, leaving her all alone on the dance floor like that," she scolded.

"I gotta go, Rubylee," he said without turning around.

She reached for him and he stopped and wheeled around to face her. Her hand fell away from his arm. "I didn't come out here tonight just to thank you, Chance," she admitted.

It was late, he was tired and still irritated every time he thought of Kathleen with Henry. His patience was running too short to play any kind of game with Rubylee. "Then why *did* you come here tonight, Rubylee? What do you want from me?"

Her expression turned defensive. "Now, what makes you think I want something?"

When he resumed his trek toward the corral, she fell in stride beside him. "I came here tonight just to see you, Chance."

"Rubylee—"

"Listen. We're two of a kind. I knew it in Virginia City. We're lucky, you and me. You started over, didn't you? And now I'm starting over too."

"And I wish you good luck," he said as he slipped through the corral rails, caught his horse, and led the animal to the gate.

"But why can't we be together, Chance? Why not?" she pressed him, lifting her skirts to edge around the muddy corral to stand beside him as he saddled his horse. He didn't look at her when she ran a hand seductively down his sleeve. "We were good together you and me," she said, her voice husky. "We had us some good times, didn't we?"

With his free hand, he took her hand off his sleeve. "It won't work, Rubylee," he said in a low voice. "Now, you go on. Open your dress shop. You find yourself a young man and start your life over again, just like you said. But it's not me. Do you understand? It's not me."

Her eyes turned hard. "You think you're too good for me, that's it, isn't it, Mr. Rancher? I'm a saloon girl from Alder Gulch and that's all I'll ever be to you. You have your little ole maid—your Kathleen." She spat out the name as though it had singed her tongue.

He released her arm so suddenly, she almost stumbled backward.

"It's her, isn't it? Your sweet little ole partner. So high and mighty and pure!"

He'd finished saddling General and had one foot in the stirrup when she grabbed his arm again. He swung around to face her again, his patience finally stretched to the breaking point.

"Go back inside," he ordered her, his voice low and ominous.

"It won't work, Ballinger," she warned him, ignoring his command. "She'll find out what you are and then what will you do? Huh? Well, here's something for you to think about while you're waiting for her to be done with you." And with that she rose up on tiptoe, planted a hand on each side of his face, and kissed him, her mouth grinding down on his, her lips open and her tongue probing.

Before Chance could shove her away, he heard a soft, gasping sound to his left. He spun around to stare into the darkness. "Who's there?" he demanded. "Who's out there?"

But the duet of crickets and the soft sighs of the other horses in the corral was all the reply that came back to him.

"It's no one," Rubylee told him. "Just a mouse or a night bird."

Chance stared another long moment in the direction from which he'd heard the sound that had seemed distinctly human.

"Now, come on. What do you say? Come back with me to my room. Come with me now," she urged him. "We'll have us a drink and then I'll show you what I came all this way to give you."

Chance eyed her cynically and shook his head. "I'm sorry, Rubylee, but you've got nothing I want," he said quietly. "Nothing at all."

"Oh, is that so?" she shot back bitterly, one hand planted firmly on each of her hips. "Well, you just never know, now do you, Mr. Rancher?"

"I know," he said as he swung up into the saddle and adjusted the reins in his hands. "Believe me, Rubylee, I know."

* * *

Kathleen had seen Jeb leave the barn less than an hour ago. No doubt he and Nolan Stubbs and some of the other men were outside sharing a jug. She'd heard voices at the corral and was following them when she'd stumbled on the scene that still had her reeling.

The sight of the blond-haired woman and Chance kissing drove a jagged blade of jealousy straight to her heart, where it twisted and turned its way into the pit of her stomach.

She stumbled back to the barn in the darkness, blinded by her jealousy. Just outside the large opened doors, she ran headlong into Henry. Swiping at her tear-streaked face, she gasped, "Henry!"

"Kathleen, what's wrong?" He hauled her against him and stroked her hair for a moment before she could pull away.

"I—I came out here to find Jeb—but—" Oh, how could she explain? "Just please, please take me home, would you, Henry?" she cried, barely containing her turbulent emotions enough to speak. "Please." Her insides quivered and she stifled another choking sob as it rose in her throat.

"Yes. Yes, I will, of course. But what's happened? Tell me, Kathleen. What's wrong?" he demanded. With his thumb and forefinger he tilted her chin so that she had to face him.

His eyes were shining and this time she knew without a doubt that it *was* the smell of whiskey she detected on his breath. "Nothing," she lied, swallowing hard to compose herself. "I'm just feeling so horrible, suddenly. Please . . . if you could just drive me home . . ."

He nodded quickly, put his arm around her shoulders and brought her with him as he hurried to where his buggy was parked. "Get in. My horse is right over there. I'll fetch him and I'll have you home before you know it."

True to his word, Henry quickly hitched the small gray gelding to the soft-topped buggy, and in five minutes he was beside her and steering the rig out of the drive.

Kathleen was relieved he wasn't trying to force conversation. The memory of the blonde in Chance's arms, of his lips pressed against hers, burned in Kathleen's mind, making any attempt at even polite conversation impossible.

What a fool she'd been, she told herself, to believe that he could care for her the way she'd come to care for him. To believe that he might want the kind of partnership that she'd dreamed of sharing with him, when all the while he'd been pining away for this woman from his past—the woman who'd waltzed into the Brewers' barn tonight and destroyed all of Kathleen's foolish dreams with one smile from her painted lips.

Drawing a weary breath, she blessed the darkness that hid from Henry the humiliating tears she felt still shimmering in her eyes. With luck she would arrive at the ranch long before Chance did. Seeing him again tonight, knowing he'd come from *her* arms, would be just too much to bear.

In the morning she would ride into town and beg Charles Settlemier to loan her the money to buy the gambler out. The time had come. There was no sense in delaying their confrontation any longer.

The surrey had traveled only a short distance from the edge of the Brewers' farmyard when, without warning, Henry jerked the reins up tight and brought the buggy to a sudden halt.

"What is it, Henry? Is something wrong?"

"Yes, Kathleen," came his curt reply. "Something is very wrong and I intend to make it right, here and now."

Even in the shadowy darkness of the carriage interior, Kathleen could see a disturbing glint in Henry's eyes.

"What are you talking about, Henry?" she asked, twisting the thin satin strap of her reticule nervously around her fingers.

"I'm talking about you and me, Kathleen. The time has come for some plain talk. I am a patient man, but even I have my limits."

Kathleen sighed impatiently. "Oh, Henry, please. It's late and I'm tired. Please, just take me home."

When he made no move to comply with her request, she prodded him. "Henry. You've been drinking. You're not yourself. Please just take me home before you do or say something we'll both regret."

"I'll take you home," he muttered grudgingly, "after I've said what I have to say."

For the first time, Kathleen grew truly alarmed. She'd never seen Henry assume such a dark demeanor, talk to her in such a malevolent tone.

"All right, Henry," she relented, clasping her hands in front of her on her lap. Steadying her hands was easier than steadying her jangled nerves. She took a deep breath of pine-scented air and said, "Go on. I'm listening."

"You know I want to marry you, Kathleen," he said almost angrily. "And you also know I'm a man accustomed to getting my own way. You will marry me, Kathleen. You will." His words echoed around her, reverberating through the still night air with unbelievable force. His sudden proposal didn't surprise her, but his blunt demand did.

"Why, Henry. I don't . . . know what to say," she stammered.

"There *is* nothing to say. It's time we were married—everyone knows it. Some would even say it's past time." His voice was bitter. "I spoke to Charles Settlemier and we have reached an agreement whereby he will rewrite the existing note on Twin Rivers and the bank will advance me the money to buy out your—your business partner. We drank to our bargain and it's all settled. As soon as we're married, Charles will draw up the papers. I'll send for a circuit preacher to give us our vows."

The air rushed out of Kathleen's lungs in a gasp. "Henry, what have you done? You and Charles Settlemier . . . ? My God, Henry!" Kathleen's voice shook. Just a few short minutes ago, she'd thought nothing could have shocked her more than seeing Chance standing in the moonlight kissing another woman, but now this . . . this was a true nightmare! "How could you have done such a thing?" she demanded. "And Charles—"

He cut her off with a savage glance. "Charles is as concerned as I am about your reputation, in light of your—well, what shall we call it, Kathleen? Your present living arrangements?"

The words with which she wished to batter him rose in her throat, choking her with their bitterness. She fought for control. "I have to assume your interference was well intentioned and that Charles was only doing what you'd asked him to do." Her voice dropped to a ragged whisper. "But I won't marry you, Henry. Not now. Not ever," she added, finding a sudden strength in her anger. "I don't love you. As a matter of fact, I don't even like you anymore, Henry."

She stared at him with new eyes and saw Henry Draper, at last, for what he was: an opportunist and a self-righteous fraud.

She turned to climb out of the carriage, bitter tears of anger and disappointment stinging her eyes. Perhaps it was best, after all, that she live the rest of her life alone. If she were no better judge of men than tonight's experiences had proved, perhaps she was better off living up to her title of old maid.

"Where do you think you're going?" Henry demanded, grabbing her arm and forcing her back down beside him.

No man had ever touched her in anger, and for a moment Kathleen could only stare at him in stunned disbelief. "You're hurting me," she said, trying to pull away from the viselike grip that held her fast.

"Am I?" he growled, tightening his hold until his fingers dug painfully into the tender flesh of her upper arm. His breath was sour; the strong smell of whiskey assaulted her, bringing with it fresh waves of alarm. Her eyes darted up and down the deserted road, and to her dismay, she realized there was no one to come to her aid.

"Let me go, Henry," she said in a low voice that surprised her with its steadiness.

"Now you listen to me, Miss McBride," he declared in a voice laden with menace, "and you listen good. I am willing to marry you. Do you understand what I'm saying? I am *willing* to give you my last name, to make an honest woman of you, as they say." His smile was both a sneer and a smirk. "I am willing to overlook the sinful nature of your past indiscretions with that saddle tramp you refer to as your business partner."

His words packed the force of a physical punch, and the heat of betrayal and rage sizzled inside her.

"And you will accept my proposal, Kathleen," he continued confidently. "For the most part, I believe you are a sensible woman. Despite the romantic notions you harbor concerning the future with your Mr. Ballinger, you must know he will never marry you."

"Let me go, Henry," she demanded again, renewing her struggle to break free of his grasp.

"Oh, it's not me you wish to escape, my dear," he chided her, "but the consequences of your own wicked behavior. After all, you know what they say about a man not wanting to buy the cow when he can get the milk for free . . ."

She raised her hand to slap his leering face, but before her palm could make contact, his hand snaked out with surprising speed and captured her wrist. Now, both her arms were pinned and she was held prisoner in his relentless grasp.

"Henry, please. You don't know what you're doing. You're not used to drinking liquor," she tried to reason with him. "Let me go, and we'll forget any of this ever happened. You needn't worry about seeing me home. I'll just go back into the barn and tell Daphne I've decided to stay over with them tonight. Please, Henry. Just go home now," she said, her placating tone belying the fear that made her heart race.

For a moment he seemed to have been persuaded by the things she'd said. Slowly, he lessened his grip and then, finally, he released her.

Kathleen kept her eyes on his face as she edged cautiously away from him and prepared to step out of the carriage. She turned slowly and had one foot on the running board when he grabbed her hair and jerked her back onto the seat. He startled her breathless with his attack.

With one hand tangled painfully in her hair, he jerked her head around savagely, forcing her to face him. With his other hand, he twisted her arm behind her back and pulled her roughly against him.

"So, we'll just forget all about tonight, huh? Is that it?" he growled against her ear. "Just as I'm supposed to forget how you humiliated me in front of Jeb and Danny and that bastard Ballinger!"

"Please, Henry," she gasped.

"I think not, my dear. For I promise you, when I've finished with you tonight, you'll never forget. You'll never deny me again. Never!"

Her shriek was a strangled gag as he lunged over her, forcing her against the seat and grinding his mouth down onto hers. Hysteria threatened to overwhelm her as she felt the weight of his body crushing her beneath him.

Though he'd released her arm, it was still pinned painfully, uselessly, behind her. With one hand Henry continued to clutch at her hair as he crushed her mouth with his own. With the other hand he grabbed at her skirt, trying to raise it.

Fighting her own panic as desperately as she fought her attacker, Kathleen began to shake her head furiously from side to side against his grip. But Henry had the advantage and he held her tighter; her struggle seemed only to spur his frenzied lust to greater heights.

"No!" she screamed between clenched teeth as he shoved his tongue against them. *No, no, no!* her frantic mind shouted over and over again. A sudden pain shot through her face as Henry dug his fingers into the sides of her jaw, forcing her mouth open. His thrusting tongue gagged her and she arched her body, trying furiously to shove him away.

When she heard her skirt tear, renewed panic shot through her. *Dear God! Henry Draper meant to rape her!*

With sudden strength born of sheer terror, Kathleen bucked desperately beneath him and finally managed to free her right arm. At the same time as she yanked a fistful of his hair, she clamped her teeth down hard on his tongue.

The pain made him rear back; a startled cry escaped his gaping mouth as he glared down at her.

"Why you little bitch!" he cried as he raised his hand to strike her. At that exact moment, Kathleen brought her knee up and drove it hard into his groin as he lunged for her again. With an agonized cry, Henry collapsed backward onto the carriage floor, writhing and curling into a tight ball of pain, his anguished moans carrying on the night air as Kathleen clambered out of the carriage and ran into the darkness without looking back.

Chapter Thirteen

———◆———

JACOB Brewer's stocky bay mare was surefooted, and in less than an hour Kathleen was riding into her own yard. While cursing the name of Henry Draper under her breath, she issued a silent prayer of thanks for her good friend Daphne.

After she'd freed herself from Henry's attack, Kathleen had slipped into the back of the barn unnoticed. She'd been lucky to catch Daphne's eye without drawing anyone else's attention. One glance from Daphne told Kathleen how she must have looked.

The pins and comb that she'd used to sweep her hair up on top of her head had been lost in her struggle with Henry, and her long hair cascaded down around her neck and shoulders in a tangled veil.

Daphne hadn't needed to say a word. Her eyes had asked all the questions. Kathleen's frantic explanation had been short and disjointed as she'd saddled the little bay. Remembering Daphne's startled stare, Kathleen worried, hoping again that she could count on her friend's promise of discretion.

Word of her encounter with Henry circulating the valley could only double the humiliation she felt welling inside. Besides her own pride, Kathleen worried about the reactions of her brother and Uncle Jeb if they somehow found out what Henry had tried to do to her.

If she was lucky, Danny and Jeb would accept the explanation she'd conjured for the presence of the Brewers' horse in the barn tomorrow morning. She had no intention of ever telling another living soul about Henry's unforgivable behavior. If pressed about why their relationship had changed, she would simply say they had quarreled. She knew that neither her brother nor Jeb would be especially disappointed to learn that she and Henry had decided to go their separate ways.

But what about Chance Ballinger? What would his reaction be, she wondered, if he somehow found out that Henry had tried to force himself on her tonight? Merely asking the question startled her. What made her think Chance would have any reaction at all? Romantic fantasies of the tall, dark cowboy racing to defend her honor were absurd in light of what she'd witnessed tonight.

Had he arranged ahead of time to meet the blonde dressed in blue satin? Or had their meeting at the Social been purely coincidental? But what did it matter whether their meeting had been coincidence or pre-arranged, they had left together, hadn't they? To share a moonlight kiss. And that fact alone was enough to leave Kathleen feeling thoroughly bereft.

The cabin was dark as she dismounted and led the mare into the barn. The bunkhouse looked deserted as well. More than likely Jeb had not come home yet.

Danny, if he came home tonight, wouldn't be riding in for hours. And Chance . . . well, he must still be with *her*, Kathleen decided grimly.

She closed her eyes and could see them together again, almost as though she were watching again for the first time.

"Fool!" she declared herself as she guided her borrowed mount into an empty stall, unsaddled the animal, and gave it water and a forkful of well-deserved hay. Patting the gentle horse affectionately, Kathleen let her head rest wearily on its satiny neck. After a moment, she collected herself and slipped quietly out of the barn.

When she was halfway across the barnyard, a movement on the porch caught her eye. Immediately she recognized the long, lean figure that lounged in the porch swing. The reddish glow from the tip of his cigarillo and the faint smell of tobacco riding the breeze unmistakably confirmed his presence.

How long had he been sitting there? Had he seen her ride in alone? Could he possibly have been waiting for her? Suppressing the tingle of excitement that last unlikely thought had triggered, Kathleen smoothed her skirts, pushed her hair off her face, and strode purposefully toward the cabin.

If she hurried past him, perhaps he wouldn't notice her disheveled appearance and she would not be forced to explain why she'd come home unescorted.

"Kathleen." His rich voice reached out to her through the darkness as she stepped up onto the porch.

She acknowledged him with a nod.

"Where's the preacher?"

Out of the corner of her eye, she saw him walking toward her. "I wouldn't know," she answered tersely.

As she reached to open the door, she fought the urge to turn around and look at him. She kept her back to him until he placed both hands on her shoulders and gently turned her around to face him.

"That party dress wasn't meant for horseback riding," he said, taking in the tattered condition of her clothes.

She bit her lip.

"Why did you ride home alone?"

She shrugged. "I don't think that's any of your business."

"I'm making it my business," he informed her, leveling her with his dark stare. "Why did you ride home on Jacob Brewer's horse?"

"It's late," she murmured. The tantalizing scent of soap and leather teased at her senses, and without warning an image of him holding the woman in blue satin flashed through her mind again. She turned her back to him and reached for the door.

"What the hell happened tonight?"

Without turning around she said, "Where I go, what I do, and how I travel is of no concern to you, Mr. Ballinger."

He edged around in front of her, blocking her access to the door. "But it is. I care about everything that happens to you, Kathleen."

"Is that so?"

"Yes, that's so," he said quietly. "Everything that affects you, affects me."

"Like what?" she asked, her throat inexplicably tight and dry.

"Like why you rode home alone. And where you were tonight when I came back to the Social looking for you." The startling revelation that he'd looked for her caused Kathleen's heart to beat double time. Was he teasing her or had he really tried to find her?

"But most of all," he said, "I'd like to know why you're afraid to stand here in the moonlight and talk to me."

"I'm not afraid of anything," she insisted, sounding anything but certain, the breathy quality of her voice betraying her bravado. "For your information, I enjoy the moonlight as much as the next person, Mr. Ballinger."

"Why, that's good, Miss McBride." His wry grin drove the gentle cleft deeper into his chin. "That's just dandy."

Kathleen asked herself if his southern drawl had ever sounded silkier.

He took her hand. "Because a moon, such as the one tonight, was meant to be shared." The sound of his voice and the compelling warmth of his strong hand wrapped securely around hers sent a wave of anticipation flooding through her.

He led her to the porch swing and sat down, patting the wooden slats beside him. "Come. Sit beside me, my fearless partner, and let's have us a good, long look at that big old Montana moon, shall we?"

She tried to glare at him, but he only smiled. "Sit down, partner."

She sat stiffly and busied herself arranging her full skirt. When he kicked the porch swing into motion, she was jerked backward against his arm, which was draped across the back of the swing. His fingers came to rest lightly on her shoulder.

"Yes ma'am, that's quite a moon," he declared, tipping his head back and gazing in rapturous admiration at the heavens.

"Quite." She stole a glance at his distinctive profile and, despite herself, noted again how very handsome he was.

He sighed. "A perfect moon on a perfect night for dancing."

She saw them together again and felt another sharp jab of envy, her nerves twisting as tight as the new wire wound around the meadow.

"Those boys sure could play the fiddle."

"Yes, they were very good," she replied impatiently. She didn't have the vaguest notion what kind of strategy he was planning, or where this simple conversation would lead them, but she'd be damned if she'd let him run her off, she told herself resolutely.

"I don't know about you," he said, his gaze still locked on the sky, "but that fiddle music made me wish I could have gone on dancing all night."

"Oh, really? One would never have guessed," she shot back crisply.

"How's that?"

She turned and addressed his puzzled expression with a syrupy sweet smile. "One would have thought by the way you and your dancing partner dashed out of the barn that you had had your fill of dancing."

He shifted slightly in the swing and his arm tightened around her shoulders. "And it seems you and Henry quickly tired of dancing, as well," he countered. "It *was* you I saw slipping into his carriage just as I was leaving, wasn't it?"

Like hot oil, his mocking remarks raised fresh blisters on her already scalded pride. She stood up abruptly, clasping her hands tightly in front of her, groping to collect the composure she felt unraveling within her. "Good night, Chance," she said, with as much dignity as she could muster before whirling around and walking toward the cabin door. The bright tears that nipped her eyes made the cabin a swirling presence before her. If she could only escape before her sobs broke.

But escape was not meant to be. Just as she reached the door, he came up behind her and took her hand again, then spun her gently around to face him.

"Leave me alone," she cried, her voice ragged.

"You don't mean that," he informed her. With one fingertip he traced a tear that had slipped from the corner of her eye and trickled slowly down one cheek.

"What happened tonight, Kathleen?" he asked gently. "Please tell me."

His unexpected tenderness caused the lump in her throat to swell. She swallowed hard and tried to speak, but the memory of the awful encounter with Henry, combined with Chance's gentleness, stole her voice.

"Kathleen?"

She shook her head. Even if her emotions weren't choking her, what could she tell him?

"All right," he said finally, releasing her suddenly. "I'll go ask that good-for-nothing preacher myself. So help me," he vowed as he stepped down off the porch, "if that bastard did anything to hurt you . . ."

She rushed down the steps after him. "Wait!"

His eyes narrowed.

"He—he proposed to me, th-that's all," she lied. "When I refused, we quarreled and I wouldn't let him bring me home."

His jaw was set, his mouth a rigid line, his eyes a deep blue-black. She watched his face, but couldn't judge what effect her words had had on him, or whether he'd believed her.

"Henry proposed?" he asked, his face still an immobile mask.

She drew a quick, sharp breath. "Yes."

"Henry Draper asked you to marry him?"

"I think you heard me the first time," she said, before turning and walking back to the porch swing.

He followed her, striding across the porch, shaking his head as he dropped down beside her. "Well, I'll be," he muttered. "I'll be damned." Suddenly he laughed, a short, dry, mirthless snort.

"What's so funny?"

He shook his head at the thought, obviously too bewildering for him to comprehend. "Why, the idea of you and that sanctimonious son of a—"

"Oh, and I suppose you and that . . . that woman I saw you kissing tonight make a more suitable match?"

"So it was *you* out their spying!"

"I wasn't spying," she snapped. "Who in their right mind would want to watch you fawn all over that . . . woman!"

He stared at her a moment before a slow, insolent grin spread across his handsome face. "Why, partner," he drawled, "I do believe you're jealous."

"Don't flatter yourself, Mr. Ballinger," she shot back indignantly even as the truth of his words stung her.

His eyes danced, and Kathleen's heart sank. If she were made of glass, he couldn't have seen through her more clearly, and she knew it.

Without a word, he rose and reached for her hand, his fingers closing around it firmly as he pulled her to her feet. "In truth, Kathleen," he admitted, "my evening was anything but enjoyable because the only woman I cared to dance with was in the arms of another. But now it seems I've been given another chance. Would you do me the honor of sharing a waltz, Miss McBride?"

Her answer was trapped in her throat and she could only stand staring at him, her heart racing as his eyes held her in an invisible embrace.

But Chance was not so immobilized, and placing one hand at her waist, he took her right hand and placed it on his shoulder and folded her other hand into the warmth of his palm. Slowly they began to move together in a gentle circle around the moonlit porch.

The tune he hummed in a deep, rich baritone seemed hauntingly familiar, and Kathleen's body responded to his graceful movements as though they'd danced together many times before. As though in each other's arms was the most natural place in the world for each of them to be. Did he feel it too? she wondered.

Time hung suspended as they held each other. A silken web seemed to have been spun around them, shutting the world outside, setting them apart from every other living thing. Nothing moved or dared make a sound. The night and all the creatures in it seemed to hold their breath. In all the universe, nothing else existed but the two of them, the moonlight, and the music, and Kathleen longed for this feeling to last forever.

But all too soon their waltz was over, the music ended. He made no move to release her and she didn't pull away. His gaze locked so purposefully, so hungrily, on her mouth that she could almost taste his desire.

She felt her eyelids flutter as her own desire rose. A distant voice begged her to run. Common sense and pride demanded it. But that aching hungry longing for him spoke louder.

His gaze swept her face. His eyes, two indigo diamonds, shone with his passion. His lips hovered over hers for only an instant. "You'll never marry Henry Draper," he promised her.

"What right do you have—" she began, only to have her words cut short when he interrupted.

"I don't," he whispered. "I have no right at all, nothing to give you, nothing to promise, only this . . ." And when his mouth came down on hers, his teeth grazed her lower lip and excitement shook her. As his kiss deepened, her mind reeled, her senses thrumming and vibrating with the pleasure his lips and tongue bestowed upon her.

The feelings and sensations that crashed over her in waves tormented and thrilled her at the same time. Her arms locked around his neck, her lithe body molded against the lean, muscled length of him. His heat radiated around them, penetrated them, igniting and reigniting their mutual passion. When his hands skimmed her breasts, she gasped with pleasure.

When her fingers tangled in the thick, dark mass of his hair, he groaned his approval. He kissed her again and again. And she kissed him back, seeking, exploring, and tasting, following his lead unashamed.

And then without warning, he dragged his lips from hers. "Can Henry . . . can *any* man make you feel this way?"

There was no need for her to answer. Her body, still trembling from his touch, spoke the truth louder than a shouted confession. Cupping her chin, he tilted her face until her eyes met his.

"I want you," he murmured before kissing her once more with such tenderness, she thought her heart might burst. She responded hungrily, but he pulled away from her and held her at arm's length, his gaze traveling over her before finally coming to rest gently on her face. "God knows I do. But as you said, I have no right . . . no right at all."

And then with her heart, her mind, and her senses crying out for more of him, she watched him turn and walk away.

Confusion rocked her. Thrust so suddenly out of his arms, she felt more completely alone than she'd ever thought possible. How could she watch the man she'd fallen helplessly in love with just walk away? But what choice had he given her?

Her thoughts whirled, trying to make sense of his rebuff. Her heart ached, but her pride would not let her run after him.

She reached blindly for the door, and her mind grappled with his words as she stepped numbly inside the cabin. He'd said he wanted her, but he'd said nothing of love. *No right. No right at all.* Scalding tears stung her eyes and scorched her cheeks as she closed the door behind her. His meaning suddenly becoming all too clear: He'd said he wanted her, but it was the woman in blue satin whom he loved. And it was to that other woman that he'd vowed to remain true.

A wrenching sob racked Kathleen's body as she stumbled to her room. Dropping down onto her bed, she reached for a quilt and drew it up around her, burying her face in its softness to muffle her cries. She trembled. Her body and her heart ached. The chill that seeped inside her wrapped its icy fingers around her shattered heart and refused to let go.

It was still dark and the cabin was cold when Kathleen climbed out of bed and stumbled into the next room to build a fire in the hearth. She'd slept little. The bittersweet memories of her moonlight waltz with Chance Ballinger, the taste of his kisses, and finally the shame of her own naked desire swirled around in her mind, taunting and tormenting her, making anything but fitful sleep impossible.

She blew impatiently on the sputtering blue flame before she went outside to the pump to fill the large black coffeepot with water. A small fire was crackling by the time she came back inside.

If she hurried, she'd be out of the cabin before the men came in for breakfast. Facing Chance this morning would be agony. She could only hope to delay the inevitable as long as possible. Perhaps if she busied herself outside all morning, she'd have recovered at least a modicum of poise by the time she was forced to finally see him.

Dressing quickly in a pair of britches and a loose-fitting cotton work shirt, Kathleen twisted her hair into one long braid before laying out a cold breakfast of biscuits, jam, jerky, and cheese. A nip of guilt tugged at her. The men would be putting in a full day's work; the skimpy breakfast wouldn't sustain them for very long. She'd make it up to them at the noon meal, she told herself as she slipped out of the cabin and crossed the yard.

The Hereford cattle were dusky mounds in the somber light of predawn. When she saw a light flickering in the bunkhouse window, Kathleen quickened her pace toward the barn.

"What a coward you are," she scolded herself as she fed and watered the chickens and gathered the eggs.

By the time she'd finished in the barnyard, the sun

was peeking over the mountains and the whole valley was bathed in the soft, pink sunlight of morning. A loud bawling sound pulled Kathleen's attention to the fenced meadow, where several calves lay in the grass sunning themselves. The mother cows were raising quite a fuss.

Kathleen walked toward them, keeping her eyes trained on one cow who was acting particularly strange. The mother's bawling was shrill and constant. As Kathleen moved closer, the cow began to paw frantically at its young. Fearing for the calf's safety, Kathleen slipped between the strands of barbed wire and ran toward the animal, waving her hands and yelling, trying to chase the cow away from the helpless calf.

But the larger animal would not be dissuaded from her frantic pawing until Kathleen picked up a large stick and chased her away. As she approached, she couldn't help wondering why the calf didn't jump up to follow its mother as it should have. A weak, gurgling sound came from deep within the small animal as Kathleen dropped down on her knees beside it. Its large, dark eyes rolled blindly into the back of it head, and in the next moment, the calf stopped breathing.

Kathleen gasped when she looked around and realized that several more of the white-faced calves lay dead or dying around her.

Jumping to her feet, she crossed the meadow at a dead run, searching her mind for an explanation for the dead cattle as she raced toward the cabin. Nothing made sense. A predator would have left some trace of an attack. The calf that she'd watched die had no marks on its small body. No teeth marks or gaping flesh. No bullet wounds.

At the fence, Kathleen's shirt caught and she cursed as she struggled to free herself and felt the barbs scrape across the tender flesh of her back.

"Chance!" she screamed. "Danny! Jeb!"

She was breathless by the time she freed herself and finally reached the porch. Jeb and Chance were emerging from the cabin when she arrived, but her eyes locked on Chance's as he bounded across the porch and down the stairs two at a time to meet her. His face was dark with concern. "For God's sake, Kathleen, what is it? What's happened?"

"Dead!" she gasped, grabbing his arm and dragging him toward the meadow. "Four or five calves, maybe more."

His features set in a grim expression, Chance turned and strode purposefully toward the meadow. She hurried after him, dark dread pounding an ominous warning like a second pulse with every step.

Chapter Fourteen

As Chance approached the first dead animal, its frightened mother bellowed in alarm. For a moment, she looked as though she might charge him, but when he waved his arms and emitted a shrill whistle, she wheeled away to join the rest of the bewildered herd bunched at the far end of the fence line.

He was bent over the small brown-and-white carcass when Kathleen came up beside him. "What was it? A wolf? Coyotes?"

He shook his head as he rose and moved over to a larger calf struggling to get to its feet. Kathleen followed him. As they drew nearer, the animal let out an exhausted sigh and collapsed to the ground, as if its legs had turned to jelly.

Chance crouched down beside the calf and motioned to Kathleen. As he held the dying animal's head between his hands, they watched a stream of blood escape its mouth and form a crimson pool in the damp morning grass.

"What is it, Chance? What's happening?"

He hesitated a moment before answering. "I can't . . . be sure."

"But you have an idea."

He nodded solemnly. "I hope I'm wrong, but it looks like these animals are tick-infested."

Her bewildered eyes posed the question.

"It's a cattle tick that carries a strain of fever."

Kathleen thought a moment. "I remember the stories my father used to tell my brother and me about how the fever nearly destroyed the cattle industry in Texas in the early forties."

Jeb arrived breathless and crouched down beside them. "Good Lord!" he exclaimed.

"It looks like tick fever," Chance said evenly.

"But how . . . how could the cattle have become infected . . . ?" She let the question wilt on her lips as a sickening thought occurred.

Chance's eyes bore into her. He didn't say a word, he didn't have to. A tiny muscle working in his granite jaw told her he knew what she'd been thinking: The Hereford cattle he had insisted would save Twin Rivers were in all probability the carriers of the infestation that could ultimately destroy it.

Kathleen saw his inner agony and her heart turned over. She longed to tell him that she would never place the blame on him, that it didn't matter how the cattle had died, that together they would find a way to survive this latest stroke of bad luck.

If only she could find the words, she would tell him that the pain she'd seen contorting his face as he'd knelt beside the dead calf had finally convinced her, in a way mere words never could, that his heart belonged to Twin Rivers. Somehow the gambler had come to love her home as deeply as she did, and Kathleen finally knew it.

Jeb broke the silence that hung achingly between them. "We'll probably never know how they got infected, missy. It could have happened at the railhead when they were brought in from Kansas. They could have picked it up on the trail when Danny and Chance drove them home. It really doesn't matter now, does it?"

"No," Kathleen answered quietly, her gaze locked meaningfully on Chance's face. "It doesn't matter. To build a herd, you've got to take risks."

Chance's eyes remained unreadable as they bore into hers.

"The problem now," Jeb said, "is that once a herd's infested, the fever spreads like a brushfire."

"Could we lose the Herefords?" she asked.

"We could lose everything," Chance said, unflinching. "The Herefords. The Longhorns. Everything."

Kathleen tasted fear. "Are you sure it's the cattle tick? Could there be some other explanation?"

"We can't be absolutely sure," he admitted. "But I don't know of anything else that hits a herd this hard."

Or with such deadly speed, Kathleen thought. "What can we do?" she asked, her voice rising desperately as the young animal at their feet breathed its last.

"We'll do everything," Chance said, his eyes flinty and his jaw set. "Jeb, have you ever dealt with anything like this before?"

Jeb nodded.

"Then you know what we have to do."

The old man nodded again. "We're in for one hell of a battle, missy," he said, pushing his hat back on his head and running his sleeve across his forehead. "We'll have to wash 'em down, every single head. And not just once, but over and over until we wipe out every last tick and every single egg it leaves behind." He shook his head. "Even then, I'm afraid we're in for some heavy losses."

Chance started for the barn, and Kathleen and Jeb fell in beside him. "We've got to move fast," he said. "First, we'll need to separate the infected animals." He turned to Jeb. "Do you have any arsenic about?"

Jeb nodded. "Your daddy made sure we always had the stuff on hand, missy. He never forgot the infestation in Texas that nearly wiped him out. There's a bottle of the stuff in the tack room," he told Chance. "I'll go get it."

"At least we can be thankful that the Herefords are contained inside the fence in the lower pasture," Kathleen said, after Jeb had left them.

Chance gave her a grateful smile. "Where's your brother? We're going to need all the help we can get if we intend to beat this thing."

The question surprised her. "Wasn't he with you at breakfast?"

Chance shook his head. "The last time I saw him, he was leaving the Social last night around ten. He and Otis Johnston were riding out for Bozeman."

The anger she felt surging through her erupted in a flash of heat across her cheeks. "I'll ride in to town this afternoon and get him."

Chance shook his head. "We can't spare you, and we haven't time to hunt him down. We've got more here than the three of us can handle. When he shows up, we'll put him to work. We're in for a long haul, partner."

"We'll do whatever we have to do," she assured him, echoing his own firm resolve.

"You bet we will," he promised her quietly, slipping his arm around her shoulders. "We damn sure will."

A hundred feet or so from the barn, they came upon another stricken animal. Despite the urgency of the situation, Chance and Kathleen stopped and stood staring down at the lifeless carcass at their feet, each lost in their own private dread.

The stinking black arsenic solution Chance had concocted simmered in a heavy iron pot suspended over an open fire in the southwest corner of the barn. For the last four days, life had taken on a grim sameness, revolving around the gurgling pot and the grueling routine of bathing, doctoring, and dragging the dead animals out of the barn.

The three of them, Jeb, Chance, and Kathleen, had survived the onslaught only by breaking the long days and nights up into shifts. During those brief respites, there had been time for little else but precious sleep. In her fitful dreams, the luxury of a hot soapy bath taunted Kathleen.

Tonight with the acrid odor especially strong, she couldn't help wondering how many baths it would take to rid herself of the noxious smell that seemed to have become a permanent part of her consciousness.

The sun had set hours ago, but Chance and Kathleen worked on into the night. Kathleen's arms ached and the muscles between her shoulders screamed with the accumulated tension and lack of rest as she scrubbed down yet another infected animal.

She glanced over at Chance as he drove a small

heifer through the wooden chutes they'd constructed that first night to drive the treated cattle back into the pasture. The chutes had proven a godsend in keeping the infected and the scrubbed animals separate.

As her arms moved in an automatic scrubbing motion over the docile animal's body, Kathleen watched Chance work. Despite her exhausted physical state, the mere sight of him soothed her overworked senses the way a sudden shower cooled a sweltering summer day.

Through it all, his steady competence and unrelenting confidence had bolstered her when she'd felt her own resolve beginning to wane. A reassuring smile, a cup of hot coffee in the middle of a long watch—all the little ways he'd shown his concern for her had made an indelible mark on her mind and on her heart.

When he turned now, and gave her one of his special grins, his eyes told her he knew she'd been watching him. "How're you doing, partner?" he asked, walking over to her.

She bit back the complaints that hovered at the edge of her mind. He had to feel as bone-tired as she—even more so, for he had carried the brunt of the workload, despite her best effort to keep up with his grueling pace. In the last twenty-four hours she'd begun to wonder if the extent of his stamina and strength was boundless.

"Just . . . about finished," she said as she tipped the bucket up and poured the remaining solution over the animal's back. "I think this fella is ready to join his mama in the pasture for the night."

Chance led the bawling animal to the chute and prodded it through. When he rejoined Kathleen, he ran a hand through his hair and sighed. She followed his gaze as it swept the empty barnyard.

"I think we're getting better at this," he declared wearily.

She stretched her brittle limbs, straightened up, and forced herself to ignore the exhaustion that radiated through her back and legs. "I guess we are at that. It isn't even dawn yet, and we're through for the night." Her chuckle was dry.

He moved around behind her and put his hands on her shoulders and began to gently knead the sore muscles bunched between her shoulder blades.

She closed her eyes and leaned into his soothing touch.

"At least we're making progress," he said.

"Hmm."

"We haven't lost an animal in over twelve hours."

When she turned around to face him, he let his hands slide down her arms. "Do you think it's over, Chance? Do you think we've actually beaten the fever?"

He nodded. "I think we might just have her licked."

She rewarded him with a smile and his heart instantly awoke. Her hair clung to the side of her face in damp swirls. Shadows of exhaustion ringed her eyes. The oversize work shirt she wore knotted at her waist was soiled and torn at one elbow. The soft woolen britches that hugged her gentle curves—so maddeningly well, he'd thought he'd lose his mind—were filthy and covered with grime. She smelled like the barn and the ever-present arsenic solution.

But when she smiled, her emerald eyes shone with a clean, bright spirit that was undaunted.

Through it all, all the dirty, exhausting work of the last four days, she'd held her own, working side by side with Jeb and him, long into the night without a murmur of complaint. He'd watched her eyes each time they'd lose a battle with death and he felt her grief.

"What's the count?" she asked, her question breaking into his tender thoughts of her.

"Twenty-one," he said with a frown. "Counting that little one over there, twenty-two." He motioned to the end of the barn, where an ailing calf was sequestered.

Together they walked toward the stall. Kathleen draped her arms over the top railing and rested her chin on her hands. The calf looked up at her with melancholy eyes.

"Come on, little one," she whispered. "Fight."

Chance stood so close their shoulders touched. "He looks better than he did a few hours ago."

"He does seem a bit stronger, doesn't he?" she agreed cautiously.

"Don't get your hopes up, Kathleen. He's still awfully weak."

But even as Chance spoke, the white-faced calf stretched his neck and let out a long, mournful bawl and began thrashing about in the clean hay, bawling and kicking, attempting to stand.

"Look!" Kathleen exclaimed, her eyes shining.

Chance shook his head and tipped his hat back farther on his head as with one last all-out effort the little animal finally struggled to its feet. Though its legs wobbled and its body trembled, the calf stood, emitting another long triumphant bawl.

"He did it!" Kathleen exclaimed, impulsively throwing her arms around Chance's neck and hugging him.

"He sure did, partner." His arms folded instinctively around her.

"We're not going to lose him," she declared. "He's

the first, Chance. The first one to recover. It's over!" she cried. "It's really over." She hugged him again.

God, had a woman ever felt this good in his arms? She tipped her head back to stare up at him. As always, her chin had a defiant tilt, her eyes a spirited gleam.

He murmured her name and her eyelids fluttered closed seconds before he kissed her. Her lips parted slowly, expectantly, her heart fluttered erratically against his own.

With a moan of desire, he feathered kisses down the long slender column of her neck. She pressed herself against him, her breathless sighs of pleasure stoking the fire of desire already rising to a fever pitch inside him.

The feel of her supple body, the taste of her soft, sweet lips drove him deeper into his passion. He took her hand and led her into the next stall and then lowered her down onto the clean, sweet-smelling hay. She didn't fight him, but clung to him as he eased her down beside him.

He bent over her, his mouth claiming her mouth again and again, branding her with his kisses, claiming her with his desire.

When his lips trailed into the open V of her shirt and between the creamy mounds of her swollen breasts, a whimper of ecstasy escaped her lips. He felt the thrill of pleasure rippling through both of them.

"Chance," she whispered, burrowing her fingers into his thick dark hair. His name was a whispered plea on her lips and he rolled over on top of her, hugging her to him with his muscled thighs. Her body arched up to meet his, and his passion mounted.

"God, how I want you," he moaned as he covered her face and neck with his urgent kisses. He wanted her as he'd wanted no other woman before. All of her. Here and now. Wasn't that really all they had? a desperate voice inside him taunted. Only now.

"And I want only you," she murmured, pressing herself against him.

A shuffling sound and the squeak of hinges as the barn door opened broke through their passion, startling them both back to reality. Chance rose quickly to his feet, tugging the breathless Kathleen up beside him.

The sound of Danny's voice filled the barn as he called out their names.

Kathleen opened her mouth to answer, but Chance touched her lips with a finger as he brushed the hay from their clothes and hair. She smiled at him and he felt his heart tighten.

"Chance, are you in here?" Danny called out again.

He winked at her and dropped a quick kiss on her startled lips before taking her hand and leading her out of the stall.

"Over here," Kathleen called out, fighting to make her voice steady. "We're over here, Danny."

At the sight of her brother's face, gaunt under a heavy growth of beard stubble, Kathleen gasped. "Danny!" she cried.

Chance only nodded, and Danny returned his greeting with a sheepish smile.

"Where have you been?" Kathleen demanded. "What happened to you? I—I was so worried," she cried as she rushed over to him and gave him a quick hug. "I thought maybe something had happened—" The strong smell of whiskey nearly overpowered her, and she swallowed the rest of her words and drew away from him quickly.

Danny lowered his eyes and shrugged. "After the

Social, I—I decided to spend some . . . time in town,"
he stammered.

For a long moment no one spoke. Kathleen drew a
deep breath. "You decided to spend some time in
town?" she repeated slowly. "Nearly a week in town,"
she said again, her voice rising. "While we were here
struggling to save our livelihood, save our home, you
'spent some time in town.'" She knew her voice had
grown harsh and that her words echoed the bitter disappointment that flooded her heart and erupted in her
eyes.

"Oh, Danny," she cried. "How could you?" Her
voice cracked. "You don't care about this ranch. You
don't care about your family. You just don't care about
anything, do you?"

Danny opened his mouth to reply, but seemed unable to find the words. He lowered his eyes and hung
his head.

She turned on him. "Pack your bags, Danny." Her
whole body trembled with the anger and betrayal she
felt churning inside her. "You don't belong here anymore."

"Kathleen!" Danny gasped. "You—you don't mean
that."

"Get out," she whispered savagely, turning her back
on him. The mental burden of the last four days, the
long hours of worry, work, and exhaustion had finally
caused her frazzled nerves to snap.

"I'm sorry," Danny began. "Kathleen. Truly. I didn't
know what was going on here. How could I have
known? I should have come home, I know that. I don't
know what got hold of me . . ."

"Cheap whiskey," she spat out. "And cheaper
women, probably."

"But you gotta listen," Danny pleaded. "You can't just throw me out. Th-this is my home."

"Was!" Kathleen shouted. "Was your home." The anger compounded with her disappointment threatened to overwhelm her.

"But it's not my fault the cattle got sick," Danny whined.

His words had the effect of kerosene on an open flame. "Not your fault?" she gasped. "It's all your fault! Why, if not for you, we wouldn't be in this mess in the first place. If not for you, the McBrides would still own Twin Rivers outright!" Her words exploded like buckshot into the air before she could stop them. And one look at Chance told her who'd been hardest hit.

Exasperated, desperate to escape an impossible situation she'd just made worse, she whirled around and ran for the door.

"Kathleen." The sound of Chance's voice reverberated across the barn, and she stopped but didn't turn around. She couldn't face him.

"Wait," he ordered. "Danny, you take watch over the herd until dawn."

If he'd kicked her or slapped her, Kathleen couldn't have been more shocked. She spun around to face him as he moved up beside her. His dark eyes pinned her where she stood.

Her anger made her cheeks burn like a thousand stinging needles. "I told you to leave, Danny," she said, her eyes still riveted on Chance. "And I meant it."

Chance glared back at her, his expression ominous. "Don't, Kathleen," he warned. "You don't know what you're doing."

"I know what I have to do."

"Don't do this," he ordered, his voice gruff.

Her pride and her eyes stung, a burning lump lodged in her throat. "This is a family matter. Between my brother and me."

"Danny," Chance said without blinking, "get out to the meadow. If any animals go down, get them into the barn immediately. I'll be out to spell you in a few hours."

"Yes—yes sir," Danny stammered as he rushed past them out of the barn.

When Kathleen started after him, Chance grabbed her arm. She tried to jerk free, but he held her fast.

"Let him go," he ordered.

"Danny!"

"I said, let him go."

"This is none of your affair."

"But it is. Danny's my employee."

"He's my brother."

"I say he stays. You just reminded all of us that I'm half owner of this outfit and I'm giving an order. He stays."

She felt his anger radiating in hot waves, scalding her with the heat.

"He stays, damn it," he growled again. "Don't push me, Kathleen."

The instinct to protect herself took over and she raised her hand to strike back before she knew what she was doing, but before her hand could connect with his cheek, he caught her wrist in midair. A strange mixture of longing and fear quivered through her, shaking her to the foundation of her being.

"How dare you manhandle me!" she growled through clenched teeth.

"Perhaps it's time you realized just which one of us *is* the man, partner," he admonished her, his voice rough, his chest heaving with his pent-up rage.

"You bastard," she hissed, the tears springing to her eyes.

For a long trembling moment they continued to glare at each other before she jerked away from him, and nearly stumbling, ran past him out of the barn.

And as she disappeared into the darkness, Chance stood and watched her go, and wondered if he'd ever felt more alone.

Chapter Fifteen

———◆———

A small cabin, constructed of rough-hewn pine and surrounded by a small stand of scraggly pines, sat directly behind and a hundred feet west of the Community Church. The church was the last building in town beyond the livery.

Though empty now, on Sunday mornings and Wednesday evenings the large clapboard structure housed the devoted flock who had, two summers ago, donated the materials and the labor to build the cabin. The rectory, as Henry preferred to call it, had been built on the small plot of land that separated the church from the cemetery. A well-worn footpath that had previously led to the graveyard, now led directly to Henry Draper's front door.

Through the window he saw her approaching on that path. Opening the door a scant inch, he anticipated her arrival as his nervous eyes scanned the darkened churchyard. It was late, long past the time for a proper social call. But Henry knew that the woman dressed in faded satin whom he ushered through his door was no casual caller.

Another darted glance satisfied him that she was alone, and that no one had observed her arrival. He closed the door behind her and bolted it.

"Nice place you got here, Henry," she said with an approving smile.

He accepted her compliment without comment.

"Aren't you even gonna ask me to sit down?"

Henry offered her the straight-backed chair at the table in the center of the room.

She shrugged out of the fringed black shawl that draped her pale shoulders and sat down. The room was hot and shadowy, the fire raging in the hearth providing the only light.

As the shadows played across Henry's face, he appeared strangely menacing. Despite the temperature of the room Rubylee felt chilled and uneasy, but quickly chided herself for her uncharacteristic nervousness— this was no time for her to lose her nerve, she warned herself. She had little money left and less time. She needed to grab the chance she'd been given.

"Aren't you going to offer me a drink? Maybe you've got a bottle of that southern bourbon you used to be so fond of?"

He shook his head, scowling at her. "I am a man of the cloth now," he informed her tersely. "I no longer partake of spirits."

"But in Virginia City . . . you used to love a good—" His pointed glare brought her reminiscing to a halt. "Oh, come on, Henry. What's so sinful about a little drink now and then?" she asked playfully. "If I remember my catechisms, there was a good deal of partakin' goin' on in the good book."

Henry studied her face. The layers of powder and rouge had been applied with a heavy hand, but they still couldn't hide the lines around her eyes and mouth. How odd. In his mind's eye, he remembered Rubylee Tyler as younger and more attractive. Though he'd known her for the better part of four years, it felt like he was viewing her now for the very first time.

She had been pretty once, hadn't she? Or had she always looked so frayed? Had the whiskey they'd consumed in generous portions whenever they were together altered his perception of her that drastically?

"Miss Tyler . . ." he began.

She winced as though he'd cursed her. "Miss Tyler! It's just plain ole Rubylee, don't you remember, honey?" Her lower lip jutted. "Why, don't you remember how you used to call me your precious gem, your own sweet little Ruby?"

At the mention of their previous intimacy, Henry felt a familiar gnawing in the pit of his stomach. It had been more than the whiskey that had altered his perceptions of Miss Rubylee Tyler on those long, sultry nights in her dingy room above Bummer Dan's saloon.

A wistful smile played across her rouged lips, and he knew she shared his memories. Striding impatiently to the window, he pushed the curtains back and peered out into the church's deserted backyard. He'd taken a risk by responding to the message she'd left for him in the collection plate last Sunday. But if she'd brought with her the damning evidence against Chance Ballinger that she claimed to possess, Henry's actions had been well worth the risk.

Besides, it was nothing compared to the risk he'd run dealing with those lowlife cowhands out of Texas, the ones who, for a price, had agreed to drive a half-dozen tick-infested Longhorns onto Twin Rivers's lower pasture.

"Did you bring the letter with you?" he asked.

"Uh-huh, sure did. Just like I promised," she said, smiling. "Now, come on, honey." She patted the seat of the chair next to hers. "Come, sit down. Relax. Why, you're as jumpy as a colt. You needn't be so skittish around me, Henry. I'm no different than I ever was, no different from them other little gals you're so fond of talking to after services on Sunday." Her lashes fluttered demurely, and she leaned forward, revealing the deep cleavage barely contained by the scalloped neckline of her faded red dress.

Henry felt the gnawing in his stomach creep lower. "Oh, but you're wrong, Rubylee," he murmured as he eased himself down into the chair next to her and slipped his arm around her shoulders. "You're nothing like those other women. Nothing at all."

She giggled under his compliment.

"They're mere children, Rubylee. But you are a desirable woman, a woman who knows how to give a man pleasure," he murmured in her ear, feeling his need for her building.

"Why, Reverend," she teased, "I hardly know what to say. I never heard a man of the cloth go on about such things."

"You know what I need," he whispered gruffly, taking her hand and bringing it slowly to his lips.

She smiled again and her small eyes flickered with obvious delight. "Now that's more like the Henry Draper I remember."

"What do you say we attend to business before we indulge in our pleasure?"

"Why, Pastor Draper!" she protested in feigned indignation, "whatever are you implying? Lord knows I only came here with the most honorable of intentions."

Henry saw her tighten her grip on her small velvet handbag.

"I'm just doin' my civic duty by coming here. We can't have criminals running about the territory, now can we?"

Henry shook his head and smiled. "No, we surely can't. Where is the letter? Did you bring it with you, Rubylee?"

"Well, I—I . . . no," she said, shaking her head.

His gut told him she was lying. "But you told me a moment ago that you had. Now, where is it?"

"Wouldn't you like to know?" she teased.

He grabbed her hand and squeezed it hard. "Yes, I would like to know. And you're going to tell me, aren't you, Rubylee?" Still holding her hand, he rose and, with his eyes locked on hers, led her into the small dark bedroom.

"Well, I just might tell you at that," she teased, smiling coyly as he pushed her down onto the edge of the bed, "if you . . . promise to treat me right."

Henry's voice was a low growl. "And just how does one 'treat you right,' Rubylee?"

She flashed him a knowing smile as she reached for his hand and drew him down beside her. He slipped his arm around her waist and pulled her roughly to him.

"You know what I want, Henry," she purred as she pressed herself against him. "And in a way I think we both want the same things: respectability, a little appreciation." Her smile was sly. "And money. The rest of it isn't all that gratifyin', now is it, luv, when you're livin' like some poor little ole church mouse?"

He released her abruptly. "How much do you want, Rubylee?"

"I don't know exactly. I'm tryin' to start a business, and I'm not sure how much I'll need. Let's see, there's the fixtures and the equipment . . . oh, and I'll need to hire me a seamstress—"

"How much?"

She dropped all pretense of coyness. "I want a husband, Henry."

He felt the blood drain from his face. "You're crazy."

Her laugh was a sharp bark. "Maybe. But you're just as crazy to get your hands on that ranch and the little gal who owns it, aren't you, Henry? So maybe you shouldn't be so quick to throw stones."

He grabbed her again, this time much less gently. She tried to jerk away, but his mouth ground down on hers and he jammed his tongue against her lips to part them. She struggled as his mouth moved lower, his breath coming in hot gasps against her breasts as he fumbled with the row of tiny buttons that lined the bodice of her dress.

Finally wrenching free, she gasped, "I came to Bozeman City for a new start, Reverend. So mind your manners." Her face was flushed and she was breathless. "Finding that letter in Virginia City after Chance Ballinger rode out, it was my ticket out." She shrugged away from him. "And you ain't gonna ruin it for me, Henry. I'm not one of Bummer Dan's girls anymore."

He glared at her.

"Henry?" she asked breathlessly. "Are you listening to me?"

"How much do you want, Rubylee?" he asked again.

"It isn't money, damn it. Aren't you listening? I want

more than money. I want—I need a new start, a new life."

He stood, straightening his shirt and adjusting his cuffs. "If the letter gets me what I want, you'll get your share," he said coldly.

She followed him into the front room. "That isn't good enough, Henry. I want it all. I want the life I never had." Her eyes filled with bright tears as she took an uncertain step toward him. "And you could give me that, Henry," she said softly. "Don't you see? You could give me that respectability, that appreciation."

His smile was chilling.

"I'd be good to you. You know I would," she insisted. "It's a fair exchange, isn't it?" she prodded. "I know your plans, Henry," she whispered, "and I have what you need to see them through. If you take that letter to the sheriff, it will take care of Chance Ballinger forever. You can force the McBride woman off Twin Rivers and then buy up that land for a song for yourself. That *is* what you want, isn't it, Henry? All that preachin' about cleanin' up the territory, ridding it of criminals, is all so much crap and we both know it."

He stared at her unblinking, his mouth a hard set line.

"I'll make you a good wife, Henry," she insisted, reaching for him and moving cautiously into his arms. "I swear I will."

He stared at her a long moment, unblinking, before he burst out laughing. "Wife! You? My wife?" he blurted. "Rubylee Tyler a preacher's wife? Are you out of your mind?" His cruel laughter followed him as he abruptly shoved her away from him, and stalked across the room.

She rushed after him, feeling shaken and desperate

and humiliated. Things weren't going at all the way
she'd planned. Only a few moments ago Henry had
been feverish with his desire for her. Though the stakes
had never been this high, she'd always been able to ply
him with her body before. But somehow he'd grown
immune to her powers, and his cool indifference and
deadly calm frightened her.

Henry opened the door. "Get out, Rubylee."

"Wait!" she protested. "You can't do this to me. I
still have the letter, you know."

He smiled maliciously. "Had the letter," he corrected, as he tossed her the velvet handbag.

"Give it back!" she screeched as she lunged at him.
"That letter doesn't belong to you! You told me you'd
pay. You said you'd take care of me."

"Get out, whore," he said again, "or I'll give you
nothing but the back of my hand."

"Liar!" she screamed. "Liar and fraud! Just you wait
till your congregation gets wind of what kind of man
the real Henry Draper is. They won't be so anxious to
build you that fancy new church, now will they,
preacher?"

As she tried to rush past him out of the cabin, he
grabbed her arm. Twisting it behind her back, he
hauled her up against him and closed the door. "Don't
threaten me, Rubylee," he snarled. The murderous
glint in his eyes sent tremors of desperation reverberating through her.

"Come on, Henry," she urged, trying to wriggle free
of his steely grip. "We don't have to go on this way.
We c-can come to . . . some kind of agreement, can't
we? I won't press you. You're—you're right. You
couldn't marry me. But it's only fair that I get a little
something for my trouble, now ain't it?"

Henry tightened his grip on her arm and glared at her a long, dangerous moment before his expression suddenly softened and he nodded slowly. "Yes. I suppose you do deserve something for your trouble." He relinquished his grip so suddenly that she had to grab for the table as she stumbled backward to keep from falling. "I'll see what I can do after I've delivered this document to the proper authorities."

Rubylee saw her hopes fading into the dark depths of his lying eyes. "But you said you'd pay. Damn you, Henry, you said you'd pay! If I'd known you were going to double-cross me, I'd have pressed Ballinger harder. Damn it, he'd have paid good money for the information in that letter. Good money."

"I'll see you home now, Miss Tyler." Henry picked up her shawl, but she snatched it away from him.

"Give me back that damn letter," she demanded. She reached for his pocket and he slapped her hard. Grabbing her by the upper arm, he hauled her back to the door.

His fingers dug painfully into her flesh. "I said I'd see you home, Rubylee. Now come along. Don't be a fool."

Rubylee tasted blood on her lips where he'd struck her. She struggled against his grip when he dragged her outside.

"Let go," she cried as he pulled her across the yard toward the small cemetery behind the church. "Let go. You're hurting me, Henry. Who do you think you are, treating a lady in such a rude manner?"

Henry tightened his grip, and she winced in pain. "Oh, excuse me, Miss Tyler," he mocked with exaggerated deference.

When she reared back to slap him, he blocked her blow and drove his fist hard into her stomach.

The eerie light blazing in his eyes as he bent over her sent a chill of raw terror slashing through her. "All right. All right. F-forget the—the l-letter," she gasped, struggling to catch her breath. "Do—do whatever you like with it. I don't care anymore. I won't say anything to anyone. I p-promise, Henry. Just . . . just let me be."

When he hit her again, her ears rang and blood gushed from her lip. "Please," she pleaded, staring up at him through startled, terror-filled eyes. "P-please just let me go."

He fell on her, clamping his hand over her mouth. "It's too late," he hissed, his face inches from hers. "No one threatens me or blackmails me. No one, do you hear? I get what I want."

As she struggled beneath him, his hand slid up to her throat. Her eyes bulged as his fingers tightened around the fleshy column. She tried to fight him, struggling with every ounce of energy she possessed, but her efforts were futile.

"No!" Her desperate plea was lost in the sigh of the night wind.

Even after her body went limp, Henry exerted steady pressure on her jugular until he felt it collapse under his hand. His heart pounded with a rush of electric excitement when he saw the startled last expression in her eyes. The power he held over life and death exhilarated him.

This wanton woman had demanded her fair share and she had received it. Just as others who tried to stand in his way would always get what was coming to them, he reminded himself.

He fetched a shovel from the cabin and hurried back

to the cemetery. As the spade bit into the cool, moist earth, Henry felt another rush of power surge through his veins. Ballinger would pay, Rubylee had said.

"Oh, yes," Henry whispered to the woman as he rolled her inert body into the shallow grave that would be her eternal home. "You were quite right, my greedy little gem. Ballinger *will* pay. And soon."

By the time Kathleen reached the cabin, her tears had subsided and she was left with an inner ache that hurt all the way to the bone. It wasn't his interference with Danny, or even his anger that lingered and stung, but his implication that she'd tried to usurp his manhood. Did that make her less than a real woman in his eyes, she wondered.

Was that the real reason he'd left her on the porch the night of the Spring Social and why he'd given his heart to the woman in blue satin—a real woman. A woman who hadn't been forced to live in a man's world, take on the responsibilities and duties of a man, a woman who hadn't had to risk everything for her pride and for her land. Her precious land.

But at what price had she purchased that pride and what was the final cost of her legacy, she asked herself bitterly. What terrible price? A life alone? The title of old maid?

He'd said he wanted her. The words that had made her feel as though her heart would burst with joy, now came back to mock her. He wanted her. But he didn't love her. He would bed her, but he'd never ask her to be his wife.

The old maid of Twin Rivers. She had indeed earned that title, she admitted to herself miserably, for she'd given her heart to a man whom she'd never marry.

And tonight, before Danny had interrupted them, she'd been ready to give him everything else—her body and her soul. He'd laid his brand to her as surely as he had the Hereford cattle they'd struggled so hard to save.

Oh, how could she hate him and love him so fiercely at the same time? she agonized as she slumped down onto her bed, hugging the pillow to her aching breasts.

As her tears flowed silently, bitterly, she swore she would get even with him if it was the last thing she ever did. Unbidden, the memory of his touch came back to her and she bolted upright. A dark fantasy for revenge swirled out of the depths of her battered pride and left her breathless.

She would go to him, she thought, beg his forgiveness, and then seduce him into her arms. She remembered the power her kisses had had over his body, and her dangerous fantasy came into sharper focus.

She could almost see herself tempting, taunting, and arousing him. She could almost taste his desire. And then, at the peak of his passion, she would scorn him, turn her back on him, belittle and betray him as she felt he'd betrayed her tonight. She'd mock him, she told herself, and leave him burning with his thwarted desire for her, even as her own body burned for his now.

Kathleen trembled at the thought of Chance's arms around her again and she knew her fantasy was only that, a fantasy that she couldn't, wouldn't, ever bring to reality. In his arms, she knew she'd be as helpless against the forces of her own mutinous emotions as she wished to render him.

Lighting a single candle, Kathleen undressed and washed quickly at the basin beside her bed. The cold water sent a fresh wave of loneliness sliding through her. Peering into the darkness beyond the window, she saw her own reflection, but she thought about Chance and her brother and her life and quiet tears of regret stung her eyes again.

She slipped into bed numbly, shaken. And long moments later, cursing herself for her cowardice and Chance Ballinger for his heartlessness, she cried herself into an exhausted sleep.

She wasn't sure what woke her, but when she heard the scuffing sound coming from the front door, she bolted upright in bed and sat holding her breath, listening. "Danny?" she called out tentatively. "Danny, is that you?"

The dark beyond her door was filled with silence. "Gideon," she whispered. "Did you hear that?" The large yellow cat sleeping at the foot of her bed raised his head and eyed her speculatively before going back to sleep.

Another sound penetrated the silence and Kathleen reached for the shotgun under the bed and tiptoed cautiously into the next room.

The cabin door was standing open. The murky light of predawn filtered in where a figure lay facedown and deathly still in the doorway. Kathleen gasped as an icy dread seized her. "Chance!" she screamed.

Her heart thudded, sending the blood and adrenaline coursing through her with such force she felt lightheaded. She dropped down beside him and carefully grasping his shoulders, turned him over so that his head came to rest in her lap.

A whimper of unconscious pain escaped his lips. His breath came in slow ragged gasps and his body quaked.

Panic welled inside her when she touched his face and realized he was drenched in his own sweat.

Easing his weight off her lap, she jumped up and ran out the door, racing through the uncertain early light for help. At the bunkhouse door, she pounded and yelled for Danny or Jeb.

In a few moments, Jeb's startled face appeared in the doorway. Grabbing his hand, Kathleen ran, pulling him with her back to the cabin.

Chance hadn't moved. "He's burning with fever," she cried as she sank down beside him once more. "Help me get him out of the draft and into the bedroom."

Jeb bent over and brought his arms up under Chance's. "Grab his feet, missy."

"He's a big man, ain't he," he groaned as together they half carried, half dragged Chance into the bedroom. With strength born of desperation, they lifted him onto the bed.

"What is it, Jeb?" Kathleen asked as she fought to steady her hands to light the oil lamp beside the bed.

Jeb frowned. "I'm not rightly sure, missy. The concoction he brewed up for the cattle packs a powerful wallop. Yesterday I got a snoutful of the stuff and almost keeled over myself. Could be he just inhaled a mite too much of the stuff."

Kathleen stared down at Chance as the lamplight sent flickering shadows across his ashen face. She remembered how he had insisted on being the only one to handle the arsenic mixture. Only after it had been diluted and portioned out in buckets would he allow Jeb and her to use it to wash down the cattle. Even then, Chance had cautioned them to avoid breathing the stuff and to keep the doors in the barn open to ensure ventilation as they worked to save the cattle.

"We've got to get him out of these wet clothes," Kathleen murmured as she worked to unbutton the vest Chance wore over his sodden shirt. "I saved some of Pa's things . . . in a trunk in the loft. Would you go get them, Jeb?"

Kathleen managed to remove his vest and drop it onto the chair by the side of the bed as Jeb moved quietly out of the room.

She started to unbutton Chance's shirt when he stirred suddenly and startled her. His eyes flickered open and he stared up at her with glazed and unseeing eyes. His breath came in gasps and the frightened confusion staring out at her from the fathomless blue depths of his eyes caused Kathleen's heart to swell.

Instinctively, she stroked his forehead and whispered, "Chance, I'm here. You're going to be all right."

Whether he heard her promises, she couldn't be sure, but in a moment his eyes drifted closed again, and his breathing became less labored. He flinched again but did not awaken when Kathleen tried to pull his arm out of his shirtsleeve. Was he in physical pain? Or had his sudden movement come from some inner pain, some pain of the soul that his unconscious state had forced him to confront?

When he lapsed into ominous stillness again, Kathleen worked quickly to remove his shirt. Beneath his clothes, his golden skin glistened with fever. She remembered how she'd seen his naked chest that first day he'd staked his claim on her ranch.

A wistful smile touched her lips now as her eyes took in the sight of him again. His was a powerful body, lean and muscled, bearing not an ounce of fat. His skin and the springy mat of dark hair that dusted it glistened just as it had when he'd stood that day at the pump. Her gaze flicked over him for another instant before she covered him with a blanket.

As she struggled to remove his boots, Jeb came back into the room carrying a bundle of clothes. After setting them down at the foot of the bed, he laid a gentle hand on her shoulder. "I'll see to the rest, missy," he said quietly. "Why don't you put some water on to boil. If we can get something hot down him, maybe we can sweat the fever out."

When she hesitated a moment at the door, Jeb gave her a kindly smile. "Go on," he prodded. "You can take over just as soon as I get him decent."

Kathleen felt the color flood her face. The urgency of the situation had caused her to forget all propriety. "Thank you, Jeb," she said softly as she left the room.

What would her old friend think if he knew how intimate she'd already been with the fever-ridden gambler who now lay helpless in her bed? Kathleen shook off her guilty speculations and stoked a fire from the embers banked in the iron stove.

Her hands shook as she filled the large black kettle with water and set it atop the stove as Jeb had instructed. Pulling a chair into the kitchen, Kathleen climbed up onto it in order to reach the top shelf of the small narrow pantry.

After a moment, she found what she was looking for, a small tin filled with a rich, dark powdery substance. Her mother had learned from an Indian woman in Bannack how to make the dark medicinal tea that, if it did not cure outright, seemed to ease the symptoms brought on by any number of ailments. Kathleen re-

membered her mother administering steaming cups of
the brew to her family for everything from croup to
dog bites.

She pried the lid open and glanced inside. The tin
was half empty. She sighed and chided herself for
never having learned her mother's recipe. Perhaps Jeb
knew the proper ingredients, which, Kathleen guessed
by sniffing, included a heavy portion of chamomile and
mint.

As Kathleen mixed the tea, Jeb appeared in the bedroom doorway, his expression grim.

Kathleen swallowed her dread. "What is it? Is he
worse?"

Jeb shook his head. " 'Bout the same, which is none
too good. He's a mighty sick man, missy."

"But he's a mighty strong man as well," she declared
with a defiant tilt of her chin as she busied herself
setting the tea and two clean towels onto a tray.
"Would you bring me a bucket of springwater, Jeb?"

He nodded. "I'll feed the fire," he added. "When his
fever breaks, he's likely to be chilled to the bone."

Kathleen accepted his optimism with a faint smile,
as he gave her shoulder a reassuring squeeze before he
left.

A muffled mewing sound drew Kathleen's attention
to Gideon, who was staring out with his one good eye
from beneath the pile of Chance's discarded clothing.

"Don't worry, my friend. He'll be all right," she declared. *He will recover. He will,* her desperate mind
insisted.

She couldn't lose him, not like this, not with the
memory of their angry words still torturing her mind
and searing her heart. Chance Ballinger would never
be her husband, she knew that now. He didn't love her,

and he probably never would. The man was a drifter. A gambler. Soon, she would figure out a way to buy him out. And when she did, the tenuous ties that bound them would be broken, as logic told her they must.

But he was the only man she'd ever loved, the one man who had captured her heart. And for that reason and that reason alone, she'd walk through hell and wade high water before she let him die!

Chapter Sixteen

———◆———

CHANCE's fever ran high throughout the long, torturous next day and late into the next night. Kathleen bathed his body with cool springwater when his
fever raged and bundled him with blankets when his
body quaked with chills.

When he thrashed violently, Kathleen covered him
with her own body and soothed and whispered her re-
assurances until he slid back into his own solitary darkness. The tea, which she administered one careful
spoonful at a time so as not to choke him, seemed to
be slowly working.

Jeb checked in regularly to refill the water bucket,
bring fresh towels and a cup of coffee and food to
Kathleen. He seemed to sense her need to stand vigil
at her partner's bedside, and he did not try to dissuade
her.

Though she'd seen him in the meadow from the window, Danny had not come into the house since that
dreadful night in the barn when she'd ordered him off

the ranch. Her angry words, words of exhaustion and anger, came back to haunt her during the long hours at Chance's bedside.

She'd never meant to hurt Danny, to hurt anyone, her only thought had been the welfare of her family's legacy. Had that been so wrong?

Her questions were her constant companions as she sat hour after hour beside the unconscious man who lay in her bed. At times he would moan or mumble, but Kathleen could never make out his words.

Just after dawn on the third day as Kathleen dozed in the chair beside the bed, his sudden shout jolted her to her feet. His eyes were closed, his face twisted in pain, as he rolled his head from side to side against the pillow, muttering and moaning. She touched his cheek and found his fever had subsided a bit, and she allowed herself a measure of cautious relief.

"No," he moaned again, his glazed eyes open but unseeing. "James!" He called out the name like a warning. "No! No!" he cried, struggling against the bed-clothes to sit up. Kathleen leaned over him, placing her hands firmly on his shoulders.

"It's all right," she assured him, easing his fevered body back onto the pillows. When he looked up at her, it was with the eyes of a confused child.

"I'm sorry," he moaned, his face contorted with regret. "Forgive me, James. I didn't know."

Her heart ached to give him the absolution for which he pleaded. "It's all right," she told him again as she bathed his forehead with a cool cloth.

Though his eyes were open and his gaze was locked on her face, his haunted expression and the sudden tears that filled his eyes told her he was locked in his

own private hell, and that she had caught only a
glimpse of his terrible inner pain.

The darkness lifted gradually. Through the heavy veil
that shrouded his senses he caught glimpses of the tangible world, the world from which he'd felt strangely
separated for how long he could only guess. A moment? A day? An endless eternity of time filled with
half-remembered nightmares and tantalizing dreams of
home, of Texas, of murder and of moonlit waltzes.

His limbs felt leaden, his skin dry and prickly. Every
time he tried to open his eyes, a scorching pain in his
head jerked him back into a dizzying darkness from
which he longed to escape.

Where was he? And what the hell had happened to
him? Over the smell of a candle burning, he detected
the delicate scent of lilac, and a longing to see Kathleen's face again, to kiss her lips, consumed him. A
desperate and helpless longing pulled at him as he hovered somewhere between fantasy and reality.

Cool fingertips feathered across his brow, their familiar touch tugging him closer to the light. He inhaled
a ragged breath. He could almost taste the gentle scent
of her, feel her satin skin beneath his fingertips. God,
how he wanted to touch her again!

When he opened his eyes, she was bending over him,
smiling gently. His apparition, his auburn-haired angel.
He'd come home to her at last.

"Kathleen?" His voice was little more than a dusty
whisper, his throat had never felt more desperately
parched and sore.

She brought his hand to her lips and kissed it.
"Thank you, Lord," she whispered, her eyes fluttering

closed. "You're back," she cried. "Oh, Chance, you've come back to us."

At the sight of her, his shadowy past became a distant dream, and his future only her. His love for her drummed through him, a living presence. And in that moment, he knew beyond all doubt that she loved him as well.

But could this woman, this extraordinary woman whose joyful tears flowed unashamedly down her lovely cheeks, become his future?

With the hand she still held, he pulled her down beside him. His arms felt weak and heavy, but when he wrapped them around her and felt her nestle against him, the joy that filled his soul gave his body an unexpected strength.

With her in his arms, there was nothing he couldn't do, no obstacle he couldn't overcome. Wherever she was, was home.

Two days later when Kathleen carried the tray into the bedroom, she cringed as the color drained from Chance's face when he scooted to a sitting position in the bed. He had regained his strength with surprising speed. And although his fever had not returned, Kathleen feared a setback.

She'd told him as much when he'd awakened this morning, demanding his clothes, insisting that he felt fully recovered and ready to return to work. Despite her best arguments, she hadn't been able to convince him to rest even one more day. He had, however, agreed to stay in bed a little longer this morning and let her bring him one last breakfast.

She held the tray out to him now. "Are you all right, Chance?"

"Never felt better," he declared. The conviction in his voice didn't quite reach his eyes. "And judging by the tempting smells coming from that tray, I'd say I'm going to feel even better after I've downed a couple of those biscuits and half a dozen strips of bacon. Lord, but I'm ready for some real food."

"Drink this first," she ordered, handing him a cup.

"Aw, partner," he groaned, waving the cup away. "A man needs coffee in the morning. Black coffee, strong and hot. And lots of it. I swear if I didn't know better, I'd think you were trying to poison me again with that damned swamp water."

She pressed the cup into his hand. "That *swamp water* as you call it, may very well have saved your life, Chance Ballinger. Now stop being childish and drink it."

He stared down at the pale amber liquid and made a gruesome face.

"No tea, no breakfast," she warned, picking up the tray and heading for the door.

"All right. All right. I know when I'm beaten." Tipping the cup, he drained the contents in one noisy gulp. "Satisfied?" He grimaced.

She smiled and handed him the tray. He set it down and reached for her hands.

"Jeb says *you* saved my life."

"Jeb exaggerates." She smiled, her skin tingling at his touch.

"Ah, but I know better. I felt you there beside me, through the fever and the pain. I remember you standing there looking like you did the first time I saw you, like an angel."

She felt the color rise to her cheeks and quickly slid her hands from beneath his. "Eat your breakfast," she said quietly as she turned to leave.

He shifted the tray to the other side of the bed and reached out and caught her hand before she could leave, pulling her back to the bedside. "It was like I was falling, Kathleen, sliding deeper and deeper into some bottomless ravine. I couldn't stop myself.

"When the darkness closed around me, it was an endless tunnel. I thought I was dying. I knew I was. And there wasn't one blessed thing I could do to save myself." His voice was low, his expression pained as he relived his fever-induced nightmares.

"Then I'd feel the touch of your hands, cool and healing on my body." He sighed. "And I'd awaken just long enough to see you there, to sense your presence beside me. You gave me the strength to fight back."

A stubborn lump lodged in her throat.

"I couldn't leave you, Kathleen," he murmured, squeezing her hand gently. "We belong together, you and I."

As he pulled her down beside him, a wave of desire curled inside her. But instinctively she held back, stiffening when he tried to nestle her against him.

"You're remembering the night I fell ill," he said, his voice somber. "The argument we had in the barn when Danny came home." He lifted her chin so that she had to face him. "But you must know by now, that all those things we said to each other didn't amount to anything. We can't let those words come between us now, Kathleen," he beseeched her. "You've forgiven me, as surely as I've already forgiven you, isn't that right?"

She felt the heat of his steady scrutiny on her face.

"And you want me, Kathleen," he said quietly. "You love me as much as I love you."

She shook her head, refusing to believe.

"But I do love you, Kathleen," he whispered as he pulled her to him again. "Now tell me, tell me how you feel. Tell me that you love me too."

The dam of her emotions burst all at once. "Oh, I do love you, Chance," she cried. "Heaven help me, I do. When I thought I'd lost you—" Her voice broke and he kissed her.

"Kathleen," he whispered. "My proud and beautiful Kathleen. There are so many . . . things I have to tell you, things you should know."

"Tell me about James, first," she said softly. Though his arms were still wrapped around her, she sensed him withdrawing. "You called out his name in your sleep."

He studied her face intently as he spoke. "James was my older brother. What else did I say?" he demanded. "You have to tell me, Kathleen."

"You asked for forgiveness," she said quietly. "And you called out the names James, Jim, and Callie. Who are they, Chance? Why do you need their forgiveness?"

She watched his eyes grow darker, as though the shadow of his past was enveloping him. He reached for her again.

"Tell me," she said again. "Who is Callie?"

"Callie," he whispered, more to himself than to her.

Kathleen sat up stiffly on the side of the bed, her hands clasped in her lap, bracing herself for his answer. Was Callie an old love from his past? Was Callie the woman in blue satin?

He shifted in the bed so that he was propped up on one elbow. "I was dreaming of Callie. I dreamed she was here. I remember now."

Kathleen held her breath. "Who is she? Chance, please tell me. I have to know."

"Callie is a young lady from Texas," he said with a tender smile. "A little gal I love very much."

"You love her?" she asked, her voice a hoarse whisper.

"I do," he admitted. "I love Callie May Ballinger with all my heart."

"Callie May Ballinger?" she choked, an unthinkable reality jolting through her with lightning speed. *Dear God, she'd fallen in love with a married man!* "Your w-wife?" she stammered.

Chance took her hand and cradled it between both of his. "Kathleen, Callie May is my niece," he explained softly. "My brother's child. Callie and her brother, Jim Jr., live with their grandmother in Texas."

The image of Chance with a family dawned slowly. "Your niece?"

He nodded. "It's little wonder I called out their names. Not a day has passed since I left Texas that I don't think of those children."

Kathleen felt a rush of relief that left her weak. "Oh, Chance," she cried, impulsively throwing her arms around his neck. "I thought Callie was the woman who danced with you the night of the Social."

"No," he murmured. "That woman was no one at all, dearest. No one at all."

The clear blue light in his eyes said he was telling her the truth, and her heart cried for joy. "Tell me about the children, Chance," she begged him. She wanted to know everything about him, about his family, the people he loved and who loved him.

"Little Callie and Jim," Chance said, shaking his head and smiling. "Now, there's a pair to draw to." His smile was warm, but there seemed to be a tinge of sadness in his eyes that Kathleen couldn't understand and couldn't dismiss.

"Jim Jr. is tall for his age," he began. "As skillful on horseback as any grown man. But inside, he's filled with a gentleness, a special goodness"—Chance hesitated, swallowing hard before he went on—"like his father," he added quietly.

"And Callie?"

"Ah, little Miss Callie May," Chance said, one eyebrow arched. "She's a real spitfire. Reminds me a bit of you," he added with a smile. "Stubborn, proud, but enough charm to talk the stars right out of the sky."

Kathleen glowed under his compliment.

"She's a beauty as well. Golden hair and blue eyes."

"Blue, like your eyes?"

"Lighter," he remembered. "Like her father's." He cleared his throat and looked down at their hands still entwined. "James was a good man, Kathleen," Chance said solemnly. "The kindest man I've ever known. He taught me everything I know about cattle, ranching, and most of what I know about life."

Instinctively, Kathleen knew that James was dead and that his passing had had a profound effect on his brother. She wondered what had happened to James Ballinger as she listened to Chance explain how after the war he and his brother had decided to start a ranch in Texas. She watched the pride gleaming in his eyes as he explained how he and his brother had chosen only the finest stock, building their herd slowly and carefully, paying special attention to proper breeding and crossbreeding.

"When Jim came along, James and Nancy asked me to be godfather." His voice dropped a notch. "Two years later, Nancy died in childbirth with Callie. It was rough on James. A month later, he asked me to be his daughter's godfather as well. It was an honor I didn't deserve," he said gruffly.

"But that isn't true," she insisted. "You love them, I can tell by the things you say about them. Those children are lucky to have an uncle who cares for them as you do."

His eyes said he was unconvinced. "I haven't always been the man you've come to know. I was wild, Kathleen. Irresponsible. Stupid. I resented James for how I thought he was trying to tie me down to the ranch. So I left, headed to the city, looking for—aw hell, I don't think I even *knew* what I was looking for. I made more mistakes in a year than most men make in a lifetime."

His self-loathing and anger filled the silence with a tension that could almost be touched.

"And when I finally found my senses and came back home it was too late . . . James was dead." His voice faded like smoke on the wind.

"Oh, Chance, how terrible for you and for the children."

His eyes turned an even deeper blue. "Afterwards, I headed north."

She squeezed his hand, urging him to go on.

"He was the best friend I ever had and I never got the chance to tell him that I'd finally realized it. A brother is a precious gift, Kathleen," he said softly.

It became instantly clear to her why he'd given Danny a second chance, why he'd come to her brother's defense that night in the barn. He was trying in some way to make amends to Danny for all the regrets he had about James. But what she couldn't understand was the glint of anger she saw sparking in his eyes, and why it sent a shiver of dread down her spine.

The silence between them grew heavy again as each of them was lost in their own speculations. Kathleen wondering how much of his troubled past he would be willing to share with her. And Chance weighing the consequences of opening his wounded heart to the woman with whom he wished to spend the rest of his life.

"What about your ranch?" she asked finally, tugging them both back to the present.

He shrugged. "Gone by now, I expect. Taken over by the . . . neighbors, probably. The children moved into town with their grandmother after I left. When I met Danny," he said, raking his fingers through his dark hair, "I was headed to Canada, looking for a place where I could build a new home for me and the children."

"But you came here, instead."

"Yes," he said smiling. "And from the moment I set eyes on Twin Rivers, I've dreamed of one day sending for Jim Jr. and Callie. Montana is a place tailor-made for those children."

"But why didn't you tell me sooner?" she demanded to know. "And for heaven's sakes, why haven't you sent for them?"

He stared at her, wishing with all his heart that starting a new life could be that simple. "But there are things to be taken care of, details . . ." he began.

"What details?" she asked incredulously. "Oh, Chance, I adore children. I've always wished I'd had a little sister. And Jim Jr. must miss you terribly. They both need you. Please, Chance, send for them right away. My home—our home," she corrected, "will be theirs, as well."

"You mean that, don't you?"

"Of course I mean it. I can think of nothing that would make me happier than to share my home with your family," she said brightly, her eyes shining.

She came into his arms willingly when he reached for her again. He held her close, pressing her against his heart, a heart that swelled to near bursting with his love and respect for her.

But loving her couldn't change the past, a bitter voice whispered inside him. And what future did he have to offer her while the murder charge that had chased him from Texas still threatened to destroy their life at Twin Rivers?

If there really was to be a second chance for him, a chance for a future with Kathleen and the children, he knew he'd have to leave her. He'd have to go back and try to clear his name. Even as he listened to her happy chatter about the preparations she intended to make for Jim Jr. and Callie's arrival, he made his own plans to leave. He let her talk, not wishing to spoil her joy, knowing that he would send for the children, but also knowing that if he couldn't change things in Texas, he wouldn't be around to watch them grow up.

The children were too young too understand and he could never tell Kathleeen, never implicate her in his crimes. It was bad enough that he planned to saddle her with his responsibilities, not knowing the outcome of his attempts to clear his name. Although the thought of hurting her broke his own heart, he knew he couldn't tell her why or where he was going when the time came for him to leave.

It would take a few days, maybe even weeks, until

he was ready to go. He needed to regain his strength. He also needed to see to it that the financial affairs of Twin Rivers were in order before he left. He'd teach Danny everything he knew about ranching. He'd educate Kathleen and her brother as to the proper care of the Hereford cattle. If he didn't make it back, at least he'd have the peace of mind of knowing that he'd left Twin Rivers a little better off than when he'd ridden onto it.

But what about his love for Kathleen? What about her growing love for him? How could he go on letting her pin her hopes on a man who couldn't promise a future? On a man with a price on his head and a hangman's noose awaiting him?

In the days following Chance's recovery, life at Twin Rivers seemed idyllic to Kathleen. She and Danny had made their peace, and she and Chance seemed to be spending nearly every waking hour together. Her devotion seemed to grow deeper with each passing hour, until sometimes she wondered how her heart could contain all the love she felt for him.

Their evenings were filled with the sweetness of quiet walks along a stream bank and murmured conversations late into the night as they sat entwined in each other's arms by the fire. Their talks ranged from the mundane concerning the day to day workings of the ranch to more serious discussions about the growing restlessness of those in the territory who yearned for statehood.

Inevitably, as the fire burned down to a few glowing embers and the moon began its western descent, their conversations became more intimate. Kathleen's voice would grow wistful when she spoke about her parents—the way her mother had taught her to make lace, how her father had taught her to trust her instincts.

Last night Chance had spoken for the first time about his boyhood days before the war in Natchez. His voice had taken on a husky tenderness that further endeared him to her heart.

And so, between their ardent caresses and soulful kisses, the long, tender evenings invariably came to a close with Kathleen sharing her fondest dreams for their future, a future that had seemed hopeless and lonely before Chance Ballinger had ridden into her life and claimed her heart for his own.

Consumed by her joy and blinded by her love for him, Kathleen found a ready supply of excuses for the way Chance seemed always to maneuver the conversation back to the present, away from the future. As she basked in the warmth of Chance's devotion, everything around her seemed happily infected with her own inner glow of well-being and happiness.

The small green shoots emerging through the plot of rich, dark earth in her carefully tended garden behind the house seemed a more vibrant green than in years past. The cattle that had survived the onslaught of tick fever were thriving and their bulging bellies and glossy coats testified to the high quality of this summer's crop of native grass.

The dozen or so white-faced calves Kathleen watched frolicking in the near meadow each morning seemed to be stronger and friskier. Each day felt like a new beginning, and Kathleen's hopes soared.

Even the financial state of things seemed to be improving. Chance had sent Jeb to negotiate the sale of twenty-five Longhorn steers to the cavalry to feed the hungry troops at Fort Benton. A fair price had been set, and next week Danny and Chance were planning to drive the steers north. With the money from that sale and the promise of another payment after the fall roundup, Charles Settlemier had agreed to extend the note at the bank.

With so much good fortune behind and ahead of her, Kathleen's heart felt light this morning as she stepped out onto the porch with a basket of wet laundry.

Even Danny seemed to be thriving, she told herself as she set about hanging the linens on the clothesline on the south side of the house. He was taking more interest in the ranch. Under Chance's patient tutelage, he seemed to be growing, at last, into the responsible young man Kathleen had always believed he would be.

Sometimes the memory of the harsh words she'd spoken to her brother the night she'd ordered him off the ranch came back to her, and each time regret welled within her. Though their tearful words of reconciliation had been spoken the same day Chance had regained consciousness, Kathleen prayed that Danny harbored no hidden resentment toward her now. If he did, he'd neither done nor said anything to reveal it.

Chance was right: A brother's love was a precious gift.

And on this morning so bright and full of promise, Kathleen felt like hugging the whole world. The McBride family had finally had a turn of good luck, she told herself as she pinned the last sheet onto the clothesline. And she was more than ready to accept all that great, good luck at face value.

After she picked up the empty basket, she stopped and closed her eyes for a moment, inhaling the warm summer air and listening to a pair of meadowlarks serenading each other across the meadow. Summer was a glorious time in the valley, and soon the sound of children's laughter would be added to the lively sounds of nature.

As always, thoughts of Chance's young niece and nephew coming to Twin Rivers filled Kathleen's heart with eager anticipation. Though she'd already begun converting her work area in the loft into a bedroom for them, there was still much to be done, she reminded herself as she hurried toward the house.

At the cabin door, she stopped short at the sound of a carriage approaching. She frowned when she turned around and recognized the black buggy pulling into the yard. She hadn't attended church services since their last wretched encounter, and the prospect of seeing Henry Draper again was something she dreaded.

Henry's eyes were already on her as he climbed out of his carriage. Kathleen set down the laundry basket, ducked into the house, and with hands shaking, grabbed her father's shotgun.

When she came back out of the house, Henry was standing at the gate.

"Kathleen," he acknowledged her and the shotgun leveled at his chest with a stiff nod, not bothering to remove his hat.

"You're not welcome here, Henry," she answered him coolly.

He seemed not to have heard. "Is your hired man around?"

"What business do you have with Jeb?"

Henry's eyes narrowed and he tilted his chin. "I was referring to Ballinger."

Kathleen felt the hair on the back of her neck prickle. "Chance Ballinger is my business partner,

Henry," she said evenly. "I thought you were well aware of that fact."

"Be that as it may." He dismissed her explanation with an arrogant wave of his hand. "Is he around or not?"

With anger that surprised her, she shouted, "Get off my land, Henry!"

She watched with grim satisfaction as the force of her words caused his back to stiffen. "I did not come out here today to do verbal battle with you, Kathleen. Nor is my visit a social one."

"There's nothing verbal about the lead in this shotgun," she assured him. "Now be on your way."

Henry swatted at a fly indignantly. "As you know, it is customary for a pastor to visit the sick and infirm. I heard of Mr. Ballinger's recent illness and I included him on my rounds. What are you afraid of, Kathleen. Is there some reason you don't wish Mr. Ballinger and me to meet?"

"He's in the barn," a voice from behind her offered.

Kathleen whirled around at the sound of Jeb's gruff voice behind her. Henry gave Kathleen a triumphant sneer.

"You don't have to protect Chance from the likes of that rattler," Jeb assured her.

Kathleen stared after the preacher as he opened the barn door and disappeared inside. "I hope you're right, Uncle Jeb." In a fair fight, there would be no question who'd come out the better man. But Kathleen knew only too well that when one dealt with Henry Draper, the rules of fair play were suspended.

Chapter Seventeen

———◆———

CHANCE heard someone come into the barn and frowned when he recognized the voice that called out to him as Henry Draper's.

"Over here," he said as he slid his left hand slowly down the small black mare's swollen right foreleg.

"Ballinger," Henry said as he appeared outside the stall where Chance was tending to the animal.

Chance glanced up at Henry but didn't speak as he continued to examine the soft underside of the mare's hoof.

"I'd like a few words with you," Henry informed him impatiently.

"What's on your mind, preacher?" Chance didn't stop working but went on gently probing the hoof with a small metal pick.

"What I have to say to you requires privacy," Henry declared.

Chance finally located the small stone that had been the source of the animal's discomfort. "There you go, young lady," he murmured as he ejected the offending stone and set the horse's foot back on the ground.

"The bunkhouse is empty," Chance said evenly as he led the mare past Henry out into a small pen and released her. Without looking to see if the black-clad preacher was following him, Chance strode toward the bunkhouse, leaving the door open when he walked in.

Situating himself in the center of the room, Chance stood with legs braced evenly and his arms crossed.

Henry stepped across the threshold, sweeping the room with a critical eye before finally focusing his attention on Chance.

"What do you want, Draper? I've got work to do."

"Believe me, I have no desire to linger on Twin Rivers soil a moment longer than is absolutely necessary. But what I have to say won't wait."

"Then say it," Chance growled. The image of Kathleen and the way she'd looked the night she'd returned from the Spring Social formed with disturbing clarity in his mind's eye. The temptation to plant his fist squarely in the middle of the preacher's face was strong, and it was taking every ounce of control Chance possessed to resist doing just that.

"I'm here to offer you a deal."

Chance said nothing as he withdrew the leather tobacco pouch from his shirt pocket and proceeded to roll a cigarillo.

Henry drew himself up to full height, his mouth tightening into a thin, hard line. "You'd do well to listen to what I have to say, Ballinger."

"I don't make deals with the devil," Chance said flatly as he started for the door.

"Very clever," Henry remarked, following on Chance's

heels. "But I warn you, Ballinger, you'd better hear me out."

"And just why would I want to do that?" Chance asked between the clenched teeth that held the tip of his unlit cigarillo.

"Because I know who you are, Ballinger," Henry said in a voice brimming with pleasure. "I know who and what you are and if you don't agree to the terms I'm prepared to offer you, I'll pass that information on to those who know how to deal with criminals."

Henry's words landed heavily.

"I think you'll find that the group of gentlemen with whom I'm associated do not take kindly to murderers taking up residence in their communities, passing themselves off as respectable landholders."

Chance stared at Henry, unblinking. Since making the decision to stay on at Twin Rivers, Chance had thought a good deal about what course he would take should his past catch up with him before he had the chance to put things right. The solution that came to him was always the same.

"I'm not bluffing," Henry assured him smugly. "I have solid proof of your past, and I'd like nothing more than to see you brought to justice."

Justice? Chance scoffed inwardly at the word. Which brand of justice should he hope for? The kind they practiced in Montana, meted out by a group of vigilantes inflamed by the phony preacher? Or in Texas: the best jury money could buy.

"Do what you have to do, preacher," Chance uttered with grim resignation as he turned to leave.

When Henry grabbed his arm, Chance spun around with dangerous speed and snatched the smaller man by the shirtfront, yanking him up onto his toes. Henry's hat fell to the floor and he blinked, astounded when the back of his head connected with a satisfying thud against the bunkhouse wall.

With the tip of the cigarillo dangerous inches from the wide-eyed preacher's ashen face, Chance growled, "Get the hell off my land, Draper."

"I—I will. And gladly," Henry stammered, struggling in vain against the iron grip in which he was caught. "I'll go," he repeated shrilly. "I'll go."

Chance relinquished his grip so quickly that Henry stumbled backward.

Keeping one eye on the big man towering over him, Henry groped around on the floor for his hat. "I know your type, Ballinger. You think you can outrun or out-gun justice." He backed steadily toward the door as he spoke. "But what about Kathleen? Have you thought about what this will do to her? To all of them?" Henry asked, a satisfied gleam flickering in his small dark eyes. "Folks don't think kindly of a woman who lives in sin with a wanted criminal."

"You son of a—"

"If she's lucky, she could probably avoid the territorial prison, but I doubt Charles Settlemier would want his bank tainted by association with her. At best she'll lose this land. And before I'm through she'll never hold her head up again in this community, that much I promise you . . ." Henry added quickly, snatching up his hat and heading for the door.

In one stride, Chance filled the doorway, blocking Henry's retreat. "What's your price, Draper?"

"Your freedom can't be bought with money," Henry informed him with a smug smile.

Chance felt the anger coursing through him, white-hot and dangerous. "What do you want, Draper?" he growled again.

"I want you to ride out of here," Henry said quickly, taking a cautious sideways step. "Leave Twin Rivers, leave the territory. I want you gone and gone for good."

Chance rolled the cigarillo thoughtfully between his thumb and forefinger. "And if I stay?"

"I'll go to the vigilantes and have them down your throat before sundown. Jeb, Danny, and your whore will be run out of the valley before your body goes cold and—" Henry never got the chance to finish his sentence, nor did he have the chance to avoid the blow that sent him sprawling backward over a bunk and crashing into the wall behind it. His startled expression mirrored the pain that exploded in his head. He seemed close to unconsciousness as he grabbed for the small pistol, the handle of which showed just above his vest pocket.

Chance reached down and clamped his hand around the preacher's wrist at the same moment Henry's fingers closed around his gun. A startled whimper of pain escaped Henry's colorless lips.

"I ought to kill you here and now," Chance hissed as he shook the gun out of Henry's hand and sent it clattering to the floor, spinning out of reach.

"Th-they'll come after you, Ballinger," Henry promised, his voice high and tremulous, his eyes glazed and wild. "Do you think . . . I'd be fool enough to ride out here without telling someone?" The fear etched in Henry's face was undisguised, but Chance had played poker with enough men to know that the counterfeit preacher wasn't bluffing. "They'll come after you, Ballinger, and when they're through with you, I'll ruin her!"

Chance grabbed a handful of Henry's shirt and hauled the wiry preacher to his feet, dragging him toward the door like so much dirty laundry. "Do what you want to me," Chance growled as he shoved Henry up against the door, "but leave her out of it." His voice dropped another dangerous notch. "If anything happens to any of them . . ."

"Th-that's entirely up to you, now isn't it, Mr. Ballinger?" Henry's cold eyes narrowed as he shrugged away from Chance's grasp. "Threatening me won't do you any good. You're a criminal and I have the evidence to prove it, thanks to your lady friend from Virginia City."

Rubylee. Chance despised the surprise he felt registering on his face.

Henry nodded, straightening his coat as he declared, "Miss Tyler came to me as a concerned citizen. She passed on an interesting bit of information the night before she left town. She tried to deliver it to you, didn't she? At the Social, remember? I think you'd find the letter she intercepted for you in Virginia City most interesting. Seems the family of the man you murdered in cold blood has raised the price on your head."

Henry touched his jaw gingerly and straightened his jacket. "Be in Virginia City day after tomorrow, Ballinger. I'll be waiting for you. If you're not there by dark, I'll send them out after you. Then I'll come and take care of *her* myself."

Chance took a threatening step toward him and Henry's hands flew up to protect his face. "Killing me won't save you!" he warned. "On my instructions, a letter is to be delivered to Charles Settlemier on Saturday. I penned that letter last night. In it I expose your criminal past and implicate the McBrides in your crimes." A smug confidence lit Henry's long, pallid face. "I will retrieve that letter and destroy it when I return from Virginia City. I guess you could call it my ace in the hole, couldn't you, gambler?"

Chance grabbed the gun up off the floor and shoved it against Henry's temple. Overwhelming anger and bitter regret churned in his gut and seeing the preacher tremble, hearing the breath catch in his lungs, and watching the last drop of color drain from his face offered Chance no solace. For a long dangerous moment he considered pulling the trigger.

But finally, with a muttered curse, he lowered the gun and shoved it into his belt. "Get the hell out of here before I change my mind and scatter your brains all over this room."

Henry groped behind him for the door. "If you try to double-cross me, I'll see you hang, Ballinger," he promised as he shoved the door open and backed outside, "and if you're not in Virginia City day after tomorrow, whatever happens to the McBrides will be on your head."

With barely contained rage, Chance watched Henry climb into his carriage and whip his horse up into a gallop. For moments after the dust from Draper's carriage settled on the horizon, Chance stared out at the road leading away from Twin Rivers.

Tonight he'd travel that road for what might be the last time. It seemed his luck had finally run out. The phony preacher from Bozeman City held all the cards.

Chance was no stranger to loss. At the tender age of ten, he'd seen his mother suffer an agonizing death of consumption. A few years later, he'd lost his father to the war. Chance had held his newborn niece and wept with his brother the night they'd lost Nancy. And then it seemed in the next moment, James was gone. The homeplace in Mississippi, the ranch in Texas, all gone.

Through it all, Chance had somehow withstood the pain. He'd closed the door on each loss, absorbed the personal casualties with the grim acceptance that had become a numbing constant in his life.

But with Kathleen things had begun to change. He'd begun to let himself feel again—the joy as well as the sorrow.

Muttering a curse under his breath, he dropped the cigarillo to the ground and crushed it angrily beneath his bootheel. When he looked up, he saw Kathleen working in the garden.

Wisps of auburn hair glistened like burnished red-gold around her pretty face. The soft cotton dress she wore swirled lazily around her ankles in the gentle mid-morning breeze. He closed his eyes, imagining the fresh scent of her and the sweet taste of her mouth. The memories tightened around his heart with choking regret.

When he opened his eyes, he saw that she was watching him. She smiled and called to him. He stared at her a moment longer, filling his senses with what he knew might be their last gentle moment. And then, without a word or a gesture, he turned and walked back into the bunkhouse.

Best to make it a clean, fast break, he told himself. He couldn't for one minute consider telling her the truth. The less she knew, the better. If Draper broke his word and set the law on her, her ignorance would be her best defense.

Too much of her life had already been tainted by the sins of the men in her life. The disgrace her brother and her father had brought down on the family had nearly obliterated any chance she might have for happiness in the Gallatin Valley. He'd be damned if he'd seal her fate with his own guilt.

Thoughts of his beautiful and loyal Kathleen wasting the rest of her life grieving for a convicted murderer made him heartsick. It would be easier this way, he told himself. Easier for her to hate him.

If by some miracle he could find a way to prove his innocence and come back to her, then he'd have to take the risk that she might not understand, that she might not forgive him. It was a chance he'd have to take. Draper and his lynch mob had given him no other choice.

In the meantime, he'd have to let her believe the worst about him, believe that he'd lied about loving her. It was her only chance for the future she deserved. He had nothing else to offer her; at least he could offer her a second chance with someone else.

At this point, with a price on his head and the law on his heels, he had no way of knowing if he'd even survive long enough to make it back to Texas to confront his past. He had no way of knowing if he'd make it, he only knew he had to try. For the children, for Twin Rivers, for Kathleen. Most of all for Kathleen.

For even as he gathered his belongings and stuffed them into his saddlebag, he wondered how long he could survive without her. The memory of her love was something he knew he'd never lose. It was one door he'd leave open for the rest of his life.

*　*　*

A few minutes later, he heard the light tapping and knew before he opened the door who was on the other side.

"Chance?" she called out. "Are you in there?"

He drew a deep breath, bracing himself for the darkness that was to come. "I'm here."

She opened the door slowly and stepped inside.

"What do you want?" he asked without turning around.

"I've prepared our noon meal," she said, her voice betraying the uneasiness she already perceived between them. "Danny and Jeb won't be back until suppertime so I fixed a basket for the two of us. It's such a lovely day, I thought we might have a picnic by the creek."

When she touched his arm, he shrugged away, steeling himself against her warmth.

"No," he said flatly

"All right," she said evenly, swallowing her disappointment. "If you have work to do, I'll go and set the table in the cabin. Come in when you're ready."

"Don't wait for me." He folded down the leather flap on his saddlebag and tied the leather strings securely before turning to face her. "I'm not hungry."

Her gaze traveled to the bulging bags. "I didn't know you were going anywhere today," she said, the brightness in her voice forced and unnatural.

"Well, I am," he stated simply.

"I see." Her stare flicked expectantly on his face. "Where, Chance? Where are you going? To town? Do you want me to ride along with you? I could bring the basket—"

"No," he snapped. "You can't come along. I'm not

going to Bozeman. If you must know, I'm headed for
Virginia City." He watched the devastating effect of his
cold words and felt her pain twisting like barbed wire
around his own heart.

"Virginia City?" she whispered.

His nod was almost imperceptible.

"Wh-when will you be coming back?" She held her
breath.

"I can't say."

He saw the panic in her eyes and her hands flew to
her mouth. "Oh, Chance," she gasped, reaching for his
arm again. "It's Callie and Jim, isn't it? Something has
happened to the children . . ."

He shrugged away from her touch again and the hurt
that lodged in her eyes turned them a bright spring
green, and the pain of losing her hit him like a hammer
in the gut. Good Lord, how could he go through with
this?

"No. Nothing has happened to Jim or Callie," he said
quietly.

"Then what? Chance, what is it? Why are you leaving?" Her voice was low and jerky. He prayed she
wouldn't cry; his own emotions were already strained
to the breaking point.

"Leave me alone, woman," he bit back savagely.
"Can't you see when a man has had enough?"

She stared at him, eyes glistening. "I don't understand." Her voice was a choked whisper.

"I have to go."

"You have to go," she repeated numbly. "And you
won't be coming back, will you?" Her eyes pleaded
with him to dispute what she'd said.

But Chance could say nothing.

"And the ranch?" she said, her voice vapor thin. "Our partnership?"

"Partnership?" he scoffed, turning his attention back to his packing. "You didn't really believe that's what I wanted, did you?"

He heard her swallow a gasp.

"I wanted it all, Kathleen." She would never know how much. A home. A family, a beautiful and devoted woman to be his true partner for the rest of his life. Fighting back the emotion that threatened to betray his plan, he said, "Don't try to tell me that grabbing back your half of Twin Rivers wasn't always first in your mind, as well. Isn't that what you've schemed from the first moment we met? Or maybe you were just trying to catch yourself a husband at last. Was that it, partner? A husband, another set of hands to work your precious ranch?"

She stared at him, disbelieving. "Why? Why are you doing this?" she whispered.

"I'm ready to move on. I never promised I'd stay," he reminded her. "And now it's all yours, at last," he said flatly. "You'll never raise enough money to buy me out, and I can't wait any longer."

"What? You don't mean . . . ?"

"Every acre," he said. "Every worthless cow. Take it all. I give it all to you, and gladly, just to be rid of the burden."

Her shattered expression wrenched his heart, but he persisted, although he didn't know if he possessed the strength to drive that final wedge between them.

"You won't need a husband, now, partner, not with this place to support you in your old age. Why you won't even have to share it with your brother . . ."

"You bastard," she gasped and her open hand blazed across his face with a smack that echoed sickeningly around them. "Damn you!" she cried, and turned and ran away from him.

Despite the sunlight streaming through the open door, the air in the room felt midwinter cold and lonely. He drove his fist into the wall, but even the tangible pain couldn't shift his focus from his inner agony.

After he'd gathered his things, he stepped outside, closing the bunkhouse door behind him. He could leave in the morning and still make Henry Draper's deadline in Virginia City. But he'd decided that tonight he'd sleep on the trail. He couldn't spend another night at Twin Rivers, his resolve to leave her was too weak. His plan to drive her away from him had worked. She despised him. She probably always would.

From this day forth, the mere mention of his name would cause hatred to boil inside her. He'd done that wretched thing that he'd set out to do, and done it well. But he had to leave now before his anguished heart betrayed him and destroyed both their lives forever.

Kathleen slumped numbly into the chair beside the fire. Never had she loved anyone so completely. Never had she known such pain. And never, if she lived to be a thousand years old, would she understand his sudden and total cruelty.

"Damn you, Chance Ballinger," she sobbed through her tears as she buried her face in her hands and wept until her sides ached. After a moment, her tears subsided and she rose and walked woodenly into the kitchen. Standing on tiptoe to reach the cupboard's

ighest shelf, her fingers closed around the delicate
ugar bowl that had been her mother's and her grandmother's before her.

She held the bowl for a long moment before lifting
he lid and quickly removing the small roll of bills and
he pouch of coins that lay hidden inside. Her hands
rembled slightly as she reached to place the bowl back
on the shelf.

In the next instant the bowl slipped from her hands,
shattering against the drainboard as it tumbled to the
loor. An anguished cry escaped her lips as she dropped
o her knees. It was hopeless. The precious bowl lay
hattered in a million pieces. Like her shattered dreams,
he bowl was broken beyond repair. The fresh tears that
lowed scalded her cheeks with their white-hot fury,
oropelling her into action.

Shoving the money into her apron pocket, she
rushed out of the cabin. From the porch she saw
Chance outside the barn and hurried over to where he
stood saddling his horse.

"The McBrides won't accept charity from the likes
of you, Ballinger," she seethed, her chin tilted with
defiant pride. "Take it," she demanded, thrusting all
he money she had in the world at him with a trembling
hand.

He seemed not to have heard, but continued to work
over the bags he was tying to his saddle. Without looking at her, he reached for the reins. When she grabbed
hem out of his hands, he turned on her, his glare simmering, his eyes a dangerous blue-black.

"Take it, damn you!"

He stared at her, still refusing to acknowledge the
money she held out to him.

"I'll send the rest in payments. Don't worry, you'll be paid in full. I'll find a way to buy back my ranch," she vowed, "or die trying."

"I can't take your money," he said quietly.

"It's the least of what you've taken from me, gambler," she informed him bitterly.

Something in his eyes told her she'd struck a nerve.

"Perhaps there is another way . . ." he said.

"There is no other way," she spat out. "I will pay you every cent, no matter what it takes to raise it."

"But if there was a way to get your ranch back free and clear, and be rid of me at the same time, you would take it, wouldn't you?"

"But how is that possible?" she challenged him.

"Poker," he said simply. "We play a game of high stakes poker. Winner take all."

Kathleen felt gutted by the depths of his cruelty. Had his heart turned completely to stone? Was there not an ounce of feeling for her left inside him anywhere?

His steady, indifferent stare gave her the answer that pierced her heart. Oh, how could she have been such a fool?

"Surely you must know how to play," he goaded, "you are a McBride, after all."

His sarcasm slashed her raw emotions like a jagged knife. "All right." She managed to utter the words despite the wretched lump that burned her throat. "Winner take all." For when one's heart and pride were lost, what more was there to lose?

Chapter Eighteen

———◆◆———

SHE watched him pull the deck of cards out of his saddlebag, still disbelieving. His eyes were on her back—she could feel them—as she walked to the cabin. But she held her head high. Chance Ballinger had seen her cry for the last time today.

Inside, a fire danced in the grate. The cabin was warm and bright, a stark contrast to the cold Kathleen felt closing around her heart. Gideon lay curled in the rocker and opened his good eye when he mewed a welcome.

Kathleen watched Chance's gaze sweep the room for one long moment before he sat down at the table and began to shuffle the cards. She sat down in the chair across from him.

"Draw poker all right with you?"

She could only nod, her throat had gone too dry to speak. Watching the cards skim across the table, Kathleen cursed the tears that threatened.

Surely this whole wretched morning was only a ter-

rible nightmare from which the real Chance Ballinge
would soon come and kiss her awake.

"Pick them up," he demanded gruffly, indicating th
five cards fanned out facedown in front of her.

She bit her cheek to keep her lips from tremblin
and picked up the cards one by one. For a momen
the numbers and symbols meant nothing to he
through the haze of her inner pain. This truly was
nightmare, she told herself, but no lover's kiss woul
save the day. For the only one who could put an en
to this wretched nightmare was the man who'd cause
it to spring to life so hellishly before her eyes.

Chance shifted in his chair. "How many?"

"Wh-what?"

"How many cards?" When she didn't respond, h
explained, "You can ask for more cards to get a bette
hand."

"N-no. None," she stammered. *Concentrate, Kath
leen.* The king of clubs, the ace of spades, and thre
fives stared back at her. Was it good enough? A surg
of panic like an angry fist closed around her hear
What if she lost? What if he held the winning hand?

But what did it matter now? With dreams of he
future laying in tatters at her feet, what did any of
matter anymore?

"Well?" His voice was icy and impatient. "What ar
you going to do? Good Lord, woman, make up you
mind. Is that the way your brother and father taugh
you to play?"

It was as though he'd aimed his cruel words straigh
for her heart. Startling images jolted through her: He
father clutching a losing hand to his chest as he la
bleeding to death on the dirty floor of that back roon

in Bozeman City. And Danny, alone and broke in Virginia City, desperate and humiliated.

"Two!" she blurted, discarding the king and the ace. "Two cards." *Damn you, Chance Ballinger, the Mc-Brides will not be beaten again without a fight.*

With a nimble flick of his wrist, he slid two more cards across the table. She held her breath and picked up the cards. Her pulse pounded in her ears and behind her eyes. The eight of hearts and the queen of spades. Her heart sank and judging by the dark glint in his eyes, she knew Chance sensed his victory.

"Three of a kind," she said, her voice nearly inaudible as she laid her cards down on the table.

Something like pain flickered in his steely gaze before he pushed back in his chair, rose quickly to his feet, and headed for the door.

With his back to her, he said quietly, "You win, partner," before tearing his cards in half and letting them fall from his hand as he walked out the door.

She could only sit and watch, the irony of their situation chilling her like a north wind, shaking her from her stupor. In the end, she'd won it all. And lost everything.

The sound of hoof beats drew her involuntarily from the chair to stand at the window. She watched him ride away, still choking back her tears. She watched him until he was lost in shadows. The feelings of emptiness and desolation that settled over her was unlike any pain she'd ever endured.

"I loved you," she whispered. "I was going to be your wife." Unable to face the stark loneliness that stared back at her from the deserted road, she spun away from the window.

When she'd lost her mother and father, Kathleen had learned to stand on her own, depend on her own judgment, trust her own instincts. Could the woman who once found happiness in solitude ever feel that contentment again?

But there could be no happiness, no contentment. Not as long as she still cared. And despite what had passed between them this terrible morning, she knew that she would always care, that she would always love him.

Suddenly the stillness of the cabin engulfed her and she ran, hell-bent, across the porch, through the gate, and out of the yard. She ran through the meadow and through a small stream, oblivious to the water and mud that speckled her. She ran until her legs ached and her lungs burned, stumbling over stones and brush, tearing her skirt and her stockings on branches that tried to stop her.

She ran until she could run no more. But she could not outrun her pain, and when it overtook her she sank into the lush grass beside the creek and poured her tears out on the ground.

An hour later Kathleen came back to the kitchen. Her eyes rested on the food basket she'd prepared for their noon meal. She should unpack the food before it spoiled, common sense told her. But instead of attending to the basket, she stood like a sleepwalker staring down at it, forgetting what it was she meant to do.

The sound of footsteps on the porch caused her heart to leap. Chance! her heart cried. He'd changed his mind, had come to his senses and come back to her!

She rushed to the door and threw it open. Nothing

could have prepared her for the sight of the blue eyes that stared up at her.

They were Chance's eyes, and yet they were not.

"Are you Kathleen?" the boy asked, his Ballinger-blue eyes wide and shining as he dragged a battered black hat from his head and held it in front of him.

Before Kathleen could catch her breath to answer, a little girl, dressed in pink calico, clambered up the steps to stand beside her brother. " 'Course she's Kathleen, you ninny," she scolded. "In his letter, Uncle Chance said she was purty, didn't he? Evenin', Kathleen," she said, extending her dimpled hand. "My name's Callie May Ballinger and this here's my dumb brother, Jim."

Behind the children, Jeb was smiling. Danny bounded up the stairs, his face bright and his cheeks nearly as flushed as Jim Jr.'s. "Well, what do you think of these two? Ain't they something?"

Kathleen's eyes sought Jeb's.

"They came in on the stage. Were waiting in Boze-man when we arrived. Seems they came in a bit ahead of this." He handed her an unopened letter addressed to Chance, and bearing a Texas postmark.

"Well, c-come in, children," Kathleen bid them, her thoughts swirling as she stepped back to let them pass.

"Where's Uncle Chance?" Callie wanted to know.

"Be quiet," Jim admonished, reaching for her hand. "Where's your manners?"

But the little girl with the blond pigtails refused to be restrained, and she shook free of her brother's clasp and walked over to where Kathleen had folded numbly into a chair. "I didn't mean to be unmannerly, Miss Kathleen," she explained. "It's just that I've been wait-in' so long to see my uncle Chance, for days and days, it seems. Even before we got on that stage in Texas.

And—and I just c-can't hardly wait much longer . . ."
When her lower lip began to tremble and the tears
began to fill her pretty blue eyes, Kathleen's heart
jumped to life.

"Come now," she said, reaching for the child and
pulling her onto her lap. "Don't cry. Don't cry, darling.
Your uncle isn't . . . that is, he isn't here . . . right now.
But he'll be back . . . soon. I promise." Her chest ached
with a swelling heart, as she patted the child and
stroked her warm little head. "And when he gets back,
won't he be surprised to see you!" she declared, forcing
a smile.

The child sniffed and looked up at Kathleen with
hopeful eyes still swimming with tears. "H-he promised
he'd find us a home, didn't he, Jim?"

Jim's eyes were downcast, but he nodded as he drew
a circle on the floor with the toe of his boot.

"Is this our home, ma'am?" Callie May asked.

Kathleen's heart turned over. "Yes," she said in a
coarse whisper. "Yes, it is, Callie."

"Come help me with your bags, Junior," Danny said.
"And then I'll show you that old saddle we were talking
about on the way home."

Jim Jr.'s eyes shifted to Kathleen. "Excuse me,
ma'am," he said before crushing his hat back on his
head and rushing out the door after Danny.

"Oh, look!" Callie May exclaimed. "A kitty." Gideon
had slipped from behind the quilt partition and he
stood now at the edge of the room eyeing the child
cautiously. "What a big ole cat!" she exclaimed, laughing as she slid off Kathleen's lap and onto the floor.
"Here kitty." Gideon, always delighted to be the focus
of attention, sidled up to the child and purred as Callie
May stroked his fur and spoke to him gently.

Kathleen rose and walked into the kitchen.

"Are you all right, missy?" Jeb asked, following her. "When you opened that door a minute ago, you looked like you'd seen a ghost."

"You—you surprised me," she stammered. "I was resting. I didn't hear you ride in." Avoiding Jeb's scrutiny Kathleen reached for the picnic basket still sitting on the drainboard. "You and the children must be half starved. I'll get you some lunch," she said over her shoulder.

"Should I holler for Chance? Where is he anyway?"

Kathleen shook her head and drew a stinging breath before turning around to face her old friend. "Chance has gone," she said quietly so Callie May wouldn't hear. Kathleen turned back to slicing beef and bread. Was there no end to the pain?

"Kathleen?"

She turned around to see the torn cards in Jeb's hand.

"What happened here this morning?"

"I-I'm not really sure I know," she whispered. With hands shaking, she took the cards he held out to her. Avoiding Jeb's searching stare, she fought to maintain her dignity as she quietly gave Jeb a clipped summation of the strange events of the morning. As she spoke she idly arranged the torn cards in front of her on the drainboard.

"Do you have any idea where he went?" Jeb asked.

"He said something about Virginia City." A sudden picture of the woman in blue satin formed with startling clarity in her mind's eye. "I expect he's left some unfinished business there."

"That little girl is going to be mighty disappointed if she don't see her uncle soon," Jeb said, his voice low.

Kathleen withdrew the envelope Jeb had given her from her apron pocket and studied it. The letter must have come from the children's grandmother, informing them of the children's travel arrangements. What if the letter had arrived a day earlier? Would Chance still be with them? Would he still be acting out the role of a man in love? Kathleen asked herself bitterly.

For a moment Kathleen wondered if she should open the letter, perhaps it contained something other than the news of the children's arrival, perhaps something had happened to their grandmother. But just as quickly, Kathleen decided against opening it.

A few short hours ago she might have decided differently, but things had changed. The empty ache she carried inside reminded her just how much.

With one hand, Kathleen whisked off her apron and tossed it onto the table. "We've got to go get him," she declared. No matter what had passed between Chance and herself, his devotion to his niece and nephew was still a certainty in her mind. And the children would be devastated to learn that he'd left. They'd already lost so much.

"Jeb, either you or Danny must ride out after him. He's only been gone a little over an hour. I'm sure if you ride hard you can catch him before he crosses the Madison."

"I don't think Danny should go," Jeb said shaking his head. "That little boy is a quiet one, shy and skittish as a new colt. But he made up to Danny right off. I think it would be a good idea if Danny stayed with him until Chance gets back."

"Then you go, Jeb."

The old man shook his head and backed away, re-

fusing to take the envelope she held out to him. "Missy,
I'm too blamed old to ride fast enough to catch him.
He'll be halfway to Virginia City before I ever reach
the Madison. You're the one's goin' to have to go after
him, missy."

"But—"

"Now, you'd better get goin' if you hope to catch
him." Kathleen saw a familiar stubbornness in the old
man's soft gray eyes.

"I can't," she said quietly, her eyes searching his
weathered face for understanding.

"Not even for those two little children?" he whispered.

Kathleen worried her bottom lip with her teeth. "I—
I don't know." Given the terms under which Chance
had left, if he spotted her coming after him, more than
likely he'd just keep right on riding. Kathleen didn't
know if her battered pride could survive another blow
of that magnitude.

"Go after him, missy," Jeb prodded gently, his eyes
locked on hers with compassion.

"Come on, little one," he called to Callie May. "Put
that old cat down and come out and help me saddle
Miss Kathleen's horse. She's goin' to go fetch your Uncle Chance."

"Hooray!" Callie May cheered, startling Gideon back
into the bedroom.

Before Jeb took Callie May's hand, he reached for
his jacket hanging on the peg by the door. "Take this,
missy. It's likely to get cool this evening. And take that
basket of food as well. I'll make these young'uns some
of my famous hotcakes while you're gone." He dropped
his voice and added, "My old Peacemaker's in the

pocket." He patted the pocket where the gun was nestled. "You know how to use it if you run into trouble."

Kathleen could only stare at him, her heart racing. "Why are you doing this, Jeb?"

Her eyes followed his to the cards she'd idly arranged on the drainboard. "Because a man doesn't walk away from a hand like that without a damn good reason. Now wouldn't you kinda like to know why Chance did?"

Kathleen walked slowly over to the cards and studied them. Three jacks and two queens. A full house! Chance had held the winning hand.

"This is your chance, missy," Jeb said, his voice gravelly, "and my money's on you. On both of you." He smiled. "Now git goin'. And don't come back alone."

Kathleen threw her arms around the old man's neck and buried her face against his rough woolen collar. "Thank you, Jeb," she whispered.

"Hurry back, won't you?" Callie May made her promise.

And for the first time in the whole long, miserable morning, Kathleen knew she wasn't alone.

The sun would not be setting for another hour, but Chance decided it was time to look for a place to rest his horse and spend the night. He'd ridden fast and hard, putting as many miles as he could between himself and Twin Rivers, lest his thoughts of the woman he loved prove stronger than the miles between them and send him rushing back to her arms.

The last leg of his ride would take less than half a day, and he had no desire to arrive in Virginia City any earlier. Chance intended to make his meeting with

Henry Draper as brief as possible. At the thought of the phony preacher threatening him, threatening Kathleen, Chance tightened his grip on the reins. If by some miracle he was given the chance to return to the Gallatin Valley, he vowed to settle accounts with Henry Draper, once and for all.

The sudden sound of a branch cracking drew Chance's attention to the dense forest to the left of the trail. It wasn't the first time in the last few hours that he'd had the eerie sensation he was being watched, being followed.

Pulling General up short, Chance surveyed the area and realized that while absorbed in his thoughts, he'd wandered a good mile away from the stream bed along which he planned to camp for the night.

With a flick of his wrist, he wheeled General around to retrace his path. The sensation of being watched grew stronger when he glimpsed a shadowy movement through the trees. When General's ears peaked forward, Chance's suspicions were confirmed.

"It's okay, boy," Chance murmured. "I heard it too." Silently, he dismounted and moved noiselessly into the forest, trying to catch a glimpse of whomever or whatever had been following him. But his searching proved futile and in a moment, satisfied that he was once again alone, Chance swung back up into the saddle. Whoever had been watching him was gone now, as confirmed by the small puff of dust on the horizon and the sound of thudding hoofbeats fading in the distance up ahead on the trail.

A short time later, Chance found a small clearing near the creek and decided it was as good a place as any to camp for the night. General blew out a long, slow sigh of relief when Chance dismounted and set to unsaddling him.

"There you go, boy," he murmured, tying his mount to a sturdy pine near the creek. But just as the horse started to drink, his long-muscled neck arched gracefully over the water, he pitched his head and emitted a long, sharp whinny.

Chance moved up beside the animal, and ran his hand down the animal's sleek back. General's ears twitched forward again, his big dark eyes wide and glistening. His second whinny was a low, rumbling warning that Chance could not ignore.

Scrambling up the side of the creek bank, Chance threaded his way through the trees, keeping a keen eye on the trail below. Keeping low as he moved swiftly and silently through the forest, he headed for the spot where the ridge curved out over the trail.

At the unmistakable sound of a horse approaching, he flattened himself against the ground, his eyes sweeping the road below. In a moment a lone rider emerged from shadows. Inching his way closer to the edge of the outcropping, Chance tried to get a better look at the man who was tracking him. But from his perch above the trail all he could see was the top of the rider's wide-brimmed black hat.

Quickly he scanned the trail ahead and behind the rider. Were there others? But suddenly there was no more time for speculation. The rider was almost directly below the outcropping. "You there, below. Stop your horse!" he shouted.

But instead of complying with Chance's command the rider ducked his head and spurred his horse into startled action. At the exact moment the rider passed below him, Chance jumped down from the ledge, lunging out and across the horse's back, taking the rider by surprise and knocking him to the ground with a breathtaking thud.

The man on the ground beneath him was small, but size did not limit the determined zeal with which the stranger fought. Although Chance possessed far superior strength, he found he had his hands full as the rider, arms flailing and legs kicking wildly, defended himself with the spirit of a wildcat.

Finally, Chance managed to grab a handful of the man's oversize jacket and haul him to his feet. As he did, the wide-brimmed black hat toppled backward and a familiar mane of flaming auburn spilled past slim shoulders, and a pair of snapping green eyes stabbed him.

"Let go of me, you idiot!" she shrieked, jerking away from his grasp and brushing the leaves and weeds from her clothes and hair. "I knew you wouldn't be all that happy to see me, but I didn't think you'd try to kill me!"

For a moment Chance was stunned speechless, but then he shouted, "What the hell did you think you were doing tracking me, sneaking up on me like that?" He grabbed her by the shoulders and, holding her firmly at arm's length, let his gaze drink in the sight of her. "Why did you sneak off into the woods when I came after you?"

"I did not sneak off anywhere," she bit back. "And I was never in the woods. I've stayed on this trail since I left Twin Rivers." She jerked out of his grasp again.

Standing there glaring at him with one hand planted firmly on the curve of each hip, cheeks flushed with fiery indignation, eyes sparking with tantalizing emotion, was the woman Chance cherished above his own life, the woman he'd wondered if he'd ever see again in this lifetime. And yet, by some strange quirk of fate, she was here now, and seeing her again left him breathless.

"Kathleen." He smiled, and before he could think or she could recoil, he pulled her into his arms and hugged her so hard, he thought he might crush her. "Kathleen," he murmured again against her cheek.

Despite herself, she clung to him. Whatever insanity had seized him had seized them both, she told herself as she tilted her face up to him and welcomed his kiss with hungry desperation.

As his lips claimed hers and their tongues met and mated, the humiliation, the pain, the bitter aching reality of a few scant hours ago, melted magically into oblivion.

"I thought I'd never see you again," he whispered.

She pulled a few scant inches away from him. "But I thought that's what you wanted, to be rid of me, of the ranch, of—" Her voice broke.

"Rid of you? My God, Kathleen you'll never know what it did to me to leave you," he admitted, holding her, stroking her hair and feathering kisses across her face and into her hair.

"Then why," she cried. "Tell me why you left me."

He tried to swallow his welling emotions. "I was a fool," he muttered. "A liar and a fool. But I swear, I only left because I loved you. Because I still love you so very much."

She stared at him, her eyes glistening with her desire to believe him.

"Come," he said, taking her hand, "there is so much I have to tell you."

"But I have *more* to tell you!" she declared. "The

children," she exclaimed. "Jim Jr. and Callie May have arrived, Chance!" She answered his startled stare, "Yes, it's true. They're at the ranch now with Jeb and Danny."

At the campsite they unsaddled and tethered her mare.

"What's this?" Kathleen asked, and lifted a delicately woven chain of wild flowers draped over General's neck.

Chance took the flowers from her, smiling as he touched their velvet petals. "We've had company," he said, his eyes scanning the horizon as he spoke. "It seems Callie May and Jim Jr. aren't the only children who've surprised me today."

Kathleen's expression was one of complete confusion. "What is this? Where did it come from?"

"It's nothing to worry about," he assured her. "It's only a gift from a young friend." He slipped the flowered garland around her neck as he imagined the small brown hands that had lovingly fashioned the gift. And he hoped little Washita and her family were well.

Chapter Nineteen

———◆◆———

KATHLEEN helped him gather wood, and in a few moments they'd built a fire. After spreading his bedroll on the ground, he took her hand and together they sat staring into the campfire as he opened up his past to her in a way he'd never done before.

As the light of day faded and the sky turned a dusky gray, he told her about the first herd of Longhorns he and his brother brought up from Mexico, that first scraggly herd upon which they'd built their plans for the future. He told her how they'd survived Indian raids and battles between neighbors for water, an element of survival more precious than gold to the West Texas rancher. He told her about his youth, about the restlessness and the longing.

By the time he told her about the way James had been gunned down, the night sky had turned a velvet black.

"I was half out of my mind when I found out he was

dead and I rode out for the Holcomb ranch—I admit it, I wanted J. D. dead."

She said nothing; she scarcely dared to breathe as she listened to the details of the night she knew still haunted him.

"J. D. was waiting for me." His hands shook as he stared into the fire. He seemed mesmerized, although Kathleen knew it wasn't the flames but a vision of the past that held him. It was almost as though he could see in the fire the events of that night happening all over again.

"I wanted to fight him—hell, I wanted to choke the life out of him with my bare hands. But his boys came out of nowhere and grabbed me from behind before I got the chance. I thought they would kill me, then and there. And at that moment it didn't matter. James was dead. Nothing they could do to me would make any difference." His voice faded.

The silence was filled by the snapping and hissing of pine logs as long, bright flames consumed them.

After a moment she said, "I know how it feels to be angry, desperate, and afraid. To want to kill. The night Pa died, I felt the same way you did when you rode out after J. D.. Had I known the identity of the man who pulled the trigger that ended my father's life, I'd have gone after him the way you went after Holcomb. And, God help me, though I never knew his name, I've wished him dead a thousand times."

Chance gazed into her eyes, somehow knowing that until now she'd never before put into words her dark feelings and lonely guilt. He realized she'd dredged up her own pain for him, let it sting her again just to assure and comfort him, to help him make the kind of confession that could heal him. Her honesty and unselfishness touched him deeply, and he fell in love with her all over again.

"Go on, Chance," she urged him softly. "Tell me the rest."

"J. D. held a gun to my head," he began. "My only fear was that he'd kill me before I could kill him. He just laughed when he told me that it was me he'd meant to kill that night when he'd gunned James down." Chance's expression grew distant, haunted, and his voice dropped another painful notch. "My brother took the bullet that was meant for me, Kathleen." He cleared his throat and turned his gaze back to the fire.

"Somehow I managed to break free from Seth and Will. I lunged at J. D. and we fought for his gun. It went off with an explosion that I'll hear till the day I die. And when J. D. fell backward and I saw that he was gut-shot, I thought I was a dead man, as well. I thought his sons would tear me apart. But they just stood and stared at me, too shocked, too stunned to move. I guess they'd never thought they'd see their old man beaten.

"They started arguing, blaming each other. And then Will took off running like the devil was on his tail, but Seth just stood there, staring. He was still standing over his father when I rode away."

The memory of that horrible night drove hard lines across his broad forehead, making him look years older than Kathleen would have thought possible. His eyes glistened with pain, with the bitter tears that still refused to be shed.

"It was self-defense," she said, reaching for his hand, tugging him gently back to the present the only way she knew how, with her love.

"Not according to the lynch mob that came riding

after me the next night. Will told them I'd gunned
J. D. down in cold blood, that his father had been un-
armed. It was my word against his. My word against a
Holcomb's," he added bitterly.

"Then you had no choice. You had to run."

"That's what I thought then. But now I know better.
I'm through running, Kathleen," he said, his voice
raspy but resolute. "Even before Henry Draper threatened to expose my past, I decided I had to go back to
clear my name." He rose.

"But you can't mean that!" she protested, coming to
her feet to stand facing him. "You won't have a chance.
It will still be your word against J. D.'s sons. I—I can't
let you go back there, Chance," she cried. "I won't! I
can't lose you again. We'll go away." Her voice rose in
desperation. "Tonight. Together. We'll pack up and go
to Canada where no one knows either of us. We'll ride
back for the children and head out at first light. We
can begin again the way you planned when you left
Texas, only this time you won't be alone. We'll all be
together."

"And spend the rest of our lives looking over our
shoulders, running down a different trail every time
another Henry Draper steps out of the shadows?" He
shook his head sadly. "It won't work, Kathleen. There's
no place far enough."

Listening to the truth, her heart felt as though an
iron band was being welded around it.

"I'm going back to Texas," he said evenly. "It's time
to settle old accounts. One way or another, it's time to
put the past to rest."

They stood without touching as the flames leaped
and danced around the fire ring. Without words, an
understanding passed between them, both accepting

that their dreams for the future could never become reality until the nightmare of his past was put to rest.

"I need you to stay with the children, Kathleen. To help them understand."

She could only nod.

"I'm glad you came after me, partner." Even his wry smile couldn't dispel the sadness in his eyes. "And I'm glad you finally know the truth."

"Good Lord!" she exclaimed. "I'd almost forgotten the letter!" When she tugged the envelope out of the deep pocket of Jeb's woolen overcoat, her fingers touched cold steel and she remembered that she still carried Jeb's revolver. "Danny picked up this letter for you when he was in Bozeman this morning. I figured it must be from Grandma Logan, letting you know the children were on their way."

He took the letter, but didn't open it right away. "You will take care of the children, won't you, Kathleen? Their grandmother is old, and she isn't well. Right now I'm all they have. And if something happens to me . . ."

She pressed her finger against his lips. "Shh. Don't say it. Nothing will happen to you. You'll come back to us. You will. And until then, I'll have their dear, sweet faces to remind me of you."

He gazed into her eyes, nearly overwhelmed by the love he saw shining back at him. "You make me believe in my own dreams again, Kathleen," he whispered, and then broke the seal of the envelope and unfolded the small piece of white paper inside.

Grandma Logan's scrawled handwriting was instantly recognizable. "It *is* from the children's grandmother," he explained as he read. He read the letter silently, quickly, front and back, and then turned it over and read it again. "It's over," he said, his voice cracking. "Seems the Holcomb brothers had a falling-out, and Will gunned Seth down. On his deathbed, Seth told the truth about the night his father died. He confessed what really happened moments before he breathed his last. Grandma Logan said he did it 'to get the last word' to show his brother up as a liar." Chance's laugh was brittle. "Just like a Holcomb, carrying an argument to the grave."

"Oh, Chance!" Kathleen cried. Happiness crowded her heart. She threw her arms around his neck and hugged him, before quickly pulling away to read for herself the news that seemed too good to be true.

"Please tell me I'm not dreaming," she demanded, her hands shaking as she read. "Say it's all true? Tell me you're free."

"It is! It's all true!" he yelped as he grabbed her around the waist and swung her up off the ground. "It's true. We can go home, partner," he said as their lips met in celebration.

The surge of pure joy that filled her made her weak. She clung to him, laughing and crying at the same time. "Oh, yes," she whispered as he feathered tiny kisses across her cheek, "we can go home."

She nearly stumbled when, without warning, he pulled her away from him and held her by each shoulder at arm's length.

"What is it?" she asked breathlessly. "What's wrong?"

"You're sure you want to marry a landless drifter who lost his ranch to a beautiful woman in a poker game?"

She lowered her lashes and smiled coquettishly. "Well," she drawled, "if that landless drifter is willing to settle down to a lifetime with a stubborn old maid, I guess we've got us a deal—partner," she added with a low, seductive chuckle.

"Why, it'd be my eternal pleasure, ma'am," he drawled, as he bowed low and doffed his hat. His smile was deliciously wicked as he straightened and pulled her to him again, kissing her with an unbridled passion that left them both breathless. But with a groan, he dragged his lips from hers once more.

"Now what?" she asked, her voice husky and impatient.

"There's just one more thing I need to know. Was it only to fetch me back to my family and to deliver that letter that you came all this way to find me?" His eyes danced. "Now tell me the truth, Miss McBride," he warned with a frown, "for I won't tolerate a deceitful wife." His mouth tugged into a smile. "Was it only for the sake of the children and for no other reason that you came riding after me?"

She sniffed indignantly and tossed her head. "The truth, you say? Well, to tell the absolute truth—no," she confessed, her eyes sparking a sensuous challenge. "Neither the children's arrival nor the letter from Texas was the real reason." Suddenly her expression grew solemn as she slid her arms slowly around him again. "It was my love for you, Chance," she admitted in a whisper, "and those heavenly kisses of yours," she declared, interrupting her confession to plant a playful kiss on his lips. "And if the whole truth must be told, then I'll have to admit that it was those kisses and caresses that sent me running shamelessly after the man who had so recently scorned my affections."

His smile was full of wicked delight and his eyes

sparkled with the flames of desire her playfulness fired in him.

"But it was not *only* for love," she added. "And not merely for those kisses, either, gambler."

"Go on," he demanded. "If not for love alone, and not for want of my kisses, then what?" he demanded. "What other reason, partner? If there is a reason stronger than love that brought you here, and stronger than your lust," he growled seductively, "then I damn well need to know what it is."

She slid her arms around his waist again and gently pressed her cheek to his chest. A deep sigh told him her playful teasing had come to an end. "I came after you because someone very dear to me . . . very dear to both of us . . . was willing to bet everything he owned on our love. And our friend," she said softly, "has never been known to back a losing hand."

"Jeb," he said quietly.

She nodded, her face buried in his chest and her eyes still averted from his. "If not for Jeb, my pride," she began, her voice bitter and filled with self-loathing, "would have kept me from you, Chance . . . my stubborn pride would have kept us apart."

"Shh," he chided, tilting her face up to his and pressing a finger gently against her trembling lips. "Don't you know by now that it was your pride, that fiery spirit, that first drew me to you?" When she searched his eyes, she saw his soul. "I've loved you from the first moment we met. We've hurt each other, Kathleen." He winced. "I'll never forget the way I hurt you this morning. Can you ever forgive me?"

She touched his cheek, wishing she could erase the lines his past had etched there. "I've already forgiven and forgotten," she whispered. "We've been given another chance, my love. And I won't allow another moment of looking back."

His smile warmed her from within as he feathered kisses across her brow. "And I won't allow another night to pass without you in my arms," he murmured in a provocative whisper, causing a swell of emotion like none she'd ever known to rise inside her.

When she thought of how close they'd come to losing each other, it made her weak. He tightened his arms around her and she clung to him. In his embrace she felt her strength renewed. The power of his love coursed through her, filling her heart and her mind with certainty and hope.

He felt her joy and her awakening radiate through him like a healing light. Never had she felt so good in his arms. Never had he wanted her more than he wanted her now. And she wanted him as badly, he knew it by the way she trembled. When he stared into her eyes, he was dizzied by their emerald depths, shimmering with anticipation.

He kissed her deeply, hungrily, yet with every taste his need for her sweetness grew more insatiable. As their breath mingled and their lips and tongues touched and teased in a sensuous dance of love, he felt intoxicated by his desire for her.

He thrilled to the feel of her hands sliding up his back, her fingertips kneading his flesh. His pulse pounded and his longing for her shot through him like wildfire.

When he eased her down by the campfire, she sighed a silky sigh and his heart raced.

A blush of anticipation flooded her cheeks as he settled down beside her. Luck had smiled on them this

day, he told himself. And though no one could predict
what awaited them tomorrow, tonight was theirs. Peering down at her, Chance vowed not to waste one precious moment.

"I love you, Kathleen," he whispered. "Dear God,
how I love you." He stared down at her for one long,
timeless moment, relishing the way she looked nestled
against him.

"And I love you," she murmured, her voice as soft
as the night air that stirred the pine boughs overhead.
"And I want you, Chance. I want you now and for the
rest of my life. Hold me. Make love to me."

The darkening of his midnight eyes told her he
wouldn't deny her—that he couldn't deny himself any
longer.

His mouth touched hers again, and he kissed her
with such exquisite tenderness that she held her breath,
lest she disturb one single silvery strand of the memory
she knew she'd treasure for the rest of her life.

Knowing Chance Ballinger was about to make love
to her caused a burst of inner joy that shook her whole
body with delicious tremors of anticipation.

His eyes followed her when she sat up and shrugged
out of Jeb's coat. He smiled and reached for her, pulling her down beside him again. She went into his arms
as naturally as breathing, raining kisses over his face
and neck with a fervor that threatened to undo them
both.

His big hands trembled slightly as they made quick
work of the row of tiny buttons down the front of her
blouse. When he reached the final button, she pulled
her arms free and the blouse fell away. Where his eyes
touched her breasts straining against the sheer camisole, she felt scorched.

An urgent desire coiled in the pit of her stomach when he reached for the ribbon that held the thin slip of material together, and he slid the delicate camisole from her shoulders.

The night air played across her bare skin for only the moments it took him to jerk out of his vest and unbutton and remove his own shirt. His breath caught when he turned back to her and realized she'd slipped out of her skirt. With an economy of motion and fluidity, he removed the rest of his clothes and eased his long, languid body down beside hers.

The campfire had died to only a few smoldering embers, but the moonlight bathed their bodies in a silvery opulence. Kathleen drew a deep, quenching breath of cool, pine-scented air as she allowed her gaze to travel shamelessly over the tautly muscled length of him. His rippling strength and stunning masculinity made her quiver.

When her eyes came to rest again on his face, he smiled and she snuggled against him, reveling in the love she felt flowing through her like warm honey. She could hardly believe that this beautiful, virile man would soon become her husband. And to him, and him alone, she longed to joyously surrender all that she had, all that she was.

As he gazed at her, he felt himself moved anew by her delicate beauty and inner strength. She was, indeed, a heavenly combination of the angel he'd first imagined her to be and the flesh-and-blood woman he'd come to love. The glow of her love and desire for him shone in her eyes, mesmerizing him. His fingers grazed her desire-flushed cheek before sliding into the red-gold wreath of her hair. He nibbled her lips before burying his face in the warmth of her neck. Inhaling the gentle lilac scent of her, he breathed his kisses into her ivory skin. When she moaned with pleasure, his heart turned over and he wondered if a man could die from happiness.

As she slid her hands down his bare chest and around his hips, he shuddered with the raw emotion she evoked. His hands roved over her body, and he committed to memory every inch of her.

As his lips followed the trail his hands blazed, Kathleen felt her need for him building, her desire increasing to an almost unbearable pitch. Her heart and her mind screamed for release, yet she prayed that he would go on touching her forever.

His breath fanning against her skin and the provocative pressure of his fingertips sent waves of pleasure radiating through her in an ever-tightening spiral. But even as her body tingled with each heightened sensation, she knew instinctively that these pleasures were merely the sparks from a larger fire that would soon devour them both.

As their caresses became more urgent and frenzied, their clutching and clinging more desperate, they lost themselves in a ritual as ancient as time itself. They spoke without words, taking pleasure from each other and giving back tenfold. When he finally lowered himself over her, she gasped in anticipation, instinctively arching up to meet him.

And in the next breathless moment, softly, lovingly, Chance claimed with his body what his heart already possessed. She groaned in sweet agony as he drew her closer to the core of their passion. As they clung to each other, their bodies and their minds moving as one, their pleasure exalted them, enveloped them, and sent them soaring into ultimate ecstasy.

As a wave of unbelievable joy flooded her, he kissed her as he'd never kissed her before, and his own body tensed and shuddered.

For a long moment they lay clinging to each other, trembling, sated, exhausted, their hearts hammering, their breath still coming in ragged gasps.

Slowly, slowly, as the tingling sensation seeped from Kathleen's body she felt a poignant sweetness filling her. Chance sighed, kissed the top of her head and rolled to his side, bringing her with him. Tugging at the bedroll, he covered them, snuggling her deeper into his embrace.

She nestled against him, feeling her body relax, her limbs grow liquid and warm, her mind pleasantly fuzzy.

They lay cradled in each other's arms, silently savoring the feeling of complete well-being and happiness. With her head on his chest she listened to the steady sound of his heart and marveled at the depths of the love she felt for him. Silently she gave thanks for the love she knew he felt for her.

From this night forward, she vowed, they would forever be as one. His love made her whole. Her love made him complete. The sheer wonder of their union brought tears to her eyes.

As though reading her thoughts, Chance murmured, "I'll never leave you or let you go, Kathleen. I love you more than life itself."

The emotion that choked her made speech impossible, but she lifted her head and kissed him before snuggling back into his embrace.

In a moment his breathing grew rhythmic and gentle and she knew he had drifted off to sleep. Carefully, so as not to disturb him, she eased out of his arms, kissing him tenderly before she reached for her clothes and made her way to the stream to refresh herself.

When she'd dressed, she gathered an armload of kindling and came back to their campsite to find him awake and dressed and kneeling by the fire, coaxing the dying embers back to life.

When he saw her he smiled, but before she could return to his arms, he whispered, "Wait. Listen."

"It's only the wind."

"Horses," he said, rising.

She nodded, still listening.

Chance moved a few feet away from the campfire and scanned the wooded area behind them. Was it Washita and her brother playing a childish game of hide-and-seek? Or had the braves from the band been scouting their campsite even as he and Kathleen had engaged in their lovemaking?

Peering into the darkened woods, Chance could see nothing. The trail that led away from the stream was shrouded in darkness, the glow of the half-moon diffused by the trees.

Kathleen watched Chance edge cautiously toward his saddle lying on the ground near the horses. But just as he reached to pull his rifle from its scabbard, the darkness was illuminated, set ablaze.

Riders, four or five of them, emerged from the darkness of the forest like evil specters. The sudden light of their flaming torches half blinded Kathleen, making it impossible for her to see the men clearly, to comprehend the madness that was exploding around her.

"That's him!" she heard an angry and oddly familiar voice shout. "The murderer. There's a bounty on his head, boys. Enough to go around. Grab him!"

She saw Chance reach for his gun and heard the sickening thud when the rider nearest Chance struck him down with a savage blow from a rifle butt.

"No!" Kathleen screamed as she rushed to where he had fallen. As she dropped to his side, stark fear stabbed her at the sight of crimson flowing from the ugly gash on the side of his head.

"Get her," a gruff male voice ordered.

"No!" she screamed as arms closed roughly around her and hauled her away from an unconscious Chance.

"It's him all right," a voice insisted. "I saw his face on that poster from Texas. We'll show the bastard he can't make a mockery of Montana justice."

As her eyes adjusted to the light cast from the ambushers' torches, Kathleen saw to her horror that the men who surrounded them wore black shrouds over their faces. With only small slits cut out for the eyes and mouth, it was impossible for her to distinguish one attacker from another. But despite their cowardly disguises, Kathleen knew these men were the infamous night riders, the vigilantes Henry had spoken so proudly of joining.

Two more men dismounted and proceeded to tie and gag Chance and haul him up onto a horse. Kathleen quickly surmised that the man who'd struck Chance down was acting as leader.

"No, stop! You're making a terrible mistake!" she pleaded, fighting against the arms that held her. Strong fingers dug painfully into the soft flesh of her upper arms. "You must listen to me," she shouted. "He's innocent. It was self-defense. You must listen . . . I have proof. I have a letter right here that proves that it was self-defense."

Her words seemed to send a wrinkle of uncertainty rippling through the group.

"What did she say?" a voice asked.

"Reckon we ought to hear what the letter says," another voice suggested.

"Please!" she begged them. "If you'll only let me explain."

"Don't listen to her," the leader ordered. "What else would you expect her to do but lie for him?" he shouted. "You saw them together, just as I did," his voice boomed from the darkness, compelling in its fervor. "This little slut has been making fools of all of us, acting like she was too good for us, and all the while living in sin on her father's ranch with a murderer."

A grumble of consent rose from the other men. The man who had spoken moved through the crowd toward her. Her father had told her once about witnessing a pack of wolves descend on a herd of sheep. A lone wolf might never have drawn blood, he'd told her. But together they acted with a mob's savage deadliness. To Kathleen, the men that circled her were those wolves. And as the leader drew closer, the contempt-filled eyes that glared at her through the slits in the black hood sent a shiver of terror-filled recognition slithering down her spine.

"Henry!" she gasped. "Dear God, you must help me!"

His bark of laughter was cruel. "Help you? But, my dear, don't you see? I am helping you. By ridding you of this criminal under whose dark spell you have fallen, I am bringing you back single-handedly into the light."

Brazenly, Henry pulled the mask from his face. The mocking arrogance with which he glared at her made

Kathleen's stomach churn, and she struggled with renewed strength against the hands that held her from behind.

"Calm yourself, Kathleen," Henry chided as he tossed a coiled rope to one of the men on horseback.

"You know what you have to do," he snarled.

The terrifying reality that these men meant to lynch Chance struck her like lightning. With a desperate lunge she broke free of her captor for a single precious moment, just long enough to blaze a trail of fiery pain down Henry's cheeks with her fingernails.

The backhand he dealt her caused a shattering pain in her jaw and nearly rendered her unconscious as she reeled backward, landing with a bone-jarring thud onto the ground.

"Get him out of here," Henry shouted over his shoulder as he stood over her, his whole body quaking with his rage. "Take their horses, as well. The stallion will bring a good price in Virginia City. You know what to do with Ballinger. I'll take care of his . . . partner."

Kathleen struggled against the shock that threatened to immobilize her and watched in utter helplessness as the men on horseback disappeared into the woods, taking Chance with them. A whirling gray mist of unreality shrouded her senses and muddled her thinking as Henry reached down, grabbed her wrist, and jerked her to her feet.

"I don't care what you do to me," she cried, almost hysterical, "but for God's sake, Henry, you must stop them from murdering an innocent man."

"Innocent?" he scoffed. "You wouldn't know the meaning of the word." His eyes narrowed and his lip curled into ugly contempt.

"Let me go," she shouted, squirming against his steely grip. "I can prove his innocence. If only you'd listen . . ."

"I have no interest in hearing any more of your lies, Kathleen. My only interest lies in that perfect piece of property you call Twin Rivers ranch. The property that I plan to make my own by week's end."

"Never!" she spat. "I'd die before I see you lay your bloodstained hands on my family's legacy."

"What a timely choice of words," he mused. "In a matter of a few short minutes, your partner will be a dead man," he declared, his eyes glinting with dark satisfaction. "I always get what I want, Kathleen. You should know that by now."

Twisting both her arms painfully behind her back, he crushed her against him and bent his head to kiss her. "It didn't have to be this way," he snarled. "I gave you a chance. You could have been my bride."

With teeth clenched she tried to shake her head away from him, but he wrenched her arms harder, holding her fast as his mouth ground down on hers. The metallic taste of his thin lips caused bile to rise in her throat.

"You betrayed me, Kathleen. You were mine and you let another man have you. And now I'll show you what happens to those who betray me."

"Bastard!" she shrieked. Her screams were that of a wounded animal as he shoved her to the ground and fell on top of her. With one hand clamped firmly around both her wrists, he pinned her arms above her head. With his legs and thighs he held her helplessly to the ground as he pressed himself down onto her. His eyes blazed as he bent over her, his free hand cruelly kneading her breasts through her clothes as his knees pried her legs apart.

As he groped to unfasten his britches and he pressed himself against her, repugnance overwhelmed panic and Kathleen struggled more fiercely, twisting and squirming beneath him. When his mouth clamped over hers again, she blocked his tongue with her clenched teeth until she gasped for breath and he thrust it savagely into her mouth, gagging and choking her.

In desperation, she fought him with all the force her fear and revulsion afforded her. At last she managed to free one hand and her fingers flew to his face. He screamed in agony and rolled off her, cursing and groaning, his hands clutching his eyes.

Kathleen struggled to get to her feet and she tried to run, but Henry's hand shot out and grabbed her ankle and she fell face first onto the ground, the impact jolting every bone in her body. Her breath came in short, strangled gasps as she clawed the dirt, trying to regain her footing.

Suddenly her hand closed around cold steel. Jeb's pistol must have fallen from the pocket of his coat in their struggle. Whirling around to see Henry starting for her again, she took aim, leveling the pistol at his heart.

He froze, his face contorted into startled disbelief. The hand he held above her, ready to strike her again, fell slowly to his side.

"Take me to him," she demanded, cursing the inner quivering that made the gun tremble in her hand.

"Or what?" Henry mocked. "You'll shoot me? You can't do it, Kathleen. You're a coward. It's in your blood. Your father wore the same pathetic look the night they gunned him down in that saloon, the same look he handed down to you and your hangdog brother."

"You saw my father killed?" she gasped, feeling dangerously light-headed.

"He was a fool. A stupid fool. He led a sinful, undisciplined life, just like you and your brother. And he came to a just end."

"No!" she screamed with a shuddering rage so dark, so foreign, it terrified her. How could Henry have seen her father killed? Was it true, or was he only taunting her?

"Give me the gun," Henry demanded in a low growl.

Kathleen took a tenuous step backward, her mind and body still reeling from the blows they'd received.

"Give me the gun," he repeated as he stepped closer.

"I don't want to kill you, Henry," she managed, sudden tears choking her voice. "Take me to him," she begged. "Please. Please stop them, Henry."

He stood motionless for an uncertain moment, his eyes narrowed and darting. "All right. This way," he said finally as he turned and walked toward his horse.

She didn't trust his surrender, yet a flood of dizzying relief swept through her, sapping precious strength.

"You'll have to ride with me," he grumbled. "They took your mare."

Kathleen nodded uncertainly. "Just take me to him, Henry. And please, please hurry." She couldn't let herself even contemplate the devastating consequences of a failed rescue.

Henry swung into the saddle and extended his hand to help her up behind him. Distrust fought with the desperate need to catch up to the vigilantes before they murdered Chance.

"Come on," Henry prodded. "You're the one with the gun. I know when I'm whipped."

Cautiously, Kathleen shifted the gun to her other hand and reached for his hand.

In the next instant, she felt herself being jerked off her feet as Henry slammed her against the horse and dismounted. Suddenly his hand was at her throat, squeezing with the unyielding strength of steel. With his other hand he fought her for the gun as he cursed her in a vile whisper.

The steady pressure he exerted on her jugular caused bright-colored spots to swirl before her eyes and her vision began to blur. Panic threatened to overwhelm her as a deadly darkness crept from the edges of her mind. With a final surge of strength she brought the revolver down against the side of his face.

He gasped and the pressure on her throat lessened slightly. Taking advantage of the momentary rush of air, Kathleen gulped a life-giving breath and continued to fight and claw at him. At last she was able to close both hands determinedly around the gun.

Henry must have sensed the sudden shift to her advantage because he released his death grip on her throat and clamped both his hands over her wrists, bending and twisting them until she thought they'd break.

Somehow she held on as the gun wavered wildly above her head in their combined grasp. Terror filled her as she realized he was slowly, steadily overpowering her, that her own strength was hopelessly waning.

She screamed when he wrenched her arms down, and her heart stopped when she realized the gun was between them. Cold metal dug into the tender swell of her breast. And when the gun discharged, the startling retort split the night air with deadly finality.

Chapter Twenty

HENRY'S last expression was one of startled disbelief as he fell away from her, the blood pouring from his chest.

In an instant she knew he was dead, knew that she should feel something, knew that someday she probably would. But right now, as she mounted Henry Draper's horse and spurred the animal into a frantic gallop through the dappled moonlight, her only thought was of Chance, of finding him and somehow finding a way to save his life.

Fighting to focus through the veil of tears that obscured her vision, she urged Henry's gray gelding through the darkness and up the steep side of the outcropping above the trail. Breathless with hope, she spotted the distant glow of torches.

Surely without Henry there she could reason with the men, convince them of Chance's innocence. If she was not too late, her trembling heart warned as she raced toward the lights on the horizon.

Low-hanging branches and brush scraped her cheeks and ripped her clothes as she pressed her mount to move faster. Oblivious to the physical pain, but sick with the fear that gnawed at her mind and churned in her stomach, Kathleen kept her eyes trained on the glowing lights. She could make out figures on horseback now, and her hopes rose even higher. In another moment she would be upon them.

But without warning, the gelding stopped and Kathleen had to grab for the saddle horn and dig her heels into the animal's sides to avoid flying head first over its neck. Her heart lurched when she saw that the horse had stopped at the edge of a steep precipice, a jagged and rocky slope where the bluff had been cut away by time and the elements.

The horse skittered and balked when Kathleen tried to urge it down the narrow incline. Afraid to squander any more precious time fighting the animal, Kathleen dismounted and tugged on the reins, trying to coax it to follow.

But the frightened gelding would have none of it and his glassy eyes rolled when he reared back, ripping the reins from Kathleen's hands before wheeling on his hind legs and galloping off wildly in the opposite direction.

Where the leather had been pulled through her bare hands, Kathleen's flesh felt seared and raw. Whispering a curse, she proceeded to negotiate the rugged slope on foot. She could hear the men's voices drifting up to her from the bottom of the hill. She stopped for a moment, straining her eyes against the darkness, searching desperately for a glimpse of Chance.

When her eyes finally focused on the scene below, her blood froze in her veins. Chance sat on horseback poised beneath a hangman's noose dangling from the branches of a cottonwood tree. His arms were bound behind him and his feet were strapped to the saddle.

Like the shadowy images of her darkest nightmare, the events of the next few seconds proved too horrendous for her startled mind to comprehend. Kathleen opened her mouth to scream as a hooded man on horseback raised his hand to slap Chance's mount into deadly action.

But her cry was reduced to nothing more than a strangled gasp when a stunning blow from behind jolted her into numbing shock before submerging her completely into blessed unconsciousness.

"She seems better this morning." The sound of a woman's voice drifted through Kathleen's dreamless sleep and tugged her awake. She opened her eyes, despite a raging, pounding headache that begged her to keep out the light.

At first her vision was blurry, but she knew where she was and she could see that Jeb was standing at the foot of her bed, his face long and tired and gray with worry. Her eyes shifted to Sam Coulter, who stood just inside the quilt partition. His expression was even more grim. Out of the corner of her eyes she noticed Danny, but before she could make sense of why they were all in her bedroom, she heard a small voice exclaim, "She's awake!" Immediately Kathleen recognized the voice as Callie May's.

And along with that recognition came another flash of memory and bright inner pain that tightened around her heart like an unrelenting fist. She closed her eyes again and remembered more. *Chance! Oh God, Chance!* her heart cried.

Responding to an insistent tug on her nightgown, she forced her eyes open again and despite the pain it cost her, turned to see the little girl standing beside the bed. Callie May's pale blue eyes were as wide as two round platters. "We thought you were dead," she whispered solemnly, her small, freckle-dusted face long and sober. "When them two big ole Indians came ridin' up this mornin', Uncle Jeb said he thought they'd killed you!"

Kathleen tried to speak, but found her throat too dry even to utter a small squeak.

"No, Kathleen, please don't try to talk just yet," Etta ordered. "Drink this first," she said, and slid her hand gently under Kathleen's shoulders to help her to a sitting position. As Kathleen sipped the cool water, the tenderness around her mouth and her stinging lips brought back the ghastly memory of the final blow Henry had delivered. She winced and bright tears sprang to her eyes.

"Easy, Sis," Danny murmured. "Take little swallows at first. It'll hurt less." She shifted her gaze to her brother where he stood beside her bed. It was her imagination, but she could have sworn he'd aged ten years since yesterday.

"Danny's right." Etta's hands closed over hers and together they tipped the cup again. "That's it. Little sips. That's better."

"Thank you," Kathleen managed.

Etta's dark brows were drawn in furrows of deep concern. "Oh, Kathleen. We were so worried about you."

"I—I'm all right. But h-how did I—" She tried to talk, but her throat still hurt and her thoughts were impossibly jumbled. "I—I don't remember . . ." She touched a tentative hand to the tender and swollen puff above her right eye.

"She's got a big shiner, Danny," she heard Jim Jr. whisper. He stood just behind his sister, his dark hair shining, his eyes as sad and mournful as the winter sky.

"What Callie May said is true, missy," Jeb explained softly. "When I came out of the bunkhouse and found you draped across the Indian pony"—he cleared his throat before continuing—"well, I didn't hardly know what to think."

"Those two braves didn't speak much English," Sam put in.

"And Lord knows, I don't speak their language," Jeb said, chuckling softly. "But between us we managed."

"It makes me shudder just to think about you riding across that pony's back like a broken doll all the way down the pass," Etta said, her voice shaky.

Jeb shook his head. "I would never have believed that mare woulda throwed you, missy. I thought she was too old for that foolishness. But it's a mighty good thing them bucks came along when they did—the way you're all bunged up, you woulda spent a mighty rough night in that ravine."

Before Kathleen could respond, Callie asked, "Where's Uncle Chance? Did you see him? Is he coming back?"

The child's innocent question broke Kathleen's shattered heart again, and she squeezed her eyes closed and turned her face away to hide her tears.

"Danny, perhaps you should take the children outside," Etta suggested softly. "Kathleen needs to rest."

Danny put a hand on Jim's shoulder and reached for Callie May's hand. "Come on, you two. We'll finish the chores and then we'll slip down to the creek and if we're real quiet we might be able to get another look at those baby ducks."

"Oh, you should see them, Kathleen!" Callie May exclaimed. "They're so little and so cute and their feathers are all fluffy and sunshine yellow! Jeb says they're only a day or two old."

Kathleen opened her eyes and turned back to the child, offering her a weak smile. "When I'm better . . ." she whispered, "w-will . . . you show them to me?"

"I will," Callie promised, her face glowing. "Bye-bye, Kathleen. I'll come see you again after your nap."

As soon as Danny and the children left, Jeb moved to the side of the bed. "What happened out there, missy?"

"I—I don't . . . remember . . . everything," she began weakly. "But oh, Jeb—" Her voice broke and she sobbed. "Wh-what . . . they did . . . to him—" The ache in her heart swelled to her throat and robbed her of her voice again. Jeb sat down beside her and took her hand, and she clung to him, borrowing the strength she needed to tell them what had happened.

A few moments later, Kathleen stopped talking and the only sound in the room was the sound of her soft weeping and the musical sound of the children's laughter drifting through the open window. But there was no laughter in the bedroom, no joy where the adults all stood speechless, shocked silent by the things she'd told them, by the details of the nightmare she'd endured.

"Oh, you poor darling," Etta finally blurted out, sinking down on the bed and stroking Kathleen's hair away from her face and wiping the tears from her cheeks

with a cool, wet rag. "We're just so lucky you were
spared."

But Kathleen's heart said otherwise; with Chance
gone, what reason did she have for living?

Jeb shook his head and ran a weary hand through
his shaggy gray hair. "It's my fault," he said gravely. "I
should have gone out after him myself."

"You couldn't have known," Sam assured him.

"Jeb, we've got to go . . . back there—we've got to
go help him," Kathleen insisted, but as she struggled
from beneath the covers and slid her legs over the side
of the bed, a wave of nausea and dizziness enveloped
her and she fell back against the pillows.

Jeb pulled the quilts over her again. "Now, you just
hold on, missy. You're not goin' anywhere. Not just yet,
anyway. Sam and me, we'll head out there right now.
But you just lean back there and behave yourself."

The pain radiating from the back of her head took
her breath away and left her too weak to argue.

"Maybe we should send Danny to Bozeman and
have the sheriff meet us," Sam suggested.

"Good idea," Jeb replied.

As Etta assured the men she would stay with her and
look after the children, Kathleen closed her eyes and
issued a silent prayer for Jeb and the others to find
Chance alive and bring him back to her. But deep in
her heart, she knew she was asking for a miracle.

The emotions and events of the past few weeks jostled around inside Kathleen's mind as the wagon jostled
her body. Danny sat beside her, handling the reins, his
eyes on the road as the team plodded over the well-
worn trail that led home.

She'd languished in the silence that had stretched
between them since they'd left Virginia City early this
morning, and she was thankful that for once Danny
hadn't seemed to want to talk either. His testimony to
the territorial governor about what he'd witnessed
weeks ago on the trail outside Bozeman seemed to
have robbed him of his usual good humor.

Along with the sense of grim victory that had re-
sulted from her meeting with the territorial officials,
came a feeling of final emptiness that Kathleen knew
of no earthly way to overcome. From the day Jeb and
Danny had ridden back to Twin Rivers without
Chance, despair had become her closest companion.

She'd never forget the look on Jeb's face, or the sudden stab of pain that knifed her when he'd handed her
Chance's leather tobacco pouch. They'd found it, and
nothing else, beneath the cottonwood tree where Kathleen had last seen her beloved. In a strange way, not
knowing if he was dead or alive gave her hope, and yet
the uncertainty was a constant tormentor.

But how could he have survived? her rational mind
insisted on asking. If he was dead, where was his body?
her heart responded. Had the vigilantes who'd lynched
him buried the evidence of their heinous crime? Or
had some passing Samaritan administered the final rites
for the dark-haired stranger?

In her heart, Kathleen couldn't accept either explanation. Her friends and her family urged her to accept
the inevitable: No one could have survived what they'd
done to him, they insisted.

And hadn't she seen enough with her own eyes to
know t' e truth? Hadn't she gone back day after day to
search every inch of that fateful site, to no avail?

But even though the evidence told her to stop believing, each time she relived those last awful moments, she was always left with some faint glimmer of hope. Always there would be the doubting, the wondering. And in the end, one very simple truth would always keep her heart wondering: When she'd last laid eyes on Chance Ballinger, he'd been alive, and until she saw his body, she would never believe that she'd lost him forever.

And so, life at Twin Rivers went on, despite the unrelenting pain that made each day for Kathleen an uphill struggle against despair. The delightful presence of Jim Jr. and Callie had helped ease some of her great loneliness. They had become the light of her days—her nights, however, were another matter.

Thoughts of Chance, of the life they could have had—should have had—tormented her each night, until inevitably exhaustion claimed her for a few short hours of fitful sleep. There were no more tears, but the aching never stopped.

But at least now, thanks to her persistence and the letter from Jim and Callie's grandmother as evidence, she'd accomplished her goal of clearing Chance's name. Her explanation of the events of the night that Chance had been killed hadn't been easy. But by the time she'd finished, the authorities were ready to accept her plea of self-defense in the death of Henry Draper. The territorial governor was in the process of a full investigation into the activities of the vigilantes. But in the end, Kathleen found these realities still offered little consolation. With Chance gone, what did any of it matter?

"We're almost home," Danny said, drawing her out of her grim reverie.

Through the trees she could see the cabin like an

old friend, waiting for her. She took a deep, cleansing breath of crisp fall air, and raised her eyes to the peaks that already wore a blanket of fresh white. The long gray days of winter would soon hang over the valley and the meadows and pastures would sleep, almost deathlike, awaiting another spring, another awakening.

Kathleen tried not to dread the winter, but instead to find solace in autumn's defiant dance, a dance never more vital than just before the killing frost. The ruddy reds of the scrub oak, the soft yellows of the willow, and the startling, shimmering gold of the aspen, gave her strength. She looked around her, drinking in all the beauty, all the glory that was Twin Rivers, and somehow she knew she would endure this long, desolate winter of the heart.

She would survive and someday her heart would smile again. For the children, for Danny and Jeb, for her dear mother and father and all those who had endured the changing seasons of life before her. But mostly for the memories of her beloved Chance and the dreams he'd dreamed for them and for Twin Rivers.

Spring will come again, she told herself.

When Danny pulled the team into the yard, Jim Jr. came bounding around the corner of the house, smiling. As always, Kathleen was struck by the boy's startling resemblance to his uncle, the same intelligent blue eyes and jet-black hair. Callie May came rushing up behind her brother, her golden pigtails bobbing behind her.

"You're home early," Jim said happily as Danny threw him the reins and he held the team while Kathleen climbed down from the wagon.

"Did you see it?" he asked Danny excitedly. "That new saddle at Shrader's leather store? Ain't it a beaut?"

Danny tugged on the brim of the wide straw hat that he'd given the boy and that Jim never took off. "Now, what makes you think I had time to run around Virginia City looking for some blamed saddle?"

Kathleen watched Jim trying to hide his disappointment and her brother trying to suppress a grin.

"Ah, come on," Danny drawled, giving Jim an affectionate slap on the back. "Help me haul the blamed thing out of the wagon."

In a heartbeat the adult expression Jim had tried so valiantly to maintain vanished, and in its place a child's pure joy shone like Midas's gold. The growing friendship and brotherly love between Jim and Danny had been a pleasure to watch.

"Did you miss me?" Callie asked breathlessly, pulling on Kathleen's sleeve.

The pale blue eyes that stared up at her touched her heart. Bending down, Kathleen tugged playfully on one frazzled braid. "Does the snow fly in Montana in the winter?" she teased as she scooped the child up in her arms and carried her into the house.

"Jeb says the snow will be here before we know it," Callie May replied earnestly as Kathleen set her down inside the cabin. "And I can't wait. I shall build a snowman and a fort," she declared, her broad smile revealing a gap where her two front teeth used to be.

"Oh no! They're gone!" Kathleen gasped in feigned astonishment. "Callie May Ballinger, I do believe someone stole your front teeth while you were sleeping!"

The child's giggles bubbled up out of her like champagne. "I wiggled them out all by myself," she announced proudly, one small hand planted firmly on each hip.

"Well, how about that! Say, I bought those ribbons to match your new dress," Kathleen said as she unpinned her hat and shrugged out of her coat.

"Sunshine yellow?" Callie asked, her eyes dancing with anticipation.

"Sunshine yellow," Kathleen affirmed. "Now run out to the barn, will you, dear, and ask Danny and Jim to bring the parcels in from the back of the wagon. I seem to remember the man at the general store in Virginia City putting some peppermint sticks in with those yellow ribbons."

"Yes, ma'am!" Callie shouted, planting a quick kiss on Kathleen's cheek before she hit the door running.

After the child had gone, Kathleen sighed and touched the damp spot on her cheek. Through these wonderful children Chance still found a way to give her his love, she reminded herself. Making a home for them, guiding their futures, would be her future now, her reason to go on. "Thank you, partner," she whispered.

"Welcome home, missy," Jeb greeted her, startling her as he stuck his grizzled face through the doorway. "Danny tells me things went well."

"They did," Kathleen said quietly, sinking wearily into a chair at the table. "I think the vigilance committees and the night riders have murdered their last innocent man." She sighed. "I'm just glad it's over and that we're home."

Jeb strode across the room and rested one bearlike paw on her shoulder. "The whole territory owes you its thanks," he declared. "You should feel proud."

She nodded vaguely. "Hmm."

Jeb pulled a chair up next to hers and eased his frame down into it before pushing his hat onto the back of his head and releasing a long, tired sigh. "We've come a long way in a short time, haven't we, missy."

Kathleen nodded. A long way indeed, she thought. Had it only been two years since they'd lost Pa? And only two months since she'd lost Chance? Without him, she lost track of time, her days melding into one long, unrelenting sorrow.

"Yessir," Jeb went on, "this here ranch has come a long way—not that we don't still have a few problems." Jeb's pronouncement grabbed Kathleen's attention.

"Problems? What problems, Jeb? We've nearly doubled our investment in the Herefords. We have a year-round income from the army, thanks to the contract Chance negotiated with them at Fort Benton. The note at the bank has been paid six months in advance—"

He held up his hand. "It ain't the cattle. It ain't the money. It's me," he said flatly.

"You?" Alarmed, Kathleen rose to stand beside him. "What is it, Jeb? Are you ill? Has something happened? Are you in some kind of trouble?"

He shook his head and reached for her hand, closing his callused fingers around hers and tugging her back to her seat. "Sit down, missy," he said, his voice gentle.

"Tell me, Jeb," she pleaded with him, her heart in her throat. "If something's wrong, I must know. We're a family and we'll face it together, whatever it is. Now, tell me, what's the trouble."

"I'm old," he said simply, his faded gray eyes resting on hers tenderly. "And I'm tired. I can't keep up the way I used to." He scratched his whiskered jaw before adding, "I know you and Danny don't complain, but lately I know you've been carrying a good share of my load."

"As you carried our share for a good many years," Kathleen reminded him. "We're glad for the chance to pay you back, Uncle Jeb."

He shook his head and pulled his hat into his hands. "But it ain't right," he declared. "There's too much work around here for the two of you. I've seen how tired you are at the end of the day. And Danny—sometimes he can hardly make it through his supper without nodding off. The herd is growing, missy. Those children are taking more and more of your time, what with their schoolwork and such. I don't think the two of you can keep up with things much longer."

"We'll manage," Kathleen said confidently as she stood again and moved into the kitchen to start a pot of coffee. "You and my mother and father worked this ranch with less muscle than we have. You three managed somehow and so will we."

"But I don't think so," Jeb said stubbornly.

Kathleen studied his face. It was clear this was something about which Jeb felt strongly. "Well then, what should we do about the situation? I suppose we could hire a hand to get us through the busiest times, roundup, branding, and—"

"Part-time help is no solution," Jeb said firmly. "What you need, missy, is another partner."

Kathleen gasped. As the blood drained from her face, she reached for the table to steady herself. "A partner?" she repeated, hardly recognizing the gruff whisper as her own.

"Yes, ma'am," Jeb said quickly. "And I've taken steps to try to find you one."

Kathleen sank down onto the chair numbly. "You—

you've done what?" The world seemed to spin out of control and she held on to the tabletop for balance.

"A partner, Kathleen," he said again. "And I think I found just the fella. He's a bright young man. Knows his business. Ranched most of his life."

"Jeb, I can't believe you're suggesting—"

"Well, I am," he interrupted brusquely. "As a matter of fact, he rode over here this morning to meet you. He's out in the yard right now. I think you should talk to him, at least give him a chance."

Kathleen could only blink in stunned disbelief. "But Jeb—"

But he was already at the door. "No buts about it, missy. I'll go fetch him."

Kathleen brought her trembling hands up to her cheeks and touched the spots of fever that had risen there. She prayed that this was some kind of crazy nightmare from which she'd awaken at any moment. But the feel of her skin beneath her fingertips and the sound of a man's voice on the porch convinced her this was one nightmare through which she would have to walk wide-awake.

When the door opened, she stood up slowly and took a deep breath. A scuffing sound on the porch announced the arrival of a breathless Callie, who burst through the door ahead of the stranger on the porch. "Th-that man," she stammered, turning an accusing glare to the tall man in the door who, with the sun behind him, was a silhouette in black. "He—he knows my name!"

Kathleen bent down to stroke Callie's hair, trying to soothe her and make sense of her excited babble. "Callie May, calm down. That man is our guest. Now, show your manners and ask him in, won't you?" she instructed the frightened child, who instead of doing as she was told bolted for the door.

The man at the door seemed not to notice the child as he stepped into the room. He was dressed in fringed buckskin and sported a thick dark beard. But although his face was shaded by a crumpled black hat and his dark hair curled around his collar, recognition dawned immediately and she stumbled breathlessly into his arms.

He kissed her long and hard, and when he finally lifted his mouth from hers, the slow smile that bloomed behind the heavy beard captured Kathleen's heart anew.

The light that shone from his midnight-blue eyes was filled with love. "Kathleen," he murmured, and the sound of his voice sent life coursing through her again, her love for him filling her mind and her soul in a dizzying rush of pure spring.

"Chance! Oh, Chance!" she cried, staring into his face, her vision glazed with her tears. "Can it be? Can it really be you?" She touched him, stroking his face and his hair with shaking, disbelieving hands.

"It can, and it is," he said, laughing, and he captured her hands and brought them to his lips and kissed each trembling fingertip. "I'm home, partner! I'm really home."

Her happiness washed over them as she reveled in his embrace and welcomed the only man she'd ever love, the only partner she'd ever need.

Epilogue

———◆———

B y the soft, pink light of early morning that filtered through the lacy curtains at the window, Kathleen spied her wedding dress where it lay in a heap of ivory lace and satin on the floor beside the bed. She blushed, remembering the fevered circumstance under which it had come to be so carelessly discarded.

Chance's black waistcoat and string tie had been similarly cast off, and Kathleen stared at his clothes a moment, letting her thoughts drift lovingly back to their wedding day. How handsome he'd looked! How tender his lovemaking last night. And how completely she loved him!

With an inner smile that warmed her, she snuggled closer to her husband. Did anyone have a right to be this happy? she wondered.

Nestling closer still, her hand strayed to his chest and she toyed with the thick mat of hair until he began to stir. His eyes opened and he smiled, drinking in a long, leisurely look at her before he spoke.

"Good morning, partner," he murmured finally, and folded her into his arms while he buried his face in her hair and inhaled deeply, and growled a hungry growl that told her his appetite for her had not been sated.

She scattered a dozen kisses into his hair and felt the warmth of his breath and the stirring feel of his hands moving in warm, enticing circles across her back. The embers of her desire sparked again, and she slid her hands up over his chest and locked her fingers behind his neck and drew his mouth slowly, slowly to hers.

He kissed her gently at first, but with her encouragement his kisses grew deeper and more urgent. She furrowed her fingers deep into the thick, dark waves of his hair and clung to him, as his hands roamed over her quivering body. She pressed herself against the long, warm muscular length of him, drinking in his strength and savoring his sweetness on her tongue.

Suddenly his hands stopped and he lifted his head. "Listen," he whispered. "Did you hear that?"

Kathleen sat up abruptly, pulling the quilt over her naked breasts. "I did," she whispered. "And I think I know what I heard."

Scrambling for her white satin wrapper, she slipped into it and then tossed him his trousers, which lay on the floor beside the bed.

"Uncle Chance? Aunt Kathleen?"

Chance smiled his thanks as he jerked his britches on and sat back on the bed and put his arm around his wife before he called, "Callie May? Is that you?"

The child took his acknowledgment as an invitation and a second later the quilt partition opened and she bolted across the room, jumping up on the bed. Breathlessly and she sat smiling at them, her legs crossed

Indian-style. "Jeb made me promise not to wake you. He said it was your wedding morning and that I was to let you sleep late. And I tried to be quiet, honest. But then it got so light and I got so lonely . . . and . . . please don't tell him, all right?"

"All right," Kathleen assured her. "Besides, we were already awake, weren't we?"

Chance's smile was wicked. "Yes. We were awake."

Just then a streak of butterscotch fur slipped around the partition and leaped up onto the bed and into Callie's lap with one bounce. "I guess Gideon couldn't wait to see you either," Callie May giggled as she stroked the old cat and he purred shamelessly.

"Who's next?" Chance laughed.

Just then a voice from the other room called, "Callie May?"

"I'm in here, with Uncle Chance and Aunt Kathleen," she sang out merrily.

"Callie May Ballinger, you better not let Jeb know you woke them. He'll skin you alive!" Jim's face was so red, it glowed when it appeared around the edge of the quilt partition.

"Good morning, Jim," Chance said. "You might as well come on in and sit down, everyone else has."

"Mornin', Uncle Chance. Aunt Kathleen." Jim sat down at the foot of the bed and let his long legs dangle over the side.

"Jim, you sure looked handsome yesterday standing beside your uncle in that black suit," Kathleen told him.

The boy beamed under her compliment. "That was some wedding party, Uncle Chance. I never knew you could dance so good." His face shone with astonished admiration.

"Maybe some day he'll teach you," Kathleen suggested.

"That'd be a *good* idea, Uncle Chance," Callie May agreed. "Old Jim dances like a three-legged mule, don't he, Kathleen?" She giggled and he stuck his tongue out at her when she dissolved in laughter. Jim lunged at her, tickling her ribs and ordering her to take back what she'd said.

"Stop! Stop!" Callie May shrieked.

"Take it back! Three-legged mule! I'll show you."

But before Jim could make Callie recant, Chance dove into the middle of the ruckus, grabbing both children and tickling them until they gasped and begged for mercy.

Gideon arched his back and hissed before leaping to safety as the bed shook and heaved.

Somebody kicked Kathleen and she dove for the side of the bed, laughing and trying to avoid the flailing arms and legs. But before she could escape, Chance grabbed her foot and began mercilessly to tickle her tender instep.

She screamed and grabbed him, gasping for breath and helpless as her laughter sapped her strength. Callie squealed in delight, jumping up and down on the bed as Jim yanked Chance's hair and Kathleen dug her fingers into her husband's ribs. When Chance tried to shrug out of Kathleen's grasp, Callie attacked him from behind, wrapping her arms and legs around his back and holding on for dear life, just as Jim escalated his own tickling attack.

Suddenly and without any more warning, the big old bed shimmied and collapsed at one end, leaving them all bunched together on the floor, momentarily breathless and stunned silent.

But just one look at one another's startled faces and the room shook with the explosion of their combined laughter.

"Now what do we do?" Jim asked, when he finally stopped laughing long enough to take in the strange, tilted angle of the bed.

"It doesn't look good, does it?" Kathleen asked, wiping her eyes and holding her sides, which ached from her laughter.

"Your bed looks like that Indian travois you told us about, doesn't it, Uncle Chance?" Callie May asked. "Like the one in the story. The travois that carried you to Canada."

Chance smiled and pulled her onto his lap and ruffled her hair. "It does look a little bit like that rig," he admitted.

"Tell us again, Uncle Chance," Jim urged him.

"Oh, please. Tell us," Callie May begged him. "Tell us about the travois and Washita and the Indians."

Chance's gaze shifted to his wife and she nodded. "Go ahead. You know how they love that story."

Chance grabbed the pillows that had slid down to the floor and slipped them behind his head and leaned back against the sloping bed. With Callie still sitting on his lap, one arm around Kathleen, and Jim sitting at rapt attention at his feet, he told the story of how he'd been rescued.

"It was like coming out of a long, deep sleep." He always began this way, watching the children's eyes grow wider as they conjured mental images from the scenes he painted for them with his words. He marveled that they never seemed to tire of the story of how their uncle's mind had been wrapped in a fog, like a death shroud, from the moment the vigilantes put the rope around his neck.

His consciousness had come back to him gradually, his senses reacting slowly, groping to identify his surroundings. His throat and his head hurt like hell. His arms and wrists felt bruised and battered. The pungent smell of horseflesh and leather stung his nostrils and sent a wave of nausea rolling through him. The sounds of excited and chattering voices left him utterly confused.

He was lying down, but not flat, exactly. And he had the distinct sensation he was moving. He shook his head to clear his befuddled thoughts, to try to find some logic in his predicament. He was injured, every muscle and bone in his body ached as if he'd been stomped by an angry bull. Perhaps he was lying in the back of a wagon, he thought. But if it was a wagon in which he was riding, he figured one of the wheels must surely have been broken, judging by the jolting and jostling that sent fresh stabs of pain shooting through his battered body.

He thought about trying to lift his head, but a searing pain above his eye made him think again. Cautiously opening one eye, he blinked against the bright sunlight that blinded him.

He moaned and drew a ragged breath and the events of the last few hours of hell crashed down on him in a shower of jagged images: the torches emerging from the darkness; the blow from behind that had rendered him unconscious; the rope that had seared its brand into his neck. The frenzied shouts. The smell of gunpowder. The grotesquely painted bodies of the Indians riding out of the darkness. The men in black hoods fleeing in fright.

Kathleen! his mind had shrieked. My God, where was she?

Fighting to put the pieces together, he'd closed his eyes again and willed his mind clear. When he opened them again, he focused on the view directly in front of him: a pinto so skinny that a man could count his ribs and the lean, muscled body of the Indian brave riding it.

The sight of the Indian and his own precarious position helped Chance finally make sense of his immediate situation. The jolting was because he was the lone passenger on a drag the Indians called a travois. He'd seen the A-shaped contraption before. The Indians used it to carry their household goods and sometimes their children and their elders when they moved from camp to camp.

But why were they moving him? And where were they moving him to?

The veil of confusion lifted partially when Chance saw his hat suddenly appear above him. He reached up and took it from the small brown hand that held it out to him.

The childish eyes behind the hat stared down at him, and he smiled, knowing at last that the Indians who had assumed the unlikely role of his benefactors were the band to whom he'd given the steers outside Bozeman when he and Danny had driven the Hereford cattle to Twin Rivers from the Richardson ranch.

"Washita," he murmured, finding his voice tight and his throat painfully dry.

She offered him a shy smile, and he knew she was pleased he remembered her.

"Where are we going?" he asked, hoping the little girl walking beside the travois had learned enough

English at Fort Benton to understand his question. "Where, Washita? Where are they taking me? Where do we go?"

Her smile grew brighter as understanding broke through.

"We go!" she proclaimed excitedly, one arm outstretched and one finger pointing proudly. "We go to Ca-na-da!"

"And you did go to Canada, didn't you, Uncle Chance?" Callie May broke in. "And the Indians helped you get better, and gave you food and a horse and a shotgun."

Chance nodded, Callie May's precocious charm delighting him as always. "That's right, little one. And this." He lifted the leather band he'd worn around his neck from that day forward. He handed it to her and she accepted the necklace carefully, studying the careful beadwork and the strange markings of animals and moons and stars with reverent awe. "When I was finally strong enough to ride, Silver Elk gave me that necklace for safe passage," he told them again.

"He said it was full of good medicine," Jim said, adding the details of the story he knew by heart.

Chance nodded. "And that good medicine brought me back to you."

Kathleen smiled up at him and kissed his ruddy cheek. "It was good medicine to be sure," she whispered, "but maybe it was a bit of Irish luck, as well, that brought you back to us, Chance Ballinger."

He returned her smile and kissed her cheek, hugging her to him and whispering in her ear, "And it's the love of an angel that makes me stay."

If you're looking for romance, adventure, excitement and suspense be sure to read these outstanding romances from Dell.

Antoinette Stockenberg
☐ **EMILY'S GHOST**   21002-X $4.99
☐ **BELOVED**   21330-4 $4.99
☐ **EMBERS**   21673-7 $4.99

Rebecca Paisley
☐ **HEARTSTRINGS**   21650-8 $4.99

Jill Gregory
☐ **CHERISHED**   20620-0 $4.99
☐ **DAISIES IN THE WIND**   21618-4 $5.50
☐ **FOREVER AFTER**   21512-9 $4.99
☐ **WHEN THE HEART BECKONS**   21857-8 $5.50

Christina Skye
☐ **THE BLACK ROSE**   20929-3 $5.50
☐ **COME THE NIGHT**   21644-3 $4.99
☐ **COME THE DAWN**   21647-8 $5.50
☐ **DEFIANT CAPTIVE**   20626-X $5.50
☐ **EAST OF FOREVER**   20865-3 $4.99
☐ **THE RUBY**   20864-5 $5.50

At your local bookstore or use this handy page for ordering:

DELL READERS SERVICE, DEPT. DS
2451 S. Wolf Rd., Des Plaines, IL. 60018

Please send me the above title(s). I am enclosing $_____
(Please add $2.50 per order to cover shipping and handling.) Send check or money order—no cash or C.O.D.s please.

Dell

Ms./Mrs./Mr._____

Address_____

City/State_____ Zip_____

DHR2-9/95

Prices and availability subject to change without notice. Please allow four to six weeks for delivery.

Be sure to read these
outstanding historical
romances by author:

CHRISTINA SKYE

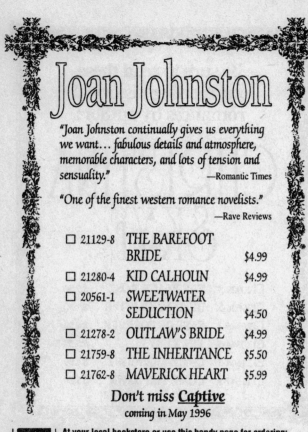